Also by Frederic Mullally

POLITICAL
Death Pays a Dividend (with Fenner Brockway)
Fascism Inside England

NOVELS
Danse Macabre
Man with Tin Trumpet
Split Scene
The Assassins
No Other Hunger
The Munich Involvement
Clancy
Venus Afflicted

DIVERSIONS
The Prizewinner
The Penthouse Sexicon
Oh, Wicked Wanda!

HITLER
HAS WON

A NOVEL BY

Frederic Mullally

SIMON AND SCHUSTER
New York

A list of real and fictitious characters
appears at the back of the book.

Designed by Irving Perkins
Manufactured in the United States of America

1 2 3 4 5 6 7 8 9 10

Library of Congress Cataloging in Publication Data

Mullally, Frederic.
Hitler has won.

1. Hitler, Adolf, 1889-1945—Fiction. I. Title.
PZ4.M958Hi3   [PR6063.U38]   823'.9'14   75-11846
ISBN 0-671-22074-8

For
CLARENCE PAGET,
bookman extraordinary

But for a few elementary mistakes, he might have succeeded in conquering the world.—ROBERT PAYNE, *The Life and Death of Adolf Hitler*

If I could have added to my material power the spiritual power of the Papacy, I should have been the supreme ruler of the world.—NAPOLEON BONAPARTE

Mark my words, Bormann, I'm going to become very religious.—ADOLF HITLER, January 12, 1942

CHAPTER ONE

HE WAS standing at one of the tall gray-curtained windows, gazing out over the Chancellery gardens, as Kurt entered the room, keeping a respectful pace behind Martin Bormann. A man of about five feet nine, impressively erect for his fifty-three years, but with the thickened waist of a sedentary worker and a stealthy assertion of silver about the ears and above the closely trimmed neckline of his flat, dark-brown hair. The field-gray jacket and black trousers spoke of quality and a valet's devotion, and as the man at the window turned briskly around, Kurt caught a glimpse of the Iron Cross, First Class, glinting low on the military pocket over the left breast before his eyes were pinned by the Fuehrer's own swift and challenging stare.

"Heil Hitler!" He had diligently prepared his salute for this moment, so that the snap to rigid attention, the click of heels, the outflung arm would come as one smoothly integrated movement. And he had remembered the instructions of the head of the Party Chancellery, now advancing to the Fuehrer's side. ("You will give him the German salute, not the military one. Don't bawl it out like some overeager *Kreisleiter*. Just so long as it's crisp and clearly audible. You will say nothing else until you are addressed.")

"Lieutenant Armbrecht, my Fuehrer," Bormann announced, half turning toward Kurt, who remained stiffly rooted to the carpet a few paces inside the salon. "His was the dossier the Doctor sent over this morning. If you would like to be re-

9

minded—" He broke off at a wave of the hand from Adolf Hitler.

"That won't be necessary. I've read it. It's all here." The Fuehrer's hand flicked on up, lightly brushing his right temple. "We shall have a little chat, Lieutenant Armbrecht and myself."

He hadn't taken his eyes off Kurt since acknowledging his salute, and it was true what they said about the magnetism of that steady gaze. You were not being looked at or penetrated so much as being *drawn* by some invisible force burning behind the sallow, homely face of the most loved and most hated man in all the world. The spell was momentarily broken as Hitler muttered a few words of dismissal to Martin Bormann, only to be renewed as soon as Kurt, in quick response to the Fuehrer's gesture, lowered himself into one of the hard-sprung leather armchairs and was once more held by that deep hypnotic stare.

"Two years ago you sacrificed an arm for your country. . . ." The voice was harsh but expressive, recalling for Kurt, subliminally, the accents of the athletic coach at his high school. It was a voice he had heard, through one medium or another, hundreds of times in the past ten years, but almost always impassioned and always amplified by loudspeakers or newsreel sound tracks. Here, in one of the smallest salons of the Chancellery's ground floor, across the few yards of hand-woven carpet separating Kurt from Hitler, the famous voice, in this lower and unstrained register, was giving off cadences quite unfamiliar to Kurt. "Compelling" would be one word to describe it. And instantly one grasped the phenomena of Neville Chamberlain's rushing back to England with his idiotic "Peace in our time," of the aged President von Hindenburg's blessing on the man who would bend and if necessary break the old Germany of inept parliamentarianism to his will.

". . . would you now be willing to give up two, maybe three years of your private life to an enterprise that will bring no glory, no medals, no recognition apart from my own personal gratitude?"

"No German could dream of a richer reward, my Fuehrer."

The quiet statement came out of him unmeditated, like a received truth, flawless and inviolate.

Acknowledging it with the slightest dip of his head, the Fuehrer continued. "There will of course be some material compensations. The person I choose is to receive the pay and allowances of a captain in the Home Army throughout his employment and will be quartered and messed here in the Chancellery, or at the Berghof, or wherever my movements take me. But there is another consideration, and I should be disappointed if a young man of your intelligence hadn't already taken it into account." He had started to measure, with precise, catlike steps, an area of carpet in front of the gray-curtained windows, but now he paused to favor Kurt with an almost roguish smile. "My literary secretary need not be too envious of the enormous royalties that will accrue to his Fuehrer from the sales of this sequel to *Mein Kampf*. He will be my automatic choice—assuming his work has pleased me—as official biographer of Adolf Hitler, whose death will therefore make him a millionaire. Have you not thought of that?"

He stopped abruptly, expecting a reply. Waiting for it. In the brief silence, Kurt's mind swiftly framed and instinctively rejected two distinct but equally insincere answers, saying instead, "I hadn't thought of it, my Fuehrer; and I'd rather not think about it now."

"You're a young man," Hitler muttered, "and I shan't live forever. Allow me to give you some facts about *Mein Kampf*." He had resumed his pacing. "From 1925 to 1933, I lived on the royalties from that book and never had to draw a pfennig from Party funds. Since 1933, when I became Chancellor, the book has never failed to sell a million copies annually. But it has become almost a source of embarrassment to me, Armbrecht, and I shall tell you why. The book was dictated by me to that lunatic Hess in far too much of a hurry. I am an artist, you understand, and an orator, but I make no claims to being a graceful writer. Later, when the first draft was completed, I permitted that renegade Hieronymite priest, Bernhard Stempfle,

11

to edit the typescript, and I will not deny that he put a polish on some of the rougher passages resulting from the speed of my dictation. But seventeen years have elapsed since *Mein Kampf* burst like a comet across the political firmament, and although it remains the philosophical cornerstone, so to speak, of my world outlook, there is a great deal in the testament that events and the passage of time have now made invalid. Alas, I have no doubt—" Hitler stopped his pacing to direct another wry smile at Kurt—"that there is a great deal that could, and perhaps should have been put more felicitously."

Kurt started to protest, but was gestured back to silence.

"Don't spoil the good impression you've already made on me, Armbrecht. *Mein Kampf,* along with Plato's *Republic,* the Bible, and Marx's *Das Kapital,* is one of the four unique books that have most influenced mankind. But, like the other three, it is a flawed work. So much so that my first intention, after I had watched our bulldozers level the ruins of the Kremlin to the ground at the beginning of this year, was to take a month off from the supreme command of the Wehrmacht, lock myself up in the Berghof at Obersalzberg, and devote myself to a completely revised edition of the two volumes. It was Reichsminister Goebbels who dissuaded me from this course. 'The document you gave the world in 1925,' he told me, 'now belongs to history. Future generations will study it for the light it throws on the mind of Adolf Hitler as he stood on the threshold of power, challenging the enemies of Germany to do battle.' But *Mein Kampf,* the Doctor went on to argue, must be read as the introduction to a work that will constitute my true epitaph. This work will explain, for the benefit of future historians, how a man of the people, a self-educated former corporal in the German army, managed in eight short years to raise a demoralized and bankrupt nation to be the masters of a Germanic empire stretching from Brest on the Atlantic to the Volga, from the North Cape to the Mediterranean.

"And it will prescribe, in definitive detail, the conditions that will guarantee the survival of Adolf Hitler's New Order for the next thousand years. It will be the story of an incredible victory —a victory over the past, over the present, over the future. And there can be only one title—the Doctor and I agreed—for this work." Hitler swung around on one heel of his brilliantly polished black shoes to face Kurt. His body became suddenly rigid, and the sagging facial muscles had contracted to reproduce in the flesh that stern and ubiquitous portrait of Der Fuehrer that had by now superseded the image of Christ for the millions of Kurt's generation. There was a glint of teeth below the neatly squared-off mustache as the next two words ripped out like splinters of steel.

"Mein Sieg!"

In the same instant Kurt was up out of his chair and fighting for balance as his right arm shot forward to the cry, "Sieg Heil!" Without the balance of a left arm, the involuntary force of the reflex would have sent him sprawling had Hitler not stepped forward and crooked a stiff forearm for Kurt to seize. For a long moment they remained linked in silence, the twenty-seven-year-old disabled lieutenant and the ruler of all Europe and Russia-in-Europe. Kurt, who had dared to put his hand to the Fuehrer's person, now dared not withdraw it without a sign.

The arm within the fine worsted yarn of Hitler's gray sleeve untensed itself, freeing Kurt's frozen hand.

"You are a good soldier, Armbrecht. I shall ask my personal surgeon, Dr. Karl Brandt, to have a look at your arm. Our German doctors are performing miracles with prosthesis these days. Sit down."

Kurt had been sitting bolt upright for more than a quarter of an hour, breathing shallowly and willing his brain to memorize every word of Hitler's monologue, delivered for the most part with didactic calm but erupting occasionally into scornful or triumphant declamation.

He had assumed that his first interview by the Fuehrer would have been brief. A few questions, maybe, about his already well-documented background, just to get him talking. A word or two about what would be expected of him in the almost inconceivable event that he be chosen for the post of Literary Assistant. But he had been asked no questions so far and, apart from the opening references to *Mein Kampf* and its projected sequel, there had been no pronouncement about the working method envisaged by the Fuehrer. Instead, Kurt Armbrecht was being honored with an inside account of Adolf Hitler's masterly strategy, diplomatic and military, over the past tremendous year, the strategy that had won him his greatest victory. It was as if the Fuehrer had already made his decision, without waiting to interview the last candidates on Reichsminister Goebbels's short list, and that he and Kurt were now launched on their first session together as narrator and scribe. Perhaps a miracle would occur and the time would come when he would be privileged to listen *and* take notes at the same time. For the moment, it was enough to listen, to memorize. . . .

"Consider the situation that faced me by the middle of January, 1941. I had already set a firm date for the spring invasion of Russia—May 15. The last thing I wanted was to stir up the neutral Balkan States. But Mussolini, without consulting me, had invaded Albania and Greece three months earlier and been given a bloody nose for his pains. On top of that, his North African army had been flung back from Egypt by the British and was now being chased back to Libya. I tell you, Armbrecht, with only four months to go before the launching of the greatest offensive in the history of warfare, I had no appetite for a Balkan campaign plus an operation in Libya. Yet something had to be done to contain the British during the six months it would take me to destroy the Red armies west of Moscow.

"I had the power to crush Greece and to halt and destroy Wavell's army in North Africa. But of what use is the exercise of power unless as an integral part of a grand design?"

Hitler paused once again, staring out over the manicured Chancellery gardens, and Kurt seized the opportunity, without taking his eyes off the Fuehrer's back, to ease himself into a slightly more comfortable position.

"There was deep snow blanketing Obersalzberg that day in January, when I summoned my military chiefs to a council of war at the Berghof," the Fuehrer went on, his back still turned to the room. "I had slept on my decisions overnight, and when I took the air on the terrace that morning and looked out over those eternal Alpine peaks, I knew beyond all doubt that these decisions were inspired and therefore irrevocable.

"My instructions were as follows: Three divisions of the Reichswehr would be sent to Albania to stiffen the Italian forces along the Greek frontier, and to secure the main mountain passes between Albania and Yugoslavia. Ten divisions would be moved from Rumania into Bulgaria, where they would take up battle positions along the Yugoslav and Greek frontiers. Three panzer divisions under the command of General Rommel—as he was then—would be dispatched to Tripoli to hurl the British back into Egypt. There would be no invasion of Greece or Yugoslavia. Meantime squadrons of Reichsmarschall Goering's Luftwaffe, operating from Libyan airfields, together with Admiral Raeder's U-boats, would bottle up the British navy in Alexandria. Do you follow my brilliant strategy, Armbrecht?" He had turned from the window and his chin was up, his eyes flashing.

"Mein Fuehrer—"

"Impeccable!" Hitler clapped his hands together and chuckled as he renewed his carpet pacing. "Defensive positions everywhere. No excuse for Turkey to become alarmed. No excuse for Stalin, with his bandit eyes on the Bosporus and the Dardanelles, to send that robot of his, Molotov, scurrying to Berlin with hypocritical protests. But, most important of all, my armies on the eastern front could go ahead with their massive buildup for Operation Barbarossa. That date, May 15, 1941, was absolutely vital, Armbrecht, and would brook no postponement. It gave me a bare six months to encircle and destroy four hundred Bolshevik divisions and to reach Moscow before the winter clamped down. I say without hesitation, looking back over that shattering but glorious campaign, that if I had permitted a Balkan adventure to delay the invasion of Russia by as much as two weeks, we should still be grappling with the Russians west of Moscow.

"Instead, what is the situation today, thirteen months after the launching of Barbarossa? Marshal Timoshenko's armies utterly destroyed. Advance columns of the Waffen-SS two hundred miles east of Moscow and threatening Gorki. Stalin cowering in Kubyshev. Four million Russian prisoners of war put to work building an impregnable system of defenses from Archangel to the Caspian Sea. Rail communications to Vladivostok cut off.

"I will let you into a secret, Lieutenant, that you will be sharing with the whole world tomorrow. At this moment, as we speak, our Wehrmacht in Bulgaria is poised to strike into Salonika, liquidate the British forces there and drive on to Athens. While this is happening, the Yugoslavs will be attacked simultaneously from the Ostmark,* Hungary, Rumania and Albania. Yes, yes, I can see that soldierly gleam in your eyes and can well understand your excitement. But that's not all! Over the past month I have been ferrying men and material, around the clock, to Field Marshal Rommel in Libya. When Rommel takes Alexandria, as he will, the British Mediterranean fleet will have to put to sea for its final rendezvous with our U-boat packs! After that—the Nile, Cairo, the Suez Canal! Have you any conception, Armbrecht, of the geopolitical significance of a German-controlled Suez Canal?"

This time, the question seemed more than rhetorical. After a moment's hesitation, Kurt plunged swiftly in.

"The Middle East will be ours, *mein Fuehrer*. Gaullist Syria will be isolated. The British, and their Empire troops, will fall back on the Persian Gulf, hoping to be evacuated by their navy. The Gulf will then be ours, together with all the oil supplies of the Middle East. When our Japanese ally completes the conquest of India, the Pact of Steel will extend unbroken from Tokyo to the Straits of Gibraltar."

* Official name for Austria under National Socialist rule, 1938–45.

1 6

Hitler had nodded his approval of each point made. Now he raised a silencing hand. "Not too fast, Lieutenant, not too fast! We have yet to take Gibraltar, and I have a few problems to settle with Generalisimo Franco. The question of India still troubles me. But these are details. The general picture is how you've sketched it. The master touches—" his smile was almost apologetic—"will be added as the major events unfold. You will not expect me to—" He broke off, his smile dissolving, as Martin Bormann entered quickly through the massive double doors and paused a few paces inside the salon, respectfully awaiting the Fuehrer's signal to advance. When it came, Bormann hurried across to murmur a few words in Hitler's ear.

"Very well," Hitler grunted, one hand gently pressing into the gray cloth over his stomach. "I shall see him in the Map Room in five minutes. Lieutenant Armbrecht—" he glanced toward Kurt, who was already halfway to his feet—"it has been a pleasure meeting you." And acknowledging Kurt's rigid salute with a dismissive half-salute of his own raised palm, Hitler pivoted on his heel and strode toward the green-baize door in the far corner of the room.

There were two anterooms between the salon and the busy hive of offices that comprised Bormann's communications center on this floor of the Chancellery. Once again, as he passed quickly through the first room close on Bormann's heels, Kurt's eyes met those of the two SS officers watchfully at ease in the immaculate but sinister black uniform of the SS Leibstandarte Adolf Hitler, and once again he bore the cold scrutiny of those blond blue-eyed giants with an inner calm, aware that the Ritterkreuz at the neck of his own undistinguished gray uniform more than compensated for the absence of silver facings. As they passed on into the second anteroom, the reason for Bormann's interruption of Kurt's interview with the Fuehrer manifested itself in the form of a short gray-bearded figure draped in a black *djellaba* and topped by a neat white "flowerpot" turban.

Easily recognizable from the photographs that had been appearing in the German press since November 1941, when he had first arrived in Berlin to launch his holy war against Britain, was Haj Amin el Husseini, the forty-nine-year-old Grand Mufti of Jerusalem. Fanatically anti-Jewish and pro-Axis, the Mufti had for months now, over the German radio, been urging his Muslim followers of the Middle East to sabotage pipelines, blow up bridges and ammunition dumps and kill British soldiers in the name of the Koran and for the honor of Islam. It was said that his influence over the Arabs in Egypt, Jerusalem, Transjordan, the Lebanon, Syria and Iraq would be worth a whole Army Corps to Feldmarschall Rommel once he had taken Alexandria.

He was seated on a sofa to the left of the room, listening with a fixed, almost cherubic smile to one of Bormann's fast-talking adjutants. Now the beady blue eyes fastened on the advancing couple and the neat feet came together, ready to push their owner to his feet. Gesturing Kurt to stand by, Bormann strode briskly across to the Mufti and his companion and engaged them in a brief low-voiced exchange of words that ended with the Mufti nodding contentedly and easing himself back in the sofa. As Bormann swung around and headed for the door on the right-hand side of the room, smartly opened for him by an SS guard, Kurt hurried after him.

The door closed, and they were back in the nerve center from which the dour Deputy Party Leader, with his locked insensitive face and thick peasant body, controlled virtually all traffic in information and human beings to and from the Fuehrer and the vast infrastructure of the Greater Reich. Half a dozen female staff members were busy at desks grouped at the far end of this long, high-ceilinged reception room, some typing, others talking into the telephone. Three male secretaries were bent over their work at the broader desks flanking the threshold of the room, one of them sifting through a deep wad of cablegrams. A fourth man, of about Kurt's age and wearing, like himself, the noncombat uniform of an army lieutenant, was tearing a strip of paper from one of the clattering ticker machines ranged against the left-hand wall. At the open door to the right of the room, giving access to Bormann's inner office, a tall gray-haired civilian, looking every inch—save for the Party badge in his lapel—a Chancellery departmental chief of prewar, even Weimar Republic days, stood clasping a slender file to his chest. Bormann hesitated, as if uncertain whether to lead Kurt on into his own room, then turned to him with a distracted, almost impatient frown.

"The post is yours, Armbrecht. I'll have one of my men show you your quarters."

"Herr Reichsleiter, I am overwhelmed! The Fuehrer said nothing to me, that is about—"

"The Fuehrer speaks to me without words," Bormann grunted. "You will receive formal confirmation of your appointment in due course. Also, your promotion to Captain. Heiden!" He snapped his fingers at the bespectacled middle-aged occupant of the desk nearest the door, and the man popped to his feet as if propelled by an invisible spring. "Take Lieutenant Armbrecht to the Fuehrer's office and introduce him to Fräulein Eppler. She will take over from there." And without another word, the bull-necked Reichsleiter marched through to his office, ignoring the respectful heel click of the official standing by the door.

"May I offer you my congratulations, Herr Captain." The man called Heiden was smiling over his shoulder at Kurt as he led the way down the length of the room. "You have triumphed over some very formidable rivals, I can assure you of that."

"I still can't believe it." Kurt was fighting an idiotic impulse to laugh out loud as he followed Heiden down a long corridor terminating in the distance at a green-baize door, larger than the one in the salon through which Hitler had disappeared, and guarded by two armed SS *Untersturmfuehrer*. Halfway down the neon-lit corridor, Heiden stopped before a pair of glass-paneled swing doors. "Here's where I hand you over to the shrews. A good-looking young hero like you . . ." He shook his head, mock-ruefully.

"You're overlooking something, Herr Heiden," Kurt muttered, glancing down at his empty sleeve. "I'm only three quarters of a hero. I'll be perfectly safe in there."

"Don't count on it. Take it from me, Armbrecht, I'd give my own left arm for that decoration you're wearing. Irresistible, my friend, to any hot-blooded female patriot of the Reich." Glancing down the corridor toward the unconcerned SS guards, he moved a step nearer to Kurt, obviously in no great hurry to do Bormann's bidding. Kurt's nervousness was not lessened by the delay.

"I almost made it myself—the western front, I mean. Think of it, Armbrecht!" Heiden turned one hand palm upwards and began ticking off his statements on the extended fingers. *"Sturmbannfuehrer* of the SA in Frankfurt-an-der-Oder in 1932. Chief of the Russian monitoring staff in Reichsmarschall Goering's *Landespolizeigruppe* from 1934 to 1936. Retained on the Reichsmarschall's headquarters staff when Reichsfuehrer Himmler took over the police, and seconded to the Luftwaffe's operations command for the invasion of Poland. Then what?" Heiden shook his head, sorrowfully. "The day after we struck in the west, on May the eleventh, 1940, I applied for a combat commission with Army Group A. The request was never forwarded to General von Manstein's staff, although I had had the privilege of attending on the general more than once during my service with the Reichsmarschall. And why? All because of these two damned languages I have—Polish and Russian. 'It's the Chancellery for you, young man,' they told me. 'Big things are in the offing. You're too valuable to use as cannon fodder against the French and British.'" Heiden gave a deep sigh, his pale eyes languishing on Kurt's decoration. "Don't misunderstand me, Armbrecht, I've not been chairbound in Berlin all this time. It wasn't exactly a bed of roses, out there in the Fuehrer's Russian headquarters last year. But to have given an arm, like you have . . ." His shoulders lifted, then dropped disconsolately.

"I didn't give it," Kurt said quietly. "It was taken away from me by the track of a French tank." He tilted his chin toward the swing doors. "Don't you think we ought to—"

"Of course, of course. Oh, and don't be unnerved by Fräulein Eppler." Heiden lowered his voice to a hiss. "I find it helps to stare at the wart on the right side of her neck."

Enthroned behind a large desk in a screened-off section of the Fuehrer's office, Fräulein Eppler was a square-shouldered gray-haired woman of middle age with the brow of a headmistress and the jaw of a woman jailer. Heiden's overly formal introduction of Kurt was cut off by her impatient "Yes, yes, I know all about it," and he was dismissed as she waved Kurt into the one vacant chair. When they were alone, she leaned back, appraising him with her keen brown eyes.

"An office has been set aside for you, Lieutenant, on the other side of the corridor. I cannot spare you a full-time typist as of now, but then I don't suppose you'll be in need of one quite yet?" Her pause indicated permission to speak.

"I'm not certain about that, Fräulein Eppler. Perhaps I could—"

"Let me know when the need arises," she cut in, with a brisk nod. "In the meantime one of my girls, Fräulein Gruyten, will be available when not otherwise engaged. Ask for whatever you need in the way of writing materials, books et cetera. Now, I understand it is a condition of your appointment that you live in at the Chancellery or wherever the Fuehrer is residing."

Kurt nodded.

"Fräulein Gruyten will take you to meet Sturmbannfuehrer Kremer who has arranged sleeping accommodation for you in the SS officers' quarters. You will not mess with the SS however, but will take your meals in the Chancellery restaurant—executives' section, of course. You will find in your office a booklet listing the internal telephone numbers of all Chancellery departmental chiefs, and it is the Fuehrer's wish that you communicate with them directly and not with subordinates. In the same booklet you will find full guidance on Chancellery protocol, security and air-raid precautions. Your appointment formally begins the day after tomorrow, and your working hours are—" the flicker of a smile momentarily disturbed the solemn cast of her features —"entirely flexible, as you must already know."

Her fugitive smile loosened his strung nerves. He said, "I'm still in a daze, Fräulein Eppler. The day after tomorrow—that is, when I start work, how shall I know when I'm wanted?"

"The Fuehrer's summons will come through me, or through Fräulein Junge, who takes over from me at six P.M. If it is any help to you, the Fuehrer rises late in the morning and seldom descends from his private apartment before eleven. But he keeps late hours." Again the spasm of a smile. "It would not be advisable for you to make private evening arrangements, outside the Chancellery, without specific clearance from myself or Fräulein Junge. However—" she broke off as a buzzer sounded on her desk, and stubbed a finger to the base of the intercom box. "Yes, Herr Reichsleiter?"

"The Fuehrer's last memorandum to the Grand Mufti," Bormann's voice crackled from the box, "wanted at once in the Map Room."

"At once, Herr Reichsleiter." She was on her feet, vibrating urgency. "You must excuse me, Captain. I'll send Fräulein Gruyten to take care of you."

Kurt rose from his chair and watched her, through the open frame of the partition wall, bustling along the aisle between the dozen-or-so desks of the general office. She called over to a girl seated behind a typewriter, then hurried on down toward a bank of steel filing cabinets. The girl got up and walked unhurriedly toward Fräulein Eppler's enclave, straightening her dress as she came. Kurt had time to register her young oval face and ripe figure before turning away politely.

"Lieutenant Armbrecht?" She had come to a halt a few paces short of where he was standing. He turned to her, answering her nervous smile with a playful click of his heels.

"I'm Helga Gruyten. I'm to show you your office." She was a near-miss at prettiness: flaxen hair plaited and coiled into "earmuffs," well-sculpted nose and cheekbones, but meagerly proportioned lips and small, deep-set eyes. From the neck downward, however, she scored impressively; and as she led the way out to the corridor Kurt had to make a conscious effort to keep his eyes off her undulous hips.

"Here we are." She had stopped in front of a plain unpaneled door inscribed with the number 14. "Your private kingdom, Herr Lieutenant, in the Reich Chancellery!" She turned the handle and waved him in ahead of her. As the overhead strip lights came on, he found himself in a room about four meters square, windowless, but newly carpeted in a deep green and furnished with a good desk, a comfortable looking swivel chair, broad leather-surfaced wall table, two visitors' chairs and a couple of steel filing cabinets. A framed photograph of Adolf Hitler hung on the far wall, and a fan was high in the corner to the right of it. "By the time you start work—" the girl's voice came from directly behind him—"I shall try to make it a bit more cheerful. A few posters of Bavarian landscapes perhaps?"

She was smiling when he turned to her, showing a row of small white teeth. Her eyes flicked between his face and the empty sleeve pinned to his army jacket.

He said, "How much more do you know about me, Fräulein Gruyten—apart from the fact that I'm a southerner?"

"Well—" Her pale-blue eyes quizzed him, seeking reassurance.

"It's all right. I shan't bite you."

"I know you are going to help our Fuehrer compile a history of the Greater Reich. And I know that the thesis you wrote for your degree from Munich University was published last year by the Eher Verlag, with a foreword by Doctor Goebbels."

"Do you remember the title?"

"Of course I do!" Her small eyes flared as she tossed her head. "I've even read it, believe it or not. *The Significance of Leadership in the German Ethos*. I can quote from it, if you still doubt me."

"You've made your point, Fräulein Gruyten. One more question, before we go to see Sturmbannfuehrer Kremer. Are you engaged?"

She wasn't avoiding his steady, teasing gaze. It was simply that his sleeveless arm seemed to fascinate her. She said, a faint flush spreading up the modest V-neck of her austere cotton frock, "There are sixteen of us in the office and we are all already married—to our beloved Fuehrer." Her eyes flicked up, answering his theatrical sigh. "However, that isn't to say, Lieutenant Armbrecht, that we don't occasionally take lovers."

Kurt put in a call to his mother in Munich just after 1 P.M., timing it to catch his sister Sophie at home. The Chancellery operator was polite but officious.

"Is this a personal call, Lieutenant, or on the Fuehrer's business?"

"It's personal."

"You appreciate it will be charged to you, on a monthly account."

"Thank you for informing me. I'd still like to make the call."

"At your service, Lieutenant."

His mother's cry of joy when he gave her the news almost shattered his eardrum. He heard her shouting to Sophie, "It's Kurt, darling! He's got the appointment! And promotion!" Then her rapid breathless interrogation. "When do you start? Where will you be living? Have you actually met the Fuehrer yet? Oh, Kurt, this is wonderful! Your father—I shall call him at the University, soon as you've hung up."

"Give him my love, Mother, and tell him I'll try to call him one evening soon. Now may I speak to Sophie?"

He could imagine his sister collecting herself, shooshing their mother as she took the receiver. Her voice was almost calm, over the three hundred miles separating them. "Captain Armbrecht, I congratulate you. But I never doubted you'd be chosen." Then it broke. "How are you, darling?"

"Couldn't be better. How are things at home?"

"Just about as usual. Father's up to his ears in exam papers,

2 4

of course, and Mother's started to grow tomatoes. When do you think we shall see you?"

"With any luck, maybe pretty soon. We're sure to be spending part of the summer at Berchtesgaden."

"And you'll get time off, do you think?"

"Time enough for me to muscle in on your boy friends," he chuckled. "Who's the hot favorite right now?"

"No one. I get so tired, bashing Spanish into thick Bavarian skulls from morning to evening. I just want to flop when I get home."

Kurt remembered what the Fuehrer had told him about the Balkan operations, starting at dawn, and the thought of dropping a hint from the heart of the Reich Chancellery to his "kid sister" (as she would always be) out there in the Bavarian backwoods was tempting. But it would be folly of the worst kind. Every call, in and out of the Chancellery, would surely be monitored by the Sicherheitsdienst.

"Sophkins, think of me when you turn on the radio, before you go off to the Institute. Especially when there's exciting news from the Fuehrer's High Command. I'm right in the center of it here."

"I'd rather think of you with your feet up here on the sitting-room sofa, with your nose glued to a book." It was true; his sister was never particularly excited by the Wehrmacht's fantastic triumphs.

"It won't be long now. Embrace Mother for me. And give Father my love."

He had decided to skip lunch in the Chancellery and accept Sturmbannfuehrer Kremer's offer of an SS driver to help him move his two suitcases from the hotel where he had spent these last two nights in Berlin to the austere cubicle of a room allotted to him in the officers' quarters. He had no appetite for food. His stomach was still fluttering from the meeting with Adolf Hitler, and a nagging ache had started up again in the stub of his amputated left arm. There was a problem bothering him and he wasn't sure of the way to handle it. The Fuehrer had talked to him for a whole twenty minutes without throwing any light on the method by which they were to approach the structuring of *Mein Sieg* or what was expected of him as "literary assistant." Werner Naumann, Undersecretary of State at the Ministry of Propaganda and Public Enlightenment, had been no more help-ful during yesterday's interview, brushing aside Kurt's tentative probes with the comment, "There'll be time to go into that, Armbrecht, if and when the Fuehrer chooses you for the post." Well, he *had* been chosen, and his work began the day after to-morrow. But what was the method to be? Was it permitted, even, for him to raise these matters with the Fuehrer at their next meeting?

There was only one person, other than Hitler himself, who could give him the answers, and Kurt now had an excellent ex-cuse for getting in touch with him again. He would try to call Reichsminister Goebbels from the Chancellery, immediately after lunchtime, and if the Ministry put him through he would thank the good Doctor for his patronage and tactfully solicit the further and inestimable favor of a personal briefing.

He made his call from the telephone in the corridor connect-ing the officers' sleeping quarters with the main guard room. From where he stood, he had an angled view through the open door of his room of a section of his iron-framed bed and the leather-framed photograph propped up on the bedside table. It was a picture of his father embracing Sophie at Munich airport on her return from Madrid in May 1941. The picture did no justice whatsoever to Professor Armbrecht, whose face was al-most completely obscured behind a cascade of chestnut hair, but it was an enchanting snapshot of Sophie, golden-brown, laughing straight into the lens and looking much nearer seven-teen than twenty-two. It had made a fine replacement for that other picture, soaked in his own blood when the stretcher-bearers had picked him up, the only survivor of an antitank unit with seven French tanks to its credit that morning of May 14,

1940, when the bridgehead over the Meuse at Sedan was held against everything the Frogs and the R.A.F. threw in. The picture had never been out of his possession since.

"Captain Armbrecht?" It was another voice in the earpiece —male, this time, vibrant with invisible authority. "This is Karl Hanke."

Kurt stiffened. Hanke. Secretary of State to the Minister.

"Herr Secretary!"

"My congratulations, Captain. Now, as to a meeting with the Herr Doktor, this would be advisable before you take up your appointment, but quite impossible over the next twenty-four hours or so. However, the Herr Doktor proposes you attend on him at his official residence the day after tomorrow at eight A.M. There is no guarantee, you understand, that you will see him there, but he will do his best to have a few words with you, before leaving for the Ministry. Is that understood?"

"Perfectly, Herr Secretary! I am greatly obliged to you."

There was a vase of flowers, next morning, on the top of the bookcase when he stopped in at his office to read the two daily papers supplied to Chancellery executives—*Voelkischer Beobachter* and *Das Reich,* the weightier journal of Reich and foreign affairs. Huge black headlines confirmed the news that had blared from the guard-room radio early that morning, when the orderly brought him his coffee (the real thing!) and the thin slices of bread, unbuttered.

BALKANS INVADED

WEHRMACHT STRIKES ACROSS FIVE FRONTIERS

He was eagerly scanning the article when the door opened and Fräulein Gruyten strode in, pushing a small office cart ahead of her. Her face was aglow.

"Good morning, Captain! Isn't it tremendous, the news?"

"Fantastic! Did you hear the radio this morning? Advance panzer columns already closing in on Belgrade! It's going to be another blitzkrieg, Fräulein Gruyten. All over in a few weeks!"

"Poor Fräulein Junge. She was on duty all night, right up to eight o'clock this morning, when the Fuehrer finally went up to bed. Here, Captain, I've brought you everything I could think of —notebooks, files, pencils, clips, writing paper. If there's anything lacking, you have only to ask." She started unloading the contents of the cart onto the table up against the wall.

"The flowers," he said, leaning back in his chair. "Do they come from the office storeroom, too?"

"Liberated from a friend's garden. No luck with the Bavarian posters, I'm afraid, but I'll keep trying." She had emptied the trolley and was dusting off her hands. "Are you lunching in the restaurant today? They usually have *Kasseler Rippenspeer* on the Tuesday menu."

"If we could share the same table I might be tempted. Oh, yes, I know—what would Fräulein Eppler think! Anyway, I'm going to spend my last day of freedom walking around the city, gaping up at buildings like a country bumpkin."

She turned abruptly around to the table, picked up a pencil and scribbled something rapidly across the front of a notebook. "Here—" she tossed the notebook onto his desk without a smile and without looking at him—"if you get lost, and it's after six P.M., you can call me at this number." She was out of the room and had closed the door behind her before he had time to think of a reply.

Kurt lunched on the Kurfuerstendamm at the officers' club he had been frequenting during that long tense Saturday and Sunday in the capital, and was treated to some fine French cognac by the club secretary, a Junker colonel of the Kaiser's army in World War I. Then he passed the afternoon strolling in the June sunshine and catching up on the places of interest he hadn't yet got around to seeing: the Bendlerstrasse War Office, the University on the Unter den Linden, the Kaiserhof Hotel on the Reichskanzlerplatz, which the Fuehrer had made his headquarters during that final and dramatic political poker game, ten years ago, ending with the collapse of the Weimar Republic and Hitler's appointment as Reich Chancellor.

On an impulse he walked north along the Wilhelmstrasse, and out through Brandenburg Gate into the Tiergarten, reversing the route taken by those endless marching columns of the Party's Storm Troopers that had so stirred German newsreel audiences, Kurt included, in the days before the bloody purge of their leadership in 1934 and the subsequent fall from grace of the brown-shirted Sturmabteiling. But an hour and a half of walking on the pavements was already beginning to take its toll of a pair of legs still far from restored to their normal vigor. He would take one more long look at the massive portico of the new Reich Chancellery, with its grandiose row of towering Doric columns, and indulge once again the truly awesome reflection that this, the political center of the Greater Reich, was to be his work place for at least another two years—two years that would decide the whole future course of his professional life.

In this administrative sector of the capital, every other man one passed on the street was wearing some kind of uniform, together with an expression of stern preoccupation with a pressing duty. And every glistening, speeding Mercedes sedan seemed to have an Army or SS driver up front and a Wehrmacht or Party pennant fluttering from its radiator. It had been a relief, his being assured by Bormann's office that morning that civilian clothes were permissible during working hours, or on private excursions within the city limits. He had had enough saluting, and being saluted, to last him a while. He was now what he had always wanted to be, not a soldier but a Party intellectual, with a God-sent opportunity to prove to himself that the pen, if not mightier than the sword, could be a rewarding extension of his right hand.

Strolling back westward, he headed for the café on the Bendlerstrasse, a few hundred yards from the Chancellery, where they had served him that delicious *schlumperwerk* of pastry stuffed with grated apples.

An hour later as he signaled for another ersatz coffee, he thought again about Fräulein Gruyten's invitation. He was killing time. In another quarter of an hour he could go to the telephone booth beside the cash desk, call the number she had jotted, tell her he was hopelessly lost and probably wind up in her bed for the night. The prospect at once excited and discomforted him. She would strip like an angel, that one, but there was also in those deep-set eyes the promise of a she-devil. He hadn't had a woman these past two years, for the services rendered by those randy night nurses in charge of the amputees' ward hardly qualified as "lays." He had ducked every tacit offer that had come his way in Munich since his discharge—not, heaven knew, out of indifference but in the bitter awareness that he could only be a sexual novelty, a fillip to the prurient imagination and inventiveness of his bed partner. It was something he would sooner or later have to come to terms with. But the more he thought about it, the more uneasy he became about plunging into the deep, as it were, with Fräulein Gruyten. It wasn't a question of keeping one's nose clean with Fräulein Eppler and the rest of the Fuehrer's staff. No one would frown, these days, at the thought of an unmarried German girl having sex with an Aryan war hero. Hadn't Hitler himself had more than once broadly hinted at the positive desirability of such liaisons? And hadn't the Reichsfuehrer SS Heinrich Himmler gone even further by setting up the Lebensborn maternity homes, where women made pregnant by his own officers could enjoy a carefree confinement in the knowledge that their babies would be proudly fostered and educated by the state?

It wasn't that. It was more in the nature of an instinct that told him that Adolf Hitler counted on owning him, Kurt Armbrecht, body and soul, and that any evidence to the contrary, especially if generated under his own Chancellery roof, would be unfavorably regarded by the Fuehrer. Nothing on earth could be worth that risk.

Finishing his coffee, he paid the bill and then spent a couple of hours in a cinema watching newsreel coverage of General Alfred Jodl's preinvasion tour of the Balkan fronts, followed by the feature film *Comrades on the High Seas*. He was in bed by ten o'clock. Tomorrow was a big day.

CHAPTER TWO

I

DURING THE short walk from the Chancellery to the private Berlin residence of Doctor Goebbels on the Hermann Goering Strasse, Kurt passed the corpses of two Russian prisoners of war, limply sprawled in the gutter about twenty yards apart. An SS trooper with an Erma submachine gun crooked in his left arm stood on the broad pavement a few yards from the first body, yawning as he stared along the Wilhelmstrasse. There were a fair number of pedestrians, even at this early hour, but they were hurrying past without even a glance at the ragged shaven-headed corpses, and as the SS guard's dull eyes swung lazily toward Kurt's empty sleeve, Kurt found himself doing the same as the others, averting his eyes from the gutter and stepping up his pace.

Curiosity goaded him to take a covert look at the second body as he hurried past; and his skin contracted with disgust. The man looked as if he had been dead for days rather than minutes. Hollow wide-open eyes fixed on the sky, sallow skin tightly stretched over bearded face, cracked lips parted in a grimace. In death, the man was ageless. There were no marks of violence on him. He was just one of the millions of Slav *Untermenschen* whose brief usefulness as slave labor to the Reich ended with their final collapse from starvation and exhaustion.

As Kurt stopped at the curb a few yards farther on, waiting

for a break in the traffic, a big garbage truck clattered to a halt beside the first corpse and two men in dirty white fatigues clambered down from the cabin. The SS guard took a few paces backward, ostentatiously pinching his nose. One of the scavengers called something out to him, and his mate let out a guffaw before turning to boot the corpse's legs and arms into line. With the practiced economy of stevedores they swung the body up and tossed it over the tailboard of the truck, wiping their hands on their thighs as they sauntered back to the cab.

It was a distasteful start to the day. One could wipe it out, however, by redirecting one's thoughts to what lay ahead. Kurt had met Doctor Goebbels only once, when the Minister's aide, Rudolf Stimmer, had collected him from his home in Munich a month ago and driven him to the airport for a five-minute interview while the Minister's aircraft was being refueled. On that occasion Kurt had been too overawed for any appraisal of the man himself, as distinct from the legend. He had concentrated so intently on answering the rapid questions shot at him from the depths of the armchair in the airport's V.I.P. lounge, he could remember only the beautiful timbre of the voice, the liquid brown eyes restlessly measuring him as he stood at attention, and the slender, almost feminine hands stroking the armchair's leather hide. His answers and general demeanor obviously had pleased the Minister for Kurt to have made the short list of candidates for the job. Perhaps this morning, if in fact he got to see Doctor Goebbels, some light might be thrown on the practical qualities the Fuehrer himself had demanded.

Joseph Goebbels . . . Reich Minister of Propaganda, Gauleiter of Berlin and comrade of Adolf Hitler since 1925. At forty-four, the most powerful and successful political propagandist in history. And, after Hitler, the Party's greatest public orator. The mind boggled at the sway this dwarf of a man wielded, unchallenged, over every medium of communication throughout the Greater Reich. Not a newspaper, magazine, novel or textbook could come off the printing press without his approval, direct or judiciously anticipated. Lord of the nation's radio through his direct control of the double-headed monopoly, Deutschlandsender and Reichssender. Dictator of the German film industry and the theater. With a headquarters staff in Berlin of a thousand specialists in propaganda and public relations and an annual budget of untold millions. And he still had time to write his brilliant weekly articles for *Das Reich,* laying down the guidelines from which a public official or Party leader might stray only at his direct peril . . .

Then there was the other Goebbels, the envied object of good-natured gossip whenever Party members discussed their leaders' personal frailties over mugs in the *bierstuben.* He had married the elegant Magda Quandt, divorced wife of the rich industrialist, in 1931 and she had presented him, by 1938, with four daughters and a son. What she had failed to do was keep him faithful to her. His appetite for aspiring young actresses was insatiable, and the power he wielded over the entertainment industry ensured that he never went hungry for fresh and nubile bodies.

Kurt hadn't succeeded in identifying Goebbels's private residence during his walking tour of the Government district the previous afternoon. Now, as he approached his destination, he could understand why. The palace Goebbels had built on the site of the villa once occupied by a Weimar Minister of Food was screened from the road by a plantation of ancient trees and was visible only as one approached the open gates of the driveway. The armed guards on duty were drawn from the regular Berlin police force, and the sergeant who inspected his Chancellery card, with its inscription "In the personal service of the Fuehrer," gave him a smart salute before leading the way toward the main entrance of the palace. A glittering black Mercedes sedan was parked in the forecourt. A liveried footman opened the door as the sergeant brought Kurt to the foot of the steps, and as he entered the spacious reception hall a young man in civilian clothes came forward to greet him with a "Heil Hitler!" salute before introducing himself as the Minister's Press Secretary, Wilfred von Oven. Kurt thought it best to decline the offer of coffee, although his mouth had started to dry the moment he stepped over the threshold. Leading him to a sofa, Oven invited him to "glance through" the daily papers neatly arranged on a beautiful Biedermeier table, then returned to the marble-topped side table, where he concentrated for a few minutes on sorting a deep stack of telegrams, before depositing them in a large red-leather briefcase. That done, he glanced at his wrist watch and reached for the telephone.

"Captain Armbrecht!" He had hung up and was smiling at Kurt across the hall. "The Herr Doktor will see you now, upstairs."

After the noise and diesel fumes of the Wilhelmstrasse, the ascent of the deep-carpeted grand stairway and the soundless passage through sunlit salons to Goebbels's private quarters was like being escorted through a modern museum outside of normal visiting hours; and the impression was heightened by the display, en route, of a pedestaled bust of Frederick the Great and several post-Impressionist canvases, among which Kurt thought he recognized a Cezanne and a Monet. A door was opened, and Oven stepped forward, motioning to Kurt to follow suit.

"Lieutenant Armbrecht, Herr Doktor."

"Lieutenant . . . ?" The mellifluous voice winged Kurt back to the private lounge in Munich airport. "I should have thought it would now be in order, my dear Oven, to recognize his promotion. Come and sit over here, Captain."

They were in what was obviously the Propaganda Minister's dressing room, a long rectangular area walled by fitted wardrobes. Apart from the Minister, whose dark head was just visible over the back of a chrome-framed chair facing the one window, there were three other people in the room—an elderly fellow in a barber's white smock, quietly fitting his tools into a square black case; a middle-aged valet standing at ease beside a breakfast cart; and a pretty manicurist with short red hair, briskly buffing the fingernails of the slender hand resting in hers. The scent of expensive eau de cologne hung on the air. There was an empty seat a few paces beyond where Goebbels was sitting

3 5

and, after giving the Minister a smart heel-clicking "Heil Hitler!" Kurt lowered himself to its edge, facing his benefactor with what he hoped was the correct expression of mingled humility and awe.

At these close quarters, with the early morning sun streaming through the tall window, the Doctor looked decidedly younger than his forty-four years, a curiously boyish figure, in fact, with his slight build, disproportionately large head and steeply sloping shoulders. He was favoring Kurt with a wide, almost conspiratorial smile.

"You won a bet for me yesterday, Armbrecht. And Reichsleiter Bormann is twenty marks the poorer for it. Emil," he called over to the valet, "give the Captain a cup of coffee. And another half cup for me."

They were alone now, except for the valet, standing by with a superbly cut dark-gray jacket at the ready while his master slipped a pair of cuff links into his cream-colored silk shirt. Kurt, balancing his coffee cup, had started to rise when Goebbels stepped down from the barber's chair, but had been gestured to stay seated. And as the Doctor limped to his dressing table, Kurt was able to steal a swift glance at the inward-turning left foot, legacy of an operation after infantile paralysis at the age of four. It occurred to Kurt then that the Minister's support for his appointment might have sprung from the fellow feeling of a cripple toward an amputee; therefore he was startled when Goebbels called over his shoulder, a second later, "That arm of yours—wouldn't it help you in your work to have an artificial limb fitted?"

"I'm afraid not, Herr Doktor. There's not really enough left of the humerus. But it doesn't bother me at all, and I've doubled the speed of my Gabelsberger shorthand since you honored me with the interview in Munich."

"Good, good." The little figure was momentarily lost to view as Emil moved smoothly in with the jacket. "I've given up trying

3 6

to persuade the Fuehrer to use a mechanical recorder. He won't be in the same room with one. Which reminds me—" Goebbels was facing him once more, shooting a half-inch of cuff from his sleeve—"I have made arrangements with Reichsleiter Bormann for you to have access to the typescripts of all Heinrich Heim's shorthand notes."

"Heinrich Heim, Herr Doktor . . . ?"

"The official who has been recording the Fuehrer's mealtime conversations since July of last year. His job is to take notes of the Fuehrer's conversations with his guests, from an unobtrusive corner of the room. The notes are then dictated to a stenographer and go to Bormann for editing, annotation and so forth. I think you will find them quite valuable, Armbrecht."

This was the opening Kurt had been hoping for. He said, rising and taking his cup over to the cart, "I am most indebted to you, Herr Doktor. I was hoping—perhaps a word or two of guidance from you as to the structure of the Fuehrer's new book and the method I should follow?"

"The structure," Goebbels said, frowning at his wrist watch, "will surely begin to suggest itself as the work progresses. I would put that out of your mind for the moment. As to method . . ." He was staring past Kurt, out of the window, softly gnawing at his sensual lower lip. "Perhaps we'd better go along to my study for five minutes. Emil, phone down to Herr Stimmer and tell him I shall be slightly delayed."

Red had been the color used by Goebbels in all those pre-1933 posters aimed at the German working class. It was a color chosen by himself and Hitler as the circular background to the black swastika, a color deliberately stolen from the Communists, for its revolutionary message of urgency and violence. It was a color that stimulated rather than soothed, and as such, it seemed proper as the dominant color in the décor of the Propaganda Minister's study. From the comfortable swivel chair behind the red-leather-topped desk, the Doctor could gaze over a vast expanse of red carpet toward the great fireplace at the other end of the room. Without turning his head, the cone of his vision would be encarmined by the lofty drapes of the window wall, muted symbols of those festive vertical banners that blazoned the Nazi charisma from the Fuehrer's platform at every important prewar rally. Kurt was aware of smaller, subsidiary assertions of red here and there in the room but was unable, afterward, to give them an identity. His eyes had been drawn, almost immediately on entry, to the huge portrait of Adolf Hitler that took up most of the wall space behind Doctor Goebbels's desk. It seemed at first the wrong place to hang a portrait of one's mentor—out of one's sight while working. But as the Doctor slipped into his chair and leaned back, propping his right knee up against the edge of the desk, the siting of the portrait made its own sense. Here in the forefront was Goebbels, the voice of the Party. And there, hugely behind him to remind any visitor of the source of this little man's far-reaching authority, was the face and form of the Fuehrer, benignly presiding over every thought and action of his *enfant prodige*.

Kurt had lowered himself into one of the tall-backed chairs facing the Minister's desk. Now, as Goebbels unbuckled his wrist watch to prop it—an unambiguous little ceremony—on the blotting pad, Kurt interpreted the Minister's silence as his cue to open the dialogue.

"These notes of the Fuehrer's mealtime conversations, Herr Doktor—I take it they are not for direct quotation in the new book?"

"They are for your reference, Armbrecht. They already run into many hundreds of typewritten pages and they embody the Fuehrer's viewpoint on an immensely rich variety of subjects. They are no substitute, of course, for the considered statements the Fuehrer will be making to you about, for example, his plans for the new Germanic Empire."

"These statements, Herr Doktor—presumably they are to be the main source material for the book?"

"Correct. But only within the framework of your own editing. This will involve the most scrupulous research on your part, so that no statement goes unsupported by the relevant historical or philosophical data. You will watch out for apparent contradictions, particularly by reference to the two books of *Mein Kampf* and to the Fuehrer's speeches throughout his political career, and you will draw his attention to any such discrepancies. And it goes without saying that you will render the Fuehrer's—um— expressive rhetoric into a literary idiom irreproachable as to grammar and general style." He was now smiling openly at Kurt, offering the shared indulgence of two university graduates toward the scholastic deficiencies of a common associate. And Kurt returned a quick nervous smile, savoring for that brief moment a harmless irreverence he suspected would be a rare enough phenomenon in Chancellery circles and utterly unthinkable in the presence of Martin Bormann.

"This aspect of your work," Goebbels went on, "the literary editing, is to be unobtrusive. You must see yourself not as a steamroller, ironing out the Fuehrer's idiosyncratic language, but rather as a kind of cosmetic surgeon, delicately removing the warts and other blemishes from the otherwise strong and immensely distinctive features of your patient. You will find it helpful that the Fuehrer does not like having himself recorded, word for word, in shorthand. He will expect you to make a note of key statements, or his more eloquent turns of phrase, but he will not want to be addressing the top of your head during the private sessions. Give him plenty of attention as you commit to memory the conceptual nature of his pronouncements. When you are dismissed, whatever the time of day or night, there will be a stenographer on duty in the Fuehrer's office to take immediate dictation, while your memory is still fresh. . . . Ah, yes, and at this particular time I would advise you to brief yourself thoroughly on Balkan and Middle-Eastern affairs. The Fuehrer is going to be greatly preoccupied over the next few months with the military and political solutions for these areas and it would be natural therefore that these will figure largely in his private discussions with you.

"Well, Captain—" Goebbels was reaching out for his wrist watch—"have I been of any help to you?"

"Immensely, Herr Doktor. I'm most indebted to you for sparing me your time."

"We will go, then." The slim figure was already limping toward the door.

As Kurt followed the Doctor down the staircase into the entrance hall, a man he recognized at once as Rudolf Stimmer, the aide who had taken him to Munich airport, snatched a briefcase from the side table and hurried to form a line with Emil, who was bearing the Minister's hat, overcoat and gloves, and Oven, who had the red briefcase grasped in both hands. There were, Kurt noticed, no "Heil Hitlers." Goebbels nodded to his aides, took his hat and gloves from the valet, but declined the overcoat, whose very appearance seemed astonishing, considering the weather. Acknowledging the salutes of the police guard, he hurried down the steps toward the waiting Mercedes, smartly followed by Stimmer and Oven, with Kurt trailing uncertainly in the rear. A Nazi salute came from the chauffeur, standing at attention by the open door of the passenger seat up front. Stimmer and Oven took their places in the back of the car. Emil stepped forward carrying the Minister's folded overcoat like a jeweler's tray, and deposited it on one of the jump seats behind the driver, and the doors of the car were closed by the policeman. From his seat beside the chauffeur, Goebbels turned to raise a slim hand toward Kurt.

"Good luck, Captain."

"Many thanks, Herr Doktor! Heil Hitler!"

Eight days went by before Kurt was summoned to his second meeting with Adolf Hitler. And while he awaited the call, busying himself with maps of the Balkans and the Middle East and the bulky briefings supplied by the Ministry of Foreign Affairs, the Chancellery buzzed like a hive to the comings and goings of generals, admirals and Luftwaffe field marshals summoned to the day-and-night Fuehrer Conferences, each commander flanked by his personal retinue of solemn staff officers and keen-eyed adjutants and all of them activated by the whims and appetites of the exigent but invisible queen bee.

The news from the battlefields came like a daily—often hourly—shot of adrenaline. In Yugoslavia, the Croatian city of Zagreb, undermined by fifth columnists, had fallen to two Hungarian divisions, and the capital, Belgrade, had been isolated by Reichswehr panzer columns. The remains of the Yugoslav front-line armies were retreating toward the mountains, and the pro-German government-in-exile, whose overthrow in March 1941 had almost caused the enraged Hitler to postpone his attack on Russia, had already proclaimed from its headquarters in Budapest its intention of abolishing the monarchy and allying Yugoslavia to the Greater Reich.

The four armored divisions spearheading the invasion of Greece from Bulgaria had ripped through Salonika and were striking south toward Athens, leaving the British expeditionary forces with their backs to the Aegean and their one hope of salvation the British navy, now under murderous attack from Goering's Luftwaffe and Raeder's U-boats as it sailed out to the rescue from its last safe base in the Mediterranean, Alexandria.

Malta's days were numbered. The island stronghold's usefulness as a base from which to scatter and sink the convoys ferrying troops and supplies to Feldmarschall Rommel's army in North Africa had ended three months ago, when five hundred of Goering's bombers were switched from the eastern front to airfields in Sicily. Since then, not a single ship of the merchant convoys dispatched by Churchill through the Straits of Gibraltar had made anchorage in Malta's Grand Harbour. The word around the Fuehrer's office was that Malta and Crete would be taken before the end of the summer by paratroop divisions now training on the Italian island of Elba.

But the most exciting news of all during these eight days was coming from the Middle East. Rommel's reinforced Afrika Korps was already bypassing Alexandria and pressing the British Eighth Army toward the Nile. Winston Churchill had just declared, in his most somber radio broadcast of the war,

Unless this new offensive can be halted and flung back, and our naval base in Alexandria relieved of jeopardy, we face the direst prospects. These would surely include the loss or, at best, the enforced withdrawal of our Eastern Mediterranean fleet, and with it the cutting of our lifeline between the Mediterranean and our empire in India. The vital oil resources of the Persian Gulf would be absorbed into the monstrous Nazi New Order. The continent of Africa would be fatally exposed to rape and plunder by Hitler's Huns.

In the Chancellery canteen, where Kurt was now taking most of his meals, a great roar of derisive laughter had greeted the reading aloud of this monitored text by the Fuehrer's interpreter, Paul Schmidt. To Kurt's left, Heinrich Hoffman, Hitler's official photographer, was choking, red-faced, over the third shot of *Schnapps,* swigged on the sly from his hip flask. "Think of it, Armbrecht," he gasped, his thick Bavarian accent lending added vulgarity to the words, "all that virgin black meat just waiting to be ravaged by us Huns! Rommel's lads are going to give a whole new meaning to the word *schwarzfahren!"*

The play on the German term for "joy-ride" won Hoffman a new explosion of guffaws, in which only Kurt and Julius Schaub, Hitler's burly chief civilian adjutant, did not join.

"It's not only in bad taste," Schaub snapped when the laughter died down, "to suggest our soldiers would consort with savages. It's also absurd to use the word 'joy-ride' in the same breath with Feldmarschall Rommel's Afrika Korps. Have you no idea, Hoffman, of the conditions they are fighting under, and still have to face, before we can win the Middle East?"

Hoffman was scowling back, but holding his tongue. The lame, hard-drinking Bavarian had grown enormously rich from the Fuehrer's patronage over these past twenty years, but he was completely outranked by SS Gruppenfuehrer Schaub, whose presence at the table was a rare enough event, made possible this day only because "the Chief"—as his closest aides referred among themselves to Hitler—was having a luncheon with Mar-

42

tin Bormann, Heinrich Himmler, and Karl Eichmann, head of the SS-controlled Jewish Office.

To take the heat off Hoffman, Kurt smoothly turned the conversation back to the Fuehrer's lunchtime guests, the topic of discussion before Schmidt had stopped by with his translation of Churchill's speech.

"I was wondering," he inquired politely of Schaub, "how Obersturmbannfuehrer Eichmann fitted into the Fuehrer's present preoccupations with the Balkans and the Middle East."

"He doesn't have to," Schaub grunted. "The Fuehrer involves himself in everything, all the time." And then, as though remembering his obligations toward the newcomer: "In this instance, however, there is a connection. It's called Palestine."

Kurt put down his fork, giving the chief adjutant his full attention.

"In the course of driving the British out of Arabia," Schaub went on, "and linking up with Rundstedt's forces in Persia, we shall be inheriting that dung heap called the Jewish National Home. It'll be given back to the Arabs, of course, but the problem will remain of what to do with the Jews already infecting the territory."

"The Grand Mufti will take care of that," Hoffman chuckled. "Didn't anyone read the report of his broadcast to the Arabs yesterday? 'Kill the Jews wherever you find them,' he said. 'This pleases God, history and religion.' I'll take a bet . . ."

Kurt said, "But there must be half a million of them, including women and children. Where do we put them, now that we've promised the Arabs their land back?"

It seemed an obvious enough question, but suddenly they were all staring at him as if he had said something provocative. They stopped staring and made a pretense of getting on with their food—all except Hoffman, whose boozy eyes were now trained on Schaub. "Our young friend," he said, breaking the silence, "has asked a question. Does the Herr Obergruppenfuehrer intend to answer it, or should I venture to give Armbrecht the facts of life?"

Julius Schaub emptied his coffee cup, shot Hoffman a look of withering animosity and rose noisily to his feet. "There are times when you bore the hell out of me, Hoffman," he said through his teeth. And without another word, he swung around and stomped away across the room.

Kurt started to say, "Look, I don't know what this is all about, but—"

"Pompous ass!" Hoffman shrugged, slipping his hip flask onto his lap. "And a moral coward on top of it." He tossed back a silver stopperful of schnapps and released a soft, contented belch. "You're one of us now, Armbrecht. We don't have to mince words, do we?"

"I shouldn't have thought so. But if I'm sticking my nose into something I—" He broke off as Professor Morell, the Fuehrer's physician, pushed his chair back and, with a mumbled "Good day, gentlemen," made tracks for the door. This left Dr. Meissner, the Chancellery protocol chief, still at the table, and he was already folding his napkin and glancing pointedly at the canteen clock. Hoffman winked at Kurt and leaned back, staring up at the ceiling.

"Well, gentlemen, time I got back to the grindstone." Meissner was on his feet, nodding and smiling.

"Naturally, Herr Doktor," Hoffman grunted, still studying the ceiling. "Good day to you!"

The two men were alone now and out of earshot, while they kept their voices down, of the next tables. Hoffman offered Kurt a cigarette.

"Thanks, but I try not to smoke during the daytime."

The photographer lighted his own, nodding. "Wise fellow, if you can keep it up. It's murder when I'm on a job with the Chief. He once caught me having a quiet draw on the open terrace of the Berghof and bawled me out for fouling the air of Obersalzberg!"

"Getting back to that question of mine . . . ."

"Ah, yes. The Palestine problem. Has nobody briefed you about Eichmann and the SS Special Action Groups?"

"Eichmann, I know about. He's responsible for delousing Germany of the Jews, carting them off to Poland and Russia, and all that. But the Special Action Groups?" Kurt shook his head.

Hoffman propped his elbows on the table and blinked at the smoke curling up from the tip of his vertically held cigarette. He kept his voice low. "What do you think happens to the Jews who are useless as slave labor for the Reich—the old men and women, the weak and the puny, the pregnant mothers and the small brats?"

"Kept in concentration camps, presumably?"

"Come now, Armbrecht! Useless *Judenlausen,* fed at the expense of the very people they've been plundering all these years? You can do better than that!"

He could, but he couldn't bring himself to say it. In fact, he didn't want to be sitting there any longer, listening to Hoffman.

"What would you do with them?" Hoffman went on. "We can't ship them off to Palestine, even if we wanted to and had the means to do it, because the British won't allow more than fifteen thousand in every year. No other country outside the Reich wants them—not even America—and who can blame them? You want to know what the Special Action Groups are doing right now, Armbrecht, in our eastern territories?"

There was no backing out now. He gave a grunt and waited, all emotion on ice, for Hoffman to say it.

"They're eliminating them, my friend. Painlessly. By the hundreds of thousands. And when the healthy ones can't work any longer, they go the same way. It's a rotten job, but someone has to do it. When it's finished, we shall have solved the Jewish problem in Europe and the eastern territories for all time."

Kurt left Hoffman spiking his coffee with another slug of schnapps, and made his way back to his office. A vulgar, unpleasant person, Hoffman, and someone who obviously wouldn't hesitate to lie or exaggerate to hold the attention of his audience. There could be only one reason why the Fuehrer tolerated the uncouth Bavarian among his personal entourage: a sense of loyalty toward one of the Nazi "Old Guard" of the early twenties; that, and possibly the fact that it was Hoffman who had introduced Eva Braun to the Fuehrer.

It was odd that he should feel so pleased to find Helga Gruyten in his office, tidying up the burgeoning files in one of his steel cabinets. Her silences over the past week—apart from the formal greeting every morning and the coolly polite responses to his requests—had become irritating, and he had been seriously thinking about asking Fräulein Eppler to allot him another assistant from her pool. Now, as she turned her head briefly to acknowledge his entry, he found himself smiling and in a mood to try breaking the ice.

"Nice dress you're wearing, Helga. My sister has one like it."

"That's hardly surprising, Herr Captain," the voice came primly over her shoulders, "these days of standardization of design." She turned around, and added, "I don't recall, incidentally, inviting you to use my first name."

"You didn't. But I don't intend to go on calling you Fräulein Gruyten indefinitely, like some stuffy Prussian bureaucrat. And inside these four walls, at least, you have *my* invitation to call me Kurt, if the idea doesn't shock you too much."

"You want me to get the sack? Fräulein Eppler has just asked me if I'd like to work full-time as your secretary."

"And . . . ?"

"If she ever heard me calling you—well, by your first name, that'd be the end of that."

"What did you tell Fräulein Eppler?"

"I said it might be advisable to check with you first. For all I know, you might hate the idea."

"And if I agree?"

She turned back to the table, not quickly enough to hide the quick flush that stained her cheekbones. Kurt's gaze stayed low on the graceful lines of her calves as she murmured, "Then I shall offer no resistance, of course," then it rose to her hips as she reached for an envelope from the far side of the table. It reached her eyes in time to catch the huntress flare as she swung around and stepped briskly over to the desk, placing the sealed envelope on his blotter.

"Starting tomorrow, then, there'll be a desk for me in here. In the meantime—" she paused to look back at him from the door —"you know where to find me." No "Captain." And no "Kurt."

He sat down at his desk and stared for a long moment at the closed door, breathing hard through slightly parted lips. He would have to do something about this soon, but not with Helga Gruyten. Shaking his head, he reached for the envelope.

It bore the usual outside inscription: "Bormann-Vermerke," in bold red characters, and below this the date: "30 June, 1942." Kurt removed the contents, a sheaf of typed pages in double spacing, and unclipped the slip of paper from the top. This read: "Notes from the Fuehrer's Conversation: 30 June, 1942, Midday. Recorded by Dr. Picker and edited by Reichsleiter Bormann. To be returned by 6 P.M., Thursday 2 July, 1942." This left ample time—more than three hours—for Kurt to read the transcript, make his own notes, and return the envelope to Bormann's office.

His eyes went straight to the underlined entry at the top of the first page.

"Special Guests: Foreign Minister von Ribbentrop and Feldmarschall Kesselring."

There followed an introductory note, presumably part of Bormann's editing:

Foreign Minister Ribbentrop had read aloud part of a report he had just received from his Chargé d'Affaires in Washington on the reaction of the American public to Germany's invasion of Yugoslavia and Greece and Feldmarschall Rommel's new thrust toward Cairo and the Suez Canal. The Fuehrer speaks:

"Of course they are split down the center. On the one hand there is American Jewry, led by its lackey Roosevelt, screaming blue murder at the prospect of losing Palestine and a so-called National Home. On the other hand there are the saner influences prevailing throughout the nation, typified by the America

First Committee, who strenuously oppose the spending of American blood and treasure on pulling the old imperialists' chestnuts out of the fire. Additionally, we can count ourselves fortunate that the powerful clique of warmongering Jews is counterbalanced by the influence of that earthy and pragmatic prince of the Roman Church, Cardinal Spellman.

"Our National Socialist solution to the Jewish problem may not be exactly to Spellman's liking, but I beg leave to doubt that the fate of these gentry keeps the good Cardinal awake at night. The Church of Rome has survived these two thousand years of vicissitudes by securing its own temporal interests first and leaving the Sermon on the Mount to take care of itself. The Catholics of America far outnumber the Jews and there's not one of them who would lift a finger to save the Soviet Union from the fate I have ordained for it. Roosevelt can rant and rave till he is blue in the face. Let him go on sending England his ships, food and war materials—most of which end up on the bed of the Atlantic, in any case. So long as I refuse to be provoked, he will never succeed in dragging America into the war against the Reich."

Foreign Minister Ribbentrop intervened. History would record, he remarked, that the Fuehrer's success in restraining Japan from attacking the Philippines and other spheres of American interest in the Pacific was the rock upon which all the hopes of the warmonger Roosevelt had foundered. It was a strategic master stroke, a policy born of geopolitical genius. The Fuehrer replied:

"It would be true to say that, but for my strenuous personal warnings to that hothead General Tojo in October 1941, the new government in Tokyo might well have taken the fateful step that winter of launching a full-scale offensive against the Americans in the Pacific. Indeed, I was under constant pressure at that time from some of our own people—notably Grand Admiral Raeder, as Bormann here will confirm—to encourage the Japanese in this act of folly. Raeder is a good fellow, but he

4 8

is totally lacking in that broad strategical vision, coupled with an infallible instinct for timing, that has won me, deservedly or not, my reputation as a military genius. All he could see was the immediate advantage of having the American fleet diverted from the Atlantic to the Pacific."

At this point, Foreign Minister Ribbentrop commented, in a lighthearted manner, on a BBC report from India that Mahatma Gandhi had called on his followers to offer passive resistance in the event of a Japanese invasion. Did the Mahatma seriously believe that the Japanese commanders would hesitate for a moment to drive their tanks over a million prostrate Gandhi-ites? The Fuehrer replied:

"We must not underestimate the effect of passive resistance on an occupying army. As a former front-line soldier myself, I am aware of the difference between the excitement of confronting and killing the enemy in military combat and the depression that often comes over a soldier when circumstances oblige him to kill unresisting civilians.

"I am obliged, against my better instincts, to concede General Tojo a free hand in the subcontinent of India as part of the price for his diversionary attack on Russia. But I would derive no satisfaction from the colonization of India by our Japanese friends, with whom we have no cultural affinities whatsoever. To be frank with you, gentlemen, I would rather the white race, in the shape of the British, retained their hold over the 350 millions of India, leaving Japan to digest its enormous gains in Burma and Southeast Asia. A day might come, once the British have accepted final defeat, when their unique talents as colonial administrators—something we Germans have never possessed—could be employed in the service of the New Order, to our mutual advantage. In the meantime, it is my hope and belief that Premier Tojo will be content with his blockade of India."

The conversation reverted to America and to Franklin Roosevelt's various stratagems for bringing his country into the war. Field Marshal Kesselring asked the Fuehrer what, in his opinion, America could now hope to gain by abandoning neutrality. The Fuehrer speaks:

"Apart from enriching its Jewish profiteers, nothing. The Japanese fleet is more than a match for them in the Pacific and Indian oceans. Fortress Europe can never be breached, least of all from the besieged base of the British Isles. The Mediterranean is now closed to them, and any attempts to land on the West Coast of Africa would be smashed by our Atlantic U-boat packs. It is important, in this connection, to realize that Roosevelt is a paranoiac. He and I came to power in the same year, 1933, and it has driven him insane to see how, in nine short years, Adolf Hitler has achieved everything he was predestined to achieve, while he, Roosevelt, has achieved precisely nothing. Roosevelt, gentlemen, is an historical irrelevance. As for me, I can only repeat what I said in March 1936, after I marched into the Rhineland and occupied it without a shot being fired (against all the dire warnings of my military and diplomatic experts): 'I go the way that Providence dictates with the assurance of a sleepwalker.' "

II

HELGA GRUYTEN had offered to stay on, taking his dictation from the shorthand notes he had made during his second session with Hitler. But he needed an hour or so to himself, as he explained to her, taking care not to ruffle her feelings.

"It will probably work out fine, doing it that way in the future. But right now my head's buzzing with the things he told me, things I couldn't jot down at the time. I'll have to set them out now, Helga, in my own way while they're still fresh in my mind. Thanks for the offer, though. I certainly appreciate it."

She lingered on, straightening the cover on her typewriter for the second time, rearranging the neat array of colored pencils on her desk. Then she said, "You're the boss. I was only concerned about the fact that tomorrow's Saturday and I have the day off. Unless, of course, you have special need of me."

He didn't have to look up from his notes to check; it was there in her voice, the innuendo and the invitation he would find in her small eyes. But he looked up all the same, teased by those two words, "special need." Making an effort to keep his voice steady he said, "It wouldn't work, Helga, you must know that. Everything's against it."

"I don't know what you mean." Her eyes, languorously focused on his empty left sleeve, gave the lie to her words. "I'm just a simple uncomplicated girl, offering her services. If you've no need of them . . ." There it was again, the one word she had found, or stumbled upon, that had the power to grip him low, causing his blood to race.

He could find nothing to say. He watched her pick up her handbag, take a last slow look around the office and walk toward the door.

"Helga."

She turned around, smiling. "Yes, Kurt?" It was the first time she had used his Christian name.

"We could have dinner together later, if you're free."

"At my place. Call me when you're ready to leave and I'll give you the directions."

When the door closed he sat quite still for a few minutes, breathing deeply. Then he drew the large writing pad closer, frowned hard over his shorthand notes, and in a little while began to transcribe in swift longhand.

Helga Gruyten's apartment was on the second floor of a modern block in the smartest part of the Kurfuerstendamm, within sight of the Gedaechtniskirche. Significantly, it was located directly above the private apartment of an official of the Reichssicherheitshauptamt, as Kurt discovered to his acute discomfiture within a few minutes of paying off the taxi driver.

A beefy plainclothes detective blocked his path as he entered the lobby. The man said nothing. His slightly raised eyebrows in an otherwise wooden face said it all.

"I'm calling on Fräulein Gruyten."

"Name, please?"

"Captain Kurt Armbrecht."

"Identification, please."

Kurt hesitated a second. Military or Chancellery credentials? He chose the latter and handed the card with its gold-embossed eagle to the detective. The man flipped it open, glanced at the inside photograph and handed it smartly back, with a heel click.

"Second floor, Herr Captain. Fräulein Gruyten is expecting you."

She opened the door to him and, pushing quickly past her, without a word, he marched on across the hall and into the sitting-room. Turning, tight-lipped, he faced her as she joined him after double-locking the front door.

"For Heaven's sake, Kurt, what's the matter?" She had un-plaited and brushed out her pale-blond hair so that it looped and flowed over her bare shoulders. The halter-neck gown of moss-green taffeta crackled softly about her thighs as she stopped a few paces short of where he was standing.

"I must have been mad to come here! Why didn't you tell me you were under police protection?"

"What difference does it make? We all are—all of us girls who work for the Fuehrer."

"Wonderful! So now the gossips can really go to work!"

"You've got it all wrong, Kurt. They're not *spying* on me, they're *protecting* me. That's why I was given this place, over the apartment belonging to an R.S.H.A. man. Automatic protection, don't you see?"

"Let's not be naïve, Helga. This will go straight to Fräulein Eppler, and from her to Reichsleiter Bormann, and before I've even—"

"Kurt, Kurt!" Laughing, she took his arm and urged him

firmly toward the nearest armchair. "Fräulein Eppler knows all about it! How else do you think I could have invited you?"

He could only stare at her in open surprise as she settled the cushions behind him and glided across the room toward the crystalline glitter of the sideboard, leaving an aural wake of whispering taffeta.

"I suppose it's up to me to put you in the picture, since no one else has. Do you like vodka?"

"I've never had it, but—"

"It's the best. Here." She glided back, handed him a small glassful of the liquor and perched herself on the arm of a fat, velvet-covered sofa. *"Prosit!"*

He had always understood one had to down the drink in one gulp, but Helga was sipping at hers and he followed suit, shuddering slightly at the first assault on his palate.

"It improves on closer acquaintance." She smiled, lowering her glass to her lap. "Anyway, back to Fräulein Eppler. You've nothing to worry about, I promise you. The Chancellery encourages social relaxation, outside office hours, between members of its staff, and Fräulein Eppler absolutely insists on it so far as the Fuehrer's female staff is concerned."

Although he was beginning to untense himself, the picture was still murky. "If she's all that broad-minded, why were you so nervous when I suggested dropping our surnames?"

"Not inside the Chancellery, silly! Fräulein Eppler's a stickler for formality, rank and all that. But you know what she said when I told her you had invited me for dinner?"

He winced and took another sip at his glass.

"Be kind and generous to Captain Armbrecht," she told me. "He didn't win that medal sitting in an office chair, like some under the roof I could mention."

She had been kind, bringing her head down to him and whispering assurances between kisses, quieting his moans of remorse as he spent himself, almost on entry. She had been generous, padding back from the bathroom, freshly scented, and readying him with unhurrying lips and knowing hands for their second and deliciously more protracted coupling. She had been inventive—more than any German had the right to expect from his woman—when they made love again, abandoning the bed to explore standing and sitting positions to which his missing arm and hand would have contributed little. And, finally she had been—well—kinky . . .

She was standing before the full-length mirror of the wardrobe when he came back from the kitchen, sipping a cold beer. He moved in behind her and they smiled at their reflection, at the way his tallness and breadth made a bronzed frame for her pale body.

"My Paros Apollo," she murmured. "It has haunted me, that one-armed statue, ever since I first saw it in the Louvre." And then, "Make it move for me again, darling."

He did it now without resentment, flexing the deltoid muscle of his shoulder to raise the short wasted stub of his upper arm, exposing the fair floss of his armpit to her probing tongue. She leaned back, looking up at him with slackened lips.

"Will you let me try something rather wicked?"

"I have one hand, and it's holding a beer. How can I stop you?"

She took the beer from him and made him lie down on his back. In the mirror, he watched her take up a crouching position with her hips over his left shoulder and her torso reversed to his, putting her head over his loins. "Raise it to me, Apollo." The plea, muffled by his hardening penis, came with a straining of her right hip against his cheek and a searching swivel and thrust of her pelvis. The stump of his arm rose to meet her and it was an incredible sensation, for the "ghost" of his severed arm was still with him and it was as if that arm were plunged through the warm sheath of her body, from womb to throat, and its prehensile hand were urging her bobbing head to its task.

When she was finished, she rolled from him and lay curled and quietly sobbing into the carpet.

She ran a bath for him and made coffee while he dressed. And he was glad they were able to sit and chat awhile, side by side on the sitting-room sofa, before he left, for he had triumphed through her and now owed her a debt transcending the bond of flesh.

"You promised to tell me about your session with the Fuehrer this afternoon."

"I'm doing better than that. I'm giving you my complete notes to type out on Monday."

"Not those, silly! I mean . . . *things.*"

"Things?"

"Things of interest. How did he look? Was he in a good mood? What room did you work in?"

"In his private study, upstairs."

Her eyes widened as she drew her legs up, all attention, like a small girl at the start of a fairy story. "What is it like?"

"Workmanlike. Unpretentious. A fine view over the Chancellery gardens." He settled down, resting his head against the back of the sofa. "There's a portrait in oils on one of the walls—an attractive young girl with long blond hair, like yours. Would that be Eva Braun?"

Helga shook her head. "Fräulein Junge told us about that. It's a painting of his niece, Geli Raubal, who shot herself in 1931 at the age of twenty-three. They say the Fuehrer was deeply in love with her. But go on, Kurt, what else?"

"Oh, I don't know. Most of the time I was concentrating too hard on what he was saying to have eyes for anything else. He sometimes speaks very quickly, I can tell you, and my shorthand's not as fast as yours."

"Just to think," she sighed, her blue eyes sparkling, "all alone with the Fuehrer in his private study for nearly an hour! I'd have melted completely away!"

"Maybe it would have been the Fuehrer who melted." He reached his hand out to stroke the curve of her thigh through the decorously draped skirt of her housecoat. "Have you never been alone with him, then?"

Again, the headshake. "But once, when I was on stand-by duty with the night shift, I was invited to join the Fuehrer's guests in the drawing room, after dinner of course. It was marvelous! Doctor Goebbels was there, and Professor Speer—as he was then—and Obergruppenfuehrer Heydrich, God rest his soul. The Fuehrer spoke to us until nearly two in the morning, and it was terrific! There's absolutely nothing he doesn't know about."

"Can you remember anything particular he said that night?"

"Oh, Kurt, how can I remember? He talked about *everything* —the old days in Munich, the works of Wagner, his plans for rebuilding Berlin. You know how it is—when the Fuehrer's speaking, you get so enthralled by the magic of his personality that time seems to fly, and afterward you can hardly remember what he was talking about."

He said, dryly, "I'm glad you're not doing my job. You'd have been fired by now."

"You mean you're not spellbound when the Fuehrer speaks?" The leg under his caressing hand had gone rigid and she was staring at him with something bordering on hostility.

"Can't afford the luxury, sweetheart, not with a book to get together. Which reminds me—" he glanced at his wrist watch— "I have a date with the Chancellery librarian at eight in the morning."

"How about the evening? I'll fix dinner again, if you like."

He would like. But he was not a free agent. He said, "I'll have to check with Fräulein Junge when she comes on at six." And then, with all the *hubris* of his newfound masculinity, "Keep something hot for me, just in case."

She came in on cue, grabbing at his hand and pressing it to her.

"There'll always be something hot for you here, my Paros Apollo."

CHAPTER THREE

IT HAD been Adolf Hitler's intention to make the triumphant journey to Athens in his own armored train, stopping en route at Prague, at his Austrian home town, Linz, then at Budapest, Belgrade, Salonika and finally Athens. The journey of over fifteen hundred miles would have been the longest he had yet made by land through the nations now integrated, through conquest or puppet alliance, into the New Order.

But it seemed that the Reichsfuehrer SS Heinrich Himmler had put his jackboot firmly down. To Kurt, snapping to attention as the slight figure with the weak chin and drooping shoulders strutted back across the anteroom where Kurt was awaiting the Fuehrer's pleasure, it was obvious that Himmler—incongruously dressed, on this occasion, in the green uniform of the Waffen SS—had had his way about something, for his very spectacles seemed to be glinting with triumph and there was almost a jauntiness in his acknowledgment of the SS bodyguards' salute.

When Kurt was finally admitted to the Fuehrer's presence, Hitler's first words explained Himmler's cockiness.

"It's a great pity, Armbrecht. I had set aside time for a good long session with you during the train journey to Athens, but Himmler now insists I should go by air, and my own security chief Rattenhuber agrees with him. I argued with them of course. But if one puts a man in charge of one's security, one must finally bow to his considered judgments."

"May I ask, my Fuehrer, why the Reichsfuehrer objects to the train journey?"

"Too dangerous. We would not only be passing through the Protectorate of Bohemia and Moravia, where Heydrich was murdered, but through Yugoslavia, where Tito's so-called partisan army has still to be crushed. Unless we line our entire route through these territories with loyal troops—a practical impossibility—we risk a derailing of the train by saboteurs in the pay of Churchill and Stalin." Hitler was pacing up and down as he spoke, making curiously uncoordinated gestures with his hands. "I must admit, Armbrecht, to some impatience with this excessive concern for my safety. If Providence—for which you may substitute 'the Almighty,' if you prefer—had disapproved of my historic mission in Europe, any one of a whole series of plots to destroy me might well have succeeded. But what in fact has happened? In every instance when my life was in jeopardy there has been a last-minute, almost uncanny frustration of the assassin's carefully laid plans. Bormann, who is not a very religious man, is convinced that I am under some form of divine protection. A few years ago, I would have dismissed this as superstitious claptrap, but today I am not so skeptical. I tell you, Armbrecht, I now have an absolute inner conviction that my life will be spared until the task to which it is dedicated is completed."

"Every German will say 'Amen' to that, my Fuehrer." Kurt's deeply felt response filled the brief silence as Hitler paused by the window, tilting his face to the afternoon sun. When he turned to face Kurt again, he was smiling.

"Do you still say your prayers, Captain?"

"Not in any conventional way, my Fuehrer. Like yourself, I was brought up as a Catholic and I suppose I still believe in a God. But I stopped going to Mass shortly after I joined the Party."

Hitler was nodding in evident sympathy. "There is no common ground," he said, resuming his pacing, "between the philosophy of National Socialism and the preposterous doctrines of the Christian churches. On the one hand, you have a movement whose dynamic stems from the natural laws governing racial purity, the leadership principle and the survival of the strongest. On the other, the disgusting theological excretion of sick brains, obstructing the evolution of an elite with its humanitarian rubbish about all men being equal in the sight of God. Armbrecht, my final task will be to solve the religious problem."

Kurt was scribbling rapidly, but managing at the same time to raise his head whenever he sensed Hitler's eyes on him. "Does that mean, my Fuehrer," he ventured, "that there will be no place for organized religion in the New Order?"

"Not necessarily. There is a sense in which the Church, despite its absurd doctrines, can never be replaced in the minds of the masses by a party ideology. Indeed, I can find no fault with the conservative, stabilizing influence it wields over the people. What we must do is eliminate the poison from the Christian ethic by encouraging the Church to adapt to the goals of National Socialism. Through this process, the Church has the possibility of revitalizing itself and surviving. If, on the other hand, it should decide to resist the process, then it will become an historical irrelevancy and will undoubtedly perish."

Kurt returned at once to his office when the session ended, to find Helga sitting at her typewriter, fingers poised high above the keyboard in an exaggerated pose of starter-tape readiness.

"Relax, *Maedel*. I'll be five minutes—" he waved his notebook—"straightening this lot out."

"And another hour straightening yourself out, if you don't stop addressing me in that vulgar Bavarian way!"

"The girls in Munich never object. And as everyone knows—"

"Yes, yes!" She made a long-suffering face. "They're the prettiest girls in the whole of the Reich. Why don't you go back there and organize yourself a whole harem of beer-swilling *Maedels?*"

Their banter was one of the fruits of a month-long intimacy. It was also—to Kurt certainly and, he suspected, to Helga herself—a kind of safety-valve against a mutual dependence that neither of them wanted and all their wiser instincts rejected. But wisdom, at its best, could be a feeble arbiter over the uneasy borderline between sexual harmony and the heart's needs, and he was challenging it now, with his retort.

"As a matter of fact, that's just what I'm going to do—go back to Munich, I mean."

From its deadpan expression her face now flickered into a strained and insecure smile. "How nice for you! You want me to help pack your *Lederhosen?"*

"I'm not joking, Helga. The Fuehrer will be flying to Athens instead of taking his train, and he has very thoughtfully given me four days' leave to spend with my family."

"Oh? And when will that be?"

"The date's still a secret. But I gather from Major Kremer that a battalion of the SS Leibstandarte Adolf Hitler has already left for Athens, so it can't be far ahead."

She was silent for a while, brushing her fingertips lightly over the keys of the typewriter. Then: "You've never told me—do you have a girl friend, down there in Munich?"

"A girl friend? Half a dozen, my little mouse!"

"How lovely! . . . Well, all I can say is, take care you spread your favors evenly over those four nights. I don't want you coming back to Berlin with your eyes scratched out."

Four nights later, as they lay side by side in bed, smoking a final cigarette, Kurt could sense the sadness in her, and he was disconcerted by his inability—or was it reluctance?—to connect.

"One thing I'm relieved about," he murmured. "Can you imagine, hours with the Fuehrer in that train, without being able to light up a cigarette?"

Helga gave a little grunt. "They say," she answered in a small spiritless voice, "Reichsfuehrer Himmler's even stricter about smoking."

She fell silent again, her head lightly supported by the ball of his left shoulder. He was thinking, *I'm not tired of her yet, and she has made a man of me again, but now she wants me to give*

60

her something in return—a word, a commitment—and it's not in me. Not yet. He said, "I was pulling your leg about the girl friends in Munich, Helga. If I take anyone out at night it'll be my sister."

Her slim white arm groped for the ashtray on her side of the bed. She rolled over and put her lips to the tapered stub of his arm, making little clicking noises as she nuzzled and kissed the puckered seam. "I don't mind how much fun you have in Munich," her voice came up shakily. "But this you keep exclusively for Helga. Promise?"

A seat was found for him on one of the Chancellery planes—a refitted Heinkel bomber—bound for Munich the next day, thereby sparing him the tedious eight-hour train journey from Berlin to the Bavarian capital. And Sophie, driving the family's old Adler (on the last two gallons of this month's gasoline ration), was at the airport to meet him. There was a blustery wind blowing down from the Alps but the early August sun was shining and the air was several degrees warmer than it had been at Berlin's Tempelhof airfield that morning.

Kurt wasn't the only tall blond man in gray army uniform on view in the Arrivals lounge, but he was the only one at that moment with an empty left sleeve and the Ritterkreuz at his throat, and he had hardly made his appearance when a slim red-headed girl in a green sweater and brown pleated skirt came at him, full-tilt, out of a loose knot of waiting civilians.

"Kurt! Oh, my brother dear—welcome home!" He barely had time to drop his valise before she was inside his encircling arm, hugging him tight. He eased away, laughing.

"Sophie! You look wonderful!"

And she did, with her wide shining green eyes and tilted nose and ripe lips slashing the freckled oval of her face. It seemed to Kurt at once an age, and also a bare moment, since that decorous, solemn embrace, seven weeks ago, on the railway platform before he climbed onto the train for Berlin.

"Let me take your valise."

"Nonsense, *Maedel*. What do you take me for—an old woman?"

The excited questions flew at him almost nonstop during the short drive from the airport.

"What's he like, the Fuehrer? I mean, is he friendly and relaxed with you or does he keep you at a distance?"

"We're the best of chums. He calls me Kurt and I call him Adolf. We have daily wrestling matches on the Chancellery lawn."

"Liar! Have you met Eva Braun yet? And don't tell me you wrestle with her, too!"

"I think the Fuehrer's keeping her away from me. She stays upstairs in his private apartment and I haven't even caught a glimpse of her yet. But she must have seen me, because I keep getting these billets-doux from her."

"Double liar! How about Doctor Goebbels? No—you wrote to us about that. Goering! Have you met him?"

"I passed him once, on his way to a Fuehrer Conference. It wasn't easy, I mean passing him." He curved his arm out, describing an exaggerated waistline. "I was almost skinned raw by his medals."

"Oh, Kurt—" her hand left the wheel and gave his arm a tight squeeze—"it's such fun to have you back! Can't you really stay any longer?"

"I was lucky to get these four days, Sophie. But maybe, after the Fuehrer gets back from Athens, he'll move headquarters to the Berghof. Think of it, only a three-hour train journey from Munich!"

"How marvelous! Oh, by the way, none of my friends will believe he wears spectacles."

"What are you trying to do, have me shot? I'm going to have to be damned careful what I write to you in the future."

"That's just what Mother said you'd say. All right, big brother—" she crossed herself, solemnly—"I won't pass on any more state secrets."

"And how is Mother? And the Old Man?"

"Both fine. They're taking us out to dinner tonight, to Humplmayr's to celebrate. And there'll be champagne for lunch —the real thing, from France."

"How did they get hold of that—a bribe from one of Father's students?"

"Idiot! Can you imagine Daddy taking bribes? You remember Herr Berchem, the locomotive engineer who lives at the top of our road? Well, he's now taking a train to Paris twice a week, and if you give him some sausages, or semolina flour—anything that's edible—he'll come back with French champagne or cognac. He makes a profit of course. And one has to be a bit discreet about it."

Kurt shook his head, chuckling. "You're making me nervous. What have I come back to—a den of black marketeers?"

"Everyone's been doing it. But you know Daddy—it took the return of the prodigal to make him unbend and have a quiet word with Herr Berchem. It's the same thing with these Russian domestic servants. He's entitled to one Ukrainian girl, to take the rough housework off Mother. But not a bit of it! 'We'll have no slave labor in this house,' he says." Sophie gave a little sigh. "I must say I sympathize with him. The way some German women treat their wretched Ukrainians!"

"Pretty badly?"

"Like dogs. I know they're not supposed to be given any free time, or allowed to go out to church or anything like that. But you *are* supposed to feed them something, a couple of times a day. Take that horrible Frau Krenkler, who lives next door. She was one of the first to get a Ukrainian, on account of her husband being the local branch leader of the Party. She worked her first girl literally to death! From dawn to midnight, practically —with hardly a break and without a proper meal ever being put in front of her. We know that because we used to see the poor thing rummaging through the garbage bin, searching for scraps. Mother and I would smuggle her a bit of something over the garden wall when Frau Krenkler wasn't around, but mostly she was existing on garbage too foul even for the pig bin. Then she died and they took her away, and the very next day another Ukrainian girl was delivered to the Krenklers."

"Is she being treated any better?"

"Worse, if anything. She's younger and quite pretty, and Herr Krenkler must have shown he fancied her, or something, because now she's locked in the toolshed before he comes home in the evening, and she has to stay there all night."

"Ghastly." Kurt grimaced. "Let's talk about something pleasant. How's your work going?"

"Same old routine. Two classes in the morning, one in the evening. I was hoping to get a holiday this month, but the Director has just landed me with another half-dozen Todt Organization overseers, who expect me to teach them Spanish in four weeks!"

"What on earth do *they* want with Spanish?"

"Didn't you know, big brother? There's something like forty thousand Spanish Reds in German labor camps. The Todt Organization has been using some of them in their workshops and now they want to start another big factory in Bavaria. Somebody has to be able to give the Spaniards orders in their own language."

They had crossed the River Isar over the Prince Regent Bridge, just east of the city center, but instead of turning right after the Haus der Kunst, and heading north alongside the Englischer Garten, Sophie took the next main turn into the Ludwigstrasse so that they could pass the University building, four blocks up on the left. The rectangular forecourt was peopled this fine Saturday morning by only a thin straggle of students wending their way to and from the Library. Kurt, in a flash of memory, saw his father waiting beside one of the columns of the main entrance to greet him and his mother the day he arrived for the graduation ceremony.

"And what," he asked quietly, "does Father think of our victories in Yugoslavia and Greece?"

Sophie gave a little shrug and concentrated harder on the

road ahead. "I don't know, Kurt. He never talks much about the war, as you know. Sometimes, I—" She shook her head and fell silent.

"Sometimes you what?"

"Nothing. Just a passing reflection."

"Well, don't be so stingy," he laughed. "Share it with your brother."

"Oh, I was just thinking—sometimes one gets the feeling Father has deliberately closed down a part of his mind. The war . . . what's happening in Germany . . . the whole big debate about our future . . . It's as if it had nothing to do with him. As if it were all happening on some wavelength he can't plug into."

"He can plug in all right, any time he wants to." The bitterness was there, and would probably always be there, embalmed in the memory of all those acrimonious, futile dialogues. It was the one anxiety clouding the prospect of these four days back home. But perhaps Sophie would prove to be right. Perhaps their father had in fact, and finally, thrown away the plug. Anyway, Kurt did not intend to find out. There would be no provocation from him, even if it meant mentally weighing every word before he spoke. And without provocation, there would surely be no lectures, none of the defunct liberal philosophizing that had so strained the love and respect he owed and had tried not to begrudge his father.

Sophie's hand fumbled for his and gave it a little squeeze. "Everything's going to be lovely, these few days. I've even booked a smashing date for you on Monday evening."

"Well you can just go right ahead and unbook it. You're my only date on this trip. Besides—" and it came out almost as nonchalantly as he had willed it—"I happen to be fully involved in that department, back in Berlin."

"*Kurt! Now* you tell me, when we're almost home! Quick, who is it? What's her name? How serious is it? Oh, Kurt!"

He couldn't help it. He was laughing out loud.

"What's funny? Kurt, if you're—"

6 5

"I'm not pulling your leg. There *is* someone. But you don't have to sound so relieved about it!"

A shade too quickly, she came back with, "Go to hell! I'm just glad I'm not going to be the only one to have to put up with your lousy dancing."

"What do you expect from a one-armed man—Fred Astaire?" They were both grinning broadly now, and out in the clear. By the time Sophie drew the car up in front of the old ivy-covered house in Nikolaistrasse, Kurt had told her as much as he wished her to know about Helga Gruyten. And Sophie had charmingly elected to make the Berlin girl a present, via Kurt, of her duplicate set of Spanish postal stamps.

The low front door in the side of the house opened up before Kurt had unlatched the street gate, and his mother came hurrying to meet him halfway down the forecourt firing off her bright vocal squibs of joy and sealing the welcome with her soft flushed cheek clamped to his.

"Dear Kurt! Let me take a good look at you! There—what did I tell you, Sophie? They're starving him up there in Berlin!"

"Rubbish!" He surrendered his canvas suitcase to Sophie and linked arms with his mother, leading her back along the side of the house. "I've never felt so fit in all my life. Looks as though it wouldn't do *you* any harm to shed a few pounds, Mother dear!"

He was joking. As long as anyone could remember, Margit Armbrecht had never noticeably lost or gained more than a few ounces in weight. At forty-six, she was something of a phenomenon for a Munich *Hausfrau* inasmuch as she could still wear one of her own daughter's tailored skirts after letting out only an inch or two at the waist. The dark-red hair, inherited by Sophie, had lost much of its luster and had been cropped short these past few years, as if to conserve its substance; but her eyes retained their full emerald sparkle, and the faint crow's-feet and the gossamer lines haunting her lips were about all there was to prevent her from passing as Sophie's eldest sister. When asked how she managed to keep so young-looking, Margit Armbrecht would reply, "By walking a mile to Mass every morning and leaving my husband to do all the worrying for both of us."

Kurt paused in the hallway to delicately sniff the air. "Goulash and dumplings! I've been dreaming about them for nights." Then he strode through the open door of the sitting-room, where his father was waiting to greet him.

"Welcome home, Kurt! The women have been almost impossible to live with since we got your message. Sophie! Fetch one of those bottles of champagne for the Herr Captain, and let the festivities begin!"

Walter Armbrecht would be fifty-two in November and, in his case, the years were stitched uncharitably into his face and physique. He had married Margit in 1914 before going off to fight the Kaiser's war as an infantryman in a Bavarian regiment, and an oval-framed photograph of him as a handsome young man with a bold challenging expression in faded sepia halftones, complete with *pickelhaube* helmet and bushy blond mustache, had been among Kurt's special treasures as a boy. Everyone remarked on the resemblance it bore to Kurt himself, as he approached the same age. But by then the portrait on the wall of Kurt's bedroom had been replaced by a photograph of Adolf Hitler.

The alienation had been gradual—a slow erosion of common ground between father and son until, with the completion of Kurt's thesis on the significance of the leadership principle, only a yawning philosophical gulf was left between them. That had been three years ago, before Kurt went off to the war.

Walter Armbrecht had not, of course, been one of the examining professors when Kurt sat for his degree, but he had read a copy of the thesis and had handed it back to his son with a defeated shake of his head.

"What's the matter, Father? Too strong for your ideological digestion?"

"Strong?" Professor Armbrecht had pushed himself up from the desk in his Nikolaistrasse study and turned to stare out through the French windows. "Oh yes, it's strong enough. It'll get you your degree. It is also one of the most odious pieces of distorted logic and makeshift history that it has been my misfortune to read."

Shakily, struggling for control, Kurt had said, "One thing I've never understood about you, Father, is why you haven't resigned from the faculty. If the National Socialist interpretation of history is so repugnant to you, what on earth are you doing at the University?"

His father made no reply for a while. When he turned around to face Kurt, all the melancholy little defeats and squalid compromises of the seven academic years since Hitler had come to power were there in his dimmed eyes, in the listless droop of his shoulders.

"I'm there, Kurt, because to resign in protest would have been to leave your mother without a breadwinner. And to resign for any other reason would have been dishonest. I'm there, if you like, because I'm the kind of person who rationalizes his moral cowardice by weighing the luxury of self-respect against the certainty of bringing disgrace and hardship upon his family. It's conceivable, of course, that I'm there because there are still a few students who might need me. I only wish that could have included you."

Kurt had turned on his heel and left him.

It had been too much to hope for—a four-day leave without a political flare-up within the Armbrecht household. And the irony of it was that the provocation, when it came, was from neither Kurt nor his father but from an outsider, and it came in the last hours of what had been, until then, the most pleasant short vacation Kurt could remember.

The family luncheon that Saturday had been a merry affair with Kurt good-humoredly lobbing answers—mostly frivolous —to the interminable questions about his job volleyed at him by his mother and sister, while Walter Armbrecht presided amiably at the head of the table, keeping their glasses topped up and chuckling at Kurt's running account of life in the Berlin Chancellery. The four of them dined elegantly that evening at Humplmayr's and the day ended with a festive seal when the professor joined them during the car ride home in a tipsy chorus of "Brave Little Soldier's Wife," to irreverent applause and cries of "Encore!" from his two offspring. Next day, after a shamefully late start, and with the professor yawning over the wheel of the Adler, they managed to make Bad Wiessee for lunch and spent the afternoon strolling in the hills above the Tegernsee.

On the way back to the city they made a detour through Bichl to call in on Margit Armbrecht's youngest sister, Uta, who was keeping a largish pig farm going while her husband, Karl, a quartermaster in Rundstedt's army, was in Georgia. Aunt Uta had been Kurt's favorite relative since his earliest remembered childhood when he used to spend weeks of his summer on the farm "helping" his maternal grandfather, now dead, mix the pig feed and clean out the sties. It was Uta who, when he was only ten, had explained to him in simple matter-of-fact terms the physical mysteries of procreation and birth which his own devoutly Catholic mother had always shied from discussing, invariably alluding to some later unspecified date when his father would tell him "all about that sort of thing." As it had turned out, Aunt Uta was no mere theoretician on the subject, for she had earlier that year been awarded the "Mother's Cross" for giving birth to a fourth child, a fine boy, at the age of forty. Now she proudly displayed the decoration to Kurt while his mother and sister cooed over the award-winning infant's pram, outside the kitchen door.

"It's so much prettier than *your* cross, don't you agree?" she chaffed him, holding the bronze medal by its slender blue-and-white ribbon against her ample bosom.

"As pretty as it should be," he acknowledged solemnly. "But then all you had to do to earn it was lie on your back, right?"

"Monster!" She poked him in the ribs and made a ferocious face. Then, turning to Walter Armbrecht, who was taking a light for his meerschaum from the kitchen stove, "To think I used to wipe this great hulk's bottom for him when he was a brat! Pah! Just ask the Fuehrer when you go back to Berlin which of our medals he rates the highest!"

"I can tell you that now—the *Mutterkreuz* in gold. He told me so himself. But you'll never make that now, Aunt Uta. By the time Uncle Karl gets back you'll be pushing fifty."

"And who says I have to wait till Karl gets back? It's a *mother's* cross, isn't it. It says nothing about fathers."

"I don't know," Walter Armbrecht cut in dryly, "if I'm changing the subject, but I didn't see either of your two Russian laborers around as we drove up. Are they still working here?"

"Yes. But they're taken back to camp early on Sundays." She stifled a giggle. "They had to work so hard last week, I gave the poor devils a bottle of apricot *Schnapps* to take into the barn this afternoon and they were flat out and snoring when the guard arrived. So I had to give *him* half-a-dozen eggs to keep his mouth shut!"

"I think that's very rash of you, Uta," Margit Armbrecht called through the open door. "There was a case only last week of a Ukrainian who went crazy after stealing some liquor and almost raped his employer's wife."

"What do you mean—almost?" Kurt grinned. "He did or he didn't."

"The dogs got him before he could do any harm. Then the woman shot him." Frau Armbrecht shuddered. "What a thing to happen!"

"More fool she, for not having her Russian castrated," Aunt Uta said primly. "Karl made sure of that before he went away. As he said, you've sometimes got to be cruel to be kind."

The wisecrack on the tip of Kurt's tongue died as he caught sight of his father's face. Instead, he said loudly, "What about this countryfolk hospitality one's always hearing about? We've been here ten minutes already and we haven't even been offered a cup of ersatz coffee!"

Kurt had planned, back in Berlin, to round up such of his Munich men friends as might be on leave or discharged from the Wehrmacht, for a Sunday-night carousal at the Buergerbraeukeller, where Hitler made his annual speech to the Nazi "Old Guard" every eighth of November. But he couldn't have chosen a worse time, for none of his close friends who had survived the war was in the city. Erich and Peter were still on the eastern front. Klaus was stuck on—of all places—the Channel Islands, an adjutant to the military commander. Hugo was with his Luftwaffe squadron in North Africa. So, instead, he did what he had intended to leave until Monday afternoon and took Sophie with him on a walking tour to refresh his memory of the places where Adolf Hitler had made his quarters during the years of his struggle for power. They followed the strict chronological order of Hitler's moves, parking the car on the Widenmayer bank of the River Isar and starting with Thierschstrasse, a short featureless street where, in 1921, Hitler had rented a small room at Number 41. From there, it was a short walk to the fashionable boulevard of Prinzregententrasse, where Hitler, on the strength of his royalties from *Mein Kampf,* had rented all nine rooms on the second floor of Number 16. Their final stop was in the Koenigsplatz, where in the early thirties, the Fuehrer had held court in the old mansion—formerly the Barlow Palace—which later was remodeled as a suitable Munich headquarters, the Fuehrer House, for a Chancellor of the Reich.

"And you know something, *Liebchen,*" Kurt said, steering Sophie across the great square. "For all his love of neoclassicist grandeur in public buildings, the Fuehrer's own living quarters in the Chancellery are surprisingly unpretentious. Almost austere, in fact. They say he sleeps in the same old iron-frame bed he slept in here in Munich."

"That must be pretty rough on Fräulein Braun, wouldn't you say?"

He glanced sideways at her. She wasn't smiling, and there

was a faint underlying note of asperity in her voice, enough to suggest to him that he had maybe overdrawn on her good will, traipsing her around the city to stare at buildings she must have seen hundreds of times. "I'm not yet in the lady's confidence," he said. And then, giving her hair a tug from behind, forcing her to smile up at him, "You've been a pal, keeping me company like this. We're going to get drunk together and roll back home singing, 'Poor Little Soldier's *Sister.*' "

On Tuesday morning, as Kurt was listening to the first flash radio reports of the airborne invasion of the island of Malta, his mother brought him a note that she had found in the letterbox from their neighbor, Herr Krenkler. It invited Kurt to do Krenkler the honor of calling on him that evening if he could find time to tear himself from the bosom of his family. Kurt scribbled a note in reply, begging Herr Krenkler to excuse him "on this occasion of a very short leave."

Kurt knew nothing about Krenkler except that he was an *Ortsgruppenleiter,* was employed on the staff of Paul Geisler, the Gauleiter of Bavaria, and that his wife maltreated foreign servants. The Krenklers had moved into the neighboring house the day after the German invasion of Belgium, replacing the former owners, who, to the astonishment of the Armbrechts, were declared to be of Jewish stock and bundled off to the concentration camp at Dachau. Until the news of Kurt's appointment to the Fuehrer's staff appeared in the Munich newspapers, the Krenklers had made no social overtures to their next-door neighbors, which had suited the Armbrechts perfectly. Margit was sure she had no common ground with Frau Krenkler, not even children or the Catholic faith, and Walter—well, Walter had always tended to steer clear of social involvement with officials of the Party, especially those with the *"Mit Uns"* plaque ostentatiously exhibited on their automobiles and residential front doors.

Now they had finished their evening meal, and Kurt and his father had lighted up cigars in the living room while the women cleaned up in the kitchen. The doorbell rang and, a few seconds later, Sophie's head appeared in the doorway. Her voice remained cool and formal while her face registered dismay.

"Herr Krenkler has very kindly 'dropped in,' Papa, with a bottle of cognac to wish Kurt bon voyage."

Father and son barely had time to exchange hunted looks when a stout pink-faced man with a completely bald cranium stepped into the room, clutching a bottle to his breast. His right arm flashed forward in the Nazi salute.

"Heil Hitler, gentlemen! Do forgive this brief intrusion, Herr Professor. A small gift—" he raised the bottle aloft—"from one loyal servant of the Fuehrer to another!" The broad smile, exposing an excess of pink gums, was beamed on Kurt, who had risen to his feet, looking to his father for a formal introduction.

"You haven't met, of course." Walter Armbrecht stood up to receive the bottle with a dignified bow. "Our neighbor Herr Krenkler—my son, Kurt."

"Whose literary and military fame has preceded him," Krenkler supplied, kneading his hands and casting an eye around for somewhere to sit. "I have only recently got around to reading your excellent treatise on leadership, Herr Captain. The Gauleiter is a hard taskmaster, I can tell you. But then, as you yourself so rightly observe, 'The language of leadership is the language of demands; its poetry lies in their fulfillment.' May I sit down for a moment, Herr Professor?"

Kurt thought as he went to the sideboard to get out the brandy glasses, *At least he seems to have read the book, which is more than can be said of half the people who have it in their bookcases. He even got the quote right. I can understand why the old man hasn't warmed to him, but that's his problem, not mine.*

"You'll join us, Herr Krenkler?" he asked, handing a corkscrew to his father.

"With the greatest of pleasure!" Krenkler, who had perched himself on the edge of a chair, now settled himself back after first unbuttoning his jacket and shaking out his tie. The small circular Party badge gleamed from the lapel of his dark-brown suit. It was the gold version, worn only by the Old Guard. All of his attention was concentrated on Kurt.

"Tell me, Herr Captain," he said, "how are you getting along in your exciting new post? Is the Fuehrer keeping you busy?"

"Oh, on and off," Kurt laughed. "Tell you the truth, I spend most of my time reading and making notes and very little time with the Fuehrer in person."

"But how privileged you are to be spending any time at all with him!" Krenkler took a sip of brandy, his pale eyes glowing at Kurt over the rim of the glass. "And to such a noble purpose!" He leaned forward a little, lowering his voice. "Tell me, my dear Armbrecht, how soon do you think we lesser mortals can hope to enjoy the fruits of the Fuehrer's literary labors?"

"Certainly not for a couple of years, at the earliest. And then only if the Fuehrer is given a respite, meanwhile, from his military preoccupations."

"Of course, of course! But our enemies' days are already numbered, wouldn't you say? There's Stalin, hopelessly sandwiched between us and the Japanese. Britain, by all accounts, is slowly starving to death. The Australians and New Zealanders have scurried back home from the Middle East, panic-stricken by the rumors of a Japanese invasion of their homelands. Now, with Malta in our hands, the defeat of the British forces strung out between the Suez Canal and Persia can surely only be a matter of months?"

"Given certain contributory factors, yes." Kurt was addressing Krenkler, but he was aware he was choosing his words—indeed, even allowing himself to be drawn out like this—to impress his father, slumped now in his favorite armchair, blandly studying the tip of his cigar. "Crete has still to be taken, but that's a detail. The British and the Gaullist French will fight as fiercely to defend their Middle-East oil resources as the Russians did in the Caucasus. But, unlike the Russians, when they realize there will be no reprieve for them in Persia they will fall back on the Persian Gulf rather than stand and fight to the last man.

A great deal will depend at this stage on whether the Japanese have pushed on into India or have taken the Fuehrer's advice, which is not to overindulge their appetites or overstretch their supply lines. Either way, of course, what is left of the democracies' Middle-East forces will be evacuated to India to await events or to help stem the Japanese advance. Thus, Britain's eventual role in the New Order will probably be determined by decisions being taken at this very moment in Tokyo." He paused. Herr Krenkler was blinking and nodding, waiting for him to go on. And he now had his father's attention. But he wanted more. And it came as he lowered his brandy glass to the coffee table.

Walter Armbrecht said, "Can you explain what that means— Britain's role in the New Order?"

"I'll try," Kurt smiled. "But you mustn't expect me to be as lucid as the Fuehrer is on the subject. Anyway, it boils down to this: The British will sooner or later have to face the fact that they made the gravest blunder in their history by not joining with us in the death struggle of civilization against Bolshevism. They will overthrow Churchill and sue for peace, and when that day comes the Fuehrer will welcome them like a father welcoming his prodigal son. They will have to pay, of course, for their lapse from sanity in 1939, just as the French are paying today. Their heavy industries will be dismantled and transferred to the Ruhr. They will have to live on what they themselves can produce, from the land and from cottage industries. In short, their status will be that of a Probationer State, such as France, Belgium, Denmark, Holland and Norway—"

"As distinct," Professor Armbrecht broke in, "from the Slave States of European Russia, Poland, Czechoslovakia, and now the Greeks and Yugoslavs?"

"If you insist, Father," Kurt nodded, "though I can think of a better way—" He bit the words off, noticing that Krenkler's attention had switched to Walter Armbrecht, whom he was now eyeing as if suddenly aware of an intruder. "However," Kurt continued quickly, "the British will be given a very generous opportunity to redeem themselves. Their reward, eventually, will be to see the upgrading of their nation from probationer to associate status, similar to the Finns, Rumanians, Hungarians and now—since they have detached themselves from all commitments to the democracies—the Turks. There!" He smiled again at his father. "Does that answer your question?"

The Professor spoke wearily, as if commenting on a student's slipshod paper. "It postulates two assumptions—one, that the British will throw in their hand; two, that they will then cooperate with the New Order. Leaving the first one aside, has either of you any conception of how odious the German New Order appears to the other side in this war?"

"An irrelevance, Herr Professor, if you will forgive me!" Krenkler was taking over, and looking far from conciliatory, with his popping pale eyes and reddening neck. "We don't need their love. What we want—and by God we'll get it—is their respect and obedience! Am I right, Herr Captain?"

"You are both right," Kurt muttered. "They hate us but they'll end up cooperating because—well, the alternative would be unthinkable."

"The evidence," Walter Armbrecht persisted, "is that they at least *have* thought about the alternative. They know what we're doing in Russia, and to the Jews, and it is precisely this that makes the New Order an abomination in their minds."

"God in heaven!" Krenkler was staring from father to son, and back again. "If I didn't know better, I'd swear we were listening to some propagandist over the BBC!"

Thoroughly uneasy now, Kurt forced out a laugh as he reached for the brandy bottle. "My father is an incorrigible academic, Herr Krenkler. He just enjoys arguing both sides of a case. . . . A little more cognac?"

"Thank you." Krenkler, still frowning, held out his glass. "It's all very well, if I may say so, for the academics, but where would National Socialism be today if its leaders had indulged in such luxuries. For Germany, and especially for the younger generation now under the Professor's tutelage, there can be no *two* sides to such questions as the morality of the New Order. Those who are not for it are against it."

"As succinct a summing-up of what I've been saying," Walter Armbrecht murmured, "as I could have wished for."

Kurt got to his feet, smiling at Krenkler. "So we're all agreed —there are in fact two sides to every issue. I've enjoyed meeting you, Herr Krenkler. Unfortunately, I'm on a very early flight to Berlin in the morning and I haven't even packed yet. Perhaps, on my next trip to Munich, you and I can—"

"A pleasure I shall look forward to!" Krenkler drained his glass and stood up. "And—" the broad smile froze almost painfully as he turned to the professor—"to your father's stimulating company. Heil Hitler, gentlemen!"

CHAPTER FOUR

I

HE HAD set his mind on being in Jerusalem for Christmas Day, 1942. He had even prepared his historic speech for the occasion and had spoken of it to Kurt Armbrecht during one of their mid-November sessions up in the Fuehrer's private apartment in the Chancellery. It was to be a speech, he confided, in the course of which he would hold out an olive branch to the world. Hitler was considering delivering the speech from the Mount of Olives itself.

"Consider the geomilitary situation, Armbrecht, as it will undoubtedly apply at that time. Yes, yes, I want you to look at this map. . . . The Gaullist forces here in Syria tied down by a massive uprising of the Grand Mufti's *Mujahidin,* or holy warriors. No relief for them from the British, who by then will be in full retreat across the Transjordan desert here, and falling back through an equally hostile Iraq toward the Persian Gulf, where their navy, now expelled from the Mediterranean, will be standing by to evacuate what is left of them to India.

"No relief for the French from Persia, because by then the British forces of occupation in that country will be under orders from Churchill to save their skins by heading for the Gulf. And no relief from the Russian occupation troops in Persia, who at this moment are being moved up here, northward, in the futile hope of stiffening Red Army resistance to Rundstedt's drive south through Georgia and Azerbaijan."

78

Hitler turned away from the map table, motioning Kurt to return to his chair. "True genius in a national leader," he went on, straightening his jacket, "consists in having the judgment to recognize the precise stage at which the political benefits of a dictated peace with one's enemy will outweigh and outlast the glory of further military triumphs.

"From the Mount of Olives, I shall proclaim that my historic mission is now accomplished. My two archenemies will have been destroyed. The Boshevik armies will be floundering in the marshes and wastelands of Siberia. The insolent Zionist dream of a national home in Palestine, where they could lick their wounds for a new assault on Western civilization, will be lying in ruins. The Grand Mufti will be appointed Civil Governor, under a Reich Commission, of Palestine, Transjordan and Syria, with the responsibility of forging a United Arabia, of which Iraq will undoubtedly form part, as soon as we have reinstalled our friend Rashid Ali in power.

"Thanks to his shrewdness in hiding from the British when Rommel reached the gates of Cairo, King Farouk is now restored to the throne of Egypt, and as I and the Duce promised him in Cairo last week, Egypt will remain a monarchy under the protection of Italy, whose mandate will also embrace Saudi Arabia and the Sudan. In my Christmas Day speech I shall hold out the prospect of a Pax Germanica from the Atlantic to the Arabian Sea and from the Baltic to the Red Sea. Under this great canopy, Moslems and Christians will live together in peace and mutual respect for the first time in two thousand years, un-exploited by Judaism and uninfected by the deadly virus of Communism." Hitler paused in his pacing to fix Kurt with a challenging stare. "Can you think of a nobler text for a sermon from the Mount?"

"A truly breathtaking concept, my Fuehrer," Kurt said, sitting bolt upright. "But what if—" He faltered, hardly daring to give voice to the question.

"What if the British reject my olive branch? Is that what you were going to ask?" Hitler seemed suddenly to grow several inches as he drew back his head and, raising one arm high, brought the clenched fist flashing down. "Total annihilation! Their armies will find no sanctuary in India or in their African colonies. Wherever they flee, I shall seek them out and destroy them! As for the British Isles, they will be reduced, as I've reduced Leningrad, to a desert of rubble and cannibalistic cave dwellers! I shall act against them, Armbrecht, as if the word 'mercy' had never existed!"

In the event, Hitler's visit to Jerusalem was unavoidably postponed until early in March of the following year, and by then he had changed his mind about offering his olive branch to the British and was back into the Anglophobic mood that had seized him after the fierce but futile resistance of Gibraltar, in September 1942, to the combined German airborne and Spanish land forces.

It had been completely in character for Hitler to have recovered his grudging admiration for the British when, six weeks later, they abandoned Cairo, to prevent the city's virtual destruction by the Luftwaffe and Rommel's artillery; and once again in character when he stormed at them to his Chief of Staff, General Franz Halder, in the Map Room of the Chancellery ten days before Christmas 1942.

"What can that drunken blabbermouth Churchill hope to achieve by blocking the Suez Canal and defending the Sinai passes? Surely even he must realize he has now lost the Middle East!"

The most unemotional and thoughtful of Hitler's military chieftains, Halder had little taste for the street-corner epithets used by the Supreme Commander. He said, "One must assume Churchill is motivated from this point by political rather than military considerations. He cannot be seen by America to abandon the Jewish population of Palestine, or by the Russians to have left open Rommel's road to Persia. In my opinion, he is counting on an early American intervention to save the Palestinian Jews."

"But that is arrant nonsense!" Hitler exploded. "There are almost half a million of those swine, penned up in Tel Aviv and Haifa. Can the Americans, or Churchill, transport them across nine hundred miles of desert to the Persian Gulf? And if they accomplished this Mosaic miracle, what then? What vast and mythical fleet exists to evacuate them, and to where? The Pope is at least being more realistic when he pleads with me to declare my intentions toward Palestine. I shall continue to ignore him, of course. But when that paralytic warmonger Roosevelt orders battleships of his Pacific Fleet into the Indian Ocean, as he has, all I can do is laugh in his face and say, 'Come on then, Yanks! Try your luck with our submarine packs and the Japanese navy!' "

"In strategic terms, you are of course right, my Fuehrer. What I had in mind was a secret understanding between Roosevelt and Churchill, whereby if the British put up a valiant enough fight in defense of the Jews in Palestine, Roosevelt would at last be able to swing Congress into a declaration of war. That wouldn't save the Jews and it wouldn't save the Middle East. But it would make all the difference to Britain's chances of survival."

Hitler had calmed down while Halder was speaking. Now he stood beside his map table, arms folded, smiling the sour smile that usually preceded an admonishment to his Chief of Staff. "You've just proved my contention, Halder," he snapped, "that generals make poor politicians. Consider the facts. Over these past two years we have been vigorously and ruthlessly purging European society of the Jewish poison without bringing America into the war. Bormann will give you the up-to-date figures over dinner tonight if you are interested, but suffice it to say that the fate of a half million Jews in Palestine is a paltry consideration compared with the sanitary operation we are already carrying out upon European Jewry. And bear in mind that, unlike the Palestinians, these are related by blood to the scum who have taken over American business and politics. Do you really imagine the United States Congress, having swallowed the camel of our Jewish policy in Europe, is going to strain at the gnat of

Palestine? No, my friend. There is no secret understanding between Roosevelt and Churchill that could possibly justify this vainglorious defense of Sinai and the coastal road to Palestine. We must therefore assume that the British are buying time for major reinforcements to reach them from India, or else Stalin has somehow managed to convince Churchill that he can stem Rundstedt's advance into Persia. Whatever the case, they are doomed."

General Alfred Jodl, chief of the Wehrmacht Operations Staff, had been hanging onto every word uttered by Hitler, supplying affirmative nods or confirmatory shakes of the head whenever appropriate. He leaped in now. "There is no question of that, my Fuehrer."

"Let us hope," Hitler muttered, "you are right. And now let's have the others in, so we can get on with the situation conference."

II

THE SUBDUED murmur, like the sound from a packed ballet audience just before the conductor strides on for the overture, gave way to an almost complete silence as Prime Minister Winston Churchill trudged in January, 1943, into the debating chamber of the House of Commons and headed for the Treasury Bench. On both sides of the chamber members were crushed tight into the tiers of padded red-leather benches, with a spillover squatting on the gangway stairs. Bombed out of the Commons chamber, the 620 elected legislators now had to make do with the smaller Lords chamber, and even allowing for those members sick or away on government business it was a tight fit. Behind Churchill, as he turned to bow to the Speaker, senior members of the Coalition cabinet heaved against one another to provide buttocks space for the P.M.

Wedging himself in roughly, to the visible discomfort of his slightly built Deputy, Clement Attlee, now sandwiched between the massive bulks of the Prime Minister and Labor Minister Ernest Bevin, Churchill fumbled for his spectacles, put them on and peered along what in other times would have been the Opposition front bench. From the corner of his eye, Foreign Minister Anthony Eden observed the tightening of his chief's mouth as the pale-blue eyes noted the presence of Aneurin Bevan, seated with folded arms on the front Opposition bench just below the gangway, gazing expressionlessly ahead.

In answer to a formal question from one of his backbenchers, Churchill rose to his feet, took the few paces to the dispatch box, laid his typewritten sheaf of notes upon it and began his speech to this secret session of the House of Commons.

As we meet in this place today, the war in the Middle East is drawing to its somber close. Our forces everywhere are in retreat—in good order, and using great tactical skill, but in retreat nonetheless. I wish I could tell Honorable Members that they are falling back to prepared lines of defense in Syria, Iraq and Persia, but this is no time for the euphemistic language of military communiqués. We have only one line of retreat, if the residue of the Eighth Army and our forces in Persia are not to perish or fall prisoner, and that is into the Persian Gulf and into the care of the Royal Navy, which must then run the gauntlet of the Japanese fleet, across the Arabian Sea to the sanctuary—if such it can be termed—of India. This House may rest assured that dispositions have already been made, to the limit of our resources, to ensure the success of this evacuation.

In my broadcast speech to the nation over the wireless last Thursday I explained that in the event of our being obliged to choose between abandoning the Middle East to the Nazis and making a stand there, sustained by reinforcements from India, we should have to take the first course. Honorable Members will not, I trust, expect any elaboration this evening, on the strategic considerations that impel us to this decision. However, there is another factor bearing on our action which I should enlarge upon. In that same broadcast speech I spoke of the disappointment felt by Britain and the Empire, and shared by the leaders of Europe in exile, with the behavior of the Arab peoples and their rulers in the face of this conflict raging upon their soil. I chose my words so as not to provide gratuitous ammunition for Hitler and his disgusting stooge, the Mufti of Jerusalem, in their hate campaign against the democracies. I am under no such constraint in this place.

Churchill paused to accommodate the deep and resounding rumble of "Hear! Hear!" from all parts of the House.

I will therefore venture [he resumed, slipping off his spectacles and urging his massive jowl forward] this judgment—that in the long history of the Islamic peoples, a history steeped as often in villainy as it has been touched by grace, there is nothing to compare with the cowardly barbaric excesses of the Moslem rulers and their subjects against the hapless Jewish communities cast upon their mercy during these past few weeks.

King Farouk! [Churchill struck the dispatch box with a clenched fist.] An obese vessel of iniquity, fawning upon the jackbooted Nazi Fuehrer in an Egyptian capital misguidedly spared destruction upon my own orders . . . The Amir Abdullah of Transjordan, [the fist came down again] dallying with his concubines while the mutinous Frontier Force, trained and equipped by this nation, yap and snarl like bloodthirsty jackals around the doomed but still bravely resisting enclave of Tel Aviv.

Half a dozen Members were on their feet, including Aneurin Bevan, who was brusquely waving Members of his own party back into their seats. Breaking off his discourse and moving a pace back from the dispatch box, Churchill turned to scowl at two of his own Tory backbenchers, up on their feet, as if holding them personally responsible for the Welshman's intervention. They sat down immediately, whereupon the P.M. lowered himself to a hastily vacated eighteen inches or so of Treasury bench, giving way to the one Member still standing.

Bevan's voice, the most lethal polemical weapon ever raised against Churchill in secret or public session, was pitched to a higher register than the war leader's; it seemed to be propelled, with a kind of reedy mellifluence, directly off his palate rather than from his lungs.

Is the Right Honorable Gentleman not aware that in the eyes of the world, and no doubt to the immense comfort of our fascist enemies, the slaughter of these innocents is as much an indictment of Britain's honor as it is a monument to the bestiality of the Mufti's followers? Has he no explanation to offer, however craven or cynical [his voice rose, cutting through the angry cries and countercries], of the shameful decision for which he himself will be answerable to history, for the precipitate withdrawal of our forces across the Jordan, thereby causing this desperate flight of the Jews into the hands of their executioners?

As Bevan sat abruptly down, Churchill came slowly to his feet.

The Honorable Member for Ebbw Vale will not, I fancy, be writing the history of this war—at least not for any publisher or institution with a reputation to cherish and inelastic financial reserves. [Over the Tory laughter, sharp cries of "Answer the question!" broke from the Labor benches.]

However [Churchill growled on] since the question just put to me so gravely impugns the honor of the Eighth Army—

The eruption of dissenting voices smothered his next words and he fell silent, glowering at the Opposition benches but standing his ground, refusing to give way to Bevan, who had sprung again to his feet.

"On a point of order, Mr. Speaker!"

Churchill glanced leftward at the Speaker, hesitated a moment, then backed away slightly, making it clear he was going to suffer only the briefest of interruptions.

The Right Honorable Gentleman once again demonstrates his unrivaled talent for distorting the words of his critics. It is not the honor of the Eighth Army I am calling in question. It is the decision made at War Cabinet level and dictated to General Alexander by the Right Honorable Gentleman himself—to abandon the Jews of Palestine to their fate—that has dishonored this nation and brought contumely on the Eighth Army in the eyes of the world. I invite the Right Honorable Gentleman to cut out the feeble attempts at humor and address himself to the question.

This time, the shouts of "Hear! Hear!" from the pro-Bevan faction brought no counter cries from the government back benches. Clearly sensing the unease of his supporters, the Prime Minister bent an ear to the urgent whispering of Clement Attlee before taking up his position once more at the dispatch box.

Let me remind those who might have been moved to question my own motives in this matter that a secure and independent Jewish homeland has long been one of the most cherished objectives of my political life. I was publicly espousing the cause of Zionism [he went on, raising his voice angrily over the supporting murmurs of his party stalwarts] when those who slander me from the benches opposite were furiously denouncing that great concept as a stumbling block on the road towards a Third International!

As he waited for the loud Tory cheering to subside, he glared across at Aneurin Bevan, who remained seated, his chubby face void of all expression.

"Answer the question!" It was a solitary, unspirited cry from the rear of the Opposition front bench. Churchill put his spectacles back on and planted himself squarely before the dispatch box, grasping it with both hands as he scanned his notes.

8 6

The issue as to whether the eastern seaboard of the Mediterranean could be defended was in fact decided against us when the British Fleet was driven from that sea following the loss of its bases in Malta, Cyprus and Alexandria and the fall of Gibraltar. There was of course a further consideration that was weighing heavily on all our minds, and that was the fate of those noncombatant Palestinian Jews and those refugees from Nazi Europe largely concentrated in the coastal cities of Haifa and Tel Aviv. The obvious solution was a mass evacuation. But to where? And by what means? President Roosevelt's plea to Hitler to allow a mercy fleet of American ships safe passage up the Red Sea and into the Gulf of Aqaba had already been rejected. Approaches were then made by the International Red Cross to Turkey, the nearest neutral and non-Arab state to Palestine. These talks were conducted in secret with the President of the Republic himself, Ismet Inonu, who appeared at first to be receptive to the idea of providing temporary sanctuary, provided the operation cost him nothing.

It was therefore arranged for the first convoy of trucks, motor coaches and ambulances, escorted by Red Cross officials, to make the three-hundred-mile journey northwards along the coasts of the Lebanon and Syria. The attack on that unarmed convoy as it crossed the frontier with Syria was, I feel sure, as abominable to President Inonu as it was to decent people everywhere. But the fact that it was carried out by *Mujahidin* irregulars, under direct orders from the Mufti, caused Inonu to reconsider his arrangement with the Red Cross. Had Ataturk still been alive, there can be little doubt that Turkey's frontiers would have remained open, even to armed convoys of Palestinian refugees. But his successor, alas, is a man of different mettle. At this point, while British and American Red Cross officials in Geneva were grappling with the well-nigh impossible logistics of a Jewish exodus across Transjordan and Iraq to the Persian Gulf, Rommel thrust north, threatening our positions at the Khatmia Pass and at Romani, on the coastal road to Palestine. This breakthrough by Rommel was also the signal for

Rashid Ali to emerge from his funk-hole and incite his Iraqi followers to the foul murder of the boy King Faisal the Second and the Regent Emir Abdul Illah. The Commander-in-chief in the Middle East reported to me as follows. [Churchill fingered a sheet of paper from the notes lying before him and cleared his throat before reading aloud.] "Palestine can now be defended only at the ultimate cost of the entire Eighth Army. Our next line of defense is the Dead Sea and the east bank of the Jordan. The Jewish Command's decision, already conveyed to you, remains unchanged."

That decision [Churchill went on] was to defend the all-Jewish city of Tel Aviv, with its remaining civilian population, if necessary to the last man, and to make clear this intention to the Germans, in the hope that as a condition of laying down their arms the safety and freedom of the civilian population would be guaranteed.

In the light of events, that might seem to be an heroic but absurdly deluded course of action. But there was good reason to believe that Rommel would bring pressure upon Hitler to accept this offer, and in fact this is precisely what did happen. It is to Rommel's credit that the Afrika Korps has been totally committed to the pursuit of the Eighth Army and that he has refused all military involvement with the Arab forces now assailing Tel Aviv. For our part, and on my express orders, we left every ton of war material we could spare to the valiant Jewish defenders before our forces withdrew from Palestine. But their days, alas, are numbered. There can, I fear, be only one outcome in this sector of the Middle-East battlefield. And the civilized world, Mister Speaker, sickened as it is by the monstrous infamies already perpetrated by Hitler's Germany, must now brace itself for the carnage that is surely to come. . . .

The Prime Minister had paused, whether out of emotion or to take breath it was not clear, when a sound no living member could recall ever hearing in the debating chamber of the House of Commons, tortured the deep silence. All heads, it seemed, were turning toward the slight fair-haired figure of Sidney Silverman, seated immediately to the left of Aneurin Bevan—all heads except that of Churchill and of the Welshman himself. The member for Nelson and Colne was sobbing, head bowed, hands limply folded in his lap. Bevan's left arm came slowly up and around his neighbor's shoulders in a tight embrace.

CHAPTER FIVE

As HITLER'S armored train, nine coaches long, came slowly to a standstill in the railway station of Berchtesgaden, Doctor Otto Dietrich, Reich Press Director and chief spokesman for the Fuehrer's headquarters, flopped into the vacant seat opposite Kurt and offered the younger man a patronizing smile.

"Excited, Armbrecht?"

"I suppose so. It's taken me eighteen months to get here, after all."

The arrival platform was now seething with troops of the SS Leibstandarte Adolf Hitler, scrambling from their coaches at the front and rear of the train. Reluctantly, Kurt switched his attention back to Dietrich. He had had less contact, possibly, with the press chief than with any of Hitler's aides since joining the Chancellery staff, and such contacts as they had made could hardly have been classed as cordial. In eighteen months, without going out of his way to solicit Chancellery gossip, Kurt had become aware of the petty rivalries and incessant elbowing for power between individuals and *ad hoc* groupings of individuals attached to the court of Adolf Hitler. And however true it might be that he himself, unmoved by executive greed, remained above —or, more precisely, *below*—this squalid maneuvering for favor, the fact remained that he had been Goebbels's candidate for the post of literary secretary, and between Dietrich and Goebbels there was now only the frostiest of relationships. They had been contemporaries and *alte Kaempfer* of the party in its early struggles, and in principle there need have been no friction between them on the executive level. In practice, however, Dietrich had been taking it upon himself, using Hitler's authority, to issue directives bearing upon certain sudden news "breaks" without bothering to consult the Minister, and there had now been several instances in which the unfortunate night staff of Room 24 at the Ministry had had to decide either to sit tight on two urgent and conflicting directives, thereby missing the editions, or else to put out only one of them, in which case it was inevitably the policy line from the Fuehrer's HQ spokesman that colored the editorials, often to the dismay and fury of Goebbels, the unchallenged *maestro* of Reich propaganda.

A particularly blatant example of this had been the handling, or rather mishandling, of Pope Pius XII's cable to Hitler, ten months back, when the Jewish redoubts of Haifa and Tel Aviv had broadcast their surrender offer to the Waffen SS. The Pope's cable, as protocol required, had been presented that morning to Joachim von Ribbentrop at the Foreign Ministry by the Papal Nuncio in Berlin, Cesare Cardinal Orsenigo, for transmission to the German Fuehrer in his advanced southern-Russian headquarters. At the same time, Orsenigo had politely informed Ribbentrop that the text of the Pope's message—a mildly worded appeal for the Jewish defenders to be afforded Geneva Convention status as prisoners of war—would be released by the Vatican press office eight hours after its delivery to the Foreign Minister. Immediately after telegraphing the text to the Fuehrer, Ribbentrop had got on the telephone to Goebbels. The two men agreed that the German press and radio should be given a "mark time" policy directive that night and that the general line should be that it would be for the Fuehrer, as Supreme Commander of the Armed Forces, to decide the terms for surrender, including the status of those laying down their arms.

The early morning radio bulletins and commentaries adhered strictly to this restrained and, by Nazi standards, unprovocative line. But the national press tore into the Pope's appeal like ravenous wolves. By what distortions of the accepted rules of warfare, it asked, could honorable prisoner-of-war status be given

9 1

to a rabble of saboteurs and stateless aggressors operating behind the lines of a national army locked in combat with the forces of a formally declared enemy? Was it in the Pope's province to rewrite the Geneva Articles?

The ensuing slaughter of the Jewish combatants and the following month-long "reduction" of the surviving civilian population by two of Eichmann's *Einsatzgruppen* were now correctly seen by the neutral nations of the world as premeditated acts of barbarism. To Reichsminister Goebbels, the whole affair was a propaganda disaster. It had also provided Churchill with all the moral support he needed—internally and abroad—in rejecting the "olive branch" offered by Hitler in Jerusalem on March 7. But the Doctor's vigorous protest to Hitler had been so toned down by the ever-vigilant Martin Bormann as to have warranted no more than a "Seen and noted" comment from the Fuehrer.

Dietrich's smile had broadened at Kurt's answer. "You can count yourself lucky the Chief's been so tied up elsewhere these past eighteen months. Take it from me, two weeks isolated up on that mountain are going to strain your loyalty to the breaking point."

"I doubt that. Remember, I was born in these parts." He snatched a glance along the platform, where some of the top brass of Hitler's entourage, including OKW chief, Feldmarschall Keitel, chief adjutant Julius Schaub, SS Oberfuehrer Rattenhuber, head of security, and Gruppenfuehrer Fegelein, Himmler's permanent representative at the Fuehrerhauptquartier, were forming into groups on either side of the red carpet laid down for Berchtesgaden's most illustrious patron.

"It's not the Bavarian Alps I'm talking about, Herr Captain. It's life at the Berghof." Dietrich simulated a huge yawn, drooping his eyelids. "A petty-bourgeois paradise, if ever there was one." His eyes opened and the grin returned, this time more spiteful than benign. "Pity you couldn't wangle accommodation for that charming secretary of yours. There's an abysmal shortage of pretty young females up on that mountain."

Kurt could have retorted, deadpan, that Helga was taking a part of her annual leave, over Christmas and the New Year. He could have said, rising playfully to Dietrich's lewd dig, that he himself needed a rest from Helga's sexual demands. Both comments would have been valid. But, seeing no profit in this line of banter, he switched back to the press chief's earlier remark.

" 'Petty-bourgeois' seems a curious term to use—I mean, of the Berghof."

Dietrich shrugged. "Semantics is our business, Armbrecht—both yours and mine—and if you can offer a more apt description, after a couple of lunch and tea sessions up there, I'll be glad to hear it." He pushed back his cuff to squint at his wrist watch. "Five more minutes for Erich Kempka to get the Chief's Mercedes off the train and another five for Hoffman to take his blasted pictures of the local *Kreisleiter's* little poppets handing out the edelweiss, and we ought to be off and away. Be a good fellow and shake me awake when you see Bormann out there, fussing about." And, with that, Dietrich slipped off into what, to all intents and purposes, was a light coma.

Kurt's own eyelids were prickling from the fatigue of the long train journey, which had begun at Berlin just after midnight and had afforded no sleep for any of the entourage until after 2 A.M., when the last of the company summoned to the Fuehrer's rose-wood-paneled parlor car returned, heavy-eyed, with the welcome news that the Fuehrer's orderly, Bussman, was about to put him to bed. After breakfasting at dawn in the dining car, Kurt had returned to his designated seat in the third coach down from Hitler's and opened the envelope marked *"Bormann-Vermerke No. 445."* The date was Friday, 3 December, 1943; the report was exactly a week old. It was of the Fuehrer's remarks at a lunch party in the Chancellery, with Feldmarschall Erwin Rommel as guest of honor. There was an introductory note by Martin Bormann:

Feldmarschall Rommel had commented on yesterday's (unconfirmed) report in the Swedish press that Sir Stafford Cripps had been involved in secret discussions in the capital of Afghanistan with the Soviet Foreign Minister, Molotov, with the presumed approval of King Zahir Shah. If this were true, he asked the Fuehrer, might it not call for an urgent reappraisal of the Teheran Agreement with Japan? The Fuehrer replied:

"We must evaluate the likely consequences of such a meeting with geopolitical realism, before goading the Japanese into a precipitate reaction. When I met Tojo and Togo in Teheran to settle the question of our respective spheres of interest, I had the greatest difficulty in persuading them against adding the vast Indian subcontinent to their empire. I will not flatter myself that it was my forceful arguments alone that won the day. I must assume that Foreign Minister Shigenovi Togo's better counsels prevailed over his Premier's military ambitions and that he had no more appetite than I had for a common frontier between our two great empires. Nor must we forget that Russia's Far Eastern armies were at that very time launching the first of their unexpected counterattacks west of Khabarovsk and threatening the Japanese supply line from Vladivostok.

"Now, as to this Kabul meeting between Molotov and Cripps, there can only have been two possible purposes behind it. One would be to trick King Zahir Shah into believing that the independence of his kingdom was threatened and to invite him to throw in his lot with Russia and Britain, thereby opening the possibility of a land link between the Russian armies east of the Caspian and the British-held warm-water ports of northwest India. The other possibility is that they have offered the landlocked monarch the whole of Baluchistan, with its seaboard, as the prize for turning his country into an Anglo-Soviet redoubt. Either way, I am not seriously concerned by such paltry intrigues and I have every hope that our Japanese ally will take a similarly detached view. Europe and the Middle East are now secure for all time against anything our enemies can throw at us. Every attempt by Stalin's generals to retake Gorki or to breach the Volga south of Engels has failed. My one fear—that Japan might provide Roosevelt with the excuse he so desperately wants for entering the war—has been put to rest by the Teheran declaration that neither of its signatories has designs on American interests in any part of the globe. We are told that when Churchill read that passage he described it as a pledge by two jackals not to eat meat. To that I can only reply, 'What jackal in its right mind would bother about poisoned meat, when it has a larder overstuffed with prime venison?' "

The long motorcade winding its way up the steep mountain road to Obersalzberg was led by the big Mercedes sedan with Kempka at the wheel, Adolf Hitler seated beside him, and the jump and rear seats occupied by Bormann, Keitel, Rattenhuber and Albert Speer, Reich Minister of Armaments and War Production. The road twisted through pine woods most of the way to the 2,000-foot-high mountain valley where the Berghof complex began, with occasional breaks in the trees affording ever-more-breathtaking views of the Bavarian Alps. All snow had been cleared from the road and from around the green-painted concrete guard-houses manned by SS troops at every vantage point on the way up. Away ahead of the motorcade, and bringing up its rear, rumbled the Leibstandarte troop-carriers and SS officers' jeeps.

In the fourth automobile behind the Fuehrer's, Kurt was wedged in the rear seat between Captain Rudolf Geissler and Captain Peter Waldheim, respectively Hitler's Army and Luftwaffe junior adjutants, with the bulky bespectacled Doctor Theodor Morell up front beside the SS driver. "For this dispensation," Waldheim had muttered to Kurt as they settled in the car, "we thank thee, O Lord!" And the young officer had pushed home the point by delicately pinching his nostrils between thumb and forefinger. Kurt breathed a pious "Amen!" He was grateful for the Chancellery protocol that gave him the companionship, at times like this, of the Fuehrer's younger adjutants, with both of whom he now enjoyed that rare Chancellery phenomenon, an easy and friendly relationship. He had remarked, glancing back through the rear window at the line of Berghof-based limousines moving off from the railroad station forecourt, "It's a bit like a funeral procession, after the corpse has been tucked safely away. Is this about average for a Berghof house party?" Rudolf Geissler had waggled his palm. "Give or take a dozen or so, yes. But we're only the advance guard. Reichsmarschall Goering and his entourage are expected in a couple of days' time, though the Goerings have their own place here, thank God. The Doctor's bound to come down for a day or two, and there'll be a stream of *Gauleiters* and *Reichsleiters* trotting in and out with their fat wives and presents over the next week or two."

"What about Fräulein Braun? I didn't see her getting on the train at Berlin."

"She'll be following with the Chief's secretaries and probably will have to make herself scarce—poor bitch—whenever the bigwigs' wives put in an appearance. Which reminds me, Peter—" Geissler leaned across Kurt to grin at his colleague— "did you manage to contact that redhead at the Berchtesgaden Hof?"

"I wrote to her," Waldheim grunted. "Got a nice letter back, from one of the SS Lebensborn maternity homes. Seems there's a future recruit for the Leibstandarte due any day now."

"The bastards," Geissler sighed. "I swear there's not an unmarried wench over fourteen around these parts who hasn't done her duty by at least half-a-dozen of the boys in black."

The motorcade had now turned into the mountain valley that was the site of Hitler's Bavarian retreat and had slowed down to allow the Fuehrer a few words with the Leibstandarte *Sturmbannfuehrer* greeting him at the opening in the two-mile wire fence enclosing the inner area. It was the second fence they had passed through. The first one, as Waldheim had explained, was nine miles in circumference and encircled the vast complex of guesthouses, office buildings, barracks and garages that had been added over the fifteen years since the then thirty-nine-year-old leader of the National Socialist German Workers' Party first rented the modest Villa Wachenfeld, as the original chalet was called, for $25 a month. Captain Waldheim, clearly as much to irritate Doctor Morell as to brief Kurt on his surroundings, was describing the lay-out as they drove into the valley.

"If you look hard up there you might just make out the shape of an exceedingly well-camouflaged building housing the main secretariat. The pine trees almost screening it are, of course, completely artificial, but the snow is real. . . . Over there to the right, visible only to the tutored eye, is the main barracks of the SS Leibstandarte Adolf Hitler, a hand-picked regiment of Germany's finest soldiers. Ah yes, and now we come into sight of the magnificent Berghof itself. You can make out the guest-house, over there on the right, built to accommodate distinguished foreign visitors but shortly to vibrate with the snores of our *Feldmarschaelle* and *Reichsminister*. Out of sight at the moment is the rather more unpretentious establishment in which lesser mortals such as you, Armbrecht, and myself are to be accommodated. . . . Please note the broad flight of stone steps leading up to the front porch of the Berghof. It was on the fifth step up, on a wet afternoon in September 1938, that the Prime Minister of Great Britain, Neville Chamberlain, nearly slipped and broke his umbrella as he climbed up to meet our Fuehrer. There is no truth whatsoever in the story that the step had been greased five minutes earlier by Reichsfuehrer Heinrich Himmler. . . ."

To Kurt, with one eye on Morell's reddening neck, it came as a relief when the doors of the car were swung open by guards, and the motorcade's passengers piled out onto the driveway to watch the Fuehrer's slow ascent between the two closed ranks of SS honor guards lining the wide stairway. As if by prearrangement, a shaft of sunlight had broken through the clouds to sparkle the silver buckles and facings on the immaculate black uniforms of the bodyguard, with their uniform blue eyes and uniform frozen features. At the top of the steps, framed by the overhanging timbered eaves of the chalet rooftops, Hitler turned and, as his immediate entourage fanned out to either side of him, raised his arm in smiling salute to the company assembled below in the driveway. Kurt's own arm shot up in "the German salute," his voice drowned in the loud chorus of "Heil Hitler!" As the Fuehrer turned away he felt Waldheim's hand on his arm. "This way, Armbrecht. There should be a bottle of *Schnapps* in my room—unless my orderly wants a posting to the eastern front."

They had arrived at the Berghof on Friday, December 10, 1943, and over the following twelve days Kurt's only contact with his family, less than a hundred miles away in Munich, was by letter and an occasional telephone call—a privilege grudgingly granted by the chief operator of the Berghof switchboard. Any hopes he had of getting away to spend Christmas—or rather "Yuletide," as the feast was now officially renamed—with them were dashed on the Monday following his arrival, when Martin Bormann summoned him to his office in the secretariat wing of the great chalet. Hitler's secretary seemed to be in a relaxed and amiable mood—lending credence, perhaps, to the Berghof gossip about his having recently acquired a young mistress, a film actress, with the enthusiastic approval of his wife, Gerda.

"Sit down, Armbrecht, sit down. . . . And how are you enjoying our fine mountain climate?"

"Very much, Herr Reichsleiter. Memories of one's youth and all that."

"That's right," Bormann nodded. "You were born in these parts, of course." Exploiting the opening, Kurt put in quickly, "In Munich itself, Herr Reichsleiter. My family still lives there."

"Of course." But Kurt might have been saying they lived in Timbuctoo, for all the significance it had for the bull-necked Bormann, who had plucked a small note pad from his side pocket and was flipping lazily through the leaves.

"The Fuehrer is concerned about not having been able to spare you more time over the past few months, but I imagine you've found plenty to occupy yourself with?"

"Indeed I have, Herr Reichsleiter. In fact I've completed a first draft covering the period 1933 to the fall of Moscow. I have it with me here, if you or the Fuehrer would like to—"

Bormann's vigorous headshake cut him short. "Don't even mention it to the Fuehrer. That's an order, Armbrecht!"

"I'm sorry. I was merely keeping you in—"

"I know. And I appreciate it. Perhaps I shall even find time to look through your draft while we're on the mountain, but I can't promise anything. I'd better explain why we mustn't impose any literary labors on the Fuehrer at this time, apart from his routine discussions with you—one of which, incidentally, you will be summoned to before lunch tomorrow." Bormann got up from his desk, gesturing to Kurt to stay seated, and began to pace up and down in a stiff-legged and totally unconvincing imitation of Hitler's catlike tread.

"The fact of the matter, Armbrecht, is that the Fuehrer has lately begun to preoccupy himself with one of the most fundamental of the challenges still facing National Socialism. As you know, these past few months have been dedicated by the Fuehrer to laying the physical and economic foundations of the Greater German Reich and to attending to such unfinished business as the Jewish problem, the question of racial hygiene and the final subjugation of our enemy across the English Channel. Which reminds me—" He broke off to stride back to his desk, take a large photographic print out of one of the drawers and toss it, smiling broadly, to Kurt's side of the desk.

"Our Yuletide present to Winston Churchill! And a box of cigars for *you*, Captain, if you can guess what it is."

Kurt's frown deepened as he studied the photograph. It had been taken from ground-level and showed what appeared by reference to the trees in the background to be a small rudimentary aircraft, more like a glider than a powered machine, with blunted wing tips and a slim windowless fuselage. The aircraft was poised halfway along an upward-sloping ramp, upon what looked like a narrow railroad track. He looked up at the grinning Deputy Fuehrer. "I can't make it out. It looks like a large-scale working model of something, but—" He shook his head, helplessly.

"You are looking," Bormann said, chuckling, "at one of the secret weapons that are going to bring Britain to its knees in 1944 without the loss of a single German soldier in combat. The first of our *Vergeltungswaffen,* Armbrecht. A pilotless plane, radio-controlled to fly to any preselected target in Britain and dive straight down on it, exploding its warhead on contact."

Kurt pursed his lips in a slow curling whistle as he looked down again at the photograph. "Fantastic!" he breathed. "A suicide Stuka dive bomber, but without the suicide!"

"Precisely. And now that I've let you in on the secret, perhaps you will understand why you cannot leave the mountain until the Fuehrer gives the order for our little reindeer to unload their first gifts on London."

He had as yet made no formal request for leave. But he had tentatively broached the possibility with Fräulein Eppler the previous day, and she had obviously reported the request to Bormann. He said, "Of course, I appreciate that, Herr Reichsleiter. May I ask if there is a date in mind?"

"You may not. But I can tell you this: We shall all have something to celebrate by Yuletide." Bormann reached for the photograph and put it back in the drawer. "But this is not the reason I sent for you. I was telling you about the Fuehrer's current preoccupations, because it is important you should prepare your mind for a new and vitally important development. In a word, Armbrecht, our Fuehrer has decided to apply himself to the solution of the religious problem." Bormann paused, staring hard at Kurt, as if expecting an instant reaction, and the young Captain could only stare back at him, feeling inadequate. What was there to say? The Fuehrer was going to tackle the Church. But that was already written large on the wall of National Socialist philosophy. True, it had not yet figured high in the order of priorities . . . He said, "This is tremendous news, Herr Reichsleiter. Not unexpected, of course, but—well—"

"Not quite at this stage, you were going to say? And yet, when you think about it, Armbrecht—" Bormann had resumed his ponderous pacing—"what better time than this Yuletide of 1943, when all the Fuehrer's enemies have been crushed, or are about to be crushed, by our invincible Wehrmacht and the priests in their pulpits are preparing to spew out their nauseating drivel about 'peace on earth and good will to all men'? I don't mind telling you, Armbrecht, that I have worked day and night over these past months to reduce the mountain of executive decisions piling up from our secular achievements—" Bormann uttered a harsh little laugh as the phrase formed itself—"so as to free the Fuehrer to grapple with their spiritual implications." The notebook was out again, for a swift entry across one of the pages, and Kurt seized the opportunity to blurt out the question now uppermost in his mind.

"About preparing myself for tomorrow, Herr Reichsleiter— had you any specific study in mind?"

"Brush up your facts. You'll find most of the relevant data in the dossiers I myself have been keeping over the years. At your disposal is a complete copy of them in the secretariat reference library. Familiarize yourself as thoroughly as you can with the infrastructure of the Protestant and Catholic churches in Europe, so as not to hold up the Fuehrer's discourse with unnecessary requests for clarification. Don't worry about dogma. That's not in your province." He looked pointedly at his watch. "You worry about the facts," he nodded as Kurt came smartly out of his chair. "The Fuehrer and I will take care of the theology."

It turned out that Hitler had hardly progressed in his thinking about the religious "problem" beyond the sweeping generalities of *Mein Kampf*. But the change in his general bearing, which Kurt had first begun to notice after Hitler's return from the Teheran meeting with General Tojo, had become even more marked.

He received Kurt in his spacious second-floor study with its two picture windows framing the distant Austrian Alps, and his first words were obviously prompted by Kurt's look of surprise at finding him in the civilian clothes of a Bavarian country gentleman.

"To all intents and purposes, the war is over, Armbrecht. I made a vow to remain in uniform until our enemies were defeated in the field. I shall now wear it only for public appearances and to reassure visiting foreign dignitaries that it has not been put away in mothballs."

Equally surprising was the complete absence of maps either on the Fuehrer's desk or on the polished rectangular table parallel to the book-lined wall on the right as one entered the room. There were several thick volumes stacked on the desk, with colored leather bookmarks in place, and a bowl of roses occupied one corner. The sanctum gave the appearance of belonging to a rather literary country squire, perhaps even a university professor with a private income. It was as congruous to a war lord as a friar's tonsure would be to a Viking.

Less surprising, because of the subtle changes Kurt had already noticed in Hitler's demeanor, was the impression he now had, as the Fuehrer motioned him to a stiff-backed armchair at the far end of the table, of being received in audience by a genial headmaster rather than the volatile human force whose very presence in the Berlin Chancellery had seemed to permeate every corridor and anteroom. Hitler looked well, and he lost no time in preening himself on the fact.

"I have a new doctor," he declared in answer to Kurt's respectful compliment. "Don't let on to Morell, but he's going to find himself out of a 60,000-marks-a-year job at the end of the year. All those drugs he's been putting into me all these years—nothing but palliatives! My stomach cramps stopped within a week of giving up my vegetarian diet—just as my new physician said they would. As for Morell's miracle pills, my valet Linge now has an extra duty—to flush them down the lavatory pan!"

But the change in Hitler was more than physical. His victories in the East, followed by the conquest of the Middle East and the Teheran Treaty with Japan, seemed to have had the effect of smoothing off the jagged edges of his personality. The mesmeric intentness of his stare, the harsh clamor of his voice—hitherto his unfailing weapons against doubt or dissent—were now replaced by an aura of serene self-assurance, suggesting an interior exaltation rooted in grace. Hitler embarked on his monologue.

"A healthy mind, my dear Armbrecht, cannot subsist in an unhealthy body. It would be like expecting a luminous painting to spring from a dirty palette. In the same way, no state can evolve to true greatness as long as its people are deprived of cultural nourishment. When I instructed Papen in 1933 to sign the concordat with the Vatican, I thereby guaranteed the Catholic Church in Germany the right to freedom of worship and the regulation of its own affairs. I did so not solely as a gesture to the twenty-two million Germans then embracing this religion —there are now, in the Third Reich, something like forty-five million—but because I believed then, and still do, that organized religion fulfills a basic social need and, provided that it permits itself to keep step with man's evolution, can play a useful role in the state, not least by its stabilizing influence on the broad mass of its adherents.

"Needless to say, I did not expect the Catholic Church in Germany to throw off, overnight, its encrusted, centuries-old shell of dogma and leap joyfully into our National Socialist bed. We had our early troubles, of course, but it was a source of some gratification to me when Pope Pius XII—the same Eugenio Pacelli who, as Papal Secretary of State, signed the concordat with Papen—declined to condemn us for invading Catholic Poland, despite the great pressures brought to bear on him by the democracies and their nationalist cardinals.

"Similarly, Pope Pius XII maintained a correct attitude of neutrality when the time came for me to settle our military accounts with Britain and Western Europe. And to this date— apart from his mild intervention on behalf of the Palestine Jews —he has steadfastly withheld any censure of our military conquests in the Balkans and the Middle East. All this, Armbrecht,

I put to his credit. But neutrality is not enough when I, as Fuehrer of the Greater Reich, embark on a crusade which, however military and political its basic thrust, has as one of its supreme motivations the extermination of the Holy Roman Church's most implacable and most dangerous *spiritual* enemies! I refer, of course, to the death struggle we have waged and won against the monstrous tyranny of atheistic Bolshevism. From the very outset of this titanic struggle we tried to persuade the Vatican to publicly confirm what every Catholic in the world gratefully recognizes—that the blood so copiously spent by our brave soldiers and airmen in Russia has been a sacred sacrifice to the perpetuation of Christianity. We failed. I am told, and I am willing to believe it, that Eugenio Pacelli was personally overjoyed by the Wehrmacht's victories in the East, but that his lips were sealed for fear of offending such strange bedfellows of Stalin's as Winston Churchill and Franklin D. Roosevelt! If I am asked to sympathize with this attitude, I can only reply, 'Since when have either of these gentlemen shown the slightest concern for the Vatican's interests?'

"But this is now water under the bridge. It is when we turn to the Church's present attitude to our racial-hygiene program in the conquered territories that I begin to have grave misgivings as to our future relationship with the Vatican. Second only to the Bolsheviks in their hatred of Christian civilization are the Jews, a cancerous virus I have already expelled from the bloodstream of our Aryan culture and am in the process of eradicating, for all time, from the rest of Europe and our eastern empire. And what thanks do I get from a Church founded on the martyrdom of the Israelite's most innocent victim? Slanderous incitement of our own German bishops by Pacelli himself! Reichsleiter Bormann will let you have a copy of a private letter we intercepted from the Pope to the Bishop of Berlin, Konrad von Preysing, a few months ago. 'Day after day,' the Pontiff writes, 'we hear of inhuman acts which have nothing to do with the real necessities of war, and they fill us with stupefaction and bitterness.' I put it to you, Armbrecht—what possible claim can

Pacelli have to understanding the necessities of war? And how, may I ask, does one commit 'inhuman' acts against subhuman trash? I tell you, there is a limit to my patience with these gentlemen of the cloth, and they have already pushed me beyond it.

"Well, I am about to teach these priests something they will not find in the New Testament—that 'he who pays the piper calls the tune.' I am giving them notice—Protestants and Catholics alike—that 1943 will be the last year they receive their billions of marks in state subsidies unless they include in their Yuletide services a prayer for the triumph of National Socialism over its enemies, both spiritual and temporal. The prayer has been composed by Bormann, and I can tell you it's going to be a hard pill for some of these gentry to swallow! But obedience to this directive must be complete, throughout the greater Reich. There will be an SS or SD man in every place of worship, from the gaudiest cathedral down to the humblest village chapel, and if only *one* of these pious ministers 'forgets' his prayer, the whole lot of them will have to manage from there on on what they can get out of their offertories, which amounts to a paltry fraction—I forget how much, for the moment—of what they've been milking from the State."

Kurt said, glancing up from his notetaking, "About three percent, my Fuehrer."

"I was merely testing you," Hitler beamed. "You may have five minutes for questions before we go down to lunch."

It seemed hardly credible, but it was all too true. Not counting his private session with the Fuehrer, Kurt had now been nearly four hours in the company of the world's most powerful man, and his jaws were beginning to ache from the effort of suppressing yawns.

The luncheon party could hardly have gotten off to a more promising start. First, there had been the thrill of being introduced for the first time to Reichsmarschall Goering within a few moments of Kurt's descent to the anteroom where the guests had gathered to await their host. Kurt had seen Germany's senior *Feldmarschall* in the flesh maybe a dozen times since joining the Fuehrer's staff, but never on an equal social footing as it were, fellow guests at an informal house party away from the rigid protocol and stifling security practices of the Berlin Chancellery.

Herman Goering's prestige as Commander in Chief of the Luftwaffe had now been almost completely restored to the pinnacle it had reached with his devastating pounding of Warsaw in September 1939. Almost forgotten was his Luftwaffe's poor showing against the British Expeditionary Force evacuating France in June 1940 and its failure to blitz Britain into surrender. It was Waldheim's contention, seriously advanced to Kurt during one of their drinking sessions together, that the personality of Germany's most illustrious and surviving World War I pilot had taken root in Hitler's subconscious as a kind of Other Ego. He was everything, Waldheim argued, the Fuehrer could not bring himself to be—an indolent, flamboyant and swash-buckling hedonist, but a proven warrior withal, twice married, and each time to spouses superbly endowed with those fleshly cushions so indispensable to a warrior's repose. Furthermore, it was notorious that Goering was relishing every fruit of his immense power and using it, quite shamelessly, to amass for himself the greatest private fortune in art treasures and industrial kickbacks in the Reich. No other theory but that of the cosseted Other Ego, said Waldheim, could persuasively enough explain Hitler's indulgence of this self-styled *Renaissancemensch,* whose whole way of life was in such complete contrast to that of the Fuehrer's.

This *joie de vivre* was radiating from the Reichsmarschall now as he held the attention of the larger of the two groups into which the waiting guests had separated, the smaller one—doing sober homage to Goering's least-favorite colleague, Foreign Minister von Ribbentrop—being made up of Speer and his wife, Otto Dietrich, Feldmarschall Keitel and Julius Schaub. As Kurt paused on the threshold, momentarily frozen by the sight of the

Reichsmarschall, resplendent in his Lord of the Luftwaffe uniform, he caught Goering's scanning eye and, seconds later, was being ushered to the presence by Peter Waldheim.

"May I present Captain Kurt Armbrecht, Herr Reichsmarschall." A heel click from Waldheim and Kurt was suddenly very much alone, stiffly at attention as the broad and expressive features of the President of the Reichstag, Minister President of Prussia and top-ranking officer of the Reich, took him in. He was aware, as through clouded water, of the smiling faces of the men and women who had broadened their half-circle to make way for the introduction: Martin Bormann, SS Oberfuehrer Rattenhuber, Heinrich and Frau Hoffman, Frau Keitel, Fräulein Eppler and—surprisingly—the blond and pleasant-faced Eva Braun herself. He also had to force himself not to glance at the Junoesque golden-haired woman standing closest to Goering, the former actress Emmy Sonnemann whom he had married in 1935. But now Goering was helping him out.

"I should explain, my dear," he said, turning his great head to her, "that the Captain has been assisting our Fuehrer in a literary capacity. Indeed, I understand his services go somewhat beyond the mere surveillance of the Fuehrer's notoriously erratic spelling."

As he joined nervously in the gust of laughter that greeted Goering's remark, it occurred to Kurt that this kind of irreverent but harmless crack at Hitler's expense was almost a therapeutic necessity, opening for a brief but heady moment a tight safety valve in one's overheated uncritical loyalty to the Fuehrer. Three hours later, he was to find himself almost wishing someone in the company would dare to create a precedent by mildly debunking Hitler to his face.

Everything else about the luncheon party seemed to promise an agreeably informal event. There was no Wehrmacht top brass, excepting Keitel, a dull-witted and fawning acolyte who held no terrors for Kurt. All three young adjutants were present, and the company was an exceptionally mixed one, as to rank

1 0 7

and vocation. They followed Hitler, after he had finished kissing the hands of the seven women guests, into the larchwood-paneled dining room, the Fuehrer escorting Frau Goering, followed by Goering with Frau Ribbentrop on his arm and Bormann squiring Eva Braun. As Hitler, with Austrian ceremony, settled Emmy Goering and his young mistress into their red leather chairs to either side of his own seat in the center of the long table facing the window, the SS orderlies guided the rest of the guests to their places. Kurt was not surprised at Gerda Bormann's absence from the party. Good *Hausfrau* that she was, she would be looking after the huge Bormann brood in their nearby villa. But he was amused to note that Professor Morell had been directed to the smaller table set up for Goering's aide de camp, Colonel Berndt von Brauchswitz, the blond and vivacious Frau Gerda Christian (another of the Fuehrer's secretaries), and a new notetaker for the Bormann Vermerke whom Kurt had not yet met.

There followed perhaps five minutes of general, rather stilted, conversation while the soup was being served, during which Hitler carried on a low-toned dialogue with Frau Goering. But it seemed to Kurt that everyone was marking time, trading platitudes while their eyes and ears stayed alerted for the moment when the Fuehrer would decide to take the stage. They were not kept waiting long. As the orderlies removed the soup plates, Hitler dabbed a napkin to his lips, leaned toward Goering and in a raised voice that instantly silenced the rest of the table, declared his conviction that the Reichsmarschall was putting on weight— "if such a personal remark is permitted." The delighted chuckles released by these words, from a person who had legally taken to himself absolute personal power of life and death over every citizen in Germany, were noticeably louder at Kurt's end of the table than where Ribbentrop held court, a conceited smile barely curling his thin lips.

Patting his belt and smiling broadly back at his host, Goering said, "I plead guilty, my Fuehrer. But, come the hunting season—" He made a pantomime of hollowing his cheeks and retracting his stomach, but the tentative ripple of genteel laughter ended abruptly as Hitler threw up his hands in disgust.

"Hunting! We shall never see eye-to-eye about this. What conceivable pleasure can a bunch of grown-up men find in waging war on a deer with a dozen repeating rifles and an army of beaters? I don't mind admitting—" his twinkling blue eyes made a quick scan of the table—"that in regard to this so-called sport I find myself on the side of the prey. Tell us, Herr Reichsjaegermeister, have you ever found yourself on the receiving end of a stag's antlers?"

"Not yet, my Fuehrer, I'm glad to say. But I make a practice of stalking only the most loyal and best-disciplined of German stags. I find they are marvelous respecters of my person."

All eyes were on Hitler, the guests craning slightly forward to check his reaction. The laughter broke out only as he rolled his eyes ceilingward and snapped, "More fools, they! And with such a gargantuan target!"

It was the high spot, in terms of conviviality, of the luncheon. From there on a creeping tedium set in as Hitler, with a curious insensitiveness to the strained and silent intentness of his audience, launched into a monologue that started with a childhood encounter with a stoat-slaughtered rabbit, went on to a prolonged and superficial examination of Darwin's theory of natural selection and progressed to a routine discourse on his own racial *Weltanschauung,* winding up as he rose two hours later to lead his strenuously smiling guests out of the dining room with a promise to regale them, as soon as they were all reassembled, with an account of how Julius Streicher had once been tricked into believing that Alfred Rosenberg was a Jew.

The Fuehrer's temporary disappearance upstairs to his private quarters was the signal for a spirited outbreak of bonhomie as one group of guests made for the toilets off the small hallway and the rest drifted into the salon, where the orderlies were already setting up to serve tea and coffee. Kurt, who had held back at the threshold of the huge room to allow the others to pass on through, found Peter Waldheim waiting for him just inside. The young adjutant drew him toward the great fireplace, faced with green faïence, and the two of them talked quietly together while the others milled about at the far end of the room sixty feet away, before the most enormous picture window Kurt had ever seen, uttering little cries of delight at the broad panorama that took in the Berchtesgaden valley, and beyond it the Untersberg and Salzberg.

"Listen to them, Kurt. The same squeals of ecstasy, the same banal comments, every time they come here. Makes one feel like heaving that bust of Wagner right through the window!"

"What's the drill from here on, Peter?" It was the first time either of them had used the other's Christian name, as if the ordeal of lunch had drawn them closer together.

"You can see the way this crazy room's arranged, with this part up here and the sunken part down there. The Chief will probably park himself here by the fireplace, with most of the ladies lined up on that sofa—plus Bormann and Keitel, of course, and either our foxy Foreign Minister or the Reichsmarschall, depending on who gets in first. I would advise you, unless you're panting for more of the Chief's reminiscences, to start studying that Gobelin tapestry over there in a few minutes' time. That way, you can move in on the second team, who'll be taking their coffee down there on the lower level. The conversation won't be brilliant, but at least you'll be able to get a comment in, if you wish."

"How about Fräulein Braun?" Kurt chose his words carefully. "I thought Geissler said she was kept out of sight when the top people's wives were around."

Waldheim shrugged. "It's about time the Chief gave her a break. The wives have all known about her for years. Anyway, it doesn't really matter what the bourgeoisie think about it. A military genius can get away with murder." There was a second or two as the two men exchanged glances, followed by an explosive guffaw, quickly damped as heads turned toward them from the far end of the room. "I claim copyright to that one," Waldheim muttered, battling to keep a straight face.

"Too bad. It would make a great subtitle for the Chief's book."

Ribbentrop and his wife were already installed by the fireplace when the Fuehrer rejoined the party, smiling and kneading his fingers as he crossed the room—the eager *raconteur,* all too conscious of his duty to keep the audience entertained. After lingering before the big Gobelin tapestry for a decent interval, Kurt found a seat on the perimeter of the group gathered about Goering, who had installed himself at the circular table near the window and was holding forth—but keeping his voice down—on his favorite subject.

"My art dealer in Holland has just come across another Rembrandt self-portrait, property of a Jew diamond merchant who 'made a gift of it,' if you please, to his non-Yid stockbroker just before he was given a free train ride by the Gestapo to Auschwitz. The stockbroker, for reasons that baffle me, considers this masterpiece to be better housed under a pile of sacks in his attic than in my art galleries at Karinhall. If that isn't Philistinism, I'd like to know what is!"

When Rattenhuber intervened to ask, straight-faced, if the Reichsmarschall could think of no way to persuade the stockbroker to adopt a less antisocial attitude, Goering's shoulders began to shake with controlled merriment. "Naturally, one is under an obligation to make such people see the light," he chortled. "I've instructed someone from the Rosenberg Organization to invite the Dutch stockbroker to make a trip to Auschwitz himself, to discuss the finer points of the situation with his Jewish benefactor. I expect to find the Rembrandt waiting for me at Karinhall, on my return."

For what seemed another eternity to Kurt, but was in fact a little short of an hour, the Reichsmarschall's group competed among themselves, under Goering's smug encouragement and patronage, in describing the various art treasures that had come their way over the past year or two, for all the world like a group of newly rich Texas oilmen, gloating in the smoking room of a transatlantic liner. Not once did the conversation rise above the

111

theme of material gain and commercial values, not even when Goering maneuvered it around to the subject of his van Gogh self-portrait.

"I've insured it, on the advice of my French dealer, for half a million marks, though of course no amount of money would compensate me for its loss. However, as I told Emmy at the time, 'If we have to cry, let it be into only the finest of lawn handkerchiefs.' He was grinning around at his circle, but their attention had been diverted. An SS officer had let himself quietly into the room and caught the eye of Waldheim, and the two men were now in close conversation by the door. In his turn, Waldheim, noticeably agitated, turned to catch the ever-watchful eye of Martin Bormann, who hurried across to join the two officers. As Waldheim spoke to him, his thick back stiffened and he glanced quickly around toward the fireplace. Whatever Bormann's intentions, the initiative was now taken by Hitler, who, aware of a distraction, glanced irritably over his shoulder, took in the situation, and pushed himself out of the armchair. Bormann met him halfway toward the door, and their heads came together. Seconds later, the Fuehrer's voice, harsh and strident with anger, froze everyone in the room.

"Herr Reichsmarschall! If you can manage to get off that fat behind, *I'll see you outside!*"

The SS officer and Waldheim had to leap aside to avoid being sent spinning by Hitler as he flung himself through the doorway. Bormann seemed uncertain whether to follow suit or rejoin the company by the fireside, but as Goering came clumping toward him, with extraordinary alacrity considering his bulk, the Fuehrer's secretary turned back into the room, chewing hard on his lip.

Kurt had sprung to his feet with the rest of the group, who now remained stock still, in petrified silence, as the Fuehrer's voice came at them in an uneven torrent of guttural bellows from the other side of the now-closed door. He was able to catch only a phrase here and there as the tirade raged on.

"... *Unforgivable slackness ... reduced to a farce ...*

112

*laughingstock of my enemies . . . disastrous . . . heads will
roll . . . utterly intolerable! . . ."*

Waldheim seemed at first reluctant to join either group, but
as the guests at the fireside closed in on Bormann, obviously
being given the news, the young Luftwaffe adjutant walked
down the steps into the sunken area, shaking his head as Kurt
and the others moved to meet him.

"Appalling! Quite appalling!"

"Well, for God's sake, man, what's happening?"

"Twenty-seven of our V-1 launching sites on the Channel—
all of them heavily camouflaged and supposedly protected by
Luftwaffe fighters—bombed and destroyed in daylight by the
R.A.F."

CHAPTER SIX

I

GOERING DID not show his face again at the Berghof that Christmas and was reported to be sulking in his country mansion of Karinhall, having sacked and disgraced three Luftwaffe generals along with their entire headquarters staffs. And within a few days Adolf Hitler, reassured by Bormann that the V-1 program was not in serious jeopardy, had recovered his good humor sufficiently to make a seasonal gesture to the junior members of his entourage. He spoke of it to Kurt at the end of their second private session in the Fuehrer's study.

"It is my intention, Armbrecht, to give a reception here at the Berghof for some of the younger people on my staff, the evening of December the twenty-third. It will extend to certain adjutants, the girls of the secretariat, some of the younger officers of the Leibstandarte and so on. Quite informal. And those with wives or girl friends not on the mountain will be permitted to invite them, subject to security clearance, of course." He turned from the window to smile slyly across at Kurt. "There will be special transport provided for any young ladies flying in from Berlin."

Kurt felt himself blushing at this first hint from the Fuehrer that he knew about himself and Helga Gruyten. He started to say, "A very great honor for us all, my Fuehrer, but there is no one in particular I myself—"

"Nonsense!" Hitler cut in. "A good-looking young fellow like you! Why, at your age . . ." He broke off, frowning slightly, to snatch up a sheet of paper from his desk with a list of names scrawled on it in his own spiky handwriting. "There's a shortage of suitable young girls in my headquarters here. I don't want to see groups of men standing around that evening, twiddling their thumbs."

"If the Fuehrer will permit me—"

"That's better! Have a word with Rattenhuber, straightaway."

"I was thinking of my young sister, who lives in Munich, my Fuehrer. She's twenty-five, and remarkably pretty."

"So? And what does this pretty young sister of yours do for the war effort?"

"She teaches Spanish, my Fuehrer—to overseers of the Todt Organization, among others."

"You may invite her on my behalf. Make arrangements through Rattenhuber's office."

When Kurt telephoned Sophie next day with the news, she thought he was joking. "But of course I accept, dear brother of mine. Shall I wear my diamond tiara, or would the emerald necklace that matches my eyes be more in keeping?"

"I'm not joking, idiot. You're to go to the *Fuehrerhaus* tomorrow morning with your identity documents and two extra photographs. Ask for Sturmbannfuehrer Schneider."

There was a brief silence at the other end of the line. Then: "Kurt, you really do mean it! *Caramba!* Will the Fuehrer be there?"

"I just told you! He's giving the party. And there's a room booked for you in the Grand Hotel at Berchtesgaden. Leave your tiara in the safe and go out and buy yourself a new evening gown—on me. Nothing too daring, you understand?"

"Fantastic! Wait till Mother and Father come back from Mass! Is it all right to tell them?"

"Of course it is. And give them my love. Tell them I'll probably be getting some leave in the New Year."

During the next five days, while the main parking lot of the Berghof hummed with the arrival and departure of *Gauleiter,* Government ministers, Party Chiefs and ambassadors bringing their greetings and presents to the German Fuehrer, Kurt spent most of the time in the reference library of the secretariat, making copious notes from the files and memoranda put at his disposal by Martin Bormann. Hitler had informed him at their last session that the religious problem in the Greater Reich would be settled "one way or the other" by the end of 1944, and it might well be that *Mein Sieg* should actually start with a chapter devoted to a review of the role played by the Christian church in German society from the immediately pre-Bismarckian era up to the revision of the present concordat with Rome, which would certainly take place in the coming year. Accordingly, the existing plan of the book should be restructured by Kurt and a new arrangement of chapters submitted for the Fuehrer's consideration early in the New Year. In the meantime, it was gratifying to learn that the priests and pastors had offered no protest, either individually or through their hierarchies, to the *Diktat* concerning Reichsleiter Bormann's Christmas prayer.

On the morning of the twenty-second, as Kurt was preparing to leave for the secretariat, an SS man brought him a message politely requesting his presence "for a few minutes" in the office of Obersturmbannfuehrer Werner Voegler, over in the administration building of the Leibstandarte Adolf Hitler.

Kurt was correct in assuming it had to do with his sister's visit to the Berghof, for there on the officer's desk, as he rose to greet Kurt with "the German salute," was a photograph of Sophie, neatly pasted to one of a small batch of identical-sized pale-green filing cards spread out on the blotter. The austerely furnished office had the mandatory framed photograph of the Fuehrer on one wall and, on another, a picture of Reichsfuehrer SS Heinrich Himmler, exactly equal in size. The second portrait bore Himmler's signature under what appeared to be a lengthy handwritten inscription.

This was Kurt's first meeting with Voegler, though he had noticed the tall, barrel-chested officer a couple of times since his arrival on the mountain—once overseeing a physical-fitness display by near-naked SS troops on the parade ground behind the main barracks, and again when he had presented himself at Oberfuehrer Rattenhuber's office, in this same building, for clearance of Sophie's invitation. Like most of the Leibstandarte officers now on duty at the Berghof, Voegler had seen action with the Waffen SS on both western and eastern fronts, as the campaign ribbons over his breast pocket testified, and moreover had been decorated with the Iron Cross, both classes. But, like all of the staff officers liable to come into direct contact with the Fuehrer, he was now wearing the distinctive black-and-silver uniform of Hitler's praetorian guard rather than the gray-green field service tunic and breeches still used by the steel-helmeted SS officers and men guarding the Obersalzberg mountainside. Kurt would have placed Voegler's age in the early thirties; with his close-cropped flaxen hair and lean, unlined face, it would be difficult to be more precise. A prominent vein snaked under the tight skin of his left brow, his jug ears stood out, and the large sharp nose was slightly askew as from bone damage. His small mouth, an almost fleshless slit, was unlocking itself now in an awkward attempt at a smile as Kurt settled into the chair facing the desk.

"A pleasure to meet you at last, Armbrecht. My old comrade Sturmbannfuehrer Kremer spoke very well of you when I last met him in Berlin." The voice was high-pitched and nasal, with a north-German—but not Berliner—accent.

Kurt said, "I'm indebted to the *Sturmbannfuehrer*. He has been very kind to me."

"Good! Now, about this reception tomorrow evening—Alas, the Fuehrer has excluded everyone above the rank of *Sturmbannfuehrer*—or *Major,* as you Wehrmacht chaps have it—so there goes a rare chance for poor fellows like myself to enjoy the company of such attractive young ladies as—" he picked up the filing card bearing Sophie's picture—"your sister, if you will permit me the comment?"

Kurt had started to say, "I'm sorry about that, Herr Obersturmbannfuehrer, but I suppose the Fuehrer—" when Voegler cut him short with a raised hand and a brittle little chuckle.

117

"A good SS man never admits defeat, Armbrecht. I have put myself in charge of the detachment from Oberfuehrer Ratten-huber's staff that is to greet the young ladies at the Grand Hotel and escort them to the Berghof. And knowing how nervous they'll be, I'm inviting them to take a glass of champagne in my mess before they meet the Fuehrer. Naturally, I should like your approval, as well as your own presence as my guest."

"It's a most thoughtful gesture, Herr Obersturmbannfuehrer. I'd be delighted."

"Excellent!" Voegler pushed his chair back and sprang to his feet. "Shall we say seven-thirty tomorrow evening, then, in the officers' mess?"

The Fuehrer hadn't touched any of the delicacies spread out on the big circular table in the salon, but he had taken a sip of champagne before thrusting the glass back at his SS orderly, Bussman. This in itself was noteworthy for one who never drank anything stronger than Faschinger water and camomile tea; and whether it was the sip of wine or the nearness of so many ador-ing young females, a slight flush had appeared on his normally pallid cheeks and a festive sparkle lit up the ever-restless pale-blue eyes.

He had entered the salon, accompanied by his blond, fresh-faced mistress, Eva Braun, about a quarter of an hour after the guests were assembled, and he had stood for a moment inside the threshold, smiling and bowing to the vigorously hand-clapping company. Then, as the champagne corks began to pop and the SS men in their white monkey jackets started on their rounds, Hitler made his slow tour of the room, kissing the hands of secretaries and young wives, greeting the men with his damp firm handclasp, reserving his pleasantries and quips for the fa-miliars among his staff, bending his ear attentively as his chief of protocol, Dr. Meissner, presented each new face—here the fiancée of one of his staff, there the wife of *Leibstandarte Hauptsturmfuehrer*. By the time he reached Kurt and his sister, awaiting their turn by the flower-decked grand piano, Sophie's evening bag had almost fallen twice from her trembling hands.

"Oh my God, Kurt, he's coming this way!"

"Calm yourself, Maedel. He's not going to eat you!" And, catching Peter Waldheim's rolling eyes, Kurt just had time to straighten his face after grimacing fiercely back at his friend. The young adjutant, with his expression, had spoken for every unattached male in the room: Sophie Armbrecht was in fact easily the most delectable of the Fuehrer's female guests that night, with her red hair done up in a dense bouquet of loose curls and her wide eyes sparkling—it had seemed to Kurt earlier, as they embraced in the officers' mess—like emeralds in the reflected light from her new green evening gown.

Hitler had spotted them and was leading Eva Braun in their direction. "My dear Armbrecht! And this is the beautiful sister you've told me so much about! You were not exaggerating." As he bent over Sophie's upraised hand, Kurt caught a quick glimpse of her face, frozen in an expression of fearful excitement. Then Hitler was introducing them to Eva Braun, first Kurt ("I believe you have already met Fräulein Braun") then Sophie, whose first name he remembered and uttered without hesitation.

". . . and the clever Fräulein Armbrecht," he added teasingly, "teaches Spanish to my Todt overseers, so let's not have any more of this nonsense about beauty and brains never going together!"

The petite, round-faced young woman by his side flushed slightly as she let go of Sophie's hand. "There will always be exceptions, my Fuehrer," she pouted. And, in a pathetic little bid to change the subject, "Your dress is lovely, Fräulein Armbrecht. You must tell me later where you shop."

To escape the drift of ear-flapping guests in Hitler's wake, as he moved on, Kurt led his sister up the steps to the higher level and signaled to the nearest SS orderly. Sophie drained her glass in a few deep, unladylike drafts and leaned heavily against her brother. She was still trembling.

"Ouff! I swear I actually felt his mustache on my hand! But

it's strange, I thought he'd be taller—about your height in fact!"

"You can credit Heinie Hoffman with that." Waldheim was at Kurt's elbow, effectively blocking a hovering SS *Obersturmfuehrer*. "He's a wizard that chap, with his low angles." He was holding his hand out for Sophie's empty glass, but she shook her head, laughing. As she turned to put the glass on the sideboard behind her, her attention was caught by a large framed canvas on the wall. It was a portrait, almost full-length, of a fair-haired and lustrous-eyed girl of perhaps twenty. A china bowl heaped with flower petals stood on the sideboard, immediately below the portrait. Sophie looked inquiringly over her shoulder at the two men.

"Geli Raubal," Waldheim supplied, keeping his voice down, "the Fuehrer's niece. The painting was done by Adolf Ziegler from a photograph, after her death in 1931. And there's also quite a good bust of her by Josef Thorak, in the Berlin Chancellery."

"It's a lovely face," Sophie murmured. "Do you think it's true she was the only real love in the F——" Stopped short by Kurt's grimace, she added, in a quick whisper, *"Well is it?"*

Waldheim had turned away from the wall to bring the nearby guests into view. He said, softly, "It's my own theory that it was the manner of her death, more than anything she meant to the Chief while she was alive, that has put her up on that pedestal. He used her as a kind of emotional safety valve, fawning over her one day, thrashing her the next with the rawhide whip he carried around at that time. But by blowing her silly brains out, after that last row with him, she achieved immortality. The Chief has enormous respect for suicides."

"Ugh!" Sophie shivered, closing her eyes. Then with a rueful smile for Waldheim: "I think I'll have that drink, after all."

As the adjutant moved away, Sophie's hand tightened around Kurt's right arm. "I have to talk to you about Voegler before the party breaks up, if we can find a quiet corner."

"Why, what's the trouble?"

"Not now. That nice captain will be back in a minute."

The opportunity arrived half an hour later, when the Fuehrer took leave of his guests to return to his upstairs rooms and the hungry young people began to crowd around the buffet table, laughing and jostling in a spontaneous release of tension. Kurt led Sophie toward the now-isolated fireside area.

"Now tell me, what's the problem?"

"Voegler wants to get me into bed, that's the problem."

"Are you serious? Christ, he's only just met you!"

"Lust at first sight, dear brother. You must have heard of it."

Grimly, he said, "Sophie, dearest, tell me all."

"Well, I could see what he wanted from practically the moment he introduced himself, down at the Grand Hotel. He drove me up here in his own car, just the two of us, and kept going on about what a smashing figure I had and how tough it was on the SS officers up here, starved of the feminine delights."

"That's a joke. They've even got their own private brothel."

"Charming! Anyway, you saw the way he cornered me over at the mess. We weren't talking politics. He wants to drive me back to the hotel later and spend the night up in my room. He said it as if he was presenting me with some kind of award!"

"What did you say?"

"The usual routine. I didn't think it would be tactful to tell him to get lost—as I wanted to—so I gave him that coy line about having to know a man better before I slept with him. And, of course, I got the routine reply to that—'So let's start to get to know each other better, tonight.'"

"And how was it left?"

"It was about then you got my distress signals and came over. I don't think I'm off the hook. He'll be waiting for me, either here or down in Berchtesgaden." She shuddered for the second time that evening. "He gives me the creeps, that one! What can we do about it?"

"I could ask for a pass," Kurt frowned, "and go down with you. Trouble is, I'd have to go to Voegler himself for it at this time of night, and he'd probably fend me off with some kind of excuse."

"I don't want you to do anything that will make life difficult for you here. Maybe I should—" She was peering over his shoulder, into the throng around the buffet.

"What are you thinking, Sophie?"

"There's that very sweet stenographer from the Fuehrer's Chancellery in Berlin. We were having a nice little girl-to-girl chat at the hotel, before the SS arrived . . . That's it!" She gave her brother a quick tight hug. "I'll tell her my problem and we'll work out an act together. Sick stenographer, solicitous girl friend. Pretty corny, but it's worked in the past." She was grinning at him for approval, and he gave it to her, nodding his head slowly.

"Now, how about being an officer and a gentleman and getting me some food?"

"Someone's got in ahead of me. Here comes good old Peter, bearing gifts."

The next evening, when he telephoned home to wish his parents and Sophie a happy Christmas, his sister let him know—in carefully guarded language—that the stratagem had worked, "quite satisfactorily."

"No bad scene, then?"

"Well, let's say he took it as I expected."

The same might have been said—though in terms of a much more massive frustration—of Adolf Hitler, when he heard how the two great Churches of Germany had presented the Bormann prayer to their congregations. Most of the Protestant pastors had offered the prayer without comment. Here and there, individual Catholic priests had done likewise. But the overwhelming majority of Catholic priests had followed the formula used by Clemens, Count von Galen, the Bishop of Muenster, who introduced the prayer with the words: "I shall now recite a form of prayer which has been distributed by our Government to the churches of all denominations throughout the Reich. I might add that there is nothing in this directive that obliges any of the faithful to utter the word 'Amen!' " In his own Church, on Christmas morning, Bishop Galen's congregation greeted the end of the prayer with complete silence. In other Catholic churches, the *amens* were as sparse—in Bormann's savage words —"as Jews in Berchtesgaden."

The story circulating around the Berghof was that, instead of flying into one of his uncontrolled rages, the Fuehrer had received the report with "a terrible icy calm." One version had it that he even smiled, muttering something to the effect that there would be more than one way to teach the Catholics to pray.

II

WERNER VOEGLER slept badly, the night of Hitler's party for the young people. At one point, tormented by images of the prize that had escaped him that evening, he switched on the light and prowled about the room, trying to summon up, if not the enthusiasm, then at least enough misogynist rancor to fuel a rampage through the SS bordello up in the pinewoods.

It was no good. He wanted Sophie Armbrecht, with an intensity no dumb and compliant whores could assuage. Her identification card, which should by now have been back in Rattenhuber's files, was lying on the bedside table, and he snatched it up again, for the umpteenth time that night, and sat staring at the piquantly smiling face, working his thin lips between his teeth. He would get this girl, sooner or later. Dedication was all —that same single-minded thrust that had propelled him in thirteen glorious years from the lowest brown-shirted ranks of the Hamburg SA to *Obersturmbannfuehrer* in the most prestigious regiment of the elite of elites, the SS Leibstandarte Adolf Hitler Brigade.

In September 1930 he had just turned twenty and had achieved *nothing* except the capacity to hate. Negative and sterile. A couple of tin-pot athletic awards. And one precious private endowment: the memory, cherished over the years, of his father.

When Werner Voegler was born, in a middle-class suburb of

Hamburg, his father, Hans, at twenty-four, was already a lieutenant in the Imperial Naval Reserve and the owner of a small but profitable coffee-importing business in the heart of the city. Voegler remembered him not as the handsome smiling image framed on his mother's mantelpiece, but as a towering tobacco-scented presence, at once warming and highlighting his childhood memories up to 1918—memories mostly to do with greeting and waving farewell to his uniformed father at the gates to the naval dockyards. He had total recall of the day they came with the telegram confirming his father's death in action commanding his U-boat on its first and last mission into the North Sea. He remembered, as if it were yesterday, all the terror of being held with his older sister against the heaving, weeping bulk of his mother, of screaming, over and over again, "What's the matter, Mother? What's the matter?" And he could still evoke, through a somewhat cloudier prism, the bitter-sweet reflected glory of remaining seated in his classroom, four days later, while the rest of the boys, in response to a patriotic speech from the headmaster of his school, stood to honor his hero-father.

The years that followed—up until 1930 anyway—were years the locusts had eaten. There was the locust of postwar German bankruptcy, with his mother struggling to save their smitten business from ruin and Voegler and his sister obliged to leave their fashionable private school for a state school. There was the locust of his mother's second marriage in 1920, to a Hamburg policeman whose feet stank abominably, who had dodged wartime service and who, in a drunken rage one day had destroyed the gilt-framed photograph of Hans Voegler. And there was the locust of those tedious wasted years locked up in a classroom with snotty-nosed working-class kids, half of whom were too hungry, most of the time, to concentrate on their lessons. This was not Voegler's excuse for being temperamentally ineducable. It was more a case of his having decided that he was cut out to be a man of action like his father. The proof of this was already becoming self-evident. At the age of twelve his prowess on the sports field was in strictly inverse ratio to his progress in the classroom. At fisticuffs and wrestling he could easily lick boys a year older than himself, and in the Protestant Youth Club, which he joined the following year, he was almost immediately marked out for special coaching by a boxing instructor, who recognized promising material for the annual interclub championships.

Until September 1930, Voegler knew little of politics and cared even less. He was thirteen in April 1924, when the Munich agitator Adolf Hitler was sentenced to five years' imprisonment for his part in the *Feldherrnhalle Putsch*. But, outside Bavaria, the Nazi Party meant little, and neither Hitler's incarceration in Landsberg Prison nor his release eight months later made any impact on Voegler or his friends. Nor would the publication of *Mein Kampf*, in July 1925, have interested the book-shy teen-ager. At fifteen, Voegler was still bent on a naval career. Alas, there was hardly a German navy to talk about. As a result of the infamous Treaty of Versailles, Germany had been left *"heerlos, wahrlos, ehrlos."* The country had also been left in penury, although that state of affairs was now beginning to right itself, through the wizardry of Dr. Hjalmar Schacht, and for the first time in years the family coffee business was actually beginning to show a small profit.

Voegler left school at fifteen and for the next three years worked in the family business, delivering the weekly orders of coffee to hotels and restaurants throughout the city. Being ingratiating to restaurant managers and kitchen staff was an inglorious way to earn his pocket money, but at least it was an open-air job, and his leg muscles throve from the hours of pedaling the heavy box tricycle from one end of Hamburg to the other. Four years later, when the worldwide depression of 1929 hit Germany with all the force of an economic avalanche, his mother's coffee-importing business was one of the first to go under, and Voegler was lucky to be taken on—again through his stepfather's connections—as casual labor in the dockyards. It was here that he was exposed for the first time to the violence and bitterness of the power struggle going on beneath the surface of the democratic Weimar Republic.

His first physical involvement in the war for Germany's soul came toward the end of August 1930, when a large group of dockers tried to break up an outdoor Nazi Party meeting at one of the main gateways to the dockyards. Voegler floored a burly docker who described the Nazi speaker's Iron Cross as "Kaiser-vomit" and, in the melee that followed, gave such a good account of himself, fighting shoulder to shoulder with the Brown Shirts, that he was whisked away to safety, together with the speaker and *scharfuehrer,* as soon as the police reinforcements arrived. He did not go back to work at the docks. He accepted membership in the SA, volunteered his services as steward at the campaign meetings for the September Reichstag elections, and celebrated with his new comrades the exciting results: 6,409,600 votes for the Party; the Nazis now were second-strongest party in the German Reichstag.

Over the next year, unemployment in Germany mounted to five and a half million, while membership of the Nazi Party more than doubled itself, reaching over 800,000 by the end of 1931. Voegler stayed with the SA, giving his full-time services and paying his way in the beer cellars with money scrounged from his mother's dwindling savings. His stepfather, an apolitical policeman fed up to the teeth with the street brawling between the Nazis and the Left, delivered his ultimatum the week after Voegler was promoted to *Unterscharfuehrer,* at the age of twenty-one.

"Get that bloody uniform off your back and find a job, or clear out of the house. You're not sponging off your mother any longer."

It was all Voegler needed. Disgusted with having to wheedle for every mark he needed, he had already set his sights on Munich, where an elite corps of bodyguards, the *Schutzstaffel,* was being built up by Heinrich Himmler into a powerful national organization, with the funds, moreover, to pay wages for full-time service. His release from the Brown Shirts was aided by his former boxing coach—now a *Sturmbannfuehrer* in the local SA —and, armed with a letter of recommendation from the Hamburg Party headquarters, Voegler took the train to Munich. He also went armed with something else, without which he would never have made first base with the SS. From the data provided by his mother, plus a painstaking search through the local parish registers and the Town Hall archives, he had documents attesting to two full centuries of Aryan stock, unsullied by Jewish blood.

When Hitler came to power in January 1933, Voegler was an SS *Untersturmfuehrer* and the holder of an SS Silver Medal for boxing. And in March of that year, when the Nazis won 43.9 percent of the votes in the Reichstag elections, he was transferred to the Berlin Chancellery as an officer of the *Stabwache* under the command of Sepp Dietrich. The errand boy of Hamburg was coming along fast. At the Nuremberg rally of September 1933 the Fuehrer renamed the *Stabwache* the Leibstandarte Adolf Hitler, constituting a regiment of three battalions. And when Voegler, eight months later, was promoted to *Obersturmfuehrer,* he knew he had at last *arrived.* But his moment of greatest personal glory was now only one month away.

On June 29, 1934, a detachment of one hundred picked men of the Leibstandarte, including Voegler, were flown to Augsburg and thence transported by trucks during the night to the outskirts of the small town of Wiessee, where they immediately took cover in some woods. All the men had been briefed before leaving Augsburg. The SA, under their commander Ernst Roehm, were planning to oust Adolf Hitler from power. The Fuehrer was going to strike first by arresting Roehm and a bunch of high-ranking SA officers in their conspiratorial headquarters, the lakeside Hanslbauer Hotel at Wiessee. The task of the SS was to surprise Roehm's guards and overcome any resistance before the Fuehrer made his avenging entrance.

Shortly after dawn a convoy of several cars and army trucks, coming from Munich, stopped by the woods and a rapid discussion took place between Dietrich and Hitler. Orders were quietly given, and an army truck pulled out and took its place at the head of the convoy, where the soldiers climbed out to make way for a platoon of armed SS under Voegler's command. Sepp Dietrich sat up front with the driver. The truck stopped a hundred yards from the hotel and, with Dietrich silently directing the operation, Voegler and his men entered the hotel and swiftly disarmed the three sleepy SA guards slumped in a room off the foyer. By the time Hitler, pale and trembling with inner fury, strode into the foyer, one of the SA officers, Julius Uhl, had appeared on the staircase, revolver in hand. At Hitler's cry, "Where's that swine, Roehm?" Uhl raised his revolver, pointing it at Hitler. A second later, as Voegler stepped squarely in front of his Fuehrer, Uhl lowered the weapon and was seized and propelled down the steep steps to the hotel cellar. Voegler was promoted by Hitler on the spot to *Hauptsturmfuehrer*.

Throughout the whole of that summer day—so inaptly named the Night of the Long Knives—Voegler and his men drove tirelessly from place to place in the Munich area carrying out the executions of SA leaders and other "enemies of the state" in accordance with orders that streamed from Hitler's offices at the Brown House. He had never killed before, and this was his baptism of blood. When the butchery was over, Werner Voegler knew himself, and his SS troops, to be apart from other men.

Two years later, his regiment was given the honor to be the first unit to enter the demilitarized zone of the Rhineland. He was cheated of front-line action during the conquest of Poland through the sheer speed with which the Wehrmacht overran that country, but on the first day of the invasion of the Low Countries, Voegler's company was in the spearhead of a Leibstandarte advance of 135 miles into Holland. He was recommended for promotion, and after the British evacuation of Dunkirk, when his battalion drove farther south in pursuit of the French Army than any other unit of the Wehrmacht, he got his promotion to *Sturmbannfuehrer,* together with the Iron Cross, First Class.

By the spring of 1941, the Leibstandarte Adolf Hitler was a

full brigade attached to Army Group A for the drive through the Ukraine toward Kiev and Rostov. It was Voegler's regiment of the Waffen SS that bore the first brunt of the surprise Red Army counterattack on Rostov and, by holding its position to the north of the city, gave Rundstedt the precious hours he needed to assess the enemy's tactics and take the necessary countermeasures. Voegler's own regiment was decimated to a little over company strength, but he himself came through with minor flesh wounds and was posted back to Germany, to the headquarters staff of the Leibstandarte.

With the fall of Moscow and Leningrad, Hitler closed down his field headquarters on the eastern front and spent the rest of the winter and the spring of 1942 at the Berghof, directing the campaign in the Caucasus and blueprinting the Eastern Wall defense system running from Archangel to the Caspian Sea. Meanwhile, Voegler received his promotion to *Obersturmbannfuehrer* and became chief adjutant to SS Oberfuehrer Rattenhuber, with special responsibility for the security of the Berghof and an area of two hundred square miles around it.

He never set foot in Hamburg again and he never answered any of the letters from his mother and sister congratulating him on the successive promotions and decorations announced in the party press. In 1936, when Heinrich Himmler took over the whole of the German police apparatus, Voegler seriously entertained the thought of settling accounts with his stepfather by denouncing him, but finally dismissed it, reflecting that if it hadn't been for his stepfather he might never have taken the train to Munich. He had also toyed with the idea, at one stage, of sending for the only one of his girl friends in Hamburg with whom he had kept a fairly regular correspondence—Margit, the full-breasted daughter of a tavern keeper. She had been an excellent cook, marvelous in bed, and would have passed the stringent racial Marriage Code for SS men. But she could never have kept up with him socially in his rapid promotion, and he was glad now that he had ended the correspondence, brusquely, a week after Hitler had made him a *Hauptsturmfuehrer*.

Now, Sophie Armbrecht—she was something else. Not for marriage, since Voegler was firmly determined to enjoy his privileged bachelorhood for several years to come, but as a nubile bourgeois girl friend he could flaunt before his men and fellow officers and a superb amenity for the small apartment in Munich where he spent most of his leave days. Fräulein Armbrecht hadn't risen as eagerly as she should have to his suggestion. Her SD dossier made no mention of emotional or sexual involvement with any male. The key that would unlock those shapely legs was right here on the mountain—the good will of her brother, Kurt.

He would have to go to work on it.

III

THERE WAS no leave for Voegler or for any of the Fuehrer's immediate entourage over the next eighty days, Hitler having decided to maintain his headquarters at the Berghof while certain structural alterations were being made to the main reception salons of the Berlin Chancellery by Albert Speer. And on the few occasions during this time that Voegler found himself in Munich on official business, Sophie Armbrecht was either genuinely or conveniently "caught up with lessons" at the language institute or able to plead from her home an "urgent job of translation that's going to keep me up most of the night." Far from discouraging Voegler, these evasive tactics by the young Fräulein Armbrecht only fanned the hot core of his lust for her.

In the meantime, he proceeded to cultivate Kurt's good will by inviting him to an occasional dinner in the SS officers' mess, to film screenings and—an especially appreciated favor—by pulling strings that gave Kurt a private sitting room, next to his bedroom in the staff quarters. It was over a drink in this same room that Kurt unwittingly provided the opening Voegler had been waiting for so patiently. He had just been telling the SS officer that he had finished restructuring *Mein Sieg* along the lines proposed by the Fuehrer and that Hitler had brought up the idea, at their last session, that Kurt should now go out and see for himself how the New Order was evolving in the conquered territories of the Greater Reich.

"Frankly," Kurt added, smiling, "I think the Chief just wants me out of the way for a few weeks while he and Reichsleiter Bormann concentrate on their war with the Vatican. I know Mussolini and Ciano are expected next week."

Voegler swirled the good French cognac around his glass. "Excellent idea, Armbrecht—provided you've got the stomach for it."

"It'll be all right. I know it's pretty rough out there, but don't forget it wasn't always a picnic for us poor gunners on the western front."

Voegler slowed the circular motion of his right hand. He said, after a long silence, "Have you the faintest idea of the superhuman tasks we are coping with in the General Government of Poland, in White Russia and the Ukraine, all the way up to the eastern front?"

"That's the whole idea of the trip," Kurt said. "Obviously I can't write about it till I get out there into the field."

"Has anyone briefed you, yet, about places like Auschwitz-Birkenau, Treblinka, Sobibor? Have you been told about our farming techniques in the Ukraine?"

"Naturally, I'll be interested in the farming techniques. The other places you mention—concentration camps? I can't imagine they'll come into the tour."

"Just as I thought," Voegler nodded slowly. "You wouldn't have the stomach for it."

"Oh, come now, it's not a question of that! Look, I'll have about four weeks and a helluva tight schedule."

"Which one *have* you seen?" Voegler asked quietly.

"None, in point of fact." Kurt tried to cover his discomfiture by emptying his glass and getting up to replenish it. "I'll take a look around one of them, of course. It's not a prospect that particularly appeals to me, to tell the truth."

Voegler said, "You'd better go with someone who knows his way around. Also, someone with rank."

"You think so? I shall have my *laissez-passer* from the Fuehrer's office."

"That's not enough. There are colonists and camp guards out there who can't bloody-well read! They pretty quickly recognize a Leibstandarte *Obersturmbannfuehrer,* however."

"You mean . . ." Kurt put the bottle down and turned to Voegler, his eyebrows up.

Voegler smiled. "Can't promise anything. But I'll have a word with Rattenhuber in the morning. Time I had a change of scenery, myself."

IV

THE FIRST-CLASS SS coach was uncoupled from the Berchtesgaden train at Munich and coupled onto the Berlin express; and there on the station platform, as planned, were Kurt's mother and sister squinting their eyes against the blustering rain as they strained for a sight of him, then scampering under their shared umbrella to greet him at the door of the coach.

"Come on up! We're not pulling out for about quarter of an hour!"

There weren't many others from the Berghof in the well-appointed sleeping-cum-restaurant-car: Werner Voegler, of course, and his SS orderly, chatting in the rear of the car with a Wehrmacht courier; an official from Reichsmarschall Goering's Economic Staff, East; a Waffen-SS *Gruppenfuehrer* and his wife, returning to Berlin from a weekend as Bormann's guests on the mountain. Kurt settled his mother and sister at a table just inside the door, meticulously avoiding Voegler's eye. He had already warned Sophie by letter that the SS officer would be traveling with him and had suggested that if they met at the station she should try to be polite to him, for the sake of harmony on the trip. He saw Sophie looking past him now, with a bright strained smile, as Voegler sauntered toward them.

"Now, why haven't I got a beautiful sister to see me off? And this, I take it, is Frau Armbrecht." He moved in, making a gesture of kissing Margit's hand. "I can see now where your daughter got her good looks."

Kurt's mother was enchanted. Sophie said, "I hope you'll look after my brother, Herr Obersturmbannfuehrer. He's the only one I have."

"I take that as a sacred order." Voegler clicked the heels of his shining jackboots. "But I'm going to start by looking after his charming mother and sister." He snapped his finger and the batman came running. "Fill two coffee cups from your vacuum-flask and bring them here on the double—" then, turning back to the women—"unless you'd prefer a glass of cognac to warm you up?"

Margit Armbrecht shook her head, laughing, and made room beside her for the SS officer. He held her in light conversation until the departure whistle blew, managing at the same time to direct at Sophie, sitting opposite him, two or three glances of such open admiration as to make Kurt almost wonder whether it was not love sickness rather than lust into which the SS officer had fallen. Whatever it was, it was clear, to Kurt at least, that his sister hadn't been infected by it, for when his mother, just before leaving them, invited Voegler to join the family for dinner the night he and Kurt returned to Munich, Sophie's nails dug so fiercely into Kurt's thigh he had to smother a yelp of pain. Well, that was something his young sister would have to get out of by herself. Her rooted conviction—which to some extent he shared himself—that their deeply religious mother somehow regarded her children as untouched by the sordid side of the battle of the sexes had obviously inhibited Sophie from briefing her about the motives behind Voegler's telephone calls to the house.

Shortly after their train pulled out of Munich, the man from Goering's economic staff, a former Reichswehr quartermaster-general named Weinbacher, took a seat beside Kurt, obliging him to lay aside his book.

"A bit early, don't you think, to start in on the hard stuff?" He gestured toward the other end of the carriage, where Voegler and the *Gruppenfuehrer* were being served *Schnapps* by the SS batman. "I myself make a point of never taking a drop until I have food inside me." They had already been introduced on the platform at Berchtesgaden. Making the best of the situation, Kurt got his pompous elderly companion talking about his job.

"Fascinating, fascinating! On the statistics side, you understand? Would you believe it if I told you the Reich is on the way to becoming richer than the United States in material resources and productivity?"

Kurt showed himself to be suitably impressed.

"Well, just think about it, my dear chap. The iron ore of Sweden, nickel from the Kola Peninsula, all that Caucasian oil, soon as we get Maikop and Grozny working full-tilt again. Lumber from Finland, iron, steel and magnesite from Austria—I beg your pardon, the Ostmark—synthetic rubber from the new I. G. Farben plants in Poland. Now consider the food-supply situation. A virtually unlimited supply of cereals, fodder and potatoes from the Ukraine. The fruit, vegetables and wine of the Black Sea. Meat? My dear fellow, do you know how much meat we lifted off the Russians last year?"

Kurt confessed his uncertainty.

"Ten million cattle! Fifteen million pigs! How can a nation like the United States begin to compete with such a setup?"

"It's a pretty big country, the U.S.A.," Kurt murmured. "Three million square miles and a hundred and thirty million people."

"Pah!" Weinbacher threw up his hands. "How does it compare with the Greater German Reich of today? Look at the miracle our Fuehrer has worked in ten short years of power! Twenty-eight individual nations conquered, annexed, or otherwise incorporated into the New Germanic Order. Are you aware what that amounts to in terms of people and territory?"

134

Kurt was finding it difficult not to yawn; he had heard all these statistics a hundred times, notably from the Fuehrer himself. Besides, he had had to get up before dawn to catch the daytime express to Berlin, and it would be nice if this Weinbacher fellow would now leave him alone so that he could close his eyes and indulge in a little erotic daydreaming about his reunion that evening with Helga Gruyten.

"You're absolutely right, sir. Perhaps we could continue this interesting chat over lunch? Unfortunately—" He gave an apologetic smile, waving his hand at the heavily bookmarked volume still open on the table between them.

"Of course, of course!" Weinbacher settled back in his seat. "You mustn't let me come between you and your studies." He closed one eye in a sage and oddly out-of-character wink. "Believe me, I'm fully aware of the important character of your work for the Fuehrer."

Picking up the book and pretending to go on reading it, he let his thoughts wander ahead to an apartment building on the Kurfuerstendamm and to the girl who had taught him that a fellow could get by enormously well with only one arm, plus an enthusiastic bed companion.

The arrangement was that Voegler would spend the evening and night visiting old comrades in the Leibstandarte Adolf Hitler barracks at Lichterfelde, a suburb of Berlin, and they would meet in the morning in the lobby of the Adlon Hotel before taking the train to Warsaw. It could hardly have suited Kurt better, and as he settled back in the cab, after telling the driver to stop at the first flower shop en route, his thoughts turned again to Helga and the unique quality of their relationship.

There had been an opportunity, after the Christmas and New Year festivities were over and Hitler had decided to stay on at the Berghof, to have Helga join the staff on the mountain, with a room in the unmarried secretaries' quarters. Fräulein Eppler had put the suggestion to him, in her brusque official way, but after reflection he had declined the offer. Helga was currently retyping a large chunk of the first draft of *Mein Sieg* and checking for him a long list of minor queries, the answers to which were readily available in the archives of the Chancellery and the Foreign Ministry. There had been no need, of course, to go into this with Fräulein Eppler; he was his own boss at this stage of the book's preparation and could direct his own secretary as he pleased. The real reason for not wanting Helga at the Berghof was simply that he was desiring her, physically and sexually, too much. The thought of daily propinquity during working hours, with no hope of sleeping together, was intolerable to him. He himself could never leave the Berghof complex, even on a twenty-four-hour pass to visit his parents, except at Hitler's own suggestion, and this showed no signs of being forthcoming. And any prospect of being able to make love to Helga within the Obersalzberg estate—short of burrowing into the snow somewhere up in the pinewoods—was thwarted by the very rules against unmarried coupling in the barracks and staff quarters that had finally prompted Himmler to permit the SS brothel.

What was remarkable was that Helga hadn't once, in her weekly letters to him, tried to pressure Kurt into having her transferred, though she must have known he could have wangled it. Conceivably, it was because she also realized what a strain they would both be under at the Berghof. Whatever the reason, he was grateful to her. He even forgave her the fact that his last two letters had been unanswered. He couldn't wait to see her face when she opened that door to him.

It was a relief to see the lights on in her flat up on the second floor. The plainclothes policeman on duty inside the entrance gave him the usual friendly greeting, as if he had been away for only a week, and offered to carry his valise with the bouquet of flowers taped to the straps. Kurt waved him off. "Surprise visit," he grinned. "Don't call her up on the house phone."

She ruined the surprise by calling through the closed door, "Who is it?" when he rang the bell, and there was a short silence after he called back, with a poor attempt at disguising his voice, "Guess who?"

The door opened. She stood there, blinking her small eyes at him as she tightened the belt of her thin cotton wrap. She had no lipstick on and her hair was tousled, as if from sleep. He felt like someone who had come to read the electric meter.

"Remember me?" He was fighting a sudden panic.

"You'd better come in, I suppose." She turned around with a shrug of her shoulders and led the way into the sitting room, with its familiar smell and all its memories. He followed her, leaving his valise in the small hallway.

"Helga, for Christ's sake—what's all this about?"

"You turn up here," she said, shaking her head slowly, "without warning, after nearly three months, and you want to know what it's all about?"

He heard a sound from the next room, like someone turning over in bed, and he strode to the open door, his heart pounding. A young, entirely nude brunette lay with her shoulders propped against the headboard. His mouth stayed open but no sound came out. The obscene object strapped about her pelvis was something one had read about in smutty books but never really believed existed. The girl was smiling at him in an incongruously feminine, reassuring way. He whirled back into the sitting room, where Helga was draining the last of a bottle of vodka into a glass.

"It's pretty obvious what's been going on," he said through his teeth. "Did you really have to sink this low?"

"What do you know about it?" She was circling the room, keeping clear of him. "Up there in the mountains, with your own private whorehouse! Did you really expect me to spend every evening home, tidying up my stamp collection?"

"I know what I didn't expect—*that!*" He flung his arm out, pointing to the bedroom.

She was looking straight at him now, with a twisted little smile. "There's an acute shortage of young men on the home front, didn't you know that? There's even talk of allowing polygamous marriages—selectively, of course, and mainly for the *Reichsdeutscher* SS. But that's for some time in the future." She looked away, frowning. "It wasn't very smart of you, dropping in without warning, like this."

"I wasn't trying to be smart. I thought it might be fun to give you a surprise." He drew a deep shuddering breath. "I'm glad I did. At least I know now just what I'm worth to you!"

It was ridiculous. She was perching herself on the arm of the sofa, her small face tight with guilt and self-pity, and the skirt of her wrap had slipped open, exposing one pale thigh, and he wanted her like hell. He also wanted to smash up the place and fling that silent obscene brunette in the next room out by the scruff of her neck.

Helga said, "What do you want me to do? I can ask her to leave."

"And break up a beautiful friendship? Don't bother!" He was heading for the hallway, forcing his eyes away from her. As he ripped the tape from his grip and sent the flowers skidding across the floor he heard the girl in the bedroom calling out, "What's going on, darling?" and Helga's low hiss, "Stay where you are!"

Kurt had slammed the front door behind him and was hesitating at the top of the steps, thinking how best to deal with the raised eyebrows that were going to greet him in the downstairs lobby, when the door of the apartment clicked open behind him and Helga's voice called out to him. He turned halfway around. She had taken a step onto the landing and was standing there, gazing solemn-faced at him. Without a change of expression, she slipped the knot at her waist and opened wide her wrap, raising the flowered cotton high, like some exotic bat's wings.

"You bitch!" It came out of him like a cry for help as he turned right around to face her. Still deadpan, she began to rotate her hips, very slowly. Only when he was close, looking down at her with his stricken eyes, did she let the wings fall and reach for him.

"You'll like my friend Hanni," she murmured. "She's from Bavaria."

138

CHAPTER SEVEN

I

THERE HAD to be one clear and indestructible image that would stay tattooed on his memory long after all the other images of that nightmare journey through the New Order had shuddered and reformed into an obscene kaleidoscope of blood, stench and brutality. It was toward the end of the tour, and their second day in Auschwitz-Birkenau, the extermination camp in southern Poland. By then, Kurt understood that he was on trial—certainly by Werner Voegler and the SS and probably by Martin Bormann. He knew, too, that they had been right to put him on trial, for he had failed them—though they could hardly judge him yet—and now they had lost him, somewhere between Ravensbrueck and this charnel house of a *Vernichtungslager*.

It was a Sunday afternoon in April, with the sky a uniform dull gray from horizon to horizon and a light chill breeze coming from the northeast. Kurt and Voegler were standing with the camp commander, SS Obersturmbannfuehrer Rudolf Hoess, and two of his senior *Totenkopfverbaende* staff, watching the last of a long column of Hungarian Jews—mostly youths over fourteen and men of middle age—wending its way, to cries of *"Los! Los!"* and blows from long rubber truncheons, toward the distant labor-camp complex of Auschwitz. A larger column, made up of older men, women and children, was packed, half-a-dozen abreast, down the long railway siding dividing Auschwitz from the extermination camp of Birkenau. The two SS doctors, who with brisk flicks of their canes had separated this new trainload of prisoners into two groups, "useful" and "disposable," were now standing together near the head of the column, tossing back glasses of *Schnapps* and, from what Kurt could hear of it, conducting a post-mortem on last night's carousal in the officers' mess.

This trainload had been the first of two, each of two thousand Jews, expected that day from Hungary. As usual, Werner Voegler was putting the questions Kurt himself should have been asking and nodding solemnly over the replies, as if he were learning something for the first time.

"At a rough estimate, Herr Commandant, how much of this rubbish would you say you can dispose of in, say, the average year?"

"An *average* year . . . ?" Hoess raised his eyebrows, dubiously. "We don't really get them here, you know, Herr Standartenfuehrer. Last year, for example, I had to take care of about a hundred thousand Jews. We're doing appreciably better this year—so far anyway. Call it about two thousand a day—mainly Hungarians and Poles—and you wouldn't be far off." He was a small man, with a gaunt, sensual face and very pale eyes. He could have been a factory foreman, wishing to impress one of his firm's major shareholders.

Voegler said, "This lot still here on the siding—there must be well over a thousand of them. Do they all get processed today?"

Hoess nodded. "We don't keep them hanging around in this camp." He glanced at his watch. "Let me invite you gentlemen to hear some excellent music."

The orchestra, about fifty strong, was made up of prisoners dressed in their civilian clothes, forming a circle around the white-coated bandmaster, who, Hoess informed them, had been the conductor of the Warsaw State Opera. The work chosen was Schubert's *Unfinished Symphony*.

From where he stood, Kurt could clearly read the faces of the Hungarian Jews as they trudged past toward the "shower rooms." Among the adults, expressions ranged from weary detachment to a kind of perplexed animation as the orchestra came into view. Some of the smaller children, trotting to keep up with the pace set by the guards, tugged at their mothers' soiled and crumpled overcoats, plying them with questions. A baby, held against the breast of a young woman with a dark sensitive face, was gurgling happily as it tugged at its mother's hair. She shook her head free and, in averting her face, her eyes locked for a second or two with Kurt's. Tears welled from them, streaking the dust and grime from the long train journey. Kurt looked away . . . Beyond the low, squat building of the "shower rooms" a tall brick chimney rising up from the well-trimmed lawn was giving off a light-gray smoke. Beyond that, again, a dense screen of birch trees afforded the last view of natural beauty to the people now being guided and coaxed into the "shower rooms" by the Jewish *Sonderkommandos,* under the watchful eyes of the SS men and women guards.

He had to stay until the orchestra had finished its performance, now exclusively directed at the music-loving commandant and his SS colleagues. Meanwhile, the great steel doors of the death chamber were closed and locked, and the blue crystals of Zyklon B fed in through the specially constructed vents. Now the bedlam of muffled screams and frantic pounding of fists on metal competed for a while with the violins, causing Hoess to frown and shrug apologetically at Voegler. But the disturbance was short-lived. The steel doors opened again and the *Sonderkommandos* went in with their hoses, their shears, their plyers and their grappling irons.

The smoke from the crematorium chimney began to turn black and thicken, and the stench of burning poisoned flesh was already coming at them when the orchestra reached the end of the symphony. With an expressive wrinkling of his large nose, Rudolf Hoess led his group toward the waiting staff cars. Kurt looked back once, as he waited to take his seat. The orchestra was packing up its music-stands and scores. The trucks were arriving to collect that afternoon's harvest of human hair, gold teeth, spectacles, wedding rings and with luck, a diamond engagement ring or two. The smoke was pouring thickly from the chimney now, forming a black polluting cloud through which the distant birch trees were barely visible. One of the guards' dogs was barking.

It was important to him, that last look back. It was a final purging, perhaps a self-imposed sentence of death.

The tour of the New Order had started with an unscheduled visit to Ravensbrueck, the concentration camp for women, about fifty miles north of Berlin. Voegler had come striding into the lobby of the Adlon, a brisk and delighted bearer of good news.

"We're in luck, Armbrecht," he announced. "By pure chance, I ran into Helga Obeheuser, one of the medicos at Ravensbrueck, last night. She has a car outside and we're going off to see her 'rabbit women' and maybe a few other interesting sights. Where's your bag?"

"Right here." Kurt reached for it, behind his armchair. "But what about our plane to Warsaw? And what the hell are 'rabbit women,' anyway?"

Voegler snatched the bag from him. "Let's get going. I'll fill you in on the way."

The staff car, chauffered by a "Death's Head" driver, reached the camp just before ten-thirty. On the way the lady doctor, prim and severe in her women's SS uniform, told them of the valuable medical experiments she and her colleagues were carrying out on some of the women inmates of the camp, experiments "of profound importance to medical science and ultimately of tremendous benefit to the human race." A whole new field of progress had been opened up by the availability in Germany of clinical human specimens—as distinct from rabbits, guinea pigs and so on—whose lives were socially of less importance than those of dumb animals and whose deaths in the pursuit of medical knowledge were therefore not only excusable but the only useful contribution these people could ever hope to make to humanity's triumph over its environment. Doctor Obeheuser had a

142

very busy day ahead of her, but she would put Kurt and Voegler in the good hands of one of her assistants. They could make a tour of the hospital wards, observe an experimental operation or two, if they so wished. After lunch, there would be time for a general tour of the camp before they were driven back to Berlin, to emplane for Warsaw.

It was the silence in this camp housing thousands of women (Polish, Czech, Dutch, French, Russian, Greek and Yugoslav) that made the first bizarre impression on Kurt—that and the ubiquitous SS *Aufseherinen,* hefty jack-booted women guards, mostly German but with a strong leavening of Scandinavian women volunteers, hardly one of whom was not swinging a long rubber truncheon or a dog whip as she marched about her business. He had steeled himself for the worst as they made their way from the camp commandant's office toward the main hospital ward, a low concrete building set apart from the bleak geometrical complex of wooden dormitories and gray-brick workshops. From the doctor's description of some of the experiments carried out on the "rabbit women," Kurt was expecting a kind of terrestrial purgatory, hideous with the moans and dying screams of its suffering inmates. Instead, he found himself walking between two long rows of iron-framed beds whose occupants were either lying quite still under their single covering of a gray blanket or with their shoulders propped up against the head rail, their lusterless eyes following the visitors' slow progress down the ward. The only sound was the low conversational tone of the young medic, answering the questions put to her by Voegler.

"There's nothing infectious in this ward, you'll be glad to know. These are all cases from our sterilization experiments. We're trying to simplify the techniques as much as possible, for a real blitz on the problem of unwanted breeding in the eastern territories. Here, we pick out only the young and the fertile, and those who recover from the treatment are mated with males from Sachsenhausen. We are already getting very encouraging results."

Behind her white-coated back, Voegler pulled a droll face at

Kurt. "When you talk," he prompted her, "about simplifying the . . . um . . . process—"

"No anesthetics. Swift intrauterine surgery or injections of acid, such as could be administered by any medical orderly. Mortality rate from hemorrhage, infection and shock has been a little disturbing, but we have another team of doctors looking into that. The object, of course, is to have the survivors up and working again in the shortest time."

The place was nauseating with the stench of blood, urine and untreated pus. It was good to get out again into the cold fresh air. Voegler expressed an interest in seeing some of the bone-graft results, and for the first and only time during their whole tour Kurt put up an objection.

"You go ahead," he said. "I can't see how any of this is going to help me with the book."

Voegler stared at him with astonishment. "You can't possibly mean that, Armbrecht. What's the New Order all about, if it's not about racial hygiene?"

"All right. But what on earth has bone-grafting got to do with that?"

Frowning, Voegler turned to their guide. "Tell the Captain," he snapped. "And then let's get on with the job we set out to do."

"A successful bone graft can give one of our German soldiers a whole new lease of life." The doctor's tone was reproachful, her eyes hostile. "Would the Captain prefer that we experimented on war heroes like himself?"

He followed them into the recovery ward. He stood apart, numb with horror, as the "rabbit women" were inspected, to a running commentary from their guide. There were women whose shinbones had been shortened or lengthened in the cause of medical science; one whose healthy hipbone had been removed and replaced by an aluminum replica. The swinging door leading to the lavatory came slowly open as they moved down the ward and a creature with shorn hair worked her way through on all fours, pausing every few seconds to summon strength. "Spinal case," the SS doctor said tersely. "Looks like a failure."

144

Over lunch the commandant got talking about his *Aufse-herinen*. "You'd be amazed, gentlemen, at the variety of types we have volunteering for this work. A Berlin streetcar driver, an opera singer past her prime, a hairdresser from Düsseldorf, a circus equestrienne, a former prison wardress, a graduate nurse, believe it or not! We train them here, you see, for all the other important camps. I tell you, if they don't make out here, they're pretty useless anywhere else."

Voegler said, dabbing a napkin to his mouth, "How do you judge failures in this kind of work?"

"Oh, by their squeamishness mostly. You'll hardly believe this, but we had a young *Aufseherin* in here, a few weeks ago— girl from a good-class family—who never stopped blubbering from the time she arrived till the day I kicked her out. There was another, only last week, who started off by saying 'Pardon me' whenever she stepped in front of a prisoner! I had a feeling about that one though, so I put her with one of our top girls, Irma Greese, for four days. You wouldn't believe the transformation!"

"Greese? They were talking about her in the mess at Lichter-felde."

"Really?" The commandant looked pleased. "Beautiful-looking animal. Hoess wants her at Auschwitz, but not if I can help it."

"What's so special about her?" Voegler asked quietly, with a sidelong glance at Kurt. "Apart from her looks, I mean."

"Special? I guess it has to do with the fact that she really *enjoys* her work. She's in there, licking the hides off slackers at the drop of a hat. Most of the poor bitches start trembling if they see her a mile off!" The commandant started to peel an apple. "How about this, for example? When she first started here a year or so ago, she found out there were still about forty survivors from the hundred and ninety Czech women put to work here after we wiped the village of Lidice off the map. Apparently, Reinhard Heydrich had been Irma's girlhood idol. She still has pictures of him plastered all over the wall of her room here.

145

So what does she do to revenge her murdered hero? She asks to be put in charge of the Czech huts. And every day, for the past year, she gets those Lidice women out of bed half an hour before roll call at four A.M., lines them up stark naked in front of the block and lays into them with that whip of hers till her arm's practically falling off. What's incredible is that she hasn't finished them all off by now. There's about half a dozen of them left. Nut cases, of course, and they don't bleed anymore. Too much scar tissue."

Kurt had glanced at Voegler toward the end of the commandant's account, looking for some slight reflection of his own feelings on that lean intent face. There was nothing—only absorption in the story and a perceptible swelling of the vein over the right brow. It might have been then that his mind's eye saw the first faint outlines of the trap that had been set for him, but this was something he would never be able to fix for certain during the trek through disillusionment and despair that lay ahead.

As the car taking them back to Berlin passed through the electrified fence, Voegler turned for a last look back before settling down beside Kurt. "Very impressive," he murmured.

"Sir?" Their ever-alert orderly looked quickly around from his seat beside the driver.

"As you were! I was thinking about what we've seen here— one of the best-run camps in the Reich." A smile for Kurt. "Wouldn't you agree, Armbrecht?"

Words were nothing. They could have his words, at least.

He said, "I certainly would."

From Warsaw they were taken to see one of the big estates on the River Bug now being turned over to German "colonists," with priority given to former Wehrmacht officers and men. Here, as in both areas of partitioned Poland, the Fuehrer's edicts were being carried out to the letter. The local population —men, women and children over ten years of age—worked the fields from dawn to sunset as slave labor under the whips of mounted *volksdeutsche* guards of both sexes. They received no pay, no food rations, no medical attention, and were hanged if they failed to report to work. Their livestock was confiscated, their schools were closed down, public transportation was forbidden and only one Mass a week was permitted them, on Sunday. The German settlers were given power of life and death over their slaves, and they used it indiscriminately.

As Voegler put it, on the way back to the Polish capital that night, "In ten years' time we Germans will truly be a nation of *Herrenvolk*. You can forget about the patricians of Rome. For every slave those fellows owned there'll be twenty working directly or indirectly for every individual German, however stupid and lazy he might be. Isn't that a fantastic thought?"

"I suppose so—if we forget about what happened to Rome."

"What's the matter with you?" Voegler turned to him with a strained grin. "Can't you see the difference between the New Order and all that other rubbish? We're Germans, not flabby Romans."

"I appreciate that. But when we've all become *Herrenvolk*? There's nothing like easy living for sapping a person's character."

"The Fuehrer has thought of all that. We'll be rich, but we'll remain a warrior state. Perpetual war, Armbrecht—the best antidote to decadence. It'll take another generation, probably, to drive the last Bolshevik into the Bering Sea. That'll put Alaska on our doorstep. Canada. While you and I are riding around our estates in the Ukraine or the Crimea, our children will be campaigning south of the forty-eighth parallel."

"And dying. Don't forget that."

"So? Can you think of a better end than dying for the glory of the Greater Reich?"

"Living for it," Kurt said dryly, "has a stronger personal appeal."

Voegler was shaking his head. "You're a strange one, Armbrecht. If I didn't know better, I'd wonder which side you were on."

It wasn't a question he would have put to himself, not in those simplistic terms, anyway. He was a German and a member of the party that had lifted Germany out of disgrace and bankruptcy. So it had been done by trampling on the weak. No nation had a monopoly of virtue and no state could stand at the bar of history with a clean conscience and unbloodied hands. But there was another question he now began to face. He was on Germany's side, all right—anything else would be unthinkable—but who or what was a German? Was it the civil administrator of Krivoyrog with his Sunday shooting parties and his boastful bag of "twenty-seven peasants and half a dozen of their brats" before lunch—or was it Professor Walter Armbrecht of the University of Munich? Was it that comely SS girl with the "Gretchen" wreath of braids he had watched flog a Crimean farm worker to death in the courtyard of their Sevastopol hotel —or was it his sister Sophie, who fainted at the sight of blood? And now Birkenau—the smoking chimney, the camp orchestra, the birch trees.

Who were the Germans? There had to be a distinction, and not simply in the convenient terms of those who obeyed orders to slaughter and those who had never had to. For example: the harmless-looking people of Essen they had passed, during that morning's drive from the airport, window-shopping or cycling home from work; was it conceivable they were unaware of the living hell created for the thousands of Jewish women and Russian prisoners of war put to toil in the city's war factories? Had none of them seen and passed on the appalling picture of starving, barefoot women clad in old sacks being flogged to the assembly lines before dawn and flogged back to their unspeakable camps, fourteen or sixteen hours later, carrying their dead and dying? And if this was in fact common knowledge among the citizens of Essen, how were they moved by it? To impotent pity? To pride in the resourcefulness of the New Order? To the escape of disbelief? Maybe, when it came down to it, this was the answer: there were three distinct classes of German, rather than two. Or perhaps even that was too pat. There was one basic German in whose conscience all three reactions interplayed uneasily, never in equal measure and changing in relative weight according to circumstances.

A kind of madness had seized Germany, and it had nothing to do with war or the survival of his people. He could clearly see that now, but he could see also that he was a part of the madness, had given substance to it and would have to live with it till the end of his days. And he saw something else, and was frightened. Werner Voegler hadn't broken him. By no word or hostile action had he given the SS officer an inch of rope for the noose he so obviously wanted to hold over him. The tour was ended. Tomorrow they would be back in Munich. Next day, Obersalzberg. What frightened him now was not Voegler but Adolf Hitler.

The first draft of *Mein Sieg* was now short only two chapters —that on religion and an end chapter reviewing the achievements and setting out the future objectives of the New Order. Relations between Hitler and the Vatican had worsened during Kurt's tour, as the result of wholesale arrests of priests in Poland and Czechoslovakia, and the Party press was now openly hostile, calling for the scrapping of the concordat. While Kurt awaited the outcome of this confrontation, he would have to start getting together the final chapter, under the Fuehrer's guidance. This would call for a careful sifting of Hitler's claims and assertions and a persuasive and credible picture of the evolving nature and purpose of the Greater German Reich— a task he would have set about with dedication and enthusiasm only a month ago. Now, the very thought of sitting down to justify and clothe in decency the obscenities he had witnessed in Germany, Poland and Occupied Russia swamped him in dismay. Where would he find the words? He hadn't been trained in Doctor Goebbels's Ministry of Propaganda and Public Enlightenment, had never pushed a pen for the servile Party press. He was an historian who had believed in National Socialism and in the genius of its leader, Adolf Hitler, and it served little purpose now to look back over his studies, over the lectures he had attended, in the hope of unraveling the skeins of self-deception, gullibility and downright cynicism that had so effectively strangled his academic conscience. The crisis he faced was a personal one, but what hope had he of concealing it from the soul-stripping eyes, the almost uncannily perceptive intelligence of the Fuehrer? How would he survive that first predictable question, "Well, Armbrecht, what impressions have you brought back from your travels?"

It was Voegler, knocking on the door of his room in the SS guesthouse.
"Make it snappy! We'd better not keep Alfried Krupp von Bohlen und Halbach waiting!"
"I'm ready, Voegler. I'm on my way."
Somehow, his words had the ring of a condemned man's last ones.

II

THEY FLEW in one of the Wehrmacht's converted Heinkels to Augsberg, forty miles northwest of Munich, where an SS staff car and driver were put at their disposal so that Voegler could indulge a fancy to retrace part of the route he and his Leibstandarte detachment had taken the night of the Roehm purge and his promotion to *Hauptsturmfuehrer*.

Kurt had already telephoned home from Essen to announce their return, and as Voegler put it, "We've masses of time. The driver can drop me off at my apartment in Briennerstrasse and take you on from there. I can't tell you, Armbrecht, how much I'm looking forward to a decent home-cooked meal at your place."

Kurt had deliberately not mentioned his mother's invitation to dinner, first extended at the Munich railway station and repeated during his telephone call. The fact that Voegler was taking it for granted both depressed and alarmed him. It had now become a routine with him to look for the ulterior motive behind every suggestion, every glancing comment made by the SS officer, and he was pretty certain that it wasn't the meal that was uppermost in Voegler's mind, nor was it solely the prospect of spending a domestic evening in Sophie's company. Clearly, his obsession with Sophie had not ended with their tour of Essen's factories. Even now, on the last lap of the journey, there was to be a turn of the screw.

"Why is he turning off here, Voegler?" They had reached Maisach, only a dozen miles short of Munich, and had swung off the main road into a secondary road forking northeast.

"Didn't I mention it? Helmut Brunner, second in command of the *Totenkopfverbaende* at Dachau, is an old comrade of mine. He'll give us lunch and show you around the place afterward."

Under cover of his army greatcoat, Kurt's hand tightened into a hard fist. Dachau—the first of Himmler's concentration camps, set up in 1933 for the "protective custody" of anti-Nazi Germans and reputedly the mildest and best-run corrective institution of them all—unless you believed the hair-raising stories and macabre jokes that had been circulating around the Munich beer halls for years.

They were stopped by the SS guards at the great arched gateway to the camp.

"Obersturmbannfuehrer Voegler and Captain Armbrecht," Voegler snapped. "Inform Sturmbannfuehrer Brunner of our arrival."

"*Jawohl,* Herr Obersturmbannfuehrer! At once!"

A brief telephone call and they were directed around the barbed wire perimeter of the huge camp toward a tree-lined avenue of attractive villas interspaced with well-kept lawns and flower beds. "Still the best married quarters and barracks of any of our camps," Voegler said, stubbing out his cigarette and straightening his belt. "You'll like Brunner's wife. Very warm and feminine."

She was waiting for them at the open front door, a plump smiling young woman wearing a Bavarian blouse and dirndl skirt, with a chubby blond child in her arms. A few yards away on the front lawn a middle-aged man with the red triangle of a political offender sewn on his pajama-striped prison garb let fall his shears and sprang to attention, sweeping off his cap. His head was shaved close, revealing an old scar across his scalp, but otherwise he looked in fairly good shape.

Frau Brunner offered a cheek for Voegler to kiss. "Werner, what a lovely surprise! Helmut will be right down. Just, you know, cleaning up." The last was said with a comical little grimace and a jerk of the woman's chin toward the distant complex of low barracks and tall watchtowers.

Voegler introduced Kurt and they followed Frau Brunner into a sunlit sitting room with matching chintz curtains and chair covers and smelling sweetly of polish and cut flowers.

"We're not staying for lunch, Kitty," Voegler kidded, keeping his lipless mouth straight. "That is, not unless you've improved your cooking since I was last here."

"Brute!" She made a face at him, hugging the child closer. "Just for that—"

"—let the miserable so-and-so go without!" It was a harsh voice, even in banter, and perfectly suited to the big rawboned man who followed it into the room, buttoning a cardigan over his tieless service shirt. He was about Voegler's age and spoke with the same North-German accent. When the shoulder slapping was finished and Kurt had been introduced, their host produced a bottle of *Schnapps* and kept their glasses primed while his wife went to see "how that new cook is getting along in the kitchen." The two SS men exchanged news of mutual friends, embroidering their gossip with allusive SS jargon, most of which went right over Kurt's head. But later, over the meal served by a crisply uniformed Ukrainian housemaid, Sturmbannfuehrer

Brunner gave way to Voegler's request to feed Kurt some facts about the camp.

There were about 40,000 "detainees" at the present time, of whom maybe a third were women and children. Most of the Jews had been deported east, but they had hung onto a few whose special skills were of value in the SS workshops. The prisoners were adequately fed, "without being spoiled, of course." Coffee in the morning before going to work—4 A.M. to sunset in the winter; 3 A.M. to sunset in the summer. A bowl of soup at midday. At night, 300 grams of bread with 15 grams of margarine or jam. Frau Brunner, however, didn't think it was enough. "We lost so many good workers during the winter," she said, helping Voegler to another thick wedge of *apfel strudel.* "Quite apart from the waste of manpower, the stench from those four furnaces installed last year was quite ghastly whenever the wind blew this way." Abruptly, Kurt asked for the lavatory and stayed there for some minutes, face buried in trembling hands. When he returned to the table, Voegler gave him a friendly smile over the rim of his coffee cup. "I was just telling Helmut about the medical experiments we saw at Ravensbrueck. He doesn't seem very impressed."

"A bunch of cranks, that lot," Brunner grunted. "The best medical research work is still being done here, under Doctor Sigmund Rascher and his team. Incredible fellow. Only last week he actually reversed the classical operation for Siamese twins by—" Brunner broke off, rolling his eyes, as his wife pushed back her chair and left the room, wailing, "I don't want to hear about it!"

"Soft as butter, that one," he grinned. "Anyway, as I was saying, Rascher actually succeeded in grafting two completely unrelated twelve-year-old kids together, using only one blood system. Claims to have kept them alive, what's more, for all of twenty-three minutes."

Over Voegler's long low whistle, Kurt said, "Did he explain the value of the experiment, Herr Sturmbannfuehrer?"

"I believe there's a report and photographs gone to Reichs-fuehrer Himmler's headquarters. Our chief takes a great personal interest in this work, as you probably know." He drained his coffee cup. "Well, gentlemen, a quick look around the camp and then I must get back to work."

The workshops were nowhere on the scale of the big factories at Auschwitz, and the *Kapos* patrolling the benches seemed far less addicted to their whips and truncheons. Outwardly, the blocks of prisoners' huts presented a neater, almost habitable aspect, but a quick look by Kurt inside of one of them was enough to explode the illusion. The wooden bunks rose three tiers high from the cement floors, accommodating five persons in each separated niche, a little over two yards wide and two feet high. The bedding was a thin straw *paillasse* and a single threadbare blanket.

As they turned the corner of Block 9, a huge sign, attached to the wall of the end hut, greeted them. In German Gothic characters it proclaimed:

"There is a road to freedom, its milestones are: Obedience, Industry, Honesty, Order, Cleanliness, Sobriety, Sincerity, and a Spirit of Sacrifice and Patriotism."

Facing the sign, at a distance of about ten yards, an elderly man, stark naked, was hanging from the crossbar of a wooden gibbet by his thumbs, his feet inches off the ground. His eyes were closed and his toothless mouth hung open. The only sign of life in him was an occasional weak flutter of his fingers. As Kurt, ashen-faced, turned quietly away he heard Voegler's calm matter-of-fact question to Brunner:

"What's this one been up to, then?"

"Recent arrival. Principal of a village primary school. Gestapo got a recent tip and found a copy of Bertrand Russell's dangerous drivel, *Education and the Social Order,* large as life on his bookshelves. Since he obviously liked shit so much I ordered him a week of latrine fatigue. Old fool decided to go on strike this morning."

After dropping Voegler and his orderly off on Brienner-strasse, Kurt directed the driver to enter Nikolaistrasse from the west, to avoid alerting the odious Herr Krenkler just around the corner on Werneckstrasse. As he dismissed the SS man, Sophie came running down the short forecourt and out onto the pavement.

"Kurt, darling! We've been worried stiff. We expected you two hours ago!"

"Slight detour en route, Maedel." He held her back at arm's length. "You look great! Another kiss!"

It was Saturday, and his father was waiting with his mother to greet him at the side door to the old house. If Walter Armbrecht was surprised by the silent warmth of his son's embrace, he didn't show it. "Let the lad go up and take a quick bath, or whatever he has to do!" he expostulated, cutting through the two women's volley of questions. "Our guest will be here in an hour or so." And, sheperding Kurt toward the staircase, "Hurry on down, Son. The champagne's on ice, waiting."

Kurt's first action upon reappearing downstairs in one of his old civilian suits was to head for the sideboard in the living room, lift the ice bucket up by its handle and hold it out to his wide-eyed sister.

"Hide this bottle away somewhere, Maedel. And tell Mother on no account to serve up anything even remotely black market." Turning to his father, whose eyebrows were also up high, "This fellow Voegler's a Party fanatic, Father. I've got to talk to you now, before he gets here."

He hadn't written once to his family during the month's tour of the Greater Reich. Now, as all three of them sat in silence, he started to tell them why.

He paused at the end of his story, lowering his eyes for a long moment before raising them to meet Walter Armbrecht's calm gaze. "I'm not going to ask your forgiveness for being such a blind and dogmatic idiot. I can't even tell you I've completely renounced National Socialism. What I do have to say is that I'm sickened and ashamed by the means this country is using to establish its New Order in Europe and the East. I've looked at it, and it's obscene. And I cannot believe that *we,* as a race, will ever be forgiven for what we are doing."

It was his mother who broke the silence. She said, her voice shaking, "Please be careful, Kurt. You mustn't do anything that might—" She broke off, staring helplessly from her husband to Sophie, then back to Kurt.

"It's all right, Mother, this is between us and these four walls. I've not had much time to think straight. I had to tell you this now because I couldn't keep it bottled up any longer, the way I've had to these past weeks. We'll talk more about it later, after Voegler has gone. But please, Father—not a word of anti-Nazi criticism while he's here, no matter what he comes out with. Don't let him goad you. The man's dangerous."

"I realize that," his father said. "It's you I'm worried about, Son. You're going back, right among the savages who have dragged us into this. How are you going to cope?"

He let out a short, joyless laugh. "I'll manage. I'll probably just keep telling myself the whole thing was a nightmare. It's not really happening."

Margit Armbrecht started to say, shaking her head, "It's terrible what they're doing to the Church. No Easter processions allowed anywhere this year. And that poor Archbishop Galen, forbidden to—" when the doorbell rang, freezing them all in their seats.

"That'll be Voegler." Kurt stood up, walked over to his father and reached down to put a swift grip on his shoulder. "I'll take over from here, Father. Just keep a tight rein on that tongue of yours."

Voegler had shed his SS uniform for a well-cut prewar suit of Cheviot tweed. In the hallway he presented a bouquet of flowers to Margit Armbrecht and a box of chocolates to Sophie.

156

"You don't have to feel badly about the chocolates," he smiled, perhaps misinterpreting her embarrassment. "They didn't come off anyone's sugar ration."

When Kurt led him into the sitting room to meet his father, Voegler greeted the professor with the Nazi salute and a respectfully modulated "Heil Hitler!" and Walter Armbrecht replied in kind but with what seemed to his tight-strung son a somewhat limp salute. The two younger men remained standing while the professor handed out the *aperitifs*.

"Herr Professor," Voegler said, raising his glass, "you will understand how much Kurt and I have been looking forward to this evening. A pleasant ending to a pretty arduous trip."

"It's an honor to welcome you here, Herr Obersturmbannfuehrer. Kurt has been telling us how much he's indebted to you for your help and guidance."

"Oh, that!" Voegler shrugged off the compliment. "We are all of us in the service of the Fuehrer. And he can be a hard taskmaster. Right, Kurt?"

It was the first time Voegler had addressed him directly by his Christian name. A month ago, he might have been flattered. Now, the familiarity was as suspect as the comradely smile that went with it. Kurt said, "I can't really complain so far as *my* work's concerned. The Fuehrer hasn't even asked to see my first draft yet."

"Wise man," Walter Armbrecht grunted. "Wish I could practice the same discipline so far as one or two of my students' handiwork is concerned."

Voegler said, "I gather your subject is history, Herr Professor. Doesn't it make you giddy, the speed at which the Fuehrer is writing it?"

To Kurt's relief, Walter Armbrecht was taking his time answering. He gave Voegler an amused smile, sipped at his drink and sat down, gesturing to the other two to do likewise. "History is the tale of what has already happened," he said. "My period ends with Bismarck and the birth of the Prussian empire."

He gave a stunted little laugh. "I certainly don't envy those whose job it'll be to condense these years into a chapter or two."

"You'll forgive my naïveté, Herr Professor, but unfortunately I never attended university. A 'chapter or two'? Is that really how you academics evaluate it?" The smile was still there, and he was leaning forward in his chair, all attention.

"In relative terms, yes. The Fuehrer has been making history for only about ten years. Alexander the Great came to the throne of Macedonia in 336 B.C."

"But *what* history! The face of Europe, completely changed!"

"I think," Kurt intervened gently, "my father's 'chapter or two' was put in the context of a single volume, if one can imagine it, of world history. In such a volume Napoleon, for example, might rate one chapter—if that."

"I see your point," Voegler leaned back in his armchair, nodding his head. "But Kurt, what is it going to feel like, having your mighty theme cut down by some future historian to a chapter or two?"

"I shan't be around to complain." He gave a wry chuckle. "Sometimes I even wonder if I'll be around to put *'Finis'* to the story." He had all of Voegler's attention now. If only he could hold it till the women took over, and the small talk. . . . "I was thinking about what you said that night we were driving back to Warsaw—about our children campaigning across Russia and Canada and down into the United States. It's perfectly feasible, I suppose. But where is *Mein Sieg* going to end—on the Volga, the Bering Sea, the Forty-ninth Parallel, the Gulf of Mexico?"

"There's a possibility the Americans might save us the journey," Walter Armbrecht put in. "I don't know if either of you read the text of Roosevelt's last broadcast—" He broke off, catching the flare in Kurt's eyes. But Voegler moved smoothly in.

"Go on, Herr Professor. Tell us how *you* interpret it."

"Frankly, I think there was more to it than his usual saber-rattling. It struck me as the language of someone who now knows he has the resources to wage war on a global scale and is not going to wait much longer to get in."

"Against the will of the Congress and the majority of the American people?"

"No. But these are delicate balances that can change overnight. Happily for us the Japanese are acutely aware of this and are still showing remarkable restraint. But all it needs is for one trigger-happy Japanese pilot to be intercepted over Philippine air space. We can easily anticipate how Roosevelt and his generals would whip that up into an act of unprovoked aggression. Roosevelt would get his vote in the Congress and America would be at war."

Voegler remained silent for a while, revolving his empty glass slowly around by the stem. Kurt sprang up to take it from him. Through the heavy silence they could hear Frau Armbrecht calling out to Sophie, and a few seconds later the girl stood framed in the doorway, her worried expression giving way to a swift smile as Voegler eased around in his chair to look at her.

"We're ready to eat, gentlemen. I'm to get you seated, while Mother puts her finishing touches to the soup."

Placing Voegler at the head of the table in the small dining room next to the Professor's study, she sat down on his left. Her mother was to sit on Voegler's right and the other two men would face each other across the bottom end of the table. As Margit Armbrecht started to serve the soup Kurt was struck by a fearful thought and, muttering an excuse, he left the room and let himself quietly into his father's study. The big mahogany desk was as littered as ever with papers and books, and after a quick glance through the titles Kurt turned to the bookshelves lining the wall behind the desk. He had to move fast but he knew more or less where to look. Within a minute he had located five works sternly proscribed by the regime, slipped them from the shelves and locked them away in a cupboard. Pocketing the key, he returned to the dining room in time to hear his mother's response to a question from Voegler.

"I suppose we could put in for one, Herr Voegler, but I really have so little to do, with the Professor and Sophie out at work all day. To tell you the truth, I rather enjoy doing my own housework."

"There speaks a good German mother," Voegler said. And, with a smile for Sophie—"How about you, Fräulein Armbrecht? Shall you take on a Ukrainian servant when you get married?"

"I haven't thought about it—mainly, I suppose, because I have no intention of getting married before the war's over."

"So?" Voegler took a spoonful of soup and gave an appreciative little grunt. "But if your father's opinion has any merit the war might go on for years. Are you going to deny some lucky fellow a beautiful wife, all that time?"

Flushing slightly as she bent over her plate, Sophie murmured, "I'd rather put it that I don't want to add to the state's burden of widows' pensions."

"*Liebchen!*" her mother protested. "If all our young girls thought that way nobody would ever get married!"

"Absolutely right, Frau Armbrecht! And may I compliment you on this delicious soup? Even better than we had at Dachau today. Wouldn't you agree, Kurt?"

It was a cat-and-mouse game, and Voegler kept it going, with amiable resolution, throughout the longest and most nerve-racking mealtime Kurt could remember. Not once did the SS officer unsheathe his claws or utter anything more threatening than a conversational purr. But his gambits, his smooth switches of topic, were as contrived as his smile. Margit Armbrecht, insulated as ever by her guilelessness, came through the ordeal unscathed and, it almost seemed, once more disarmed by her guest's flattering attentions. Sophie, unnaturally silent throughout most of the meal, had to face her own moment of decision after they had returned to the sitting room for coffee. The polite brush-off she gave Voegler left Kurt with badly mixed feelings, rather than the wholehearted approval he should have felt.

"Nine-thirty." Voegler looked up from consulting his wrist watch. "It means I now have to face one of those tiresome conflicts between personal pleasure and the call of duty." His pale-blue eyes came to rest on Sophie. "Perhaps Fräulein Armbrecht will help me to decide?"

Sophie returned his gaze, her lovely face composed and non-committal.

"Your next-door neighbor," Voegler went on, "is the worthy Herr Krenkler, the local branch leader of the Party and a member of Gauleiter Geisler's headquarters staff. But you know all that, of course."

"We've met Herr Krenkler," said Sophie.

"I'm sure you have. I myself had no idea he lived around the corner until I bumped into him just outside, walking his dog. I'm invited to discuss one of his projects over a brandy. On the other hand, there's an informal party just started at the Bayrischer Hof, to celebrate an SS colleague's promotion to *Standartenfuehrer*. Ladies are welcome, and it would give me the greatest pleasure to take you to the party, Fräulein Armbrecht, and escort you safely home afterward. There! What shall it be —Krenkler, or champagne at Bayrischer Hof?"

Sophie said, "I'm afraid the decision's out of my hands. I have to be up at the crack of dawn to catch a train to Nuremberg. In fact, if you'll all excuse me—" she turned to her mother, her eyes signaling for support—"I'd better clear up the kitchen and get off to bed right away."

The car, with its SS driver, was still parked in the street an hour later, when Kurt drew back the curtains in his bedroom to check. He was shrugging awkwardly into his pajama jacket, with its abbreviated left sleeve, when Sophie tapped on the door. She came in, hairbrush in hand, her long tresses looping about the shoulders of the old pink velvet dressing gown she had brought back from Madrid, three years ago.

"To bed so early, brother dear! I was just going down to fix you and Father a nightcap."

"We've had it—out of a bottle." He sat down on the bed, buttoning up his jacket. "How about that crack-of-dawn train you're supposed to be catching?"

She frowned. "I'm going to run out of stories for that one. Can't you use your influence with the Fuehrer to get him posted to the eastern front or somewhere?"

"What influence? Voegler could run rings around me. Which is why—" he puffed up his pillow and sprawled back against it—"I wonder if it's wise to keep giving him such an obvious cold shoulder?"

"Kurt! What's that supposed to mean? I should let myself be pawed by that horror, so we can all keep in his good books?"

"I don't know, Maedel. Maybe we should dig up a phony fiancé for you from somewhere. I don't think Voegler's going to let up, and there's a lot of nastiness there, hidden behind that revolting façade."

"Well, let him try it on someone else." She sat down at his dressing table and went to work on her red hair with long vigorous brush strokes. "I'm much more interested in what's happening with you and Helga. She's owed me a letter for about three weeks."

He had been prepared for this, but he was still uncertain how to handle it. The memory of that voluptuous night's excesses with Helga and her brunette girl friend had already begun to fray and fade, leaving only certain disjointed images, sharply remembered, vivid dislocated jump-cuts in an otherwise out-of-focus blue film. But the guilt remained, haplessly enmeshed in the prurience. He had written to Helga only once—a few stilted lines from Warsaw.

He said, "Helga's in Berlin and I'm in Bavaria. So, nothing's happening."

"Hm-m. Can't say I like the sound of that. Girls who are attracted to one-armed fellers don't grow on trees, y'know."

His sister could make cracks like that now with a perfectly straight face, and it was good. But what Helga had done for him in restoring his male ego had been even better.

She came over to embrace him before she left. "Look after yourself, Herr Captain."

"You too. And listen—make sure Father burns those damn books in the morning, promise?"

"You know Father. I'll take care of it myself, soon as he's out of the house."

"And about Voegler—" He held her face between his hands.

"Yes, brother dear?"

"Tell him to get stuffed!"

CHAPTER EIGHT

I

WILLIAM SHAW, chief Washington correspondent of the weekly *News Summary,* had earned his *persona grata* standing in the White House by scrupulously observing both the spirit and the substance of President Roosevelt's "off-the-record" briefings. That is to say, he not only took care never to put in the President's mouth the actual words that had issued from it during the short privileged sessions Shaw enjoyed in the Oval Room, but also so "doctored" his copy as to effectively camouflage its source from all except the President himself, the President's immediate entourage and just about every other Washington-based newspaper and radio correspondent. As cover for the President, Shaw habitually used a ubiquitous "fly on the wall" in the White House. His publisher, the dyspeptic multimillionaire Hudson Smith, was of course privy to the special relationship between his top Washington man and the White House; had he not been, Shaw would have been out on his ear within a month of taking up his assignment to the nation's capital back in 1940. For whereas Shaw privately held the President in high esteem, Hudson Smith loathed with an almost radiant intensity everything Franklin Delano Roosevelt stood for. He tolerated Shaw's nonpartisan coverage from Washington for one good reason: as the acknowledged best-informed weekly summary of the Presidential scene in American journalism it was knocking spots off its

nearest rival and bringing in all the prestige advertising a vain
and venal publisher's heart could desire.

The new Lincoln-Continental waiting for Bill Shaw on the
Pennsylvania Avenue side of the White House had been a 1943
Christmas present from the publisher. The long-legged and nubile brunette waiting for him on the rear seat had been Shaw's
1942 Christmas present to himself. He gave her responsive thigh
a quick squeeze as the driver moved off into the traffic.

"Great stuff, honey. Ready to get some of it down while its
good and fresh?"

"Why, Mister Shaw, suh—" the notebook flipped open on
her knees—"what are those pickets out there gonna *think!*"

He dictated rapidly during the short ride to the office—key
phrases neatly stored away in their contexts as they had
emerged, Harvard-accented, through the smoke curling from
the President's long cigarette holder; phrases and patterns of
allusion he would have to work over, transpose, reshape into the
impersonal journalese of any good newsman with his ear close
to the ground. A stern training kept his secretary silent during
the swift ascent from the street to the *News Summary* suite of
offices in the National Press Club building. The same discipline
rationed his colleagues in the newsroom to knowing grins as
Shaw thumb-upped his way to his own room, to his stripped
desk, his uncovered portable typewriter and the neat stack of
copy paper. There was a nod and a pursed lip-smack for Mary-
Lou as she deposited his vacuum-flask within reach and quickly
withdrew to her guard post outside.

Shaw got his pipe going and started to type.

The pickets parading outside the White House were a micro-
cosm of the nation's divided conscience, and fears. The slo-
gans on the banners ranged from "WE'RE NOT SAVING
STALIN'S SKIN" to "EUROPE TODAY: TOMORROW
THE U.S.A.," with almost every shade of America-Firstism,
Catholic neutralism and pro-British sentimentalism represented
in between.

Inside the White House it was another story. The latest Gallup Poll had arrived on the President's desk. It showed that while 49 percent of the American people still wanted to keep their country nonbelligerent, the "Undecided" portion had shrunk from 9 to 5 percent, and the difference had clearly been picked up by the "Let's Get In" fraction, now mustering an impressive 46 percent.

The latest Gallup findings seemed to bolster the growing evidence of a significant shift of opinion in U.S. Catholic circles. And this, combined with the secret report to the White House last week by the President's personal representative in the Vatican, Myron Taylor, could provide another precious plank for the coffin Franklin D. Roosevelt has been so diligently constructing for American Neutralism.

With 24 million American adherents, the Catholic Church constitutes the most powerful single religious denomination in the U.S. Until now Catholicism, through its formidable lobbies in Washington, has been one of the mainstays of Congressional resistance to the President's pro-war politics. Its powerful Irish element is largely unmoved by the plight of its historic enemy, Britain; and its Polish constituency positively rejoiced over every Wehrmacht victory against the hated Russians. Above all Rome, the home of the Vatican, was also the capital city of Hitler's Axis partner, Catholic Italy, and it was clear that the Holy Father, while presenting a neutralist's face to the world, was far from displeased by the outcome of Hitler's death-struggle with atheist Russia. Reflecting the Pontiff's viewpoint was a formidable front line of lay Catholic leaders in the United States—Clare Booth Luce, United Steelworkers President Philip Murray, Joseph P. Kennedy, Jersey City Mayor Frank J. Hague and John W. McCormack. In any case, there was a concordat still in existence between Berlin and the Vatican, and it was up to the Holy Father himself to decide if and when it had been dishonored.

The first militant rumblings came from the liberal wing of the United States Catholic press last Christmas when Martin Bormann imposed his obligatory Yuletide prayer on all the churches of the Greater Reich. The rumblings were swelled by outraged growls from the conservative R.C. newspapers at Easter, when the traditional Catholic processions were banned and hundreds of parish priests in Poland and Czechoslovakia flung into concentration camps for such crimes as hearing confessions in their own native languages. When the Bishop of Muenster, Clemens von Galen, was put under house arrest for speaking out against this persecution, for the first time Archbishop Francis J. Spellman of New York came right out and coupled Adolf Hitler with Josef Stalin as agents of the anti-God, thereby earning the pontifical displeasure, it was said, of Pope Pius XII, who stubbornly clings to the belief that in a head-on clash between the Vatican and the Nazi Government the Church can only emerge the loser—a thesis that, to a growing body of American Catholic opinion, is not only unproven but spiritually irrelevant.

Hitler's announcement, before leaving for Madrid, that he would cut by half the state's next annual subsidy to the Catholic Church was greeted at first with shocked disbelief by the Catholic hierarchy of Spain and Portugal. The timing seemed perverse. Here was the German Fuehrer, about to sit down with those two Iberian pillars of the Holy Catholic Church, Franco and Salazar, to argue them into accepting a Wehrmacht role inside Spain and an extension of the Atlantic Wall to include Portugal's coastline—and the best preconference sweetener he could dream up was this unilateral breach of his concordat with the Vatican!

Cardinal Cerejeira, the Archbishop of Lisbon, in Rome for a briefing on the Madrid conference from the Pope's Secretary of State, Cardinal Maglione, was of two minds whether to bring pressure on President Salazar to withdraw from the conference as a mark of solidarity with the beleaguered Church in Germany. But Maglione counseled restraint. These were among the most difficult, perhaps the most dangerous, days in the Church's long history. But the Rock of Peter would weather the storm. Meanwhile, patience and conciliation, rather than provocation, were the path they must all tread.

From the Segreteria dello Stato, Cerejeira paid a call on Eugene Cardinal Tisserand, Secretary of the Eastern Congregation and the only non-Italian member of the Curia. The Frenchman was not among Cerejeira's best-loved brothers-in-Christ. His politics were, in fact, decidedly to the left of the Vatican center, to which Cerejeira believed he belonged. The cardinal from Lorraine made no bones about his contempt for Italian fascism and his dislike of practically everything Hitler stood for. He had even been reported as asserting that Bolshevism represented a much less serious danger for the Church than National Socialism. However, his views on Hitler's extraordinary diplomatic *gaffe* might be worth hearing.

"It's no *gaffe,* my dear Cerejeira," Tisserand said firmly. "There's a well-thought-out motive behind every one of Hitler's crude and bombastic *démarches.* When he can't use a carrot to get his donkeys moving, he picks up the stick. Hitler wants something Spain and Portugal are rightly unhappy to give—Wehrmacht bases throughout the peninsula. But he's not going to Madrid empty-handed. His timing is perfect. 'Let my men in,' he's going to say, 'and I'll lay off the Church in Germany, and the Vatican.' And if the Caudillo and your president fall for that, my dear Cerejeira, they deserve to be treated as donkeys, because no deal Hitler ever made has been worth the paper it was written on."

Kurt was spared the ordeal of a personal confrontation with Hitler on his return to the Berghof from Munich. For one thing, the Fuehrer had already begun an intensive study of Roman Catholic doctrine and dogma, with the object of isolating all articles of faith inimical to the New Order and preparing a common ground upon which National Socialism and a reformed Catholic Church might coexist. This would require radical changes in the Catechism and New Testament and a "purging of

Jewish mumbo jumbo" from the Old Testament. It was to be an open question, according to leaks from Bormann's secretariat, whether Jesus was the son of God, but an accepted fact that he was not Jewish but Aryan—the illegitimate son of a Roman soldier. The doctrine of transubstantiation was out—"a metamorphosis that is a mockery of all that is divine." Divorce would be permitted within the Church for Aryans married to Jews. The doctrine that all men are created equal in the sight of God would be rewritten "to conform with biological reality and National Socialist truth."

In addition to his theological preoccupations, the Fuehrer was bent on completing the security of Europe—in particular the Atlantic Wall—as the prelude to a final all-out assault on the shrunken but still vast territories held by Stalin and the Red Army. From Norway down to the French Pyrenees he had no worries. The fact that Britain, his last European enemy, had four and a half million men under arms gave him no restless nights. Even with her still-formidable Navy and impudently aggressive R.A.F., she utterly lacked the resources for a successful invasion of Nazi Europe and would be annihilated if she tried. The threat, if one existed, lay in the poorly defended Atlantic coastlines of Spain and Portugal—that and the imponderable twists and turns of Japanese foreign policy. Hitler distrusted his Oriental ally. He was convinced that when General Tojo deemed it opportune he would break his word and invade the Philippines. America would then launch the global war so dear to Roosevelt's heart, and Germany would have no option but to take sides with Japan. The stepping stones to a United States invasion of Europe were clearly marked on the map: The Azores, Madeira, the Canary Islands, the West African coast. Thence, an Anglo-American amphibious invasion practically anywhere they chose on the Iberian peninsula.

Two days after Kurt had set out on his tour of the New Order, Hitler had sent Admiral Wilhelm Canaris, head of the Wehrmacht Intelligence Bureau, on a mission to Madrid. He was to sound Franco out about an early heads-of-state meeting in the

Spanish capital to discuss Iberian security, linked with the prospect of German aid for the crumbling Spanish economy. From Madrid, Canaris was to proceed to Lisbon—provided that Franco raised no objections—to seek the participation of President Salazar.

From Madrid, Canaris had reported that Franco was more than ready to discuss German economic and military aid, provided that the sovereignty of Spain was not at issue. Similar sentiments were expressed by Portugal's dictator, and the conference was set for the week beginning May 15.

"The Fuehrer wants you in his Madrid entourage," Martin Bormann informed Kurt in a brisk two-minute interview. "You have two weeks in which to brief yourself about Spanish politics. I suggest you spend them at the Berlin Foreign Ministry."

For Kurt, any escape at this time from the Bavarian power-house represented a reprieve, even though it precipitated an emotional decision that he was not yet prepared to make vis-à-vis Helga Gruytens. And the later prospect of a week abroad in a country free of the stench, which still stayed with him, of human crematoria at once set his mind racing—only to stop short at the same dead end that had loomed across every tentative solution to his acute moral dilemma. He would lose himself in Madrid, make contact with underground Republican circles and find sanctuary—as many German antifascist fighters had done—while he planned his next move. But it was a selfish, stillborn idea. Within hours of even a suspicion of defection by anyone from Hitler's staff, the suspect's entire family would be put to torture by the Gestapo. Against that prospect, his own mental torment was a trifle.

There remained a minor service he should render his sister before leaving for Berlin. That night, after dinner, he paid his first call on Werner Voegler since their return to Obersalzberg five days previously. The SS officer, who was working at the desk in his quarters, closed his file and sprang up, smiling, as Kurt walked in.

"You must be psychic, my dear fellow! I was just going to drop in on you for a drink."

"You'd have found me packing, I'm afraid. I'm off to Berlin tomorrow for two weeks. Then Madrid, with the Fuehrer."

"I know about your Madrid trip, lucky bastard! Unfortunately there's only a company of Leibstandarte going with Oberfuehrer Rattenhuber, and he's just passed on to me his entire backlog of paperwork."

It was some relief at least to know that Voegler probably wouldn't be taking time off in Munich over the next two weeks. But after that, with the Fuehrer away from the Berghof . . .

Kurt said, "I doubt if I'll even get to a bullfight. I've had to promise Sophie I'll spend any spare time I get with this Spanish fellow she keeps writing to."

"Oh?" Voegler's eyebrows went up but the stiff little smile stayed graven on his long face. "What's this—Cupid's arrows, across the Pyrenees?"

"It would seem so. They've made a pact to get married when the war is over. I'm under orders to reassure this fellow—Pablo whatever-his-name-is—that my dear sister is remaining true to him."

Voegler made a face. "What a sacrilege, losing a lovely German girl like that to a dago! Well—" he raised his glass—"here's to your trip, but don't bother to pay my respects to Señor Pablo—" a second's pause as his eyes locked with Kurt's—"whatever-his-name-is."

Kurt was not going to spend his first night in that clinical little room in the Chancellery's SS quarters while he made up his mind what to do about Helga. He could have afforded the Adlon or the Bristol, and a room would have been found for him, on the double, on production of his gold-embossed Chancellery card. But he had had his fill, lately, of Party bigwigs and strutting Schutzstaffel officers, and so he chose the Europeischer Hof on Dorotheenstrasse, conveniently placed for both the Wilhelmstrasse and the Chancellery Secretariat. He had just returned to his room from his first day's work in the Foreign Ministry when the telephone rang and Helga's coolly reproachful voice came over the line.

"I'm still technically your secretary, you know. Why didn't you tell me you were in Berlin?"

"Hardly necessary, was it? You've found out quickly enough."

There was a grunt of displeasure in the earpiece and he could visualize the flash of her eyes, the contraction of her thin avid lips.

"Only because Fräulein Eppler happened to call me from the Berghof. Apparently you found time enough to let *her* know your whereabouts."

"Chancellery routine—you should know that. Anyway, how are you and what are you doing?"

"I'm back in the typists' pool, that's what I'm doing. But I'm to put myself—" her voice switched to a harsh imitation of Fräulein Eppler's—"at the Herr Captain's disposal, should he require my services."

"I don't think I'll have to bother you. I'm stuck at the Foreign Ministry for the next ten or twelve days, reading and note-taking. Then straight back to Obersalzberg."

There was a long silence. Then her voice again, much lower, barely audible. "I'm leaving the office in five minutes. Shall I drop in to see you?"

His hand tightened on the receiver. He was tongue-tied. Again her voice, warmer. "It's on my way home, Kurt."

"All right." *How did one fight it, when the anger really wasn't there?* "I'll meet you in the lobby."

They sat facing one another in the leather armchairs, with potted palms on one side and the reception desk a few paces away on the other. They spoke quietly and with outward politeness as they ripped into each other.

"Didn't you enjoy that night with Hanni and me?"

"Like a pig at a trough. It's taken me till now to get the taste out of my mouth."

"You're a prig, Kurt Armbrecht. I could think of a hundred men who'd give their right—" She broke off, twisting her mouth.

"I wish you the joy of them."

"Do you want to come home now and have me, just the two of us?"

"What would that prove—that we're a couple of nice normal people?"

A silence. Then: "What's bothering you most, Kurt—that Hanni and I did it together or that you did it to the two of us?"

"This is getting us nowhere. I have to dine with the head of the Spanish department, out at Wilmersdorf. May I give you a lift?"

It was getting on toward midnight when the taxi arrived to take him back to the hotel from the Foreign Ministry official's house. Directing the cab along the Kurfuerstendamm, he stopped it outside Helga's apartment building. Her windows were dark, and the guard in the downstairs lobby informed him that Fräulein Gruyten had gone out to dinner and wasn't back yet. He scribbled a note and slipped it under her front door.

"You were right. I *am* a prig. I'll call you tomorrow."

The first thing he noticed as he let himself into the hotel room was her scent. There was a bedside light on and she was asleep under the covers, her clothes neatly draped over a chair. She stirred as he slipped in beside her, then turned and reached down to him.

"My Paros Apollo," she murmured. "Don't send me home."

II

ACCOMPANYING HITLER to Madrid went—apart from his adjutants, secretaries, chauffeur, orderlies, interpreter, cook and his new doctor—Reichsmarschall Hermann Goering, Reichsleiter Bormann, Feldmarschaelle Keitel and Jodl, Joachim von Ribbentrop, Admiral Canaris, Albert Speer, Otto Dietrich and Heinrich Hoffman. The old Royal Palace overlooking the

173

Campo del Moro had been redecorated and refurbished to accommodate the German Fuehrer and his entourage and a company of the Leibstandarte Adolf Hitler paraded twice a day in the magnificent forecourt for the benefit of an admiring throng of gaping Madrileños. The Fuehrer's personal standard with its central swastika wreathed with gold oak leaves and the golden eagles at each corner flew from one of the palace flagstaffs.

Daily conferences took place between the heads of state every morning at the Generalisimo's official residence, El Prado, where Hitler's SS men shared guard duty—by special dispensation of Franco—with the Spanish dictator's colorful Moorish guards. Every evening around 6 P.M. a prepared statement was read out to the world's press by a Foreign Ministry official at the German Embassy on the Paseo de la Castellana, and Stimmer was there to answer more general questions concerning the Nazi regime and the New Order.

It was said that you only had to call for a waiter in English, from one of the pavement café tables on the Gran Via to be surrounded at once by a dozen plainclothes Gestapo agents and invited to sample the hospitality of the Seguridad HQ at the Puerta del Sol. Peter Waldheim, who had offered to show Kurt the city, while Hitler and Goering visited the Prado the second evening of the conference, thought there were probably about two hundred of Gestapo Mueller's lads shadowing every blue-eyed civilian venturing onto the virtually traffic-free streets and plazas of Madrid. "They're looking for British agents, émigrés, Dutchmen, and so on," he chuckled. "Half the time the poor fools finish up tailing one another."

They had wandered into the maze of narrow smelly streets to the east of the Gran Via and were trying the wine and *tapas* at their third port of call along the Calle de la Ballesta. The narrow shell-littered room was packed with the usual democratic assortment of white-collar and cloth-capped workers, whose ear-splitting *brouhaha* had dropped to a corporate murmur at the entry of the tall young Germans in their Wehrmacht uniforms.

"How can they eat this stuff?" Kurt muttered, palming a half-

174

chewed cube of salted cod from his mouth and letting it fall to the stone floor.

"They were eating cats and dogs not so very long ago. If the Chief really wants those bases in Spain he's got to come up with food, on top of everything else Franco's asking for."

A shabbily dressed Spaniard who had been sidling ever closer to the two German officers now whipped off his black beret, made a stiff bow from the waist and nervously introduced himself in halting German as former *Sargento* Alberto Arias, late of the Spanish Army. He turned back the lapel of his threadbare black jacket with a hand from which two fingers were missing.

"There, *meinen Herren!* You know this medal, yes?"

Kurt craned closer. Embossed in relief on the visible side of the white-metal disc was a steel helmet and swastika with a sword horizontally suspended behind two shields, one bearing the eagle emblem of Nazism, the other the Falange bundle of arrows. He turned the medal over, holding his breath against the garlic-laden sighs of the Spaniard. The inscription read, *División Española de Voluntarios en Rusia.*

"The *Ostmedaille.*" Waldheim gave Kurt a soft nudge. "Better known as the Frost Medal. Rare decoration, only given to 47,000 Spaniards who served with the Blue Division."

"Is right!" ex-*Sargento* Arias broke in eagerly. "Blue Division! See!" He spread his dismembered hand. "How you say—*vom Froste beschaedigt!*"

"No wonder they called themselves the Blue Division," Waldheim slurred the words quickly as he smiled and nodded to the Spaniard. "We were just leaving, *Sargento,* but allow me to offer you a glass of wine."

"*Con mucho gusto, meinen Herren!* Is great honor for my country, the Fuehrer in Madrid. Here—!" He fished a paper ticket out of his wallet and waved it before them. "The *corrida* on Sunday. I go. Manolete, Domingo Ortega, Pepe Luis Vásquez—but *que vale eso! I* go to salute Adolf Hitler, greatest matador in history of the world!"

"Is he putting us on, do you think?" Waldheim murmured.

And then aloud, as he handed the glass of wine to the *sargento:* "The Fuehrer won't be there, my friend. He's too fond of animals. But Herman Goering—he'll certainly be at the *corrida."* He made a gesture with his arms and hands, signifying girth. "Provided they can find a chair large enough for him in the Presidente's box."

The Spaniard cackled his appreciation of the German officer's pleasantry and translated it for other patrons of the *tasca* now crowding that end of the bar. And it seemed to Kurt that their roar of laughter was exaggerated, a release of tensions following a tilt at authority and about as natural as the outbursts at that first luncheon party in the Berghof. Offering Arias a cigarette, he slipped the pack quickly back in his pocket as the Spaniard raised the gift reverently to his nose, rolling his eyes in delight. Waldheim used the distraction to settle with the barman and drain his glass.

They left to a round of handclaps but were no sooner out on the pavement when the ex-sergeant came hurrying after them, the unpinned *Ostmedaille* nestling in the palm of his hand.

"For your cigarettes, *meinen Herren?"* His other hand gestured to their tunic pockets. "Rare decoration? Memory of Madrid?"

Waldheim turned away, chewing his lip in embarrassment. Kurt, frowning, dug his hand in his pocket and thrust the pack of cigarettes at the man. "Keep your medal," he snapped. "You earned it, didn't you? For God's sake, Peter, let's get out of here!"

On a loftier level, at El Prado, the would-be trading of honor for commodities was making sticky progress. Franco, and to a lesser extent Salazar, needed food (particularly wheat), heavy armaments, including shore batteries, and sophisticated weapons of all types. But neither of the Latin dictators saw the need for Wehrmacht divisions on Iberian soil or for the full-scale militarization of their coastlines, as Hitler was urging. Franco would concede a stiffening of German technicians in the Spanish army and air force; Salazar would accept the principle of a mutual-defense pact between his country and Spain and the deployment of tactical divisions of the Spanish army along the land frontier between their two countries, but both rulers politely but firmly declined Hitler's offer to "improve" the defenses of Madeira, the Cape Verde islands and the Canaries.

The weather being exceptionally warm for May, it was decided to give the reception for the diplomatic corps, Falange chiefs and Madrid aristocracy in the Retiro Park, a few blocks south of the German Embassy. Entrance was gained through the majestic gates of the Plaza de la Independencia, which were closed to all general traffic from 6 P.M. and the entire plaza ringed by the *policia armada* wearing the field-gray uniform recommended by Heinrich Himmler at the end of the Civil War. Kurt's instructions were to seek out any minor notabilities with whom he might have a language in common and to let slip an "unguarded" allusion or two to Germany's new secret weapons, shortly to be deployed against Great Britain and on the eastern front; but for the first hour or so he was cheated of prey. The dark bejeweled ladies with their strutting undersized escorts alighted from prewar Rolls-Royces and Mercedes and advanced through the honor guard of blond Leibstandarte giants to be greeted by Hitler and Franco. They then immediately attached themselves to one of the several circles congealing around Goering, Ribbentrop, Bormann, Admiral Canaris and the two *Feldmarschaelle* on Hitler's staff. None of the ambassadors of nations at war with Germany, or of émigré European governments, had been invited to the reception, but the United States ambassador had been advised by the State Department to put in a brief and formal appearance, and Kurt noted, to his amusement, the rigid thumbs-to-the-seams postures of both the American diplomat and the Fuehrer as the mumbled introduction was made by Franco.

There was a stir of interest and a craning of heads when a short stocky figure wearing the black cassock with red piping, the red *moiré* zuchetto and sash, and the buckle shoes of a papal nuncio advanced slowly and broadly smiling between the ranks of the Leibstandarte, to be received by Adolf Hitler. As Kurt edged around the fringe of the loose crowd to get a better view of the prelate, he heard the name muttered from all sides.

"Monsignor Giovanni Donati . . ."

Hitler had taken the archbishop's hand and was now averting his face as the nuncio addressed him with unmistakable affability, though his words did not carry to where Kurt stood. It was extraordinary how unlike the northern European concept of a prince of the church was this tubby, neckless Donati, with his craggy face, wide mouth and broad hooked nose. As the nuncio muttered something quietly to the Fuehrer before moving on through the dictator's immediate entourage, Kurt was piecing together what he remembered from his Berlin research notes.

Born in 1881 of *mezzadri* peasant stock in the tiny mountain village of Manostrana in the Abruzzi. Ordained a priest at age twenty-three, served as military chaplain in World War I. Toured France and Germany in 1921 as secretary of the Council for the Propagation of the Faith, was made a bishop a few years later, then sent to Bulgaria as Apostolic Delegate. Moved, as an archbishop, to Istanbul, in 1935, and remained a Vatican diplomat in Turkey and Greece until 1942, when he succeeded the papal nuncio in Madrid on that prelate's transfer to France. Held in affection by Eugenio Pacelli, who, as a young Roman priest, had invigilated Donati's written examination for his doctorate. A man of deep but unpretentious piety. No intellectual.

Ten minutes later, when Kurt broke free from a would-be Spanish biographer of Hitler, he noticed that the Leibstandarte honor guard was no longer in its place and, as he scanned the reception area of the Retiro enclosure, it occurred to him that the Fuehrer had made a characteristically brusque exit to show his irritation with Franco's stance at the conference. Then he looked away toward the far end of the lawn, and his jaw fell open. A long line of Hitler's SS men stood at ease facing the marquees and buffet tables. Beyond them and thus protected from any interruption, two figures paced the grass side by side, clearly absorbed in deep and earnest conversation: one of them was Adolf Hitler, the other Giovanni Donati.

The man calling him on the telephone at the Royal Palace identified himself as Federico Jiménez, a friend of Sophie's from her student days in Madrid. He said that he had an urgent message for Kurt from Munich which he was required to deliver personally. If the Herr Captain could meet him in five minutes outside the Teatro Real, across the Plaza de Oriente from the Royal Palace, they could take a little walk and he could pass on the message. The man's German was not very good and the voice crackled with nervous tension.

There were a fair number of pedestrians taking their Saturday evening *paseo* around the huge plaza, but as Kurt, breathing hard, reached the pavement outside the theater a young man standing on the corner of Calle Felipe V quickly folded up his newspaper and came toward him.

"Captain Armbrecht? Federico Jiménez." They shook hands, and Kurt fell into step with the Spaniard as he headed for the next corner and turned into Calle Carlos III. Sophie's friend was a good deal too thin for his height. He wore thick-framed spectacles. His white shirt was crisp and clean, but neatly patched just below one of the tips of the collar.

He said, "I have bad news for you, Captain Armbrecht. Your father has been arrested by the Gestapo and is now in the concentration camp of Dachau."

CHAPTER NINE

I

MARTIN BORMANN was staring at Kurt across the desk in the Royal Palace library as if the younger man had taken leave of his senses.

"You are asking me to interrupt the Fuehrer at this moment over a purely personal matter involving your father? What's the matter with you, Armbrecht? Have you been overindulging in this filthy Spanish wine?"

Kurt swallowed hard. If there was one person he couldn't afford to antagonize at this stage it was the dour, bull-necked watchdog of Adolf Hitler's waking hours. He said, "Please forgive me, Herr Reichsleiter. The fact is, I've only just heard that my father has been arrested and sent to Dachau. I'm naturally upset. Obviously there's been some mistake, somewhere."

"Obviously?" Bormann snapped. "How do we know that?" He snatched up a sheet of paper and tossed it to one side in a gesture of irritation and impatience. "Look, Armbrecht, you know perfectly well I can't allow the Fuehrer to be bothered with such trivia—"

"My father—"

"*Trivia,* Armbrecht, to one with the Fuehrer's responsibilities! From midday today he has been engaged in the most profound theological discussion with Monsignor Donati, and they're still talking! The whole future of our relations with the Vatican might be hanging on the outcome. At the same time I'm being pestered by Ribbentrop to get the Fuehrer's approval of the draft text for a final joint communiqué. The Chief won't even talk to him on the telephone! And you come in here, with this tale about your—!"

"It's no tale, Herr Reichsleiter," Kurt cut in quietly. "My father is a professor at Munich University—"

"I know that! Look here, Armbrecht—"

"—and at this moment," Kurt persisted, "is behind barbed wire with a bunch of criminals, in conditions I've seen for myself—"

"Armbrecht!" The deputy leader of the Party was up on his feet, glowering. Kurt sprang swiftly to attention.

"Herr Reichsleiter!"

"Don't try my patience! The interview is over. The best I can do for you is have a word with Gruppenfuehrer Mueller. Try calling him at our Embassy in about half an hour."

Half an hour seemed an eternity. He decided to take a taxi across the city to Number 4 on La Castellana and try to see Mueller in person.

The taxi took him through the heart of Madrid, the Puerta del Sol, but the young German officer staring fixedly out of the side window saw nothing of the crowded pavements, the crippled lottery-ticket sellers, the dawdling *putas* and the street vendors, still hawking their little paper Nazi flags. All he could see—and he couldn't blot out the image—was a naked elderly village schoolmaster hanging by the thumbs from a gibbet.

He was saluted by the *policia armada* guarding the front gates of the German Embassy but had to produce his Chancellery card before being allowed to pass under the two huge stone eagles dominating the entrance to the building. The taxi ride had taken less than a quarter of an hour, and he was kept waiting another twenty minutes in an entrance hall alive with the comings-and-goings of bureaucrats and messengers before a burly civilian marched over to him, gave him the "German salute" and invited him up to the first floor.

Kurt knew "Gestapo" Mueller only by repute, which was how

181

the vast majority of Germans ardently hoped they would ever know the chief of the Secret State Police. He had never even set eyes on him and was at first somewhat disarmed by the pleasant-featured little man who greeted him politely from behind an orderly, almost document-free desk.

"My apologies for keeping you waiting, Captain, so much traffic at this time over the teleprinter and telephones to the Reich. Please sit down." Carefully adjusting the trouser creases of his well-tailored gray suit, Mueller resettled himself in his chair and studied Kurt for a few minutes in silence, his bright-blue eyes seeming to flicker over his visitor rather than bore into him. His expression had become solemn, even touched with concern.

"It is a fact, I'm afraid," he began slowly, "that your father, Professor Armbrecht, has been taken into protective custody on suspicion of activities inimical to the state." It was a well-worn formula covering arbitrary arrest and imprisonment without trial, but Mueller made it sound almost innocuous, a rather tiresome formality—until the image of the village schoolmaster flashed in again. Kurt remained silent, sitting stiffly upright on the edge of his chair.

"I must confess, Armbrecht," Mueller went on, "that I am not totally surprised by this turn of events. You will be aware that our people looked very thoroughly into your parents' background before you were recommended for your present post. We found, then, that your father had never been more than . . . lukewarm, shall we say? in his attitude to National Socialism. In point of fact, if it had not been for the acute shortage of faculty staff at Munich University, the Senate would probably have dispensed with his services by now. Your own background was of course unexceptionable. We had ample proof of your loyalty to the regime and of the political friction between yourself and the Herr Professor. In such circumstances"—Mueller indulged a gentle smile—"we try to avoid visiting the sins of the father upon the son."

"Sins, Herr Gruppenfuehrer?" Kurt asked, shakily. "What sins is he supposed to have committed?"

"The case comes under Section IV A of the R.S.H.A., subsection Ib, concerned with liberalism, rumors, undermining of morale, defeatism, et cetera. I understand our Munich people have taken some very damaging depositions from the faculty, the Students' Association and one or two Party officials. It's all very distressing for me, Armbrecht, as I'm sure you will appreciate. I haven't even been able to bring myself to send the Chief a memo about it. In fact, Bormann says he would hold it up, anyway, to avoid upsetting him at this time." He spread his hands, giving Kurt a sad smile.

"Herr Gruppenfuehrer—" Kurt swallowed hard—"my father is not a criminal, and I don't believe he's been disloyal to Germany. I ask, as a personal favor, that he be released from Dachau and put under house arrest, at least until your investigations are complete."

"Armbrecht, you must be reasonable. This kind of investigation takes time, maybe months. We just haven't the men to spare to keep a run-of-the-mill academic—if you'll forgive me —under constant surveillance."

"A civilian prison, then. Anywhere but—"

"With common criminals?" Mueller waggled his head. "The concentration camps were established precisely to accommodate cases like your father's. He won't be ill-treated. Dachau is the best-run camp in the whole of the Reich."

"I was in the place, only four weeks ago, Herr Gruppenfuehrer. I can't bear the thought of my father being there now."

Mueller's long upper lip seemed to freeze solid. He was looking over Kurt's shoulder, all amiability sapped from his pale compact features. "We all of us have to put up with certain unpleasantnesses these days, Captain Armbrecht," he muttered. "I would suggest you don't press the matter at this stage."

The communiqué released at midday on Sunday, May 21, 1944, was an arabesque of diplomatic noncommunication. It spoke of the "fruitful and fraternal discussions between the heads of state of Germany, Spain and Portugal and of the "spirit of ideological harmony informing the talks."

Stripped of its euphemistic verbiage, the communiqué spelled out the almost complete failure of Hitler's initiatives in Madrid. As Otto Dietrich put it to Kurt while the Fuehrer's train sped northward from Hendaye, "We're coming away with nothing we wouldn't have anyway, if our enemies ever decide to have a go at Spain and Portugal. What have we got for the extra wheat and gas that that little so-and-so Franco squeezed out of us? A pair of bloody bull's ears, given to the Reichsmarschall by Manolete at yesterday's *corrida!*" The Fuehrer's press spokesman let out a harsh laugh. "Did you hear what the Chief said when Bormann told him about it?"

Kurt shook his head.

"He said, 'If Goering comes anywhere near me with those obscenities I'll have his own ears sent to Franco, with his fat head still holding them apart.' " Dietrich put out his cigarette and stared past Kurt toward the distant Atlantic horizon. "Incredible, the calm way the Chief is taking this whole Madrid fiasco. After the first day's talks last Monday he kept Ribbentrop, Bormann and me up till about three o'clock, screaming his head off about Franco's ingratitude. On Tuesday he damn near walked out, when Salazar started to hem and haw about the defense pact. It took Muñoz Grandes the whole of lunchtime to coax the Chief into going back into the conference room. And then—presto!—he meets Donati at the Retiro reception that night and he's been a changed man ever since. 'Let's settle for what we can get,' he tells Ribbentrop, 'I can't waste any more time on these little tin Caesars.' I don't know what you make of it, Armbrecht, but something very peculiar's going on."

Kurt's thoughts were a thousand miles away, but the uttering of his name and the sudden pause in Dietrich's chatter interrupted his brooding. He blinked inquiringly at the press chief.

"Donati—" Dietrich stared back at him, irritably. "What do *you* think he's been up to in these private sessions with the Chief?"

"I've really no idea. Trying to sweet-talk him into laying off the Church, presumably."

"Brilliant!" Dietrich snorted. "Our Fuehrer goes into virtual seclusion with an Italian archbishop in Madrid for the sole purpose of being lectured about his feud with the Catholics. You can do better than that, my dear fellow."

"To be perfectly frank—"

"I know, I know," Dietrich cut in. "You're not particularly interested. Well, all I can say is you'd better be! I've been with the Chief for eighteen years now, and I've never known anything like this happen before."

"Like what, in fact?"

"Like the Chief taking to an absolute stranger—and a Vatican diplomat, at that—as if he had found a long-lost brother. There's something extremely odd about it, Armbrecht, and I don't mind admitting it's got me worried."

Kurt was not an eyewitness to Doctor Otto Dietrich's reactions, a week later, when Bormann requested the press chief to prepare a "guidance" memorandum to the Party press concerning an impending announcement in the *Osservatore Romano* and over the Vatican Radio. This would state that Monsignor Giovanni Donati was being relieved of his duties as Apostolic Nuncio in Madrid to take up, with immediate effect, the office of Special Papal Legate to the Obersalzberg headquarters of Adolf Hitler.

"We don't want any editorial comment or speculation on this," Bormann grunted, averting his eyes from Dietrich's flabbergasted face. "We want no photographs of Donati, but they are to run a brief biography, emphasizing the Archbishop's peasant background. Oh yes—and get them to recall that a similar appointment was made by the Vatican to Kaiser Wilhelm's head-quarters at Kreuznach during the war of 1914–18. The special Papal Legate then was the present Pope, Eugenio Pacelli."

II

FRÄULEIN EPPLER had seen no reason why Kurt should not leave the Fuehrer's train at Munich and spend the night at his parents' home, provided that he would be back in the Berghof by noon next day. She gave no hint whatsoever that she knew about his father's arrest, and in the light of Bormann's apparent concern not to "upset" Hitler it was conceivable that no mention had yet been made of the matter to any of the staff in daily contact with the Fuehrer. Certainly, no reference to the professor's arrest had yet appeared in the German press, copies of which had been freely available to Kurt during his week in Madrid.

His mother answered the doorbell at No. 17 Nikolaistrasse and fell against him at once, weeping her relief.

"I've been praying for you to come! Oh Kurt—promise me you'll get him out of that terrible place!"

"There, Mother, there! Of course we're going to get him out." He eased her away, closing the front door behind him. "You and I are going to sit down quietly and you're going to tell me all about it." He guided her toward the sitting-room. "Where's Sophie?"

"I don't know!" His mother collapsed into the nearest armchair and buried her face in her hands. "She's disappeared and I haven't had a word from her! I'm going out of my mind with worry, Kurt! *What's happening to us?!"*

"Now, try to calm down, Mother—please. I want to know everything, about Father and about Sophie. Start from the beginning, and try to leave nothing out."

The story emerged, haltingly, between sobs. And as it unfolded it began to make its own hideous logic to the tense young officer sitting facing his mother, to confirm all the fears he had

186

been assailed by during these past three days. There had been a telephone call for Sophie from Obersturmbannfuehrer Voegler two days after the Fuehrer's train left for Madrid. It had left her upset, but she had volunteered nothing to her mother, and Margit Armbrecht hadn't tried to press her about it. The loud banging on the front door at about three o'clock next morning had aroused them, and when Sophie and her mother came hurrying downstairs after Walter Armbrecht they found him arguing heatedly with four uniformed SS men, all wearing the SD insignia on their left sleeves. The leader, a *Hauptsturmfuehrer,* had cut the argument short by pulling a revolver, pointing it at the professor and giving him "exactly five minutes" to get dressed and pack a small "overnight bag." Kurt's mother and sister had been ordered into the kitchen but, before leaving, the professor had shouldered their guard aside and embraced them both. "It's all a ridiculous mistake," he had told them. "Don't worry about me. I'll be back in time for breakfast." Two more men, these in civilian clothes, had entered the house while the professor was being taken out to one of the waiting cars and, with the two women still confined to the kitchen, had searched the house—"God knows for what!"—from basement to roof, concentrating for over an hour on Walter Armbrecht's study and eventually making off with two cardboard cartons full of papers and books.

When 9 A.M. came around and there was still no sign of their father, Sophie had left her mother in a state of nervous collapse and hurried to the Munich headquarters of the Sicherheitsdienst. After being kept waiting for nearly two hours, she was curtly informed that her father had been taken into protective custody under Article 1 of the Decree of February 28, 1933, for the Protection of People and State, and would be transferred to Dachau later that day, when his present interrogation was completed. He would be allowed no visitors, no food parcels or correspondence. Further requests for information should be put in writing, through the appropriate channels. For a while after Sophie's return home the two women had sat in stunned, impotent dismay. Then Margit Armbrecht had proposed putting a call through to the Berghof, to find out how they could contact Kurt in Madrid. But Sophie had stopped her, arguing that they should not involve him until she had tried another channel, which she seemed quite optimistic about.

"Poor Sophie—" Margit Armbrecht shook her head distractedly—"I wasn't much help to her, the state I was in by then. She said if I didn't get some sleep I'd be no use to anyone, so I let her give me one of her tranquilizers and put me to bed. But it didn't work very well, and I was still awake when the doorbell rang—I don't know how long afterward—and I went to the bedroom window and saw a car outside in the street and an SS driver standing in the forecourt. Then Sophie came out, and got into the back of the car, and off it went." His mother found a handkerchief and gave her nose a hard blow.

"And that was the last you saw of her?"

She nodded. "But she telephoned me the next day, which was Thursday. She refused to tell me where she was, but she said she was all right and I wasn't to worry about her, because what she was doing might take a little more time, but it was all to do with getting Father released. Then she gave me the name and telephone number of this Señor Federico Jiménez in Madrid and said I was to try to contact him if I didn't hear from her by noon the next day and to ask him to get in touch with you, very discreetly, and give you the news of Father's arrest. Well, she didn't call me back and it took me all day Friday and most of Saturday to get through to Señor Jiménez. I gave him Sophie's message and—oh, Kurt, there's been no word from poor Sophie since, and nothing from your father!"

He got up, walked over to sit on the arm of her chair, and held her tight to him. "I'm back now, Mother, and I'm going to take care of everything. The first thing is to find Sophie, and I've an idea where to go. But I haven't much time, so I want you to stay here until I call you. Will you be all right?"

She blew her nose again. "I'd better get you something to eat, if you're going out."

"I'm not hungry. No, honestly, Mother," he insisted over her protestations. "I had lunch on the train. Just try to be brave and stay quietly here and I'll telephone you very soon."

He took his suitcase up to his room, tidied himself up in the bathroom across the landing and, after another few reassuring words to his mother, set off for the Briennerstrasse, a brisk twenty minutes' walk southward along the broad Leopold and Ludwig Strassen.

The house Voegler had stopped off at after their visit to Dachau was an imposing old four-story mansion at the Tuerkenstrasse end of Briennerstrasse, lying back from what obviously had been a railed-off concrete courtyard before the scrap-iron collection squads had gone to work. A broad flight of stone steps led up into a lofty entrance hall, where half a dozen private mailboxes showed that the house had been converted into separate apartments. Kurt studied the nameplates fixed to the boxes. No "Voegler" on any of them, but the one on the box marked *Stock 4* was blank. He started to climb the carpeted steps toward the top floor.

There was a single door of broad polished mahogany on the landing and a bell-push in the wall to one side. He put his finger to it and pressed once, then again with four quick jabs, the way he had always heralded his return home from college in the old days. After a long silence, a latch clicked and the door opened inward, first a fraction, then wide. Sophie was standing in the shadowy hallway, blinking at him with red-rimmed eyes. She had a bathtowel wrapped about her and was barefooted.

He had thought about this moment during the walk from Nikolaistrasse, and how they would both handle it. He said, "I came as soon as I could, Liebchen. Now let's you and I get this ghastly mess sorted out."

Sophie didn't embrace him, and Kurt hadn't expected it. She moved aside to let him in, closed the door and followed him into a spacious sitting room comfortably, if incongruously furnished with a mixture of Biedermeier and late-nineteenth-century *Jugendstil,* reflecting the taste of a petit-bourgeois Philistine come

189

up in the world. A third-rate Alpine landscape oil painting and two framed photographs, one of Heinrich Himmler wearing an expression akin to a smile and one of a squad of half-naked men, decorated the walls.

Sophie hadn't uttered a word yet. She had crossed to one of the two windows overlooking the Briennerstrasse, and was standing there with her back to him, one hand pressed to the knot in the bath towel. There were bruises on the back of her upper arms and what looked like welts on the pale flesh below the coil of her red hair. Kurt closed his eyes tightly for a moment. Then, "Get some clothes on, Sophie, I'm taking you home."

"It's no use." Still, she wouldn't face him. "I have to stay on here. There's another small point—my clothes have all been locked away."

She didn't resist when he went to her and turned her gently around. But the deadness in her green eyes was something worse than outright rejection.

"I'll call a taxi," he said. "You can come as you are." And then, with a spurt of anger, "you're certainly not staying here!"

Turning away from him, she said, "How is Mother?"

"Worried to death, wondering what's happened to you. Is there a telephone in this place?"

"Please, Kurt, don't call her. Not yet. Not till we've talked." She was moving erratically about the room, like a sluggish, captive animal. He stayed silent, waiting for her to start. When she finally lowered herself to the edge of one of the two facing sofas, he lit a cigarette and gave it to her. Then he sat down opposite her.

"He phoned me last Monday, while I was having lunch at home, inviting me to meet him here that evening. When I made one of my usual excuses, he said, 'All right, but I would suggest you make a note of my telephone number. It's very likely you might want to talk to me tomorrow.' I suppose Mother has told you how they came for Father that night, and what they told me next day at the Sicherheitsdienst headquarters?"

"She did. But I'd like the name of whoever it was you saw there."

"I'm sorry, I was too upset and confused to ask. All I can remember is he was a *Sturmbannfuehrer.* Anyway, I called Voegler on my way back home. I couldn't believe he had anything personally to do with Father's arrest, but obviously he had known something was going to happen and, with you away in Madrid, he was the only person I knew with any kind of real authority. He acted very cool. He said he could promise nothing but that he was staying in Munich until the Fuehrer got back from Spain and if I wanted to keep him amused—as he put it —while he looked into the matter I'd better come prepared for a few days' stay. She drew hard on her cigarette and let the smoke slowly out as she stared past him, frozen-faced. "So I came—"

"Why didn't you try to reach me in Madrid—right then?"

"I thought about it. But I decided not to do anything that might jeopardize you until I heard what Voegler had to say. Above all, I wanted to talk to Father and I felt sure that Voegler could at least arrange that. And, as a matter of fact, he did. . . ." She leaned forward and took a long time crushing her cigarette stub into an ashtray.

"Tell me about it."

"It was the next morning—Thursday. He hadn't done a thing about Father, like calling anyone or anything. 'We'll get around to that,' he told me, 'after you've earned the right to ask favors of an SS officer.' "

Suddenly she was out of the sofa and over by the window again.

"Well, I thought I had more than earned the right, that first afternoon as well as most of the night. Do you want me to tell you, brother dear, how an officer of the Leibstandarte Adolf Hitler expresses his respect for German womanhood?"

He said through his teeth, "Don't twist the knife, Sophie. Go on about Father."

"I told Voegler in the morning that he was a louse and a cheat and had neither the intention nor the influence to do anything about Father. He just laughed, picked up the telephone and got through to the commandant's office at Dachau. I was ordered out of the bedroom while he talked, but about ten minutes later he yelled for me and handed me the receiver and there was—" her voice faltered, "there was Father, on the line. They gave us hardly any time at all, just enough for him to say he was in good spirits and we weren't to worry because when Kurt got back from Madrid he would get everything straightened out. But you know Father. I could tell from his voice what he must have been going through.

"After that, I forced myself to keep Voegler in good humor. I cooked meals, laundered his shirts and did all the household chores, while he lounged about reading or just watching me with that ghastly grin on his face. The one thing I couldn't do, how-ever hard I tried, was show any enthusiasm when he put his hands on me, which—" she gave a little shudder—"was almost incessantly for the first twenty-four hours. He went out Thursday afternoon, telling me he was going to have 'a little chat' with his friends at SD headquarters, and that's when I phoned Mother and gave her Federico's number, because by then I was begin-ning to realize that Voegler was in no hurry to get Father out of Dachau and I had decided to give him till noon the next day, or else I was going to walk out.

"Well, when he came back he brought a lot of food and said he had put certain wheels in motion. But when I gave him my ultimatum he turned nasty. All he had to do, he said, was make one phone call and Father would be shot 'while trying to escape,' which he would do if I left here without his permission. From then on—" Sophie paused, then continued in a quieter, almost expressionless voice—"until yesterday, when he left for the Berg-hof, he treated me like a whore. It didn't matter, because that's just what I felt like anyway. But the evening before he left, when I refused to let him do something—" the voice fell to a whisper —"unspeakable, he laid into me with his belt."

She turned away from the window to gaze across the room at her brother, sitting bolt upright and motionless on the sofa. "I came very close to killing him that night in his sleep. I had the kitchen knife ready in my hand. I couldn't do it because I realized that it would amount to murdering Father and Mother and probably you. Don't you think it's amusing, Kurt, the thought of me stabbing someone to death—all that blood?"

"Where are your clothes, Sophie?"

"It's no use, even if you could get the trunk open. If I don't answer that phone in there, anytime he calls from the Berghof during the next couple of days, he's going to give the signal to Dachau immediately. If I behave myself he's going to call me on Thursday and tell me where he's hidden the key to the trunk. There'll be an SS car downstairs, half an hour later, to take me to see Father at Dachau. I'll get my 'further instructions' when I report back here afterward. Oh yes—and he advises me to think up a good convincing story for you and Mother and not to answer anyone who rings the front door. He's already been in touch with my boss to tell him that I've been given a special assignment by the SS. A very thorough gentleman, Obersturmbannfeuhrer Voegler."

"And unbelievably stupid!" Kurt stood up, tight-lipped. "On your evidence alone, I'm going to have Father released and that swine broken. Come over here, little sister."

She came, hesitantly, to him and he put his arm around her and nuzzled her hair. "Now listen to me. Voegler's almost certainly bluffing about Father, but we can't take a chance on it. Can you bear to stay here another twenty-four hours?"

"Just tell me what to do."

"Call one of your girl friends and ask her to bring you some clothes and anything else you need. Leave me to explain things to Mother. I'm taking the next train to Berchtesgaden and I'm going to speak to the Fuehrer. But if Voegler should call you before I do tomorrow, don't let on that you've seen me or told me anything about what's been happening here. Let him believe that as far as Mother or I know you've just disappeared. And listen, Maedel—whatever you did here, you did out of love of Father. No one's going to forget that."

III

THE EAGLE'S NEST was an octagonal pavilion isolated six thousand feet up on the summit of the Kehlstein, towering above and behind the Berghof. Acting on a whim of the Fuehrer's, Martin Bormann had the plans for this fantastic man-made eyrie drawn up in 1936, and the project was completed three years later at a cost of more than 30 million marks. From the Berghof a nine-mile-long road wound upward, to plunge deep into the heart of the rock below the peak. At the end of the underground road a lofty bronze portal opened into a marble hall. Here the visitor entered a capacious elevator of polished brass, furnished with comfortable seats, a deep carpet and two telephones. The elevator shaft rose vertically 165 feet into the colonnaded pavilion itself, whose lofty windows offered breathtaking views of the Bavarian and Austrian Alps, with Salzburg in the distance. One of the few foreigners ever to set foot in the Eagle's Nest, the French Ambassador François-Poncet, had asked himself whether this extraordinary edifice was "the work of a normal mind or of one tormented by megalomania and haunted by visions of domination and solitude?" That had been back in October 1938. In fact, Hitler's interest in the eyrie had quickly waned and he hadn't visited it since the invasion of Poland. He reported the air on the summit to be "insupportably thin," to the chagrin of Bormann, who could think of no practical solution to the problem—according to Peter Waldheim's apocryphal account—except to reduce the height of the mountain, "a self-defeating solution if ever there was one!"

Now, it seemed that the Fuehrer had undergone a change of heart, or was at least oxygenating his lungs better under the more robust diet prescribed by Doctor Morell's successor. He had made an ascent to the Eagle's Nest within an hour of his return to the Berghof and had given orders on his return for it to be made habitable and for his orderlies to install cooking facilities and sleeping bunks for themselves in the marble hall at the foot of the elevator shaft.

When Kurt sought an interview with Bormann the evening of his arrival from Munich, he was told that the Reichsleiter was in private and continuous conference with the Fuehrer but would probably be able to spare him five minutes the following morning. An appointment was later confirmed for noon the next day.

Bormann's eyes narrowed as he stared at Kurt across his desk in the Party secretariat. "You want to see the Fuehrer on a matter of great urgency? If so, you'd better tell me what it's about."

"It's about my father. I now can prove that his arrest was an abuse of the law."

Bormann drew in a long breath. "Let me have the circumstances. But make it short, Armbrecht."

Kurt, who had been prepared for this, said, "The arrest was trumped up between a certain SS officer and the Munich SD. The officer is using it as sexual blackmail against my sister, Sophie. At the right time we can produce all the necessary evidence."

"I see . . . And the name of this officer."

"With your permission, Herr Reichsleiter, I would rather divulge that to the Fuehrer himself."

"Well, then, Armbrecht," Bormann said heavily, "we'd better get one or two things straight. In the first place, you're going to say nothing about this affair to the Fuehrer. I wouldn't permit it in Madrid, and there are even better reasons for not bothering him with such trivialities at this time. Is that perfectly clear?"

Kurt remained silent.

"Now, as to the arrest itself. I was given a full report by Gruppenfuehrer Mueller on the train journey from Madrid, and this business of the unnamed SS officer and your sister—even if it's true—has absolutely no bearing on your father's guilt. Depositions have been made by members of the university faculty proving his hostility to National Socialism and citing among many examples—" Bormann's eyes flicked to a sheet of foolscap typescript on his blotter—"the outrageous criticism of Alfred Rosenberg's work on Charlemagne, in an article contributed by your father to the *Historische Zeitschrift.*"

"But that's absurd!" Kurt burst out. "A purely academic periodical, completely unknown to ninety-nine percent of the public!"

"The same could have been said of the Communist Manifesto back in 1919, and look where that got us! There's a deposition from the Students' Association accusing Professor Armbrecht of a thinly disguised slander of the Fuehrer in a lecture he gave on Robespierre only last year."

The room had suddenly become chilly.

"A deposition has been filed by your father's neighbor, Ortsgruppenleiter Krenkler, listing a number of defeatist statements by the Herr Professor, including—and I quote—that 'the New Order is an abomination in the minds of every civilized person.' "

"That's a downright lie. I happened to be present at that conversation. Krenkler's completely distorting my father's words."

"Of course he is," Bormann grunted sarcastically. "When did any enemy of the state not complain about his words being twisted?"

"Herr Reichsleiter, my father hasn't been tried yet. With the greatest respect, isn't it a bit early to be referring to him in those terms?"

Bormann's scowl dissolved slowly into a little smile. "I stand corrected. I understand that at a specially convened meeting of the university senate this afternoon Professor Walter Armbrecht is going to be stripped of all academic honors."

"Before he's even been tried! But that's monstrous!"

"Some of us might call it patriotism and loyalty to the state.

But you would agree, Armbrecht, that this business of your sister and the SS officer looks like pretty thin evidence in the light of these depositions taken by the SD?"

"My sister," Kurt said, struggling to keep his voice steady, "could have saved my father from being arrested by going to bed with a certain Leibstandarte officer. Since then she has been tyrannized and debauched by him as the price of my father's eventual release from Dachau. If the Fuehrer wishes it, she is ready to—" He stopped in mid-sentence as Bormann's clenched fist came down on the desk.

"For the *last* time, Armbrecht, leave the Chief out of this! When will you grasp the fact that loyalty to the Fuehrer—and that includes concern for his peace of mind—comes far above any feelings a son might have for his parents? The charges brought against your father will be thoroughly investigated and he will receive a fair trial. And if he's found guilty, you should rejoice that another enemy of the Reich has got his deserts. As for your sister—" Bormann leaned back in his chair, frowning— "your *unmarried,* twenty-six-year-old sister, it seems to me there's something neurotic about her behavior. No normal patriotic German girl would bring such a complaint against an officer of the Leibstandarte Adolf Hitler. These men are our elite. They've taken a sacred oath to lay down their lives for the Fuehrer. It should be regarded as an immense honor to share the bed of a Leibstandarte officer, and an even greater honor to bear a child by him. My best advice to you, Armbrecht, is to get your priorities straight. The work you've been given to do by the Chief is of great importance, and I know he holds you in high regard. It would be sheer madness to let the disloyalty of your father and the eccentricity of your sister spoil this relationship. However—" a little of the harshness went out of his voice —"we don't want you distracted from your work by having to worry unnecessarily about your sister, so if you would like to give me the name of this SS officer I promise to have a—shall we say 'unofficial'?—word with him. She won't be bothered after that."

"And about my father, Herr Reichsleiter?"

"I can promise nothing, except that justice will be done."

Kurt hesitated for only a short moment. He had made no pledge to Bormann. Hitler, with his personal power of life and death over all Germans, was still there as his last resort. And the mere fact of Bormann's intervention, even "unofficial," would at least guarantee his father's life, pending trial. He said, "The officer is Obersturmbannfuehrer Werner Voegler" and drew some comfort from the look of malicious anticipation that displaced the surprise on Bormann's face.

"Leave Voegler to me, Armbrecht. And now to serious matters. The Chief wants to see you in his study at precisely twelve forty-five. His eyes hardened as they caught Kurt's expression. "You will listen attentively to what he has to say and return immediately to your quarters to fill out whatever notes you may have taken. Make one carbon copy only, for my files. And speak to no one—I repeat, *no one*—about anything the Chief tells you at this meeting." He stabbed one of the buttons on his intercom box. "That will be all, Armbrecht."

From where he sat, notebook ready, at one end of the table near the bookshelves, Kurt's view of the mountain landscape was broken by Hitler's silhouette as he stood at the window, as still and as crisply outlined by shafts of sunlight as the distant peaks he was gazing upon. The silence in the paneled study was almost palpable. There was a sense of isolation not just in space but in time itself, as if this moment had nothing to do with anything that had gone before or with what was to follow.

Hitler's physical presence, which should have shattered this fragile illusion, seemed only to fortify it. For this was another Hitler, a long remove from the demagogue of the Berlin Chancellery and equally unrelated to the self-assured and genial pedagogue of that first "literary session" in the Berghof, almost six months ago. He was wearing a civilian suit of dull-black hopsack, more appropriate to a mortician than to a country squire, and the blue mesmeric intensity of his eyes had given way to a curiously abstracted gleam, as though lighted by, and at the same time blinded by, some inner exhaltation. When he turned around now to face the stiffly attentive Kurt, the younger man noticed something he had missed when greeted by the Fuehrer on his arrival a few minutes earlier: the unique "Fuehrer's badge," that gold symbol of sovereignty depicting the eagle with a swastika in its talons, was nowhere visible on his person.

He hadn't said a word in greeting, merely acknowledging Kurt's salute with a fleeting smile and waving a hand toward the chair already drawn up at the foot of the table. It was when he embarked on his monologue that Kurt became gradually aware of a change in Hitler's voice and demeanor. The change wasn't easy to define; it had, perhaps, as much to do with his choice of language—less incantatory and categorical than usual—as with the manner of his delivery, which was exceptionally calm and curiously ruminative, as if he were alone and thinking aloud. And this impression was reinforced by the fact that after a first thoughtful gaze he hardly glanced at Kurt again until he was finished. While he spoke, he slowly paced the length of the room before the two ceiling-high windows, pausing occasionally to stare out at the distant Alps.

"Most of what we have written so far will not be lost, my dear Armbrecht—that is the first thing I want to tell you. But some of it will have to be revised here and there to fit into a new framework, the shape of which I shall outline, if not definitively now, then at some later stage, when the edges begin to harden about its ultimate dimensions. For the moment, I want you to suspend work on the chapter dealing with the churches and prepare yourself for a radical departure from the premises upon which that section of *Mein Sieg* was founded.

"You will recall how in Vienna six years ago, on the eve of the Anschluss plebiscite, I publicly declared my belief that it was God's will to send a youth from Austria into the Reich, to let him grow up, to raise him to be the leader of the nation so as to enable him to lead back his homeland into the Reich? Well, I have a confession to make. The words I chose to use on that

199

occasion were deliberately tailored for a Catholic audience, to window-dress what I never doubted was the real reason for my victory—not God's will but the might of the Wehrmacht and the strength of our party in Austria. And I never had cause to doubt, since then, that the key to every victory I have achieved over my enemies lay in the boldness and skill with which I deployed that awesome power in the field. Never, I say, until that evening in Madrid, a week ago today, when I met Archbishop Giovanni Donati.

"We were of course predestined to meet, I see all that now. What astounds me, when I think about it, is that it took this pious priest—out of all the brilliant and perceptive minds with which I have always surrounded myself—to illuminate the mystery and the phenomenon of Adolf Hitler and to clarify his historic mission on this earth.

"The whole world, Armbrecht, has been asking itself how a totally unknown and underprivileged child, born to the son of a poor Austrian cottager, could in the span of fourteen years' political struggle raise Germany up from defeat and disgrace to become the greatest power in Europe, and how that same person, in the briefer span of seven years, could become overlord of the whole European continent, half of Russia and the entire Middle East. History certainly offers no precedent. But during that first evening in the Retiro Park, and in later discussions at the Royal Palace, Giovanni Donati gave me the key to the mystery.

"I have been divinely appointed, beyond any shadow of doubt, to work the will of God on earth. My mission is twofold: first, to cleanse the world of the Jewish-Bolshevik evil; then to rescue Christianity from the fatal consequences of its own decadence and decay. My military task is now almost accomplished. The spiritual mission facing me will in many respects be more formidable. But Donati will be at my side, with his comfort and his wise counsel. He is at present in Rome, seeking the Pope's consent—which had better not be withheld—to his appointment as special papal legate to my headquarters. As soon as he arrives here we shall go into retreat, up there on the Kehlstein, and there we shall stay while he interprets for me the divine inspirations for which, as he puts it, I am the vessel and the viaduct on earth."

Hitler had paused again to gaze out upon the Alpine landscape. Without turning around, so that Kurt had to strain not to miss a word, he went on: "I am telling you this for two reasons, my dear Armbrecht. In the first place, I want you to read carefully through your first draft of *Mein Sieg* and to make careful notes wherever the text needs to be revised in the light of this transcendental truth now revealed to us. You will especially look for, and establish, the parallels between events in the life of Christ and in my own life. As an obvious case in point, there was the defection of one of my closest disciples, Rudolph Hess, to my enemies—a Judas betrayal if ever there was one! You will find an abundance of similar parallels. My second reason is that I shall be asking you, on my descent from the Kehlstein, to take whatever edicts and pronouncements I may have decided upon and put them into an idiom that is not only unambiguous but recognizably in semantic tune, as it were, with the spiritual authority behind its message. Archbishop Donati makes no pretensions to literary skill. Bormann is a good fellow and immensely efficient but incapable of communing with the faithful of the Church. You, as a former practicing Catholic, will be sensitive to every doctrinal nuance, and you will be couching my pronouncements in terms acceptable to the lay Catholic intelligence. The susceptibilities of our Protestant and Evangelical Churches need not concern us. They will fall into line or be condemned to penniless obscurity in the backwaters of our national life."

In the silence, as Hitler ended his monologue and moved slowly toward his desk, Kurt floundered for a foothold. The Fuehrer had obviously crossed from delusions of grandeur into a hallucinatory state of chronic paranoia. The nation was doomed in Hitler's lifetime to a role beyond the pale of reason and humanity. But with Hitler's talk of going "into retreat," it was a case of now or possibly never, as far as Walter Armbrecht's fate was concerned. Kurt had to quickly weigh the risks involved in disobeying Martin Bormann against the possible leverage provided by the Fuehrer's new image of himself as God's appointed.

Taking the plunge, he said, "May I ask your indulgence, my Fuehrer, and possible intercession in a personal matter?"

"That's something else I shall seek guidance on," Hitler said sharply. "The whole preposterous mystique of so-called holy indulgences needs thorough examination." Glancing quickly over at Kurt, as if surprised to see him still in his place, he raised his right hand in a curiously uncoordinated gesture, half salute, half blessing. "But we'll have time to go into all that, later." He gave a nod and walked around to his chair.

"It's about my father—" The notebook fell from Kurt's shaking hand as he stood up. He retrieved it and slipped it into his pocket. "He's been sent to Dachau on false charges, my Fuehrer. If you'll forgive me, for just one minute—"

"Of course I forgive you!" Hitler snapped, sinking into his chair. "Now be a good fellow and get down to those revisions we talked about. So much to do before I am taken away!"

"My Fuehrer, if you would grant me—" The plea died on his lips, muted by the look Hitler sent him across the room. It was the old, glassy basilisk stare that could freeze the blood in one's veins. Despairingly, Kurt raised his arm in salute and turned toward the door.

Sophie answered the telephone at once. "Kurt? Oh, thank God it's you!"

"Are you all right, Sophie?"

"Fine. Just—well, what's happening up there?"

"Has anyone called you?"

"Not yet. I have some clothes now, so I can—"

"I don't think you'll be hearing from him again. But about Father—"

"Good or bad? Tell me quickly!"

"Undecided." His eyes were closed tight. "It's going to take more time than I thought."

"But Kurt! Remember where he is!"

"I know, I know. We've all got to be— Listen, Maedel: go home right now. Tell Mother I've at least seen to it that he's safe, you know what that means. I'll find some way to— Sophie, are you still there?"

There was a whispered affirmative.

"I'll get a letter to you by tomorrow." And then, deliberately for the ears of any SD monitor: "I'm sure the Fuehrer will intervene. It's just a question of timing."

CHAPTER TEN

I

WITHIN TWENTY-FOUR hours of the Vatican's announcement of Monsignor Donati's precipitate transfer from Madrid to Hitler's headquarters, the top Party leadership had converged on Obersalzberg.

Something of profound consequence was afoot, they all knew that. And whatever it was, it was certainly not covered by Bormann's bland explanation that "the Chief and his religious adviser are working on a formula for our future relationship with Rome." Above all, why this secrecy—to which Bormann was evidently privy—about the Fuehrer's intentions, when he had always in the past been so ready to bore them with his monologues on religion?

None of the leaders had been allowed into Hitler's presence between their descent on the Berghof and Hitler's ascent to the Eagle's Nest, almost immediately upon Donati's arrival from Rome. They had to be content with a message conveyed by Bormann, inviting them to remain within call during the Fuehrer's absence and to treat the Berghof as their home until his return. This they were doing, not for the splendid view from the broad terrace where they assembled before lunch every day but in the hope that one of them might have heard something through his own private grapevine that would throw some light on the Chief's eccentric behavior. And as the days went by, with no break in the clouds of obscurity figuratively wreathing the Kehlstein's bare peak, nerves began to tighten and fray as the lords of the Greater Reich, each in his own style, vented their spleen on one another and on the upstart Italian archbishop.

The afternoon of the second day of Hitler's "retreat," Kurt received a summons to call on Doctor Goebbels in his suite at the Platterhof guesthouse, a little way down the road from Kurt's own quarters. It was five-thirty, and he had just made up his mind to seek out and confront Werner Voegler, who had so far completely ignored two separate written requests to visit Kurt in his rooms. It would have been a good time to catch the SS officer after his daily workout in the gymnasium, but Goebbels's adjutant, Hauptsturmbannfuehrer Schwaegermann, strongly advised against keeping the Herr Doktor waiting.

"Very well. I'll be right over."

In fact it was a relief to postpone the confrontation with Voegler, which he had secretly been dreading. And now he could rationalize the relief by hoping that the Propaganda Minister might be persuaded to intervene on his father's behalf.

Goebbels received him in the sitting room of his suite, dismissing his adjutant with a nod and gesturing Kurt into an armchair. He was wearing an immaculately pressed gray lounge suit and seemed physically unchanged from the person who had first interviewed Kurt two years ago at Munich airport, except for a slight retreat of the hairline from his lofty brow.

"A pleasure to see you again, Armbrecht. How's the work going?"

"Reasonably well, Herr Doktor. It's now mostly a matter of revisions."

Goebbels nodded abstractedly and sat down at a small escritoire by the window, turning the chair to face Kurt. "Revisions —the carpet sweeper in every historian's closet . . ." His dark-brown eyes focused for a moment on Kurt's empty left sleeve. "I can imagine this new development in the Fuehrer's thinking is going to call for some pretty drastic revisions to the book?"

The reason for Goebbels's invitation was now out in the open. The third-most-powerful man in the land, after Hitler and

Himmler, had been reduced to pumping an army captain for information about what was going on in the Fuehrer's mind! But Kurt's heart sank as he realized that he had nothing to trade for Goebbels's good will. To reveal, in defiance of Bormann and the Fuehrer himself, the insane truth behind Hitler's ascent of the Kehlstein would be to seal the fate of his father and his own into the bargain. Groping for something to offer, he said, "There's no doubt about that, Herr Doktor. The whole chapter on religion will almost certainly have to be rewritten."

"Quite so," the Minister murmured. "But of more immediate concern—from my standpoint, anyway—will be the task of re-educating the public to the Chief's new policies. I should welcome any suggestions you might have, Armbrecht, for putting this across."

He had one suggestion. It was that Goebbels, through his control of the Reich propaganda machine, should announce that the Fuehrer had lost his mind and was no longer to be trusted with Germany's destiny. As the heresy momentarily stopped his tongue there came an encouraging smile from Goebbels.

"You find it surprising, my asking you that?"

"It's immensely flattering, Herr Doktor. Unfortunately—" he groped for the right words—"except in the most general terms, the Fuehrer's intentions—"

"—have yet to be clarified," Goebbels put in crisply. "We all realize that. It's why we're gathered here. I understand, however, that the Fuehrer spoke to you in private only a few days before the announcement of Monsignor Donati's appointment. No doubt he alluded to that event?"

"He did mention it in passing, Herr Doktor. I—well, I have the impression he is going to lean very much on Donati's judgment in his future dealings with the Church."

The little *Reichsminister* was showing signs of exasperation. "My dear fellow," he said, with less than genial sarcasm, "you surprise me! May I ask what other immensely perceptive conclusions you drew from the Fuehrer's remarks?"

"Forgive me," Kurt muttered, blushing fiercely. And then, in a miserable effort to deflect Goebbels's hostility: "I'm finding it hard to concentrate these days. A family problem. My father has been sent to Dachau."

"Nobody's going to hold that against a good National Socialist like yourself. Banish it from your mind. Getting back to this man Donati—"

"It's the circumstances of the arrest, Herr Doktor," Kurt blurted out. "The charges against him are false and malicious. If you would permit me to give you the—"

"Why *me?*" Goebbels threw up his delicately tapered hands. "You're at the center of all executive power, here on the mountain! A word from the Fuehrer, to Reichsleiter Bormann—" Frowning, he flipped back the cuff from his wrist watch. "Which reminds me—"

Kurt stood up at once. He was being dismissed. With a last desperate attempt he said, "If the Herr Doktor could spare a few minutes, perhaps later today—?"

"We'll see, we'll see . . . Be a good fellow and send Schwaegermann in on your way out, will you?"

Voegler was still in the gymnasium below the main SS barracks, lolling in a canvas chair as he watched two blond giants pummeling each other about the boxing ring. He was wearing a long bathrobe with the "key" motif of the Leibstandarte Panzer division sewn on the breast. He glanced around as Kurt strode across the otherwise deserted gymnasium, but immediately redirected his attention to the ring.

"Scheffer, keep that right hand up! You're throwing away points like a drunken Baltic sailor!"

Kurt, halting a few paces from Voegler's chair, said, "I believe we have something to talk about, Voegler."

Voegler kept his eyes on the ring. "If it's about your sister, you can save your breath. I have no further interest in her."

"We'll settle my sister's account sometime, you and I. I want to talk about my father."

Softly, through the narrow slit of his mouth, Voegler said, "I don't like your tone, Captain. Watch it, or I might give you something else to go running to Bormann with."

"I'm not a defenseless girl, Voegler—or an elderly academic. I want my father out of Dachau. What are you going to do about it?"

The vein on the left of Voegler's brow was beginning to pulse. "Your father's a traitor, Armbrecht. I wouldn't lift a finger to help him, even if I had the power."

"You'll have to do better than that, Voegler. I'm only just getting my teeth into this."

"I'll tell you what I'll do . . ." Voegler stood up suddenly and barked at the men in the ring. "That'll be enough for today! Get your showers and rub down! On the double!" As the men scrambled under the ropes, he strolled over to the wall and came back dangling a pair of four-ounce boxing gloves in one hand. "Let's settle this in a man's way. We're about the same weight and you've got four years' edge on me. If you can step down from one three-minute round in that ring, without help, I'll see what I can do for your father. Otherwise, you need not bother me again with your family problems."

"Aren't you being rash? An SS Silver Medal for boxing, not to mention the fact that you're one arm up on me?"

"The medal was twelve years ago. As for the arm—" He held up the two gloves. They were both right-handed. "If I use my left, even to block you, you're the winner."

Kurt turned away and started to strip down to his underwear. He had seen Voegler in the ring and he knew what he was letting himself in for; but he had boxed for his grammar school at sixteen and if he could manage to stay on his feet for three minutes, riding the punishment of those lethal four-ounce gloves, he would have Voegler honor-bound as an SS officer to keep his part of the bargain.

From the entrance to the locker room Voegler called out to him, "What size shoes?"

When he walked back to toss the ring shoes at Kurt's feet, he was wearing the regiment's PT "minimum": a pair of triangular black briefs. His deep chested muscular body seemed to ripple with bridled power as he adjusted a mechanical round-timer and propped it on his chair. Kurt thought of Sophie, and the hatred chased out the fear.

He stayed silent as Voegler fastened the laces, first of Kurt's glove and then, deftly employing his teeth, of his own. They climbed up into the ring, went to opposite corners and waited for the clock's starting bell.

Voegler came in arrogantly erect, left arm dangling as he experimented with a series of lightning feints and hooks. A couple of blows connected, not damagingly, and it quickly occurred to Kurt that he might, after all, have one advantage over his opponent: his own right arm and feet, the general balance of his body as he blocked and weaved, were better coordinated than Voegler's. He tried circling counterclockwise as he parried the SS man's flashing glove, forcing his opponent into continuous left-foot corrections of balance; and it was working, until Voegler, scowling hard, telegraphed a swing to Kurt's face, and the younger man stepped into the trap. He had bobbed to counter-hook under the swing and sensed, a fraction of a second too late, the swing's contraction into a lightning chop that exploded against his cheekbone and sent him down on one knee. Voegler stood back, grinning, as Kurt mentally ticked off the seconds. He was up at eight, using his feet, the ropes, his strong right arm to keep Voegler at bay while the pink mist cleared from his head and his eyes were able to focus again.

They were about halfway through the round when Voegler changed his stance, went into a loose crouch and came weaving and boring in for the kill. His arm was a piston, tirelessly feinting, double-feinting and jabbing viciously through every opening to Kurt's head and solar plexus. The end came when Kurt found himself pinned in his own corner, riding or blocking most of Voegler's punches with one eye closing fast and blood dribbling from a split lower lip.

"Had enough, Captain?" Voegler's voice seemed to be coming from a great distance. The pummeling had stopped. Gasping,

Kurt opened his guard to blink in the direction of the voice. He had no memory, afterward, of the vicious uppercut that sent him to the floor.

On the evening of Sunday, June 4, 1944, Adolf Hitler and Giovanni Donati descended from the Eagle's Nest and retired immediately to the Fuehrer's private rooms upstairs in the Berghof. Half an hour later, to the Reich leaders hurriedly assembled in the downstairs salon, Martin Bormann announced that the Chief was sleeping—an unheard of thing at that time of the evening—but would meet them next day at noon. Also in attendance at this meeting would be the Chief's literary assistant, Captain Kurt Armbrecht.

What Bormann omitted to mention was that Hitler would be accompanied by the new special papal legate. And when he entered the salon the next day, side by side with Donati, the individual reactions of the Nazi bosses gave Kurt—standing unobtrusively apart—something of a quick insight into their characters. Bormann needed no introduction to the prelate, and whatever private anguish he was suffering was well concealed behind his usual expression of flinty attentiveness to the Fuehrer's every word and gesture. Goering and Ribbentrop, who had responded so frigidly to Donati's greetings at the Retiro reception in Madrid, were the first to step forward, beaming and with outstretched hands, as Hitler began the introductions.

"You've already met the Reichsmarschall and Reichsleiter Ribbentrop, Monsignor."

"I had that pleasure," Donati murmured in his soft accented German. And his smile as he greeted the two men in turn absolved them of past sins of hostility and present hypocrisy.

Doctor Goebbels, when his turn came, was formally polite. Heinrich Himmler clicked his jackboots loudly and delivered the German salute, his prim features giving nothing away. Hitler took no one's hand and silenced Goering with a gesture when the fat Luftwaffe chief tried to speak to him. He looked pale, but more composed than Kurt had ever seen him, and as he ushered Donati to a comfortable armchair by the fireside and then turned to address his old comrades, the famed hypnotic quality of his light-blue eyes blazed out from under an uncharacteristically smooth and serene brow.

"When I left here for Madrid, three short weeks ago, it was as a soldier and world statesman, concerned to safeguard my military and diplomatic successes in the West. I returned, gentlemen, as a visionary and a revolutionary destined to make a more profound and enduring impact on the history of mankind than any military victory or political treaty has ever achieved. If I am asked, How came this transformation? I can only turn and point to the man who sits there behind me, Giovanni Donati." He neither turned nor pointed, but as all other eyes focused on the squat little priest, Donati lowered his hooded lids and moved his lips in what might have been a soft disclaimer of the Fuehrer's tribute.

"The reverend Monsignor will deny this. He will protest that it was nothing but a geographical accident that made him the instrument, in Madrid, of a higher will. But you will come to realize, the more you know him, that in Donati we have found a teacher whose personal humility is exceeded only by his saintliness. I myself have no doubt whatsoever that his whole life up to our meeting in Spain was a divine preparation for that moment, just as I now come to accept that everything *I* have done in life has been a divinely directed footstep toward the Retiro Gardens.

"Bormann will confirm that I have often in the past expressed an inner conviction that I was chosen by Providence for a unique mission on this earth. How else can one explain, without reference to a higher will, my otherwise incredible diplomatic and military triumphs over a hostile world welded against me by the satanic forces of Judaism, Bolshevism and Freemasonry? How explain my truly miraculous escapes from so many determined attempts on my life?

"Giovanni Donati had meditated on these phenomena long before our paths crossed in Madrid. For a while—as he quite

211

frankly confessed to me—he could not, as a good Catholic, reconcile divine protection of my person with certain measures I have had to take as Fuehrer of the Greater Reich to achieve the ends of National Socialism throughout Europe and our eastern empire. Revelation, as he put it, was slow in coming. But it came, when it did, with a shattering and blinding force, precisely comparable to Saul's experience on the road to Damascus. At once, Giovanni Donati was able to grasp the apparent paradox of a National Socialist salvation of Christianity. He saw how the Church of Rome was in danger of becoming the greatest anachronism of the twentieth century, how its worst enemy was its own thoroughly decadent and preposterous philosophy. Why 'love thy neighbor,' if he is about to debauch your wife and children? How can all men be regarded as equal in the sight of God to anyone who contrasts one of our pure Nordic specimens with a sniveling Jewish moneylender or a Neanderthaloid subhuman from the Pripet marshes? Such a God would have to be totally blind, apart from being stupid!

"The truth, as it came to Giovanni Donati, is that Christianity over the years has gradually abandoned the revolutionary sustenance of its founder, the militancy of its medieval princes, for a milk-and-water diet designed for the slothful, the weak and the feeble minded. With its outmoded doctrines and inept mumbo jumbo it is digging its own grave. But to Donati, as a man of great piety and unshakable trust in his Creator, has been revealed a truth still withheld from his own spiritual leader, Pope Pius the Twelfth. The faith of five hundred million Catholics throughout the world is too valuable an asset of Western culture to be squandered by the palsied old men of the Curia. 'A man will come . . .' A man *has* come!

"My old comrades—" For the first time, Hitler lowered his gaze from the mountain peaks visible through the great window and spoke directly to the *tableau vivant* of silent, immobile Reich leaders. "You have been asking yourselves what was the purpose of my retreat to the Eagle's Nest with Giovanni Donati. The answer is simple. With Donati at my side, I have been pleading for further guidance from the Almighty. It was given to me the very first evening we knelt down in prayer. Since then we have been engaged, the Monsignor and I, in the task of translating this guidance into a new theology which synthesizes the doctrines of Catholicism with the philosophy of National Socialism. I shall not take up your time this morning by talking to you about this aspect of our labors. A paper presenting a broad outline of the new doctrine will be prepared by the Monsignor, in collaboration with Captain Armbrecht, and will then be circulated among you—for your own eyes only, at this stage. What I *will* say is that this new theology, if accepted by Rome, will not only ensure the Church's survival for the next thousand years but will give it a positive and vital role to play in the New Order. But I am under no illusion, my friends, that the Vatican will embrace my teachings with gratitude, and neither is Giovanni Donati. The hard and bitter struggle that lies ahead will exact all my energies and will-power, all your individual loyalties and collective authority. We shall know what an awe-inspiring task I have set myself—or to be more precise, has been entrusted to me—when Giovanni Donati returns from his first mission to the Holy See."

Thinking back over it, as he waited for Donati in the private office set aside for them in Bormann's secretariat, Kurt found it hard to believe he hadn't been dreaming. The fact that Hitler had convinced himself he was divinely inspired was neither here nor there; Lenin apart, and possibly Stalin, Kurt could think of no great national leader in history who hadn't suffered from a similar delusion. But it was one thing to believe that God was on one's side, quite another to don the cloak of a radical religious reformer, supernaturally inspired to rewrite the dogma and doctrines of the oldest and most powerful Christian faith. The fact that Hitler seriously believed he could either blackmail or browbeat the Church of Rome into accepting his "new theology" was positive proof that he had become completely mentally deranged.

More astonishing even than this was the way Hitler's chief lieutenants had received his lunatic "revelations." Had they all become as mad as he? There was little evidence of this. Were they all so intent on weighing personal advantage and disadvantage in this sensational development as to have temporarily blinded themselves to its folly? Or was it simply that they were scared stiff of incurring the Fuehrer's disfavor or of giving Bormann ammunition for his ceaseless intrigues inside the Nazi power structure? Whatever the individual motives, this group of the most ruthless and powerful men in Europe had crowded forward when Hitler finished his address to reaffirm their loyalty and devotion and, as he left his armchair to join them, to pledge to Giovanni Donati their unstinted support.

Donati . . . Unless he was engaged in some obscure and sinister papal conspiracy to undermine Hitler as Fuehrer—which certainly couldn't be ruled out—the only conclusion was that he was a charlatan who had traded his faith for some glittering future reward. But he obviously had Hitler's ear as no one had ever had it before, and in this, if Kurt played it properly, might lie the salvation of Walter Armbrecht. Kurt had been introduced to the archbishop after the party chiefs had finished playing up to him, and Donati had drawn him aside to make arrangements for the next day's rendezvous in the secretariat building. The conversation had been brief, but in those few minutes, as Kurt gazed into the priest's dark-brown eyes, he was able to understand something of the man's power to disarm and deceive. Here were the eyes of a child, steeped in innocence, but all-seeing, unpracticed in guile but as seductive as a Turkish odalisque's.

He had decided upon his ploy as he waited for Donati to join him, but his resolution faltered as he came again under the spell of the legate's soft smile and unclouded gaze. He wasn't a good enough actor to get away with it. He would end up by losing

Donati's good will and, with it, maybe his last hope of getting his father out of Dachau. But courage returned to him, gradually, as he sat making notes while the tubby little archbishop outlined the major tenets of Hitler's "new theology."

An hour or so later, when the subject of Confession was broached, Kurt said, "Could we take a break here, Monsignor, while I ask a personal favor?"

"By all means." Donati, who had been showing signs of flagging, looked positively relieved.

"It's—well—I'm afraid I've been harboring sinful thoughts, and I should like to take Holy Communion tomorrow."

"I shall be celebrating Mass in the Fuehrer's study. I'm sure you would be welcome. You wish me to hear your Confession?"

"Yes, Father."

"Come and kneel here, beside me." Donati groped inside his soutane, took out a neatly rolled silken stole, kissed it and draped it around his neck.

Kurt said, "Bless me, Father, for I have sinned. My last confession was about ten years ago."

Donati gave a disapproving grunt.

"I have sinned in thought, word and deed, Father, but the worst of these sins has been my intention, these last few days, to break the Fifth Commandment."

"Go on, my son."

"I have been planning to kill a certain officer in the Leibstandarte Adolf Hitler. I might even still do it."

"If you want absolution and to take Communion tomorrow you must make a full and contrite confession. Why do you want to kill this man?"

Kurt then told him the whole story omitting Voegler's name but mentioning the fruitless approaches he had made to Bormann, Mueller and Goebbels on his father's behalf. When he had finished, the priest, who had been listening in silence, his eyes closed, murmured, "Go on with the rest of your confession, my son."

He rattled out a routine list of mortal and venial sins, including his fornications with Helga in Berlin. And he came back, at the end, to his murderous intentions toward Voegler.

"Tell me, Father—under the new theology will a Christian like myself be expected to feel only love for a man who has degraded his sister and thrown his father into a concentration camp?"

"You heard yesterday what the Fuehrer thinks about that. For the present, however, the old laws of our religion still apply, and if you are seeking absolution you must first put aside all thoughts of revenge."

"Help me, Father! A few words from you to the Fuehrer—"

"My son, my son!" Donati's hand came up from his lap to rest on Kurt's shoulder. "I shall do my best for you. But don't ask me to intervene yet—not until I have returned from Rome. And do nothing rash in the meantime, I beg of you . . . Do you remember the Act of Contrition?"

He stumbled at the beginning but, prompted by the priest, managed to complete the prayer. Donati's hand made the sign of the cross over Kurt's bent head. "I absolve you from your sins in the name of the Father and of the Son and of the Holy Ghost. For penance, you will recite one decade of the rosary."

II

New York's Archbishop Francis J. Spellman was resting after a good Roman lunch in the North American College on Janiculum Hill when his secretary brought him a message from Luigi Cardinal Maglione. It was the day following Giovanni Donati's departure from the Italian capital, and Francis Spellman had kept his day clear in anticipation of this summons by the Secretary of State to Pope Pius XII.

After an hour closeted with Maglione in the Cardinal's office, the American prelate was escorted to the Pope's private apartments on the third floor of the Apostolic Palace, overlooking

St. Peter's Square, and there spent ten minutes in conversation with his old friend and onetime colleague in the Vatican secretariat, Eugenio Pacelli. They spoke in English, a language Pacelli had acquired back in 1911, with much help from the young Spellman. From this audience, Spellman returned at once to the North American College, where he instructed his valet to pack his bags for the journey back to New York.

Two days after his return, he was received by President Roosevelt in the Oval Room of the White House. The only other person present was Secretary of State Cordell Hull, who arrived, breathing hard, a few seconds after the archbishop was ushered in.

As the grim-faced prelate gave his account of what he had learned from Maglione, the President of the United States had some difficulty in controlling his feelings, which were of unalloyed delight. It emerged that Giovanni Donati had been the bearer of an outrageous ultimatum—thinly disguised as an "exploratory approach"—from the Fuehrer of the Greater Reich. The Pope was invited to go in person to Berlin, where Hitler was now back in residence, to discuss with the German leader certain contradictions between the dogma and doctrines of the Roman Catholic Church and the political and racial ideology of the New Order. In return for "substantial revisions" (unspecified) of the Church's teachings, the ruler of the Reich was prepared to negotiate a new concordat with the Holy See, which would in effect guarantee the Catholic Church's permanent religious ascendancy throughout Europe.

As Archbishop Spellman drew breath, the President said, "Did no one ask Donati what kind of revisions Hitler has in mind?"

"Certainly not!" Spellman retorted with asperity. "In fact it was only his long record of faithful service to the Vatican that saved Donati from being severely disciplined for letting Hitler believe there would be any point in the mission. He was instructed to inform Hitler that His Holiness would in no circumstances make a journey to Berlin and that the dogma and doctrines of the Church could never be bargaining counters at a conference table. Revision was possible only by divine authority, expressed through the Holy Father as the successor to Saint Peter."

"Did you get any impression," Roosevelt asked, keeping his face straight, "that the Pope might be prepared to consult divine authority, if Hitler really puts the pressure on?"

"His Holiness is of course praying for divine guidance. Both he and Cardinal Maglione regard this as potentially the gravest crisis in the history of the Church. The Pope agreed to my informing you, in the strictest confidence, of this ultimatum by Hitler and of his response. But unless and until Hitler himself brings this out in the open, His Holiness asks us to keep it under wraps. He's most concerned that nothing should be said or done to provoke Hitler into any further acts of hostility against the Church. Incidentally, he sends you his blessing."

After Spellman had left, the President wheeled his chair to the window and stared over the White House lawns. A long silent minute later he wheeled around again to face Hull. "You know something, Cordell?" he said. "This thing could turn out to be a helluva lot more earthshaking than that Manhattan District Project of ours—assuming we ever get it off the ground."

"You mean a kind of *spiritual* atom bomb . . ." The Secretary of State pursed his lips. "I wish I could be sure Pacelli won't make some kind of a deal."

"There's one way to keep him dug in there, you know. The Vatican's an independent and sovereign state. How about a mutual defense pact? Anyone invades the Vatican, the United States declares war on them. In turn, anyone who attacks the U.S.A. has to reckon with the Pope's Swiss Guard."

"Maybe I have what you want right here, Mister President." Hull took a folded sheet of paper from his pocket and opened it out. "It's from our Berlin decoding people and it reached me just as I was leaving my office. From Yosuki Matsuoka to his ambassador in Berlin, General Hiroshi Oshima. Boiled right down, it instructs Oshima to secure from Ribbentrop a firm commitment that in the event of Japan's entering into war with the United States a full-scale Wehrmacht offensive will be launched across the Soviet Union's western frontiers."

The President said, quietly, "Let me have a look at that." And when he had finished reading the full decoded text of the message, he laid it on his desk and settled back in the wheelchair, his patrician features a shade paler but serenely composed.

"Looks like the long wait is over, Cordell. You know the first thing I'm going to do, before calling in the Chiefs of Staff? I'm going to get off a private message to Winston. Something loaded with meaning for us both. Maybe some appropriate lines from Whitman's 'Long, Too Long America'?"

In his private apartment at the Berlin Chancellery, Adolf Hitler listened in silence to Giovanni Donati's careful report of his discussions with Maglione and his audience with Pope Pius the Twelfth, interrupting only at the beginning to ask, "Who else was present?"

"Only his secretary, Monsignor Avanzo," Donati replied. "Our first meeting was brief, seven minutes precisely, and left me with the impression that the good Cardinal is not much longer for this temporal world." Observing the tightening of Hitler's lips, and correctly ascribing this to impatience rather than sympathy, Donati went on with his report. "After conveying your respectful greetings to His Holiness and taking the liberty of expressing your concern for the Cardinal's health, I told him how discontented you were with the worsening relationship between the Vatican and the Third Reich and of your concern that the stabilizing influence of the Church should not be further eroded by unrealistic doctrinal conflicts between Roman Catholicism and National Socialism. I expressed your opinion that these conflicts could be reconciled, given a sufficient degree of good will and flexibility on the part of Rome and that, as a first step toward this end, His Holiness might consider breaking tradition by accepting an invitation to the capital of the Reich, thereby showing the world at large that he accepts the accomplished and irreversible fact that the German Fuehrer is now the sole political director of Europe's destiny. It was your earnest hope, I said, that in the course of such a visit the foundations could be laid for a fusion of interests between the Holy See and the Reich. At this point, Cardinal Maglione asked me to give instances of the doctrinal reforms you had in mind, and I did so. He listened without interrupting. When I had finished, he ended the meeting by telling me that he would be taking instructions from the Holy Father before framing a formal reply to your overture.

"As you know, I was kept waiting for eight days before Cardinal Maglione sent for me. Our second meeting was a good deal shorter. I was to continue, the Cardinal told me, to serve as special papal legate to the Fuehrer's headquarters. His Holiness was aware of the delicacy and gravity of my mission and trusted me to uphold in all things the authority and spiritual independence of the Church. I was to thank the Fuehrer for the invitation he had extended to the Holy Father and to convey His Holiness's regrets that as spiritual leader of the Church it would be out of the question for him to accept the hospitality of either side in a war that had so bitterly divided his universal flock. As for the doctrinal conflicts instanced by the Fuehrer, His Holiness could only pray that the Almighty would reopen the Fuehrer's heart and mind to the eternal truth of the Gospel and the infallibility of the Church in matters of faith and morals."

It was the end of Donati's report, but Hitler couldn't believe it.

"Is that all?" he asked sharply. "A pat on the back for you and a prayer for me?"

"I report only the Cardinal's *words,* which were much as I expected them to be. His manner was not that of a man closing a door."

"You mean—?"

"A dialogue has begun. If its object had been totally unacceptable to the Pope, I believe I should have been told to come back here and ask for my credentials—"

"—which I should not have returned to you, my dear Monsignor," Hitler cut in tartly. "But enough of these diplomatic niceties! The Pope refuses to meet me—"

"That is not so. He refuses to leave Rome."

"It amounts to the same—" Hitler broke off and sprang from his desk. From his comfortable high-back chair, Giovanni Donati watched him with a gentle smile as he started to pace the room.

"It could be arranged, of course," Hitler was muttering, almost to himself. "He wouldn't dare refuse me! We would be meeting on neutral ground—the Vatican City. The spiritual and the temporal leaders of Europe, face to face, while the whole world held its breath! I tell you, Father—" he rounded on the archbishop, his eyes ablaze—"this is the explanation of a dream I had two nights ago, which I now see to have been divinely contrived. In this dream, I found myself standing on the bank of a river, and on the opposite bank a vast multitude was gathered in utter silence, all eyes focused on me. I started to speak to them, Father, and it was like no other speech I have ever delivered. It sang and swelled and reverberated like a Wagnerian opus, and as it reached its crescendo a man dressed in flowing white robes stepped out of the multitude and started to walk across the surface of the river, his arms open to embrace me. Can there be any doubt that the river was the Tiber and the white-robed figure a personification of the new theology of which you and I, my dear Donati, have been appointed architects?"

Donati spread his hands in a gesture of humility. "I am not fit," he murmured, "to judge the Fuehrer's inspirations, only to accept them as revelations of the Divine will."

"We must lose no time," Hitler went on, clasping his hands tightly against his chest. "There is every possibility that our Japanese ally will strike at America soon, in which case the war will become global and new demands will be made upon my military genius. The Pope and I must close ranks before the Jews and Freemasons of America make an unholy alliance with Stalin's godless rabble. We must immediately prepare the text, Father, of a letter from myself to the Pope proposing a meeting in the Vatican as soon as it can be arranged. In the meantime, I must advise my dear friend Mussolini of my intentions so that arrangements can be made on the secular front for the accommodation of myself and my entourage in Rome." He paused, struck by an incidental thought. "Your own accommodation here in my quarters—do you find it suitable?"

"Sumptuous would be a better description." There was a twinkle in the priest's eye. "I must admit, however, to being somewhat embarrassed when my valet comes across a lady's hairpin in one of the dressing-table drawers."

"Fräulein Braun," Hitler frowned. "I told you about her, in my confession."

"So you did . . . so you did."

Kurt was in his office at the Chancellery, sampling the new "soft" editorial line on the Vatican in the German press, when the door opened and Monsignor Donati ambled in.

"Don't get up, my son." The priest's eyes took in the room, the empty chair at Helga Gruyten's desk. "Is this a good time for you and me to have a little chat?"

"My secretary's away, sick, Father. I'm not expecting any visitors." His tone was deliberately cool. More than a week had passed since Donati's arrival in Berlin, without a word from the priest or anyone else about Walter Armbrecht. In the meantime, the Italian dictator, Benito Mussolini, had come and gone, all his misgivings put to rest by the Fuehrer's promise to add Monaco and Nice to an Italian empire that now incorporated Corsica, Malta and Tunisia plus protectorate status over Egypt, the Sudan and the Somalilands. The Italian papal legate obviously had taken part in the Hitler-Mussolini discussions, but they had been concluded three days ago, since when Donati had been enjoying virtually exclusive and continuous contact with the Fuehrer—time enough, surely, to have put in a word about Kurt's father.

"So this is where *Mein Sieg* has been put together, these past two years." Donati gathered up the skirts of his soutane and wedged his broad rump into Helga's swivel chair. "Here, and of course at the Berghof."

"Not completely, Monsignor. I was out for quite a while, doing field studies. Poland, the Ukraine, the Crimea. You should arrange a tour for yourself, sometime. Most instructive, believe me."

"I have not forgotten your father, Armbrecht. The opportune moment will arrive."

"His health can be shattered in the meantime, Monsignor. Maybe it already is. He's allowed no visitors, no food parcels."

"Your bitterness is understandable. Now, about your sister—Is she grieving as much as you are for your father?"

"More so. She was always much closer to him than I was."

"And I think you told me her Spanish is perfect?"

Kurt could only gape. It was a statement of fact, but not one that he could recall ever making to Donati.

"I was mentioning to the Fuehrer this morning," the priest went on, "how I had to leave so many loose ends dangling in Madrid because of his impatience to have me join him at Obersalzberg. I said I should like to brief someone here in Berlin—someone with fluent Spanish and a good Catholic of course—to go to Madrid to tidy up some of my private affairs. He was good enough to say I could choose whomsoever I liked, and when I mentioned your sister he said he had met her and thought she would be an excellent choice."

"But this is crazy! She's not a party member. She's under a cloud, so far as the SD are concerned. My father—"

"I have made my choice, Captain, and the Fuehrer has endorsed it. There will be no interference by the SD. Can you think of a better way to take your sister's mind off the plight of your father?"

"Frankly, yes. You could ask the Fuehrer to have him released."

Donati's gentle smile at once accepted and deflected the rebuke. "All in God's time, my son. Let me commend you to an inscription, said to be the words of Saint Bernard, which I first

223

read as a boy on the wall of the presbytery in my parish church. I have tried to live by those words ever since." He recited them slowly and with grave emphasis.

Do not believe everything you hear;
Do not judge everything you see;
Do not do everything you can;
Do not give everything you have;
Do not say everything you know.

"Speak to your sister on the telephone. Tell her she need not commit herself until she has spoken with me here in Berlin. Urge her to come at once." His eyes were locked unwaveringly with Kurt's as he spoke, and it was absurd but, at this moment, from that almost grotesque face lumped upon the Humpty Dumpty body, there radiated a quiet force, a resolution, as great—it seemed to the younger man—as Adolf Hitler's. Kurt heard himself saying, "I'll speak to her at once." And then, as Donati rose to his feet, "You surely realize the Fuehrer has taken leave of his senses. Why are you encouraging him?"

It seemed the Italian was going to leave the question unanswered. But halfway toward the door he paused and, without turning, quietly murmured, "The second line of that inscription, my son. 'Do not judge everything you see.' "

And then he was gone.

Sophie was waiting for him, as arranged, by the Brandenburg Gate. They crossed the road in silence and entered the Tiergarten. Kurt, who had told Sophie all he knew about Donati on the way from the airport, was the first to speak.

"Well, how did your second meeting go?"

"Fine. Papers are being prepared for me tomorrow and I'm off to Madrid the next day." She looked even more strained now than on her arrival at the Tempelhof airfield. What little color there had been then on her drawn face was gone, the shadows under her wide green eyes seemed deeper, and there was more nervousness now in her voice, in the restless movement of her hands.

He said, "And what do you make of our renegade papal legate?"

"Judgment reserved." There was a new tone to her voice, hard, clipped, and totally uncharacteristic. "And that ought to go for both of us."

"If you know something I don't know, I think you'd better tell me."

They walked on in silence for a while. Suddenly, his sister let out a flat laugh. " 'All in God's good time'—hasn't the Monsignor ever told you that?"

"Don't be cryptic, Sophie. What's going on?"

Another silence. Then, "You've been to Dachau, Kurt. How long do you think Father can hold out, I mean without cracking up in mind or body?"

"Hard to say. Some of the poor bastards have been there for eight years and still aren't broken. One thing's certain—they'll keep him alive so long as I'm in the Fuehrer's good books."

Sophie nodded her head slowly. "That's how we—well, I mean *I* see it." She slipped her arm through his, and her voice softened. "You mustn't ask me why or how, but I believe Monsignor Donati is our best hope now—that and the fact that the Fuehrer obviously still trusts you. It's important you don't do anything to upset Bormann or any other of those swine at the Fuehrer's headquarters. Now, how well do you get on with the chief military adjutant?"

"Colonel Schmund? Pretty well, I suppose. He's even told me he's going to drop a hint to the Fuehrer it was time I got a promotion."

"Good! Now, no questions, brother dear, but there's something we want you to do."

"We?"

"No questions!" she repeated firmly. "Next time you're having a friendly chat with the colonel, just mention casually that you think you ought to make another tour of the Reich and the occupied countries. Maybe this time you should talk to some of the military commanders, about recruitment, the men's morale, that sort of thing. No hurry. Just something to do next time the Fuehrer leaves you cooling your heels. But plant the idea, and see how Schmund reacts."

"For God's sake, Sophie, what *is* this?"

"I don't know," she said with a return to her hard little voice. "I'm passing on a message. You must do what you think best about it."

CHAPTER ELEVEN

I

ADOLF HITLER'S arrival in Rome, first set for August 7, was postponed at the Vatican's request until August 16, because of the death of Luigi Cardinal Maglione. It was simultaneously announced in the *Osservatore Romano* that Pope Pius XII would from now on be acting as his own Secretary of State.

The Italian monarch, King Victor Emmanuel III, had offered to put his Quirinale Palace at Hitler's disposal—as he had during the German dictator's state visit in 1938—but Hitler had turned down the offer. "First, this is not a state visit," he curtly reminded Ribbentrop. "Secondly, I'm doing nothing to honor that absurd little popinjay, who would have been packed off the throne years ago if I'd been in the Duce's shoes." He elected, instead, to stay in the Palazzo Venezia, with Bormann and Goering, while Ribbentrop was foisted onto the German ambassador to the Holy See. Archbishop Giovanni Donati, at the express wish of the Holy Father, was accommodated within the Pope's Apostolic Palace.

The first discordant note was struck with the report, brought by Donati, that the Pope was not agreeable to a private dialogue with the German Fuehrer, but would receive him only in the presence of six of the senior Cardinals in the Curia. Nor would Donati himself be permitted to attend this meeting. As the legate spread his hands in resignation, Hitler broke a glowering silence.

"What's all this nonsense? Pacelli speaks perfect German!"

"It's not a question of that, but of—"

"Well I didn't journey here to put on a one-man performance for a bunch of decrepit Italian clerics—with the greatest personal respect, my dear friend!"

"I made the same point," Donati sighed, "though not quite in those terms. There is no objection to your being accompanied by six senior members of your entourage."

Donati's second piece of news brought another explosion from Hitler. It seemed that Myron C. Taylor, President Roosevelt's personal representative in the Vatican, had been received in private papal audience that very morning and would be having a further audience of the Pope "in the near future."

"This is a gratuitous insult and quite intolerable!" the Fuehrer shouted, pounding the desk in Mussolini's *Salone*. "I shall cancel the whole thing and fly back at once to Berlin! From there I shall issue an ultimatum that will shake the Vatican to its foundations!"

"Calm yourself, Fuehrer! Heed the advice of Saint Francis de Sales—'Do not get anxious when the waves batter against your boat; have no fear while God is with you.' We have a great mission to accomplish here. We mustn't let pride divert us from our purpose."

In the event, Hitler gave notice through Donati that he would be accompanied the next day not only by Bormann, Goering and Ribbentrop, but also by the Chief of the permanent Wehrmacht mission in Rome, General Albert Weisener, and that any Vatican objection to the general's presence would lead to the Fuehrer's immediate return to Berlin.

No objection being made, the Hitler motorcade set off from the Piazza Venezia at 10 A.M. on August 17, traveling through streets packed with cheering Romans and lined from the start of the Corso Vittorio Emanuele to the bridge of the same name by troops from the Italian Piave Division. Officers from Mussolini's personal 800-strong bodyguard had been attached to the two Leibstandarte companies, one of which remained on guard over the Palazzo, the other being stationed where the Via della Conciliazione met the outer limits of the Vatican City at the entrance to St. Peter's Square. Mussolini himself remained ensconced in his Roman residence, the Villa Torlonia, and all ambassadors to the Holy See representing countries at war with Italy had been instructed to remain within the walls of the Palazzo Santa Martha during the German leader's presence in the Vatican. Accredited reporters and photographers from the Italian and foreign press and radio networks were herded into an enclosure near the central Egyptian obelisk of St. Peter's Square, which had been closed all that morning to the general public.

Wearing—for the first time in ten years, and only at Donati's insistence—a morning suit and top hat, Hitler was met by the Maestro di Camera, Monsignor Arborio di Sant' Elia, at the Angelic Gate entrance to the Apostolic Palace. Here he cursorily inspected a detachment of the colorfully dressed Swiss Guard while Hermann Goering, banks of medals glittering in the sunshine, stood twiddling his marshal's baton and Ribbentrop, in the green ceremonial dress of the Foreign Office, looked on with a barely concealed sneer on his pale and fastidious features.

The one concession to Hitler's earlier insistence that this was to be a "man-to-man" meeting was the place chosen by Pope Pius XII to receive his guest—his own study rather than either of the throne rooms. And so it was in this spacious study, almost bare of ornamentation, that the sixty-eight-year-old Eugenio Pacelli, tall but frail-looking in his elegant white cassock, rose to greet the fifty-five-year-old Fuehrer of the Greater Reich, while the red-soutaned cardinals ranged behind him came to their feet with a rustle of silk not completely masking an audible creaking of joints. The younger man, with literal power of life and death over 450 million human beings, advanced toward the smiling Pontiff, looking—as Ribbentrop would later recall in bitterness—"like the chief cashier of the Vatican Bank, about to present a rather unsatisfactory half-yearly report."

Ritual required that Catholics should go down on one knee on entering into the Pope's presence, then again halfway across the floor, and for a third time as they knelt to kiss the Fisherman's Ring. Non-Catholic males were expected to make a single deep bow, after which the Pope would motion them to a chair. It had been Hitler's view, in which Donati had concurred, that although he was nominally a member of the "one true faith" it would be preposterous for the dictator of Europe to kneel before any man and a particularly inappropriate gesture given the circumstances of this encounter. He therefore made his bow, with his companions following suit, and acknowledged with brief nods of the head the introductions to the senior cardinals, all Italians and including, significantly, the Prefect of the Congregation for the Propagation of the Faith.

He bowed again when the Pope, before resuming his seat, uttered a few words of conventional greeting, welcoming the German Fuehrer to the Holy City and expressing the hope that "We shall have only pleasant memories of his visit." Hitler then sat down and, after an awkward silence, during which the Pope fixed him with a steady and amiable regard, began to speak.

He started by reminding His Holiness that the Concordat of 1929 between the Vatican and the Kingdom of Italy, recognizing the full and independent sovereignty of the Holy See, had been negotiated with his Axis partner and comrade-in-arms, Benito Mussolini. If, he went on dryly, the Vatican was now a sovereign city-state "with a hundred acres of territory and a population of less than a thousand souls," it was not only through the good will of the Italian dictator but, in the wider context of an integrated New Order in Europe, through Hitler's own respect for the institution of the Church. It was with pain and disappointment, therefore, that he had learned of the untimely private audience given to the personal representative of President Roosevelt—a sworn enemy of the Berlin-Rome axis—and he felt he must go on record as stating that any interference in Axis-Vatican relations by the warmongering President of the United States would invite immediate and drastic countermeasures by himself, as Fuehrer of the Reich.

Only Goering's heavy breathing and the rasp of silk soutanes as two or three of the cardinals stirred in their seats relieved the short silence when Hitler paused for the Pontiff's reply.

Pope Pius XII answered quietly, in his excellent German. "We take notice," he said, "of the Fuehrer's remarks, while at the same time reminding him that We are not only sovereign but neutral, taking no sides in this agonizing conflict between nations, but earnestly pleading to God, through Our tears and Our prayers, for a reconciliation of all His children.

"At the same time," the Pope went on after only a slight hesitation, "We cannot help but take note of the fact that the Concordat of 1933 between the Holy See and Germany has already been breached, unilaterally, in many of its most meaningful provisions, and that for no reason apparent to Us the government of the Reich has now reduced by half the state's annual grant to the Church in Germany. We have striven in vain to reconcile these facts with the Fuehrer's professed respect for our religious institutions, not to mention his own baptism and confirmation in the Mother Church."

The Pope's aristocratic features had taken on severity toward the end of his statement, and the expression remained as he stopped speaking and folded his pale hands in his lap. Now all eyes in the room were on Adolf Hitler, sitting bolt upright and almost visibly bursting with suppressed rhetoric. For a moment, as his hands tightened on the gilt arms of his chair, it seemed that he was going to spring to his feet and deliver his retort in the customary Hitlerian manner—pacing about the floor, flailing his arms in emphasis, coming to a halt only to spin around, chin up and eyes blazing. Of those present, perhaps only Martin Bormann knew the supreme effort it was costing his Chief to remain seated, to keep his voice under control.

"His Holiness speaks of breaches in the Concordat. To this I reply that the document was never intended to provide a one-way flow of benefits from the state to the Church, but clearly implied, in both letter and spirit, that the Church in Germany would at all times and in all circumstances loyally respect the

231

temporal authority of the Reich. This has not been the case. Time and time again, individual clerics and entire ecclesiastical bodies have deliberately attempted to thwart the realization of National Socialist principles in our German society and to undermine the political and ideological morale of my people. This is no frivolous complaint. It can be supported by a mountain of evidence—of case after case of plots and other activities inimical to the State.

"His Holiness has referred to my own original adherence to the Roman faith, and I welcome this reminder because of the direct connection between my subsequent 'loss of grace' and the current failure of the Church in Europe to accept a constructive role in the New Order. It is no secret—certainly not from His Holiness, who is well informed in such matters—that at an early stage in my career I found much of the Church's teachings to be totally in conflict with the realities of the world I lived in. I never abandoned my faith in God, however, and if His Holiness will permit the liberty, there is abundant—some might say overwhelming—proof that the Almighty has never faltered in His faith in Adolf Hitler, whose mission on this earth, if not inspired and guided by the Supreme Being, must put in serious doubt the very existence of an omnipotent and omnipresent God."

Ignoring, or more likely oblivious to, the tightening of the Pontiff's lips and the outraged murmuring of the cardinals ranged behind him, Hitler sailed right on, his voice rising and falling now with something approaching its normal declamatory vigor. He well understood the immense gravity of the challenge which he was now presenting to His Holiness. He was limiting his proposals to those doctrinal issues that were blatantly irreconcilable with Nazi ideology on the one hand and with certain undisputable findings of modern science on the other. He had come to Rome with a full list of the minimal revisions necessary to a *rapprochement* between Church and state, and his secretary, Martin Bormann, would present a copy of this document to His Holiness at the conclusion of this audience. It remained only for the Pontiff, who, as the Catechism taught us, was infallible when he defined or redefined a doctrine concerning faith or morals, to take immediate guidance from the Almighty—as Hitler himself had sought guidance in communion with God on the Kehlstein. It was Hitler's intention, he concluded, to remain in Rome as long as the Holy Father needed him for further interpretation of the proposed new theology.

The Pope made his reply without so much as a glance at the cardinals, now frozen into a tableau of hostility behind him. He would not wish to detain the Fuehrer of the Reich unnecessarily in Rome, when so many pressing and—he managed a faint smile—"less fanciful demands" were being made elsewhere on his time. The doctrines of the Holy Catholic Church were not immutable; but, as befitting a faith that had survived two thousand years of heresy and persecution, doctrinal revisions or reinterpretations were never made precipitately. The Fuehrer would appreciate that the recent and grievously lamented death of Cardinal Maglione had imposed many new burdens on the Pontiff's unworthy shoulders, but in courtesy to the Fuehrer, for whom the Pope had always had the highest personal regard, the document referred to would be studied in due course and a considered reply given by the Holy See, through the good offices of the special papal legate.

Pope Pius then signaled the end of the audience by rising to his feet.

"We understand arrangements have been made for the Fuehrer and his colleagues to inspect the Vatican palaces and museums. We wish you an interesting tour, and may God go with you." It was the moment for the parting papal blessing, when visitors of any or no denomination might, without loss of dignity, go down on one knee. As the Pope's hand rose and his lips began to form the words, "Benedictio dei omnipotentis descendat—" Adolf Hitler started to genuflect, corrected himself immediately and made a stiff little bow. Behind him, as if activated by a single string linked to the Fuehrer's discomfiture, the right arm of Bormann, Goering and Ribbentrop shot forward in the Nazi salute.

As a German-speaking cardinal escorted the Pope's guests through the seemingly never-ending succession of magnificent rooms, loggias, chapels and museums containing some of the world's richest collections of paintings, classical sculpture, precious jewelry and priceless documents, Hermann Goering's broad thin mouth was almost visibly watering. Hitler suffered the tour in an almost complete and brooding silence, opening his lips only once, after he had held up the company to stare intently, for a full minute, at the massive gold and bejeweled reliquary framing the image of Christ's face.

"Quite obviously Aryan," he muttered to Bormann, before striding on.

When Giovanni Donati presented himself to the Fuehrer at the Palazzo Venezia two hours later, he found Hitler in a state of intense nervous excitement.

"I'm issuing an ultimatum to that man Pacelli!" he declared. "Frame it any way you like, my dear Donati, but make it clear that I mean business and will not tolerate any more papal procrastination. I want either a decision on my proposals or a further meeting with the Pope within the next twenty-four hours!"

"I can give you the Holy Father's answer right now," the Italian prelate said, with a sigh.

"I want it from his own lips. Twenty-four hours—not a minute more!"

At 1:30 P.M. on Friday, August 18, Adolf Hitler began his private war against the Vatican by ordering his air fleet at Ciampino to stand by for an immediate return flight to Berlin. Mussolini, depressed by the last-minute cancellation of his banquet for the Fuehrer and nervous about Hitler's intentions, could only offer boastful reassurances as he sat beside his German comrade on the drive to the airport.

"We Italians can do without the Vatican. My people go to church only because they know their Duce has never forbidden it. I can tell you, I have only to lift my little finger and all the latent anticlericalism of the Italians will come gushing forth to sweep those reactionary old eunuchs into the Tiber."

"Don't underestimate them, Duce," Hitler muttered morosely. "They're really convinced they have God on their side. When men believe that, they become the most formidable of opponents." His hands went to the lapels of his black civilian suit, fingering the lapels. "Have you noticed any change in me over the past month or so?" he asked, staring straight ahead as the Italian dictator blinked quizzically at him.

"M-m-m . . . there *is* something. It's difficult to define. An aura of—" Mussolini wagged his great jowls—"but you'll think I'm being facetious."

"Say what's on your mind, Duce," Hitler snapped. "An aura of *what?*"

"I was about to say 'saintliness.' Not in the conventional sense, of course. It's more an impression of—well—of intense spiritual and intellectual refinement. Do I make sense, Fuehrer?"

Hitler's features softened into a wistful little smile. "More than you can possibly imagine, my dear friend . . . But as to saintliness, that quality belongs in overwhelming measure to your countryman, sitting in the car following us." He shook his head, sadly. "There, beyond any doubt, is the man who should be sitting on the throne of Saint Peter at this grave but historic moment in the Church's destiny."

"Giovanni Donati?" Mussolini swallowed hard. "A most worthy man, I agree. Indeed," he went on, recovering quickly, "if the decision had been ours, instead of the Sacred College of Cardinals'—"

"I'm at war!" Hitler broke in fiercely. "The gauntlet has been thrown down by Pacelli, and I, Adolf Hitler, have picked it up! From now on, *I* make the decisions—guided as ever by the unerring hand of Providence!"

THE DRAFT treaty of alliance between the United States of America and the City-State of the Vatican was pushed through a special session of Congress so speedily that—as one embittered Congressman of the dissenting minority put it—"you would think the Constitution had been rewritten by Archbishop Spellman."

In his message to the Senate, urging its immediate ratification, President Roosevelt described the treaty as "totally devoid of religious significance or commitment, any more than would be a similar defense treaty with some future Zionist state." The treaty formally recognized the sovereignty and independence of the Vatican State—"no less and no more than was enshrined in the Concordat of 1929 with the Italian Government"—and provided for military and economic sanctions against any nation threatening that sovereignty. But it was something more. It served notice on the dictators of Germany and Italy that the United States, "speaking through this treaty for all nations, inside or beyond the Nazi writ, that share our own Christian civilization and culture, had no intention of standing by and watching the desecration of the one remaining European institution still unravaged by the brown- or black-shirted barbarians of the so-called New Order."

The news of the treaty, and of its ratification by the Senate, threw Hitler into one of his more spectacular rages. Mussolini was summoned at once to Berlin and ordered not only to denounce the treaty but to instruct his Fascist Grand Council to rush legislation specifically invalidating any such treaty between the Vatican and the United States. The stocky little Italian dictator listened glumly as Hitler's orders flew at him. He would do as the Fuehrer asked, he said; but he very much doubted if such a law would be acceptable as binding on the Vatican State. And he could see little possibility of enforcing it without risking civil war throughout Italy.

"So much for that magical little finger of yours!" Hitler screamed. "You get back to Rome and take care of the legislation! My Waffen SS will take care of your civil war!"

Kurt and Helga were tidying up their desks next evening, when the telephone rang.

"It's that Italian Rasputin," she called over to him, cupping the telephone's mouthpiece. "Wants to know if he can come down and see you in ten minutes' time."

"Well, tell him yes, of course."

She was tight-lipped as she hung up and turned around. "What am I supposed to do—hang around outside till you're finished or find my own way home?"

"Do as you please. How do I know how long he'll keep me?"

"Wonderful! So do I make dinner for two at home, or would the Herr Captain prefer that we eat out—at his convenience, of course."

He had been living in her apartment on the Kurfuerstendamm for nearly two months now, ever since Hitler moved his headquarters back to Berlin, and they had recently begun to snap at each other like an old married couple. It had been a mistake, of course, moving in with her. After an average day closeted together in their airless Chancellery office, they should have been able to take a break from each other, to be free to decide whether or not to sleep together that night. Instead, they had fallen into a routine which, however suited to Helga's sexual needs—and they were prodigious—was, in most other respects, changing their earlier lover-mistress relationship into something as predictable as it was tacitly contractual, and thereby robbed of delight.

It was a classic-enough situation and it had been further aggravated by extraneous tensions neither of them could do much about. There were the family worries: Walter Armbrecht was still being held incommunicado in Dachau, and there had been no word from Sophie—not even a postcard—since she had left for Madrid. And there was the fact that since Kurt and Donati had drafted the outline of Hitler's fatuous "new theology," now circulating among the Party hierarchy, Kurt had been virtually idle. The opening chapter of *Mein Sieg,* earmarked for the "religious problem," was now in suspense pending the outcome of Hitler's challenge to Pius XII, and the rest of the book was still in the first draft, unread as yet by the Fuehrer and therefore not susceptible of rewriting or amendment. On top of all this was the conflict of loyalties now silently eroding the Kurt-Helga relationship. The Fuehrer's delusions of spiritual grandeur had in no way diminished him in the idolatrous eyes of Helga and her female colleagues of the Secretariat. On the contrary, such reports as had already reached the girls about Hitler's transcendental "experiences" on the Kehlstein peak had only added to his charisma. As Helga had declared during Hitler's abortive mission to Rome, "It's as if Christ himself had come down, to put His own house in order. Let's hope the Pope has the humility to ask for the Fuehrer's blessing."

The strain upon Kurt of having to hold his tongue, of not giving away even by a grimace the disgust such rubbish aroused in him was beginning to get him down. He wanted to let loose, tell Helga she was a stupid bitch and pour scorn on Hitler's absurd pretensions. But too much was at stake. Giovanni Donati was not what he appeared to be, and whatever he was and whatever his game, Sophie was now a part of it, and he himself had been allotted an as yet undefined role. It was like walking a tightrope in pitch darkness. At the same time—and for the first time since his tour of the abominable New Order with Werner Voegler—he no longer felt oppressed by impotence and alienation. Something was moving, out there in the darkness—lurking, perhaps, like an iceberg across the course set by this mad mariner, Hitler. Kurt couldn't even see the tip of it yet, but it was there and it would grow closer, and after it struck, though the impact on Germany would be frightful, his country would survive.

He said now, as Helga snatched up her handbag and glared at him from across the room, "Don't make difficulties. Just wait at home for my call—all right?"

She left without another word, slamming the door behind her.

Giovanni Donati came in without knocking, closed the door carefully behind him and gave Kurt a surprisingly smart military salute as he made his way to Helga's vacant chair.

"Good evening, Major Armbrecht!"

"The rank is Captain, Monsignor."

"Not any more. I was with the Fuehrer when he signed the order for your promotion, half an hour ago."

"I'm very flattered. I mean, that at a time like this—"

"—the Fuehrer can be bothered with such trifles?" Donati filled in, smiling. "Proof of his greatness, wouldn't you say?" He waved his hand, forestalling a reply. "He agrees with Colonel Schmund—if you're going to tour the military headquarters, a little more rank will not come amiss."

"Surprise upon surprise! I haven't even yet asked the Fuehrer's permission."

"Schmund did it for you. The Fuehrer is all for it. He had been unhappy about having to suspend his literary sessions with you."

"Sophie gave me your message," Kurt said, looking hard into Donati's dark eyes. "Since then, I've heard nothing from her, and neither has her mother."

"Your sister is well, and at this moment in Lisbon, attending to my personal affairs most efficiently. You appreciate, of course, that Portugal and Spain are full of enemy agents—" Donati's eyes rolled as he blessed himself swiftly—"and that for reasons of security I cannot disclose her various addresses. However, I spoke to her on the telephone yesterday and she sends her fondest love to you and your mother."

"When shall we see her, Monsignor?"

"Not before the storm has passed." Donati's voice had become almost inaudible. "And you, Kurt—will you ride the storm with me?"

His heart pounding, Kurt nodded.

"The Fuehrer and I," Donati went on in his normal voice, "go to the Berghof shortly and then up to the Eagle's Nest, where we shall be totally absorbed in theological matters. This will be a most convenient time for you to make your tour, and I wanted to say goodbye to you now and to give you my blessing." As he spoke he drew an envelope from inside his soutane and stood up to lay it on Kurt's desk. Kurt walked around to face him, then went down on one knee as the Italian archbishop's hand rose for the benediction.

At the door Giovanni Donati turned to look back at Kurt.

"God goes with you, my son."

There was no inscription on the envelope. He slit it open and took out the sheaf of folded, handwritten pages. Across the top of the first page, in large block letters, underlined, were the words: TO BE READ IN STRICTEST PRIVACY AND IMMEDIATELY DESTROYED. He put the letter in his pocket, locked up his desk and set off for the men's lavatory.

Donati's instructions were set out in a legible forward-slanting handwriting.

You will be visiting most of the command centers of the Army and the Luftwaffe in the Reich, as well as the headquarters of Military Governors in German-occupied countries, with the exception of the Soviet Union. I have listed on a separate sheet the names of certain commanders who must be included in your itinerary, and you will note that with the exception of the last person on the list—to whom I shall return—all those named are Catholics and nonmembers of the Nazi Party. Let us call them Category A. Category B will comprise all other commanders visited, apart from those listed here. Your discussions with this latter group will be confined to matters of morale, recruitment, logistics and so on. To those in Category A you will reveal that you are a practicing Catholic by questioning them about the facilities for Catholic worship inside their command. Almost certainly you will be asked, as a member of Hitler's personal staff, if you have any inside information as to the real purpose of Hitler's visit to the Holy Father and the reason for the apparent failure of his mission in Rome. At this point, I beg of you to tread very carefully. Tell them, as one Catholic to another, what you know, but tell it dispassionately. If they should ask you about me, as they almost certainly will, you have my prior forgiveness for anything scathing and derogatory you care to say. Make a careful note of each commander's reactions and comments. Judge, if you can, the degree of outrage produced by your confidential information and, in particular, their reactions when you tell them that Hitler now sees himself as the Lord's appointed one on this earth. Arrange your tour so as to finish it at the Paris headquarters of General Karl Heinrich von Stuelpnagel, the Military Governor of France. To this general you will divulge everything you have learned about the responses of the individual Catholic commanders to the news you gave them. Speak freely to Stuelpnagel. He is one, among others, who will ride the storm with us.

May the blessings of Almighty God and the Holy Virgin Mary comfort and sustain you until we meet again—G.D.†

Having read, reread and committed to memory the names listed on the last sheet of paper, Kurt reduced the letter to small fragments and flushed them down the lavatory.

Hitler's departure for the Berghof was delayed by the news from Rome that the Vatican had now signed the defense treaty with the United States and had rejected an edict from Mussolini's Grand Council proscribing any such pact.

A Fuehrer Conference was immediately convened in the Berlin Chancellery, where, for the first time in the Third Reich's eleven-year-old history, Goering, Goebbels, Bormann, Himmler and Ribbentrop found themselves sitting around the long table in the rarely used Cabinet Room together with Feldmarschall Keitel, General Halder, Chief of the General Staff, Feldmarschall Jodl, Chief of the Operations Staff, Luftwaffe Feldmarschall Albert Kesselring and Grand Admiral Doenitz, Commander in Chief of the Navy. Incongruously planted among this spectacular assembly of Party and Wehrmacht executive power was the tubby sacerdotal figure of Archbishop Giovanni Donati, occupying the seat immediately to Hitler's right.

The Fuehrer, speaking with conspicuous calmness, began by recalling his historic and "predestined" meeting with Donati in Madrid and went on to describe the earnest efforts he himself had made, in person, to win the Pope's collaboration.

"I went to Rome," he declared, his pale eyes misty with emotion, "to offer the Church a glorious escape from the moral and material dilemmas brought on by its own regressive and absurdly outmoded philosophies. I brought to Pacelli the message given to me up there on the Kehlstein, the clear message from the Almighty that, just as He had taken human form two thousand years ago to show all mankind the way to redemption, so I, Adolf Hitler, had been charged with leading his Church out of the medieval darkness and into the sunlight of our National Socialist New Order.

"Inconceivably, this man, with his papal claim to infallibility, not only rejected the hand extended to him but has now had the effrontery to form a ridiculous alliance with that puppet of international Jewry, Franklin D. Roosevelt—an alliance clearly directed against the Greater Reich. I ask you, gentlemen, how am I expected to respond to this act of blatant provocation?"

The question was almost certainly rhetorical; but Foreign Minister Ribbentrop, catching Hitler's eye at that moment, took it as an invitation to speak up.

"The treaty is nothing but a bluff, my Fuehrer. It will never be put into effect, whatever countermeasures you decide upon. It assumes that a hundred and thirty-two million Americans are willing to take on the military might of Germany to preserve the doctrinal purity of twenty-four million fellow-countrymen. An arrant piece of nonsense!"

Hitler had been nodding his agreement as Ribbentrop spoke. Now, as he was about to resume his discourse, he caught sight of Goebbels, who was shaking his head slowly.

"The Doctor has some comment to make?"

"We should not forget, my Fuehrer," Goebbels said nervously, "that there is a Trojan horse already within our fortress. I speak of course of the Catholic presence inside the Greater Reich—forty-three percent of the population—and in countries like Spain, Portugal, France, Italy, Poland. The Vatican's writ runs large throughout Europe. It's the one reason, for example, why Reichsfuehrer Himmler, quite rightly, won't permit a Lithuanian national formation inside his Waffen SS." The Doctor turned to Himmler for confirmation, receiving instead a look of cold contempt.

"Speak up, Himmler!" Hitler shouted. "Let's have your answer to that!"

The Reichsfuehrer's thin and colorless lips moved like a marionette's as he flatly intoned his solution. "The moment you give the word, my Fuehrer, every Catholic Church in Europe will be closed down, every priest put into a concentration camp, every pfennig of Church funds impounded, every Catholic in our armed forces required to renounce his loyalty to the Pope or be marched off to face an SS firing squad." He made a dismissive gesture with one of his small, well-manicured hands. "We'll make firewood of this so-called Trojan horse!"

As Hitler, chuckling softly, glanced sideways at Giovanni Donati, the prelate let go of his filigree gilded cross and brought his hands up to grasp the edge of the conference table.

"It would be better, in my opinion," he said, "if Reichsfuehrer Himmler's remarks were stricken from the record of this meeting. It has never been the Fuehrer's intention to destroy the Church of Rome or to antagonize its vast flock. On the contrary, he is offering it not only survival but the promise of increased vitality and dignity through a realistic program of reforms, which I and many of my coreligionists believe to be long over-due. It grieves me that the Holy Father seems to have set himself so stubbornly against such reforms. But it is my opinion that if the Fuehrer stands firm in his divinely inspired resolution, the cardinals in the Curia will prevail upon the Pope to seek an accommodation with him."

"Let's hope you're right, Monsignor," Hermann Goering grunted. "But what happens if they refuse to budge?"

"I shall march into the Vatican!" Hitler shouted. "I shall whip the whoremongers and moneychangers from the temple of God!" His expression, as he raised his right fist and brought it flashing down, was almost beatific. Of the military chiefs sitting at the table, only Keitel and Jodl nodded approvingly. Halder and Kesselring exchanged quick glances, and Karl Doenitz closed his eyes for a full seven seconds.

Kesselring said, "It will mean civil war in Italy, my Fuehrer, and revolt by large sections of the Italian armed forces—possibly also the police."

"I've no doubt you're right," Hitler retorted briskly. "That's precisely why I asked you here and why our adjutants are now standing by in the map room. But before we go into that, gentlemen, I would like to have your comments on my revised version of the Sermon on the Mount, which I shall now ask Monsignor Donati to read aloud to you."

III

THE TEAHOUSE, half-an-hour's walk from the Berghof, afforded a superb panoramic view over the Berchtesgaden valley. Two days after the Fuehrer Conference in Berlin, Giovanni Donati was sitting on a bench outside the little round pavilion, when a pretty blonde in her early thirties came walking toward him up the pathway from the direction of the parking lot. At the sound of her footsteps he turned his head, then nodded a smiling greeting.

"We haven't been introduced, Monsignor—" Her blue eyes, normally one of her most attractive features, were distinctly puffy and red-rimmed. "—but I'm Eva Braun. Perhaps you have heard of me?"

"Indeed I have, Fräulein Braun." The priest moved along the seat, making room for her. "And I'm very glad to meet you at last."

She sat in silence for a while, tugging nervously at the hem of her skirt. Then she blurted out: "I followed you here deliberately! I want you to tell me what I've done to deserve this treatment from the Fuehrer!"

"What treatment do you refer to, my child?"

"You know perfectly well, Monsignor. *Everyone* knows! For more than three months now—ever since you arrived and went up to the Eagle's Nest with him—I've been banished! First, my things were moved from the Berghof into my sister Gretl's quarters without a word of explanation from the Fuehrer—" The tears were flowing now, copiously. "—and now I hear he's given you my room, here *and* in the Chancellery! After all these years, how can he be so—"

"My child, listen to me—"

"—so cruel! He won't even answer my letters! What have I *done?*"

"Listen to me, Fräulein Braun. Here." Donati fumbled in his cassock and brought out a handkerchief. "It's perfectly clean and it has miraculous powers of drying young ladies' tears. There! Give it a good blow and I'll try to explain something to you." When she was quiet, he took one of her hands and spoke to her gently.

"The Fuehrer needs your understanding and your help more than at any other time in the years you have known him. He cannot even allow himself to *think* about you, much less to have you close to him, while he is grappling with this monumental spiritual challenge."

"I don't ask that! All I ask is—"

"Shush, my child! Tell me this: How much love do you *really* have for Adolf Hitler?"

"Enough to die for him, of course. But—"

"Then you must prove it by continuing to die a little, as you are now, for a while longer. Tremendous issues are at stake, my dear, not only for the Fuehrer and Germany but for the entire world. You must believe me when I tell you that the greatest service you can do for the man you love is to deny him, even if he were to seek it, those womanly comforts and allurements that could so fatally distract him from this, the last and greatest mission of his career."

The empty-headed blonde was drinking in every word. The agony was over. She was a Bavarian Jean Harlow, nobly sacrificing her own happiness for a Clark Gable locked in combat with nameless enemies. She drew a deep breath.

"How long, Father, must I sacrifice—that is, when do you think we can be together again?"

"The end of his mission is near, my child. But you must be patient, and strong in your love. Tomorrow, the Fuehrer and I go into retreat up there in the Eagle's Nest. When we come down, you may start to count the days. Meantime, remember us both in your prayers."

"I will, Father. Would it be—I mean, could I ask you to give him just one little message from me?"

Donati nodded.

"Just tell him that his *Tschapperl* is praying for him, night and day."

Hitler's instructions to Martin Bormann were brief and precise. He and Donati were not to be disturbed during their second "retreat" on the Kehlstein summit except for matters of the utmost importance and urgency, such as a communication from Pope Pius XII. The telephones in the Eagle's Nest were to be disconnected from the Berghof switchboard and a simple one-way communication system was to be installed to enable Hitler to summon his orderlies up to the peak whenever they were required. The sealed trunk that had arrived from Munich for the papal legate was to be taken up to the Eagle's Nest at once.

Bormann kept his notebook out, waiting for further instructions. But there weren't any. He said, "And the approximate duration of your retreat, my Fuehrer?"

"That's not in my hands. I shall send a message when we are ready to descend." Hitler nodded briskly and returned his attention to the missal lying open on his desk. But as Bormann was halfway to the door of the study, the Fuehrer's voice brought him around on his heel.

"I was almost forgetting . . . Instruct SD headquarters in Munich to place Cardinal Faulhaber under house arrest immediately. No visitors allowed until further notice."

"The charges against him, my Fuehrer?"

"You'll think of something. Wait a minute—hasn't he been kicking up a stench over the closing down of Catholic publishing houses in Bavaria? That will do."

Bormann hesitated, chewing his lip. This was something new —locking up the head of the Church in Catholic Bavaria on such a minor charge. There had to be such a reason for the *Fuehrerbefehl* and it didn't take much insight to see the scheming hand of Giovanni Donati behind it. Bormann felt his blood rising. Ever since the arrival on the scene of this ambitious Rasputin, his own sense of closeness to the Fuehrer, of being able to read his thoughts—as Hitler himself had often good-humoredly admitted—before he expressed them, had been steadily weakening. Three and a half months ago, it would have been inconceivable that the Fuehrer would have cut himself off from daily contact with his faithful secretary, as he was now proposing to do. And now this airy command to arrest Faulhaber without a word of explanation.

"My Fuehrer, there will be strong protests from Rome. In your absence on the Kehlstein, I shall have to deal with them."

"Then deal with them, Bormann! Tell the Vatican its protest has been noted—period. And increase the SS guard on His Eminence's palace!"

Five days later, when the news of Japan's massive assault on the Philippines came hard on some bad news from Rome, Bormann was tempted, in malice, to leave the Fuehrer undisturbed with his new friend and confederate. The Japanese adventure, he could argue, was no "urgent" concern of Germany's. It called for a declaration of moral support and a new Wehrmacht offensive in the East—both of which could await the Fuehrer's convenience. As for the Italian situation, that was Mussolini's plate of spaghetti. But curiosity as to what was happening up there on the Kehlstein easily triumphed over Bormann's pique, and so at 9:35 A.M. on Sunday, September 17, 1944, he set out in his car on the nine-mile drive into the heart of the mountain below Hitler's eyrie.

Two hundred yards short of the entrance to the tunnel, he found the road blocked by a Leibstandarte half-track, mounted with heavy machine guns. The young SS *Rottenfuehrer* in charge of the platoon leaped from the truck and saluted smartly.

"Herr Reichsleiter!"

"Get that thing out of the way at once!"

"My orders are to—"

"—prevent me reaching the Fuehrer?" Bormann yelled. "Who's in command here?"

"Obersturmbannfuehrer Voegler, Herr Reichsleiter." The officer jerked his head toward the tunnel.

"Well, get in, man, get in!" Bormann gestured to the passenger seat. "Maybe you can put in a good word for me with your commander!"

Voegler, summoned to the bronze portal inside the mountain, was coldly cooperative.

"Reichsleiter Bormann may of course proceed," he snapped to the SS troopers guarding the great gate. And to the shaken young *Rottenfuehrer:* "Get back to your post at once!"

Bormann brusquely declined the duty orderly's offer to take

him up in the elevator. He had installed the damn thing, probably to his lasting regret; he knew how it worked. The well-oiled brass gates closed silently behind him, and he remained standing during the 165-foot ascent to the summit.

As the elevator stopped, the gates opened automatically. A year or so back, in the hope of encouraging the Fuehrer to make more use of this extravagant folly, Bormann had ordered the construction of a two-room apartment, with bathroom *en suite,* on the east side of the Eagle's Nest. Now, as he advanced into the pavilion, there was a murmur of voices from the direction of these rooms. He paused, straining his ears, and a look of almost comical astonishment spread over his face as he identified the separate voices of Hitler and Donati.

"Dominus vobiscum."

"Et cum spiritu tuo."

Bormann took another few steps forward until he had a clear view, between two of the concrete columns that girdled the main chamber, through the wide-open door of the built-in sitting room. And then he froze.

A small altar had been set up against the far wall, and Hitler was standing in front of it, his back to Bormann, his hands busily but invisibly occupied. He was dressed in the long white alb under the Gothic chasuble worn by Catholic priests when celebrating Mass. Standing behind and slightly to the right of him was the corpulent figure of Giovanni Donati, wearing the black cassock and white, *broderie*-hemmed surplice of an altar server.

Hitler leaned forward over the altar toward the ornamented box immediately facing him. As he straightened up, he turned to the missal lying open on his right, and began to intone another passage of Latin. Rooted where he stood, Bormann could only gape in horror when the Fuehrer turned slowly around and declared:

"Ite, missa est."

He had shaved off his mustache!

249

CHAPTER TWELVE

I

THEY CAME unhurriedly to meet him, Hitler smiling as he bent an ear to Donati's murmured words of approval. The shock of the missing mustache, shattering as this had been in its first impact, was amazingly short lived. True, the naked upper lip gave new emphasis to the Fuehrer's large beaked nose and took a few years off his apparent age. But his eyes remained, as ever, the dominant feature.

"Well, Bormann, I trust there's a good reason for this intrusion." The tone was good-humored and there was a complete absence of self-consciousness.

"My Fuehrer—" Bormann stammered. "Those clothes! Your—" His hand went to his mouth.

"Ah, yes—it's right that you should be the first to know. You must congratulate me, Bormann. I've been ordained a priest of the Holy Roman Catholic Church, by Archbishop Giovanni Donati."

"But, that's—I mean, it surely can't be—" Bormann was staring at Donati, who had fallen back a few paces and was calmly studying one of the fingernails of his left hand.

" 'Valid,' you were going to say? Come now, Bormann, you are well aware that Cardinal Faulhaber is at present unable to carry out his diocesan duties. In such circumstances it is perfectly in order for a papal legate of the Monsignor's rank to ordain a properly instructed aspirant to the priesthood. If we have had to dispense with certain formalities—well, as you yourself are so fond of reminding everyone, there *is* a war on!"

"But, my Fuehrer—" Bormann swallowed hard before blurting it out—*"why?"*

Hitler's scowl dissolved almost as quickly as it had formed. He said, "You must use that brain of yours more flexibly, Bormann. Have you ever known me launch a military campaign without being absolutely mentally and physically attuned to victory?"

"Never, my Fuehrer."

"Very well, then apply the comparison. I have set my mind on reforming and revitalizing the Church of Rome. I look to a spiritual victory, a victory of the new theology. How should I arm myself for this struggle—in the gray-green of the Wehrmacht or the white robes of Divine grace?"

Bormann could only gape, speechless, from Hitler to Donati and back again.

"The Monsignor and I are going to break our fast. You had better join us, Bormann, and tell me what's going on down there."

They sat around a table at one of the eyrie's windows. They drank tea from a vacuum flask and munched digestive biscuits, but not before Hitler, at a nod from Donati, bowed his head and said grace:

"Bless us, O Lord, and these thy gifts, which we are about to receive from your bounty, through Christ our Lord." Bormann's hasty "Amen" came a fraction of a second after Donati's.

"Well, get on with it, man! Is the Vatican beginning to make conciliatory noises?"

"There has been no word from them, my Fuehrer. But the Duce is in serious trouble. His proposal to abrogate the 1929 Concordat has split the Fascist Grand Council right down the middle. The King sent for him yesterday and demanded his resignation."

"What impertinence!" Hitler chuckled. "I assume the Duce has clapped him in prison?"

"The Duce appears to be paralyzed. Foreign Minister Ciano has flown to join Marshal Badoglio in Cairo, and there's a rumor that they're preparing an ultimatum to Mussolini, backed by the commanders of Italy's imperial forces in North Africa, the Balkans and the Middle East. For the past twenty-four hours St. Peter's Square has been jam-packed with a vast crowd of Roman civilians, all down on their knees, praying in silence."

"Get Keitel. He is to inform Kesselring that Operation Damp-Down may be imminent. Forces sufficient to take care of any revolt by the Italian army are to be moved to the Italian frontier. Get Himmler. Tell him to fly to Rome and do what is necessary —with or without the Duce's consent—to clear the sniveling rabble from St. Peter's Square. Who is our Gestapo man in Rome?"

"Standartenfuehrer Herbert Kappler, my Fuehrer."

"Of course. Have him arrest all the fainthearted Fascists of the Grand Council and fly them to the camp at Mauthausen. Keep the Duce informed. Tell him not to worry, and send him my warmest regards. Does that take care of your problems?"

"There is one other small matter," Bormann said, with a sour glance at the tea-sipping papal legate. "Japan has invaded the Philippines. President Roosevelt has ordered full war mobilization."

Hitler's cup stopped, halfway to his lips. He put it down, stood up and walked to the window. "So be it," they heard him murmur after a long silence. "Not my will, but Thine be done." He turned around. "The word has come to me," he said, addressing Donati.

The priest nodded gravely.

"The Japanese will have overrun the southwest Pacific by the end of this year and will engage and defeat an American expeditionary force in Australia early next year. After consolidating their new empire they will turn their attention to South America, with its rich resources of oil and other raw materials. It is of no concern to me whether the Latin-American republics are in the hands of our Asiatic friends or the present disreputable assortment of Indians and *mestizos*. By then we shall have conquered the whole of Russia and will have all the living space and natural wealth we can absorb. But the North Americans will, of course, either have to sue for peace or commit themselves to a ruinous and protracted war with the Japanese south of the Caribbean Sea. In either case, I shall have established, in God's name, an impregnable Christian-Aryan civilization from the North Cape to the Cape of Good Hope and from Iceland to the Sea of Okhotsk. Against such a civilization, the gates of hell itself shall not prevail." Hitler had been addressing himself mainly to Donati. Now, with an expression of pious resignation, he slipped the stole from his shoulders, kissed it and folded it up reverently. "Bear with me, Father," he said, "while I turn from things that are God's to the things that are Caesar's. They will not occupy me for long."

In actual fact, they occupied him for three days, during which he made a formal declaration of war on the United States of America—"ending at last," as he declared in a recorded radio speech put out through *Deutschlandsender,* "the hypocritical farce of American 'neutrality' "—and laid down the strategy of a new offensive in the East aimed at encircling and destroying the Red Army west of the Ural Mountains. As soon as the High Command of the Operations Staff had left for their base headquarters, Hitler summoned Heinrich Himmler, who had been cooling his heels in the Berghof for two days, and gave him his orders. He was to leave at once for Rome and present Mussolini with a list of emergency measures for dealing with the threat to his authority. These included the arrest of King Victor Emmanuel and the dissident members of the Fascist Grand Council, the recall to Rome of Marshal Badoglio and Count Ciano, under pain of being charged with treason, and the imposition of a civilian curfew throughout Italy. Gestapo Mueller was to take over internal security from the Italian Ministry of the Interior. The panzer division of the Leibstandarte Adolf Hitler was to entrain at once from its base at Lichterfelde to barracks north of

Rome, which would be provided by Mussolini. Foreign Minister von Ribbentrop was to advise Pope Pius that the Fuehrer would be seeking a further audience in ten days' time.

The news that the Fuehrer was to pay another visit to Rome, this time "of indefinite duration," threw Feldmarschall Keitel into a panic, for he had assumed that Hitler would be personally directing the new campaign in the East from field headquarters in Russia.

"You'll have to learn to fight some of Germany's wars without me," Hitler snapped. "I shan't always be around to hold my Wehrmacht generals' hands. I've laid down the plan for a victorious campaign. All that you, Halder and Jodl have to do is to see that it's effectively carried out. Am I asking too much?"

"Certainly not, my Fuehrer! But the most brilliant plans can run into difficulties. Without your genius, your superb military instincts—"

"You'll have to use your own judgment, for a change. Have you no idea, Keitel, of the enormity of the task I have set myself in Rome?"

"As a mere soldier, my Fuehrer, such matters are beyond my—"

"So *be* a soldier!" Hitler snorted. "Fight my wars for me, while I'm down there in Rome fighting for the soul of Europe! I may be omniscient, Keitel, but I've never claimed to be omnipresent."

II

GENERAL HANS GRAF VON KLAGES, commander of an infantry corps of the Replacement Army stationed in the Rhineland, received Kurt in the library of a requisitioned mansion eleven miles west of Cologne, and a ten-minute car ride from his staff headquarters. He was the fourth Catholic army commander Kurt had met so far on his whirlwind tour and the first to have invited the young major from Hitler's headquarters to a meeting at his private residence.

Tall and spare, his aquiline features accentuated by the black patch over one eye, Klages looked exactly what he was: a professional soldier and aristocrat cast in the mold that had personified German militarism since Bismarck. What was not so immediately evident about the fifty-two-year-old general was the fact that he was a deeply religious person who believed in God and Germany, in that order, and regarded Nazism as a distasteful though historically expedient aberration.

He acknowledged Kurt's smart military salute and gestured him to one of the two leather armchairs angled toward the open fireplace.

"You will be staying for lunch, Herr Armbrecht?"

"With great pleasure, Herr General." Kurt remained at attention until Klages was seated. At a nod from the general, he went into one of his now routine opening gambits.

"It's on Colonel Schmund's advice that I've taken the liberty of seeking a personal interview with you, Herr General, instead of talking to your staff. As the Fuehrer's chief military adjutant, the colonel takes the view that the future peacetime role of the Wehrmacht has not been given adequate attention by myself, as researcher for the Fuehrer's new book. And since this is an area in which national philosophy—if I may put it that way—has perhaps as much bearing as military administration, the colonel and I agree that the individual views of the field commanders themselves might prove most useful and instructive."

The general's one uncovered eye, which had been focused expressionlessly on Kurt as he spoke, now crinkled slightly at the corner. "I am a soldier, Herr Armbrecht, not a philosopher. The future of the Wehrmacht will be to safeguard the frontiers of the Reich against our enemies. In that connection I would commend a study of the *Military Works* of Moltke rather than Kant's *Perpetual Peace*."

"I've read them both, Herr General. I take it you agree with

Moltke, that war develops the noblest virtues of man, rather than with Kant's view that it spawns more evil than it removes?"

"Moltke was a field marshal and Kant a philosopher. Shall we leave it at that?"

It was a sidestep, but in the right direction. Mentally crossing his fingers, Kurt carried on.

"I believe we share the same religious faith, Herr General. I myself have had trouble from time to time, as I'm sure many loyal German Catholics have, in reconciling the gospel of Christ with certain aspects of National Socialist ideology. Happily, in my case all these doctrinal doubts have been put to rest by Archbishop Donati. There remain certain—well—reservations about some of Reichsleiter Bormann's proposals. For example, he insists young men with a vocation for the priesthood must do two years' military service before going into a seminary. I was wondering how you felt about that."

He had hooked Klages with the Donati bait. Bormann and the priesthood were dangling irrelevancies.

"This Monsignor Donati," the general said, bringing the fingertips of both hands together, "must be a remarkable person to have won the Fuehrer's esteem so swiftly. What's his secret, Armbrecht?"

"It's hardly a secret, Herr General—at least not at our headquarters. Donati is a realist. He believes the Church not only *can* find common ground with National Socialism, but *must* do so if it is to survive in Europe. He also sees with absolute clarity something the Church still stubbornly refuses to recognize—that it is the Fuehrer alone who today represents God's will on earth."

During the silence that followed, Klages's cold blue eye stayed on Kurt without blinking. To the younger man, battling to retain his expression of imbecile fervor, the seconds passed like minutes. Then:

"And the Holy Father is being asked to accept this—proposition?"

"Donati is a diplomat, Herr General, as well as a man of great piety. He sees his first task as the moral integration of the

Church with the New Order. Once that is achieved, the question of divine authority will be the more easily resolved."

"Meaning?"

"A new theology will have emerged. Its inspiration will have been the Fuehrer's, its preservation the sacred mission of successive popes."

Another silence, shorter this time. Klages uncrossed his legs, drew his heels back as if to spring up but remained seated, hands clamped to the leather armrests of his chair. He said, and the words came out like splinters of ice, "And if the Holy Father rejects this new theology?"

"He will have proved himself unworthy to guide the destiny of the Holy Roman Church. A suitable successor will be found."

The general was on his feet, frowning at his wrist watch, before Kurt had time to spring to attention.

"Luncheon will be in twenty minutes," he snapped. "If I'm not able to join you, one of my adjutants will do the honors. *Guten tag,* Herr Armbrecht!"

Stiffly erect now, Kurt followed the tall aristocrat's brusque exit from the room with as much satisfaction as if he had just had a medal pinned on him by the general.

It was an extremely harassed-looking Benito Mussolini who greeted the German Fuehrer at Ciampino Airport on September 30, 1944. They drove together into the city at the head of a heavily escorted motorcade, with Donati, Goering, Himmler and Ribbentrop directly behind, and the heads of the German diplomatic and military missions bringing up the rear. There were no Romans lining the streets this time to cheer the uniformed and bemedaled Duce and his black-suited, clean-shaven companion —only long cordons of the Leibstandarte Waffen SS division and detachments of the *Carabinieri* manning the roadblocks at every intersection along the route to the Palazzo Venezia. Hitler seemed surprisingly unperturbed by the absence of cheering crowds, merely inquiring whether it was the curfew or the "political crisis" that was keeping them off the streets.

"Neither," Mussolini muttered. "The curfew doesn't start for two hours, and I remain at the helm of the state. The people are staying indoors because that's what their priests and the Vatican Radio have told them to do." He stared glumly through the side window, his hands toying nervously with the ornamental Fascist dagger dangling from his belt.

"I underestimated those priests!" Mussolini blurted out at last. "I beg you not to make the same mistake, Fuehrer!"

"Mistake?"

"This demand for another audience of the Pope. The whole of Italy now knows what it's all about. I've kept the news of the Ciano-Badoglio ultimatum out of the press, of course, and the Vatican Radio hasn't dared break the concordat by giving it publicity. But the Italian broadcasts from London keep pumping away at what they describe as 'the Vatican's courageous resistance' and calling on the Catholics of Europe to rally behind their Pope." The Italian dictator shook his head dolefully. "I stand foursquare beside you, Fuehrer, as always. But I urge you to do nothing rash should Pacelli persist in his obstinacy. I can think of circumstances in which the loyalty of my Home Army and police force could no longer be counted upon."

"Such as, for example?"

"The arrest of Pacelli, for one."

"You are worrying unnecessarily, Duce. The religious problem is going to be settled once and for all during this visit, for we have both of us—Pacelli and I—already consulted the Almighty and He has made his choice."

Mussolini turned his stricken face away, closed his eyes and moved his lips silently, as in prayer. He took leave of Hitler inside the main entrance to the Palazzo and was escorted at speed to the Villa Torlonia, where he ordered his bodyguard to be redoubled.

A short time later, Giovanni Donati presented himself in the private apartments of Pope Pius XII. The pontiff, sitting alone, received him in his study and after accepting the papal legate's obeisance, invited him to give his report.

"The whole world trembles for you, Your Holiness, and I myself am cast down."

"Say what you have to say, in the plainest of words."

"I am asked by Herr Hitler to advise Your Holiness either to accept his proposals for doctrinal reform or to make way immediately for a new pontiff who will."

A faint expression of disgust flitted across Pacelli's ascetic face. He said, "You have, of course, informed Herr Hitler that such 'advice' is totally unacceptable."

"I did my duty, as I see it, Your Holiness. I now fear for your personal safety."

"Are you telling Us that if We reject Hitler's demands he will invade the Vatican and take Us prisoner?"

"He has the power to do that, Your Holiness, and I believe it to be his intention."

Pope Pius drew a deep breath and exhaled slowly. "Go back to your new master, Giovanni Donati, and tell him We have nothing further to say on the subject of his absurd demands and that We are unmoved by his threats. And tell him something else—"

Donati, who had lowered his head at the reproach, raised it to meet the Pope's contemptuous eyes.

"Tell him that We are aware of his intentions, particularly as they concern you yourself, and that they are doomed to ridicule and failure. And inform him, that, as of this moment, both he and yourself are excommunicated from the Church. The audience is ended."

The papal chamberlain, waiting to escort Donati from the Pope's apartments, stared in astonishment at the stooped, short figure emerging from the study. Tears were streaming down the chunky face. The chamberlain, falling into step beside Donati, murmured one of the conventional platitudes of his calling. But there was no response from the man who plodded on beside him, mute, one hand clamping the gold filigree cross to his corpulent midriff.

The limousines carrying Adolf Hitler, Donati, Goering, Bormann, Himmler and Ribbentrop drew up alongside the Palazzo Ceci in the Via della Conciliazione at precisely eight forty-five that evening. A three-hundred-strong corps of the Leibstandarte, armed with automatic weapons and under the command of Werner Voegler, came to rigid attention as the black-suited Fuehrer descended from his car and, with Donati at his side and the four Nazi chiefs walking abreast behind, strode to the head of the troops and stood still for a while, gazing across the vast and completely deserted expanse of St. Peter's Square toward the towering façade of the Basilica. His head moved slightly to take in the severer lines of the Vatican Palace, rising above the curving Bernini colonnade to the right of the Basilica. No light shone from any of the windows. An eerie stillness lay over the smallest state in the world, as if some gigantic clock which had measured the centuries of Christianity's growth had now suddenly stopped.

Hitler said, without turning around, "How many years ago was it, Goering, when you and I led the march on the Feldherrnhalle?"

"Twenty-one," the Reichsmarschall replied promptly.

Hitler nodded. "We both of us nearly paid with our lives at that time. Now we march again." His voice rose. "If I should not be so lucky this time, I want it understood that my successor as Fuehrer of the Reich will be Hermann Goering!"

The fat Reichsmarschall bowed his head in a theatrical gesture of humility. Bormann's puffy cheeks turned a dark red, and Himmler's face remained completely expressionless.

With his SS bodyguard forming a great black echelon behind him, Hitler began the oblique 250-yard march across the *piazza,* heading for the Bronze Doors, which gave access to the Apostolic Palace. A few paces short of the broad stairway leading up to the doors, he stopped. Eight of the Swiss Guards stood shoulder to shoulder at the head of the steps barring the way with their bodies and their seven-foot-long medieval halberds. Their young officer stood a pace forward at the center, left hand resting on the hilt of his sheathed sword. At a nod from Hitler, Werner Voegler ran up the steps and engaged the officer in a brief, clipped conversation, conducted in German. Then he ran back down to salute the Nazi leader.

"He says they won't give way, my Fuehrer, unless we can produce our invitation to an audience with the Holy Father."

Giovanni Donati spoke up quickly over the belligerent growls from Goering and Bormann. "It's a purely token resistance. The entire corps has been ordered to stay in its barracks, but these men are obviously making their own personal gesture. Let me talk to them."

Hitler shook his head. "They are armed soldiers, Monsignor, and this is soldierly business." He snapped his orders to Voegler. "Dispatch half of your forces to the Saint Anne Gate to seal off the barracks! Then give those fools up there one minute to step aside!"

The lay Italian press offered conflicting versions next day of what happened then on the steps below the Bronze Doors. All agreed that a warning was given to the young Swiss Guard officer and that he rejected it. According to one Roman newspaper —closed down by Himmler's orders within an hour of the story's publication—Obersturmbannfuehrer Voegler then seized one of his troopers' automatic weapons, sprang halfway up the steps and emptied the magazine into the unresisting little cordon of guards. Other versions had it that Hitler had already started to climb the steps when the Swiss Guard officer drew his sword and took a menacing pace forward—straight into Voegler's fire. Not in dispute was the fact that nine young Swiss Guards wearing the white ruffles and blue, yellow and red uniforms designed for them by Michelangelo were left dead or dying on the threshold of the Bronze Doors as Hitler walked through, one hand tightly clamped to the arm of a shaken Giovanni Donati.

There were no guards to be seen in the long, narrow hall leading to the Royal Stairway, but twenty paces along on the right at the foot of the Stairway of Pius IX stood the Bishop-Prefect of the Casa Pontificia flanked by two of his assistants. All three maintained a stony silence as Hitler halted a few yards short of them and asked for the whereabouts of the Pope.

"You are being addressed by the Fuehrer of the Third Reich!" Goering bellowed. "Speak up or take the consequences."

Donati, in a voice trembling with emotion, said to Hitler, "If there is one more murder committed in this place I shall abandon you. The Pope is not in his apartments. We shall almost certainly find him in the Sistine Chapel."

The march was resumed, up the Royal Stairway, through the Sala Regina and into the 140-foot-long rectangular chapel built for Sixtus V and famed for its Michelangelo ceiling and altar-wall frescoes. Here, Pope Pius XII awaited them, seated in the pontifical throne on the far side of the marble balustrade dividing the presbyterium from the nave. Around him were gathered the cardinals in the Curia, a dozen or so purple-robed dignitaries of the various Congregations and Tribunals—all of them Italian, except for the youngest among them, the French Cardinal Tisserand. As Hitler paused inside the chapel's entrance to take in the scene, Heinrich Himmler edged closer and whispered in his ear. The Fuehrer murmured a few words back, then straightened his shoulders and started to walk. Donati followed, in line with Goering, Bormann and Ribbentrop. Behind them came Himmler and Voegler. Voegler still carried the gun. His SS troops remained outside the chapel.

Hitler came to a halt. "Your time is come, Eugenio Pacelli," he said. "I call upon you to serve God and the Church by stepping down from that throne."

"And We call upon you, Adolf Hitler, to withdraw with your soldiers from these sacred precincts and to pray that God may forgive this desecration."

"It is you who must pray, Pacelli, for you have fallen from grace. You will have ample time in the monastery already prepared for you in Germany. I call on you once more to step down."

The Pope, visibly agitated, remained seated while his cardinals clustered closer around the throne. Twenty long seconds elapsed before Hitler turned and motioned Werner Voegler forward. As the officer's gun came into firing position, Cardinal Tisserand stepped in front of the papal throne. Behind him the other cardinals were closing their eyes and moving their lips in prayer.

"Be it on your own head, Adolf Hitler." Pope Pius rose slowly to his feet and, gently urging Tisserand aside, stepped from the presbyterium into the nave. Here he turned to give the pontifical blessing to his kneeling cardinals, several of whom were now openly weeping.

"Remember," he added softly, "they are not taking the Pope, only Cardinal Pacelli."

As soon as Pius XII, with Voegler closely escorting him, had passed into the Sala Regina, Hitler drew a folded sheet of paper from an inside pocket.

"Which among you," he asked, "is the Cardinal Camerlengo?"

The elderly prelate who had been standing closest to the Pope advanced slowly toward the balustrade.

"In the proper exercise of your office you will immediately convoke the Sacred College of Cardinals in order to choose a successor to Pius the Twelfth." Hitler handed the sheet of paper to the Camerlengo. "This will guide you and your colleagues in the selection of a pope acceptable to the New Order in Europe."

The Camerlengo glanced at the paper, stiffened, then stared incredulously from Hitler to Donati and back again. "Only one name," he breathed.

"Precisely," Hitler nodded. "It will make your task all the more easy."

Cardinal Tisserand stepped forward to the Camerlengo's side, took the sheet of paper from him and without even looking at it screwed it into a ball and tossed it to the floor.

"Pope Pius lives, Herr Hitler," he said. "But if he should die, his successor can only be elected by the Sacred College, which consists not merely of us present here but also of all other cardinals throughout the world." The Frenchman made a contemptuous gesture toward Donati. "Your puppet of an ex-priest should have told you that. He might also have advised you that it is from among the members of the Sacred College that a new pope is elected."

Not since the early days of internecine Nazi Party conflict had anyone stood up like this to the Fuehrer, and Goering, Bormann and Ribbentrop could hardly have shown more consternation if the Michelangelo ceiling had started to collapse upon them. Himmler, tight-lipped, took a threatening step forward, but was stilled by a brusque gesture from the Fuehrer, who, incredibly, was now smiling.

"I was waiting to hear from you, Eugene Tisserand, and you haven't disappointed me. You shall be rewarded in due course. In the meantime, allow me to clarify this matter of the election. The Vatican State is now under German occupation and no foreign-based cardinals will be permitted entry. Therefore the Sacred College will be convened without them, and it will be the duty of seventeen Italians and one Frenchman to elect the new Pope. As for the question of who is *papabile*—as our Italian friends put it—you appear to be inadequately instructed in the laws of the Church. Let us remind you that the Sacred College is not limited in its choice of a pope to the cardinal members of that august body. Any male who has been baptized in the Church is in fact eligible." Hitler turned to Heinrich Himmler. "Have all these saintly gentlemen escorted to the Borgia Apartments, where they will remain until the Master of Ceremonies and Marshal of the Conclave have made their arrangements for an election." Then, turning to Donati: "Come, my dear Monsignor. We shall find a quiet place somewhere until our valets have made the papal apartments ready."

Voegler's instructions were to get Pope Pius XII out of the Vatican Palace without delay and to rush him to Ciampino airport, where he would be joined, in due course, by his confessor, his doctor, his valet and his assistant (the "powerful virgin")

Sister Pasqueline. On the way, he was to be relieved of the Fisherman's Ring and, at the airport, searched to make sure he was not carrying any of the papal seals. Thus, within ten minutes of Hitler's invasion of the palace the tall thin figure of the Pope passed through the Bronze Doors, with Voegler a couple of paces behind.

At the approach to the steps leading down to the *piazza,* Pius XII stopped to gaze with anguish upon the limp and bloodsoaked bodies of his Swiss Guards. He closed his eyes for a few moments, then reopened them to focus on the SS detachment lined up at the foot of the steps and the black Mercedes limousine waiting for him in the square beyond. He then started to go down the steps.

If Voegler had not been so intent on covering the frail descending figure with his gun, he might have observed that the butchered young Swiss slumped on his knees at the base of the marble Tuscan column a few paces to his right was in fact not quite dead but was staring fixedly at him over the slender glinting spearhead of the halberd still tightly grasped in his hands. Voegler whirled swiftly as the dying guard lunged, and his shriek, as the steel pike tore into the femur muscle of his right leg, rang out over the vast *piazza,* momentarily drowning the clatter of automatic fire from the foot of the steps.

Eugenio Pacelli had sunk to his knees when the gun barrels below him snapped up, a second before Voegler's scream, and the reflex—born of a certainty that it was he who was the target —put him out of the line of fire and saved his life. When the firing stopped he rose to his feet and looked back up at the sodden, tattered remains of the young Swiss Guard and the writhing, cursing Werner Voegler. His blessing embraced both of them.

Benito Mussolini sat at his desk in the library of the Villa Torlonia staring at the notes he had made for his radio broadcast to the Italian people. His shoulders were slumped, and his face was gray with fatigue. With a sudden savage motion of his hand he swept the notes to the floor, got up and started to pace the room, muttering to himself. Three days had passed since the arrest and exile of Pius XII and already, in that brief span of time, the repercussions had been *spaventoso*. A general strike of workers throughout Italy had paralyzed all industry and transport, and the Home Army and Air Force had barricaded their barracks and bases and imprisoned all loyal Fascist officers. There were reports of naval mutiny on the high seas, of warships changing course and heading for Alexandria and of other warships leaving port in Naples and La Spezia for the same destination. The *Carabinieri* were staying off the streets and in two northern cities—Bologna and Ferrara—had arrested their own commanders and locked up the Fascist mayors and councilors. Overnight, almost, it seemed that Mussolini's famed March on Rome of October 1922 had been a pipe dream, the symbolic bundle of *fasces* an emblem written in quicksand. There were no Blackshirt legions dedicated to death-or-glory, only rebellious monarchists making common cause with outraged Catholics and militant republican-socialists.

Across the Adriatic, in Yugoslavia, Mussolini's old fascist friend Ante Pavelic, now dictator of the independent and fiercely Catholic state of Croatia, had added his voice to that of the Archbishop of Zagreb, Monsignor Stepinac, in a denunciation of Hitler's actions and a reaffirmation of loyalty to Pope Pius XII. From Madrid and Lisbon, the Italian ambassadors reported in virtually the same terms the horrified reaction of the two Catholic dictators to the violation of the Holy See and their formal demands that the Duce intervene with the Fuehrer "before all that we hold dear lies in ruins."

Throughout the Reich, and notably in Bavaria and the Rhineland, the Catholic communities were packing the churches in response to a call from the priests for "continuous prayer for the safety of the Holy Father." There were reports of troops quitting their barracks to join in the vigil and of individual commanders deliberately closing an eye to this insubordination. Millions of Catholic foreign workers in the war factories and on the farms were either downing tools or "going slow," and the *Gauleiter* offices were being besieged by jittery employers and district Party leaders calling for urgent SS reinforcements. "If only half of these demands were to be met," Obergruppenfuehrer Rudolf Brandt cabled his chief Himmler, "we should have to deprive the Eastern Command of ten Waffen SS divisions." Himmler's answer, "Do the best you can, pending an imminent decision by the Fuehrer," was pure temporizing. Like Keitel, Bormann, Goering and Ribbentrop, he had been denied all contact with Hitler since the invasion of the Vatican Palace and the expulsion of Pius XII. The cardinals had now been "walled up" in the first-floor conclave area of the Sistine Chapel and the adjoining apartments. On the third floor, behind a Leibstandarte cordon under personal command of Oberfuehrer Rattenhuber, who had flown in to take over from the temporarily incapacitated Voegler, Hitler and Giovanni Donati were said to be fasting and praying. The rest of the vast Apostolic Palace and its adjoining museums had been cleared of all Vatican functionaries and sealed off. A Leibstandarte Guard had been put on the Palazzo Santa Martha, where the ambassadors from the free world were confined, and an SS cordon circled the "Casina" of Pius IV, where the Nazi chieftains could be seen slumped in chairs on the terrace or nervously pacing the surrounding lawns, their eyes constantly seeking the roof of the Sistine Chapel and the smoke signal that would release the Fuehrer from his crazy, self-imposed vigil.

Partly to kill time, but mostly for the sheer anticipatory thrill of it, Hermann Goering had sent for the official catalogues of the Picture Gallery and the Museum of Antique Sculpture and had drooled over them, inside the Piccolo Casino for a whole morning, ticking off for future reference a Raphael masterpiece here, a Praxiteles statue there. He was humming to himself as he pondered the relative values of a Titian and a Caravaggio when Heinrich Himmler stopped by the marble-topped table where the catalogues were spread out.

"Making out another shopping list for Karinhall?" the Reichs-fuehrer SS asked, tartly.

Goering looked up at the round-shouldered little Bavarian who had taken over control of the Gestapo from him ten years ago; but if he was expecting a disarming smile, he was disappointed.

"I would counsel," he growled, "a little more respect for the Deputy Fuehrer, my dear Heinrich."

"Respect has to be earned," Himmler snapped, as, with a last contemptuous glance at the catalogues, he marched on out of the room.

In the library of the Villa Torlonia, Mussolini was talking over the private telephone line to his mistress, Claretta Petacci, at her parents' house overlooking Rome from the top of Monte Mario.

"Do you want me to come to you?"

"Not now, *piccola*. I've got to work this out for myself. But what do I *tell* them?"

"Why not tell them the truth, that Hitler's gone mad?"

"Do you want me *shot*, Clara?"

"He wouldn't dare! You are the Duce!"

"And Pacelli was the Pope, remember? . . . I'm living a nightmare, *piccola!* Everything I've fought for . . . everything I've achieved . . ."

"Fly to Cairo. Go to Badoglio!"

"You want me *shot*, Clara?"

The circumstances of Pope Pius's expulsion from the Vatican were the subject of a special directive from the office of Reichsminister Goebbels to all German newspapers, news agencies and radio stations. Acting swiftly on his own initiative, the Doctor hammered out a text—"for inconspicuous presentation in all media"—attributing the Pope's yielding up of the Holy Office to "a sudden and grave physical and mental incapacity." Because of the importance placed by the Fuehrer on the question of a suitable successor, the Fuehrer would remain in Rome for discussions with whomever the Conclave elected. No mention was to be made of Pius XII's present whereabouts.

The story appeared on the day Kurt Armbrecht returned to Berlin from his tour of the military command centers, which had ended, as Donati had directed, in the Paris headquarters of General von Stuelpnagel in the Majestic Hotel. He had spent an hour, making his report to the general. When he was finished, and Stuelpnagel had put away his notes, they talked for another half hour or so. From what Kurt had learned then, together with this news from Rome, the pattern of the plot to overthrow Hitler was now almost all of a piece.

He had telephoned Fräulein Eppler from the Europaeischer Hof to tell her that he was back and that he wanted to rest up in the hotel for at least a couple of days before resuming work in the Chancellery. He hadn't spoken yet to Helga. When he did, it would be to tell her that the affair was over and that he was no longer in love with her—which, true as it was, now happened to be only one of his reasons for ending the involvement. In the meantime, he had to catch up with what had been happening inside the hierarchy during his month's absence from Berlin.

Peter Waldheim, the young Luftwaffe officer, now a major, met him in the downstairs lobby and leaped at Kurt's suggestion that they should dine at Zum Schwarzen Ferkel, a stone's throw away on the Dorotheenstrasse.

"So you've noticed her, too—you randy bastard!"

"Noticed *who,* for God's sake?"

"The redhead on the cashier's desk. Who else?"

"Must be new. Last time I was there, there was only this old hag with a mustache."

The redhead gave them a sexy smirk as the aged waiter led them to a deserted corner of the restaurant, and for the next five minutes Kurt had to compete with her for Waldheim's attention.

"Look, she's not going anywhere, Peter! Can I crave just a fraction of your time?"

"Sorry, Kurt. You were saying—?"

"I wasn't saying, I was asking. How's the general morale inside the Chancellery?"

"Awful, and getting worse by the hour. Our offensive in the

east is practically back to where it started and no one can get to the Chief. The Yankee aircraft carriers are pounding the shit out of the Japs in the Philippines and practically the entire Italian fleet has gone over to Badoglio. Churchill's in Washington, cooking up something nasty for us with Roosevelt. War production in the Reich has dropped to about half capacity, and Albert Speer's threatening to resign if the Chief doesn't put the Pope back where he belongs."

"What are the odds against that happening?"

"If you mean against the Chief coming to his senses, I'd say a hundred to one. According to Julius Schaub, he's now completely around the bend and is convinced he's a second Jesus Christ!"

"Well, what's the leadership doing about it—waiting for him to produce a miracle?"

Waldheim grimaced in disgust. "What do you expect from that bunch of lily-livered self-seeking yes-men. If anyone's going to get us out of this mess it'll have to be the generals." He lowered his voice. "They've been in and out of Halder's office in the War Ministry today like a bunch of traveling salesmen. Something's cooking, all right."

"Like what, do you suppose?"

"Like the Wehrmacht taking over from the Party, what else? Like setting up a Reich Defense Council and inviting the Fuehrer to take a long holiday at Obersalzberg."

"The Party would never stand for it, Peter. Himmler would have the generals' heads off in a flash."

"Don't make me laugh! We're talking about the Wehrmacht High Command, not a bunch of SA perverts. Little Heinie would be bargaining for his own neck, the minute the Council took over. Come to that," he added, grinning, "so might you and I, my lad!"

"Speak for yourself. I'll be in Argentina, writing my memoirs for the highest bidder."

"Best of luck to you. They just came into the war an hour ago —on the Allies' side."

Later that night, impelled by an urge to unburden himself, Kurt gave his friend the true account of the events leading to Walter Armbrecht's arrest. By the time Kurt finished, Waldheim's face was a mask of pent-up hatred.

"That swine!" he hissed through clenched teeth. "I'll get him, Kurt, one of these dark nights on the mountain—I swear it!"

"It won't help my father, Peter, or I'd have done it myself."

"Leave it to me. I'm posted back to the Berghof tomorrow. I'll be there when the circus returns from Rome."

President Roosevelt was resting after his second round of talks with Winston Churchill and their respective military staffs, when his valet came softly into the room.

"Mister Hull wishes to speak to you most urgently, Mister President. He has Mister Ernle Massingberd with him."

"Massingberd?" The President grunted, heaving himself into a sitting position and reaching for his pince-nez spectacles. "What's he doing here? He should be in Madrid."

"Can I do anything for you, sir?"

"You can pass me my cigarettes, and that holder over there." Roosevelt forked a hand through his rumpled thin gray hair and gave out a long sigh. "And you'd better show the gentlemen in."

Cordell Hull came in first. He was shaking his head and muttering, "Incredible . . . quite incredible!" as though he had just been nominated for the Nobel Peace Prize. Behind him, solemn as a judge, came Ambassador Massingberd, the wealthy fifty-five-year-old Baltimore Catholic sent by Roosevelt to Madrid after the fall of Gibraltar. After advancing to the bedside to shake hands with the President, Massingberd lowered himself into a nearby chair, while Hull explained his presence in Washington.

"It's the most extraordinary thing I've ever heard, Mr. President! But it hangs together in a weird kind of way, and if it really *is* true, we're going to have that bastard Hitler over a barrel."

"It's not my bedtime yet, Cordell, but I guess I was always a sucker for fairy tales. Let's have it, gentlemen."

"It all started with a telephone call to the Madrid Embassy three days ago from a Spanish-speaking woman who gave the name of—what was it, Ernle?"

"Graciella. Just that."

"Right. She wanted to meet with the ambassador on a matter of vital interest to the United States government, but in view of the well-known fact that our embassy in Madrid had been under day-and-night surveillance by Nazi agents since Hitler declared war, the meeting would have to take place somewhere else and in complete secrecy. So Ernle talked it over with our security people, and they decided it was too risky for him to keep a rendezvous on his own—which this woman was insisting on—and that if she had anything to say she had better say it inside the Embassy. She was given this answer when she came on the line again, half an hour later. Shortly after that she presented herself at the Embassy. She wouldn't have a secretary in Ernle's office, but she finally agreed to his daughter, Margaret, taking notes for him. And she started off by stating that she was a German by the name of—of—"

"Sophie Armbrecht," Massingberd supplied.

"—Sophie Armbrecht, and that she was acting on behalf of the special papal legate to Hitler's headquarters, none other than Giovanni Donati!" Cordell Hull paused for effect. Satisfied by Roosevelt's slow, smoke-laden whistle, he went on: "Then she told her story. It's—" he broke off again, throwing up his hands —"well, all I can say, F.D., is, prepare yourself for one of the most fantastic tales you've ever heard. Over to you, Ernle."

The ambassador was beginning to feel the effects of his long flight via Sweden, Iceland and Newfoundland. But he straightened up in his chair, cleared his throat, and then told the story more or less as he had heard it from the pale and beautiful girl who had walked into his office three days ago.

Monsignor Donati had been leading Hitler step by step to his doom since their first meeting in the Retiro Park on May 17 of that year. But the events that had started the Italian priest on his lonely and perilous path went back earlier, in particular to the imposition of the "Bormann Prayer" on the parish priests of Germany. This, more than any other single breach of the 1933 Concordat, had finally convinced Donati that the Nazi leadership was set on a collision course with the Roman Catholic Church, which would be reduced to a servile role in the abominable European New Order.

Any illusions that Donati might have indulged about the overthrow of Hitler by force, either from within or from outside of Fortress Europe, had been shattered by conversations he had had with Admiral Wilhelm Canaris during the Abwehr commander's frequent visits to Madrid in 1943. He and the little, beetle-browed secret-service chief had established a rapport based at first on a common enthusiasm for Aranjuez asparagus —supplied daily, in season, to the nunciature—and later, as mutual trust developed, on a shared belief that Hitler's power mania would one day lay Germany and most of Europe in ruins. Canaris was at pains to assure his Italian friend that he was a loyal patriot who believed in Germany's right to be the dominant power in Europe and the colonizer of the eastern territories. Where he parted company with the Nazis was over their treatment of the defeated European democracies and their contemptuous underestimation of the United States. What was needed now was a policy of conciliation and consolidation, but there was no hope of this while Hitler held the reins of power and the German people were united behind him. Only in defeat, or as the result of some unforeseeable miracle, would the Wehrmacht generals summon up the courage to wrest power from Hitler and his gang. But defeat was unthinkable, and Canaris didn't believe in miracles.

Donati did. Which is why, on the evening of May 17 that year, he knelt down to pray before setting off for the reception in the Retiro park.

"I don't know whether he got this particular inspiration while he was praying," Ernle Massingberd went on, "but it certainly did the trick. He met Hitler, went out of his way to show that he had no bad feelings toward him, and as he moved on he murmured, just for Hitler's ears, 'Your epitaph, my Fuehrer, is already written—the fourth sentence of The Magnificat.' Well, Mister President, that's a prayer I happen to know by heart, and I guess this Fräulein Armbrecht—who is a staunch Catholic, by the way —was quite impressed when I recited the fourth sentence."

"You have the advantage of me," Roosevelt murmured.

"Well, it goes: 'He has shown strength with his arm, he has scattered the proud in the imagination of their hearts; he has put down the mighty from their thrones, and exalted those of low degree.' It seems that Donati kept an eye on Hitler from the distance and saw him send Bormann off on an errand and, five minutes later, saw Bormann hand Hitler a piece of paper. Next thing, Donati was being led to an open stretch of lawn, where Hitler joined him behind a barrier of bodyguards and the two of them walked up and down, talking for about a quarter of an hour. This was when Donati clinched his appointment as special papal legate to Hitler. He told him everything he wanted but never expected to hear from the lips of a dignitary of the Church. He not only was the savior of Europe but was clearly inspired by the Almighty in everything he did and would be preserved to fulfill his last great mission on earth, which was to reform and revitalize the Faith into which he was baptized and to create a European civilization based on a fusion between the doctrines of National Socialism and a new Roman Catholic theology.

"Well, Mister President, we don't need Fräulein Armbrecht to tell us that Hitler gobbled down Donati's bait—hook, line and sinker. What I wanted to know was, who else was in the plot? And, how could Donati, reputedly one of the most pious of priests, take the risk of unleashing such a madman upon the Vatican? This is what she told me. She said that Donati acted entirely on his own for the first couple of months, just feeding Hitler bigger and bigger doses of this monstrous heresy. At no time—right up to the present—has he confided his plan to anyone in the Vatican, for the very good reason that to do so could lead to his immediate recall to Rome. He was guiding Hitler, step by step, to the brink. He would push him over and there'd be an almighty crash in which a lot of people, not least of them Donati himself, would get badly hurt. But the Church itself would be saved, which is all that matters to this extraordinary man.

"However, it had become pretty obvious to Admiral Canaris that his friend was up to something, and when Donati returned to Berlin after his first abortive mission to the Vatican the two of them had a meeting. But Donati admitted nothing. Even when Canaris gave him the names of a dozen key generals, starting with Halder, who were now convinced that Hitler was off his rocker and were actively plotting his removal, Donati remained cagey. He told Canaris not to go off half-cocked, or words to that effect. The time was not yet ripe. The people were still behind their Fuehrer and the Party leadership was still firmly in the saddle. The signal for action, when it came, would come from Rome. It would be unmistakable, for it would take the form of blue-white smoke. Until then, and regardless of what happened in the meantime, the generals must hold their hand.

"It was shortly after this, and a few weeks before Hitler had his first audience with the Pope, that Sophie Armbrecht and her brother Kurt—Hitler's so-called 'literary assistant'—were taken into Donati's confidence. I should explain here, Mister President, that these two young people, for reasons I shall go into later, are ready to go to any lengths to bring about an early collapse of the Nazi regime. Anyway, having apparently satisfied himself about this, Donati gave Fräulein Armbrecht a job to do for him in Madrid and asked her brother to contact certain Catholic commanders of the Wehrmacht and then make a confidential report to General von Stuelpnagel in Paris—one of the key people in the Canaris conspiracy.

"Now here's where we come to the crunch, Mister President. Canaris's motives and Donati's differ in one vital respect. The admiral wants the Nazis out in order to save Germany from Hitler's follies and bring her back into civilized society. Donati wants Germany so weakened by internal conflict and external pressure that she'll be forced to sue for peace. His plan is already succeeding so far as Italy is concerned. He told the Armbrecht girl that when the final act is played out in the Vatican City, Spain and Portugal will swing over to the Allies, Occupied Europe will erupt, and the German nation will be split right down the middle. An Allied invasion force will be greeted as liberators, and the New Order will be crushed with only a fraction of the bloodshed that it would otherwise cost. But this was to be for our ears alone, as soon as she received Donati's signal to act, and in no circumstances was it to reach the ears of Canaris or the Spanish and Portuguese leadership."

Ernle Massingberd slid the handkerchief from his breast pocket and dabbed it delicately about his lips. He cleared his throat. "Monsignor Donati told her there was another, and purely personal reason why his story should go on record. It was his hope, he said, that after the storm had passed he might be able to kneel and receive absolution from the Holy Father for all his sins."

Franklin D. Roosevelt remained silent for a while after the ambassador had finished speaking. Then he asked, "And Fräulein Armbrecht—where is she now?"

"We don't know. She accepted my invitation to stay in the Embassy and I had three of our security men drive her to a house in the old town, where she had taken a room. They waited downstairs while she packed her things. After twenty minutes or so they went up, but her room was empty." Massingberd swallowed hard. "There were traces of fresh blood below the skylight leading to the roof."

"I see . . . The Gestapo, or Canaris?"

"Our guess is the Gestapo."

"So she's now back in Germany, and talking, and the whole conspiracy—if we can swallow this story—is blown wide open?"

"I'm not at all sure of that, sir. There was something about that girl—I just don't think she'll talk."

CHAPTER THIRTEEN

I

FIVE DAYS after dining with Peter Waldheim at Zum Schwarzen Ferkel, Kurt received a summons to the War Ministry on the Bendlerstrasse, where he was to report at once to Colonel Buelow of the Medical Corps. No reason was given for the 9 A.M. summons, but he assumed that it was for a routine check on his amputated arm.

The slightly built gray-haired man in his late forties who greeted Kurt in the third-floor office might well have been an army doctor in civilian clothes. In fact, he introduced himself at once as Admiral Wilhelm Canaris and invited Kurt to be seated while he made a telephone call that took all of ten seconds. ("Well? . . . I see . . . And there's no doubt about that? . . . Right!") He replaced the receiver slowly and sat staring at a row of rubber stamps for another few seconds before raising his eyes to meet Kurt's.

"You must brace yourself, Major," he said softly, "for very sad news."

"My father . . . ?"

Canaris shook his head. He said, "Your sister, Major Armbrecht, was an incredibly brave woman."

"Sophie—" He was up out of his chair. "What are you saying?"

"She was arrested in Madrid three days ago by the SD, on the

orders of Brigadefuehrer Walter Schellenberg. Look, Major—"
the admiral fumbled behind his desk—"Let me offer you a
Schnapps or something."

"No, thank you. Just—" He had to sit down. There was no
strength in his legs. "What has happened to my sister, Herr
Admiral?"

"She was observed entering and leaving the United States
Embassy. She was flown here, to SD headquarters on the Prinz
Albrecht Strasse. She—" Canaris looked away. "She died only a
few minutes ago, under interrogation."

It was a lie, of course. A monstrous, inhuman device to catch
him off guard and trick him into betraying Sophie and Giovanni
Donati.

"I want to see my sister, Herr Admiral—at once."

"I understand your feelings. But you must be as true as she
was to the cause for which she died. I can't arrange for you to
see her, even if I wanted to. At this moment, her arrest and
death is an SD secret—or would be if I hadn't my own Abwehr
man in Prinz Albrecht Strasse. We know for a fact that she gave
nothing away to those swine but stuck to her story, right to the
end, that all she wanted was political asylum in the United
States. Let me be quite blunt with you, Major. If you go storm-
ing over to Prinz Albrecht Strasse, you could expose my man in
there, myself, and of course your own self."

"Why did you send for me?"

"I found out only two hours ago that the girl they were inter-
rogating was your sister. There is nothing she could tell them
about me, but she could obviously have incriminated yourself
and our friend Donati."

"Incriminate? For *what*, Herr Admiral?" Kurt's agony hadn't
completely bludgeoned his wits. Donati had said nothing to him
about Canaris. He was not going to be conned into giving away,
out of gullibility, what his sister had— He stiffened as the delayed impact of what the admiral had told him hit him suddenly,
with the sickening force of a hammer blow under the heart. His
mother . . . If it were true, he would have to go to her, for the

second time in six months, and find words to convey the un-utterable.

Canaris's voice, a blend of sympathy and impatience, brought him back from Munich to this aseptic geometrical limbo of an office on the Bendlerstrasse.

"You must trust me, Major Armbrecht. All the fuses are lit, and in a matter of days, now—" The Abwehr chief broke off, as if seized by sudden doubts of his own. Then: "I want you to leave Berlin at once and fly to Rome. You're still in the clear, so far as Schellenberg is concerned, but there's no guarantee that he won't have second thoughts. I'm giving you an Abwehr lais-sez-passer, which, together with your Chancellery credentials, will get you into the Vatican. It's vital that you see the Mon-signor and tell him about your sister. And you must give him a message from me. Just tell him this: "The asparagus is now ready for eating." He had taken a sheet of paper from a desk drawer while he was speaking, and now he reached for a rubber stamp, pressed it to the paper and put his signature over the im-pression. He stood up. "My assistant, Colonel Oster, will drive with you to your hotel and then straight to the airport, where one of our planes is standing by. Any questions, Major?"

"My sister—"

Canaris shook his head.

"The people who did it—"

"—will pay, never doubt that. Keep a tight hold on your hatred, young man. Germany will find use for it."

After packing his things, he wrote a short note to Peter Waldheim. "Sophie is dead. What they left of her lies in the Prinz Albrecht Strasse. I shall return to Germany one day, to pay my debts. Please break this as gently as you know how to my mother."

He gave the sealed envelope to Colonel Oster on the way to the airport. "Can you get this to Major Waldheim at the Berghof —not through the usual channels?"

"It'll be done, Armbrecht."

About the time Kurt was boarding the army plane at Tempelhof Flughaven, Heinrich Himmler was hurrying up the Stairway of Pius IX in response to a summons from the Fuehrer. He found Hitler pacing the floor of the exiled Pius XII's study. Monsignor Donati was at the window, gazing at the façade of St. Peter's.

"There you are, Himmler! What took you so long?"

"I came at once, my Fuehrer. We've made our headquarters in the Casina, which is—"

"Never mind about that. There's God's work to be done and He is growing impatient. Now, what about those cardinals?"

"The cardinals, my Fuehrer . . . ?"

"Six days, Himmler, and still no sign from them! And their insolence, refusing to answer my messages! Another thing—where are the crowds who should be out there in the *piazza* waiting to honor the new Pope?"

"Your instructions, my Fuehrer, were to clear the square. All the approaches are sealed off. If it's your wish—"

"The hour has come, Himmler! Let them in! And let in the world's press!"

"At once, my—"

"Now listen carefully. I am not permitting the will of God to be frustrated another minute by those blind and obstinate old men perched on their thrones in the Sistine Chapel. Tell Rattenhuber to take them away! And have the signal go up at once from that chimney that a new Pope has been chosen. Where are Bormann and the rest?"

"In the Casina, my Fuehrer."

"I want them and the heads of our missions assembled in the Sistine Chapel. And I want every German priest and prelate in this city there as well. If any refuse, pack them off with the cardinals! Now, what about the bells?"

"The bells, my Fuehrer . . . ?"

"The Basilica's bells, Himmler! They have to ring out over the whole city when the new Pope is announced."

"Leave it to me, my Fuehrer."

"Good, good." Hitler drew a long breath and turned toward Donati, who had moved away from the window and was standing with his pendant cross in his hands and his eyes cast down.

"Come, Father," he said with extraordinary tenderness. "The time is now."

The small company that was assembled in the Sistine Chapel an hour later included Goering, Bormann, Himmler, Ribbentrop, Feldmarschall Keitel, Gestapo Mueller, Doctor Otto Dietrich, SS Oberfuehrer Rattenhuber, the German ambassador to the Holy See, the heads of all service and economic missions and the two German Monsignors attached to the Vatican administration. Benito Mussolini wasn't there—or, indeed, anywhere else in Rome, having last been seen in a fast-moving convoy of army trucks heading south for Naples.

It was a curiously still and mutually uncommunicative assembly, as if each of the men present was an island to himself, wrapped in his own private fears and misgivings. All of them knew that behind the closed doors leading to the sacristy of the Sistine Chapel the ultimate sacrilege was being enacted. All eyes were trained either on those doors or on the *sedia gestatoria*— the papal throne—which now stood on the altar platform, facing them. The sacristy doors opened slowly, and one of Hitler's SS orderlies, dressed in cassock and surplice, took a few paces into the presbyterium and sank to his knees. The bizarre congregation, led by Hermann Georing, did likewise.

Donati made his slow solemn entrance, resplendent in a full-length *ferraiolone* and purple moiré skull cap. A few paces behind him came Adolf Hitler, arms crossed upward against his chest. Except for the red stole and socks marked with the cross, he was clad entirely in white, from his silk slippers, up through his cassock and cloak to the white papal skull cap on the back of his bowed head.

In the nave of the chapel, immediately behind Joachim von Ribbentrop, one of the German Monsignors uttered a sharp cut-off cry and crumpled sideways into the aisle in a dead faint.

Before the horrified eyes of his stunned colleagues and minions, Hitler ascended the throne, settled himself, and then held out his right hand for the kneeling Donati to place upon it the Fisherman's ring. The archbishop kissed the ring and remained kneeling as another orderly emerged from the sacristy and made his way toward the throne, bearing a cardinal's red silk hat across the palms of his hands. The orderly knelt beside the throne. Hitler took the flat hat, stood up, and addressed the gaping assembly briefly.

"We rejoice, in this Our first act as Bishop of Rome and Vicar of Jesus Christ, in appointing Our dearly beloved brother, Archbishop Giovanni Donati, a Cardinal of the Holy Church." He made a slow sign of the cross over Donati's head before lowering the red hat in place and resuming his seat on the throne. Donati bent low to kiss one of Hitler's white slippers and then the Fisherman's Ring. He rose to his feet and made a sign to the orderly standing by the opening in the balustrade across the nave.

Martin Bormann was the first to walk through the balustrade, kneel at the throne, kiss the papal ring and receive a blessing. Goering and Ribbentrop followed suit, returning to their seats in an obvious state of shock. Others of the small congregation held back as Himmler, peaked SS cap tucked under his left arm, stepped through the balustrade, came to a halt a few paces short of the altar platform and suddenly stiffened. His right arm shot out and the cry "Heil Hitler!" reverberated around the chapel.

Hitler's hand, half-extended for Himmler's lips, bunched itself into a tight fist and he started to rise from the throne, eyes glaring, lips twisting into a snarl. With an obvious effort, he controlled himself, sank back in the throne and waved the trembling *Reichsfuehrer* away. The rest of the assembly took turns doing obeisance, with the exception of the still-conscious of the two German Monsignors, who remained kneeling beside his colleague, massaging his hands and intoning prayers in a low and doleful voice.

When the ring-kissing was finished, Hitler stood up and nodded to Donati. "Our flock is awaiting Us, Your Eminence. Lead Us to the balcony of the Basilica."

An orderly carrying the papal cross led the slow procession out of the chapel and on through the Hall of the Benedictines to the lofty windows opening on the second story loggia above the entry to St. Peter's and reserved for pontifical blessings. Donati went ahead of Hitler onto the balcony and looked down at the broad forecourt beyond the six steps leading up to the portico. About a hundred journalists, hastily rounded up by Dietrich's staff from the Italian newspapers and the Foreign Press Club, stared up at him. He raised his eyes to look out over the vast Bernini square, to its central Egyptian obelisk brought to Rome by the mad emperor Caligula, to the 104 evenly spaced statues of saints looking down from above the *piazza*'s encircling colonnade. Except for the clusters, here and there, of black-uniformed Leibstandarte troops, the square was entirely empty.

Donati filled his lungs and let his voice ring out over the twenty loudspeakers installed around the *piazza*.

"Habemus Papam!"

In place of the answering roar from twenty thousand Italian throats there came the clatter of a camera falling to the stones from the excited hands of a press photographer.

"Adolfum—"

The corporate gasp that went up from the journalists carried clearly into the lofty chamber where Hitler stood with his back to the loose semicircle of Nazi chiefs. Goering, alone, wore a relishing smile, as if he had personally stage-managed this sensational piece of theater and would realize 50 percent of the box-office take. Martin Bormann looked dazed; Ribbentrop seemed to be fighting hard not to vomit; Himmler's pale mask of a face was twitching spasmodically. Wilhelm Keitel's expression was a study in imbecile soldierly abstraction. The great bells of the Basilica began to ring out and, at a gesture from Donati, Hitler

283

stepped out onto the balcony. His light-blue eyes, blinded from within, ranged the empty *piazza* and suddenly took fire.

"Magnificent" he breathed. "The Nuremberg of God's anointed!"

He began to speak, deaf to the bells reverberating above him and totally inaudible to the journalists below. Those in the room behind him, straining their ears, caught only snatches of his Bavarian-accented German.

". . . a new era . . . the rebirth of Christ's mission on . . . like Julius the Second, wielding his mace in one hand . . . and with the scourge of Judaism and Bolshevik atheism . . . and everlasting peace on earth to all. . . ."

As the bells suddenly stopped ringing, Hitler broke off in mid-sentence and blinked around at Donati, as if jolted from a dream. The newly appointed cardinal made a covert motion with his right hand and Hitler nodded and turned again toward the *piazza,* his own hand moving through the sign of the cross.

II

BUT FOR the Leibstandarte transport unit now operating at Ciampino airport, Kurt would have had to walk into Rome. All public transport had come to a halt, and any unguarded vehicle belonging to a German or an Italian Fascist was being set on fire by marauding gangs of young Romans, many of them led by army deserters.

His Chancellery and Abwehr documents got him past the road block in the Via della Conciliazione and as far as the Bronze Doors of the Vatican Palace. Here he was informed by the officer of the guard that Pope Adolf I and Cardinal Donati had retired to the papal apartments and were "indefinitely inaccessible."

Kurt had heard the day's staggering news immediately on touchdown at Ciampino. And, hard on the shock, had come a sense of awe at the genius of Giovanni Donati. He said, "Reichs-leiter Bormann, then?"

"With the rest of the *Fuehrung,* up there in the Borgia apart-ments. If the matter is of great urgency, I could have a message taken to him."

"It's vital that I should speak to the Cardinal."

The officer shook his head. "Out of the question. It's precisely what Reichsleiter Bormann, Reichsmarschall Goering and everyone else wants to do. I can only suggest that you try again tomorrow."

Kurt walked back to where his SS driver had parked the car. "I'll need a bed for the night, Sturmann. Any suggestions?"

"The regimental billeting officer, Herr Major. You'll find him just back there in the Palazzo Ceci."

Fifteen minutes later, Kurt was being ushered into a pleasant attic room in the *palazzo* itself by an attentive and respectful SS *Oberscharfuehrer.*

"What a day for Germany, Herr Major! What a brilliant coup by the Fuehrer!"

"Are you a Catholic, *Oberscharfuehrer?*"

"Not yet. But I'm applying for membership, first chance I get!"

When he was alone, he unpacked his bag, took out the photo-graphs of Sophie hugging her father at Munich airport and low-ered himself to the edge of the bed.

"Kleines—"

He let go then, and sobbed out his heart. . . .

There were no Roman newspapers in the morning, but the Vatican Radio, now taken over by Doctor Dietrich, was putting out quarter-hourly bulletins, sandwiched between bravura se-lections from *Tannhäuser.* The bulletins called on the Italians to do homage to their new Pope in St. Peter's Square and promised them that under this, the first non-Italian pontiff for four-and-a-half centuries, the spiritual supremacy of the Holy Roman Church throughout the world would be assured for the next thousand years. As he listened to one of the bulletins over a cup of coffee in the Palazzo Ceci's commissary, Kurt decided on his next move.

Otto Dietrich had installed himself, with his staff, in the offices of the *Osservatore Romano* within the eastern walls of the Vatican City. An SS man escorted Kurt from the Saint Anne Gate, past the cordoned-off barracks of the Swiss Guard into the Pilgrim Street entrance to the newspaper building. Dietrich was being shaved at his desk by an orderly. He was haggard from lack of sleep, but he seemed pleased to see Kurt.

"Well, well, my dear fellow! What can I sell you? A rosary, maybe—blessed by the Holy Father himself?"

"Better than that. You can tell me how I can do what I'm supposed to do here and then get back home out of this madhouse."

"You think *this* is a madhouse? The whole world's gone berserk!" Dietrich swept a hand over the cables stacked on his desk. "All our missions have been expelled from Spain and Portugal, and the Spanish frontier has been sealed off. De Gaulle has landed in Dakar and the Cape Verde islands, and the Yanks have occupied the Canaries and Madeira without a peep of protest from Franco and Salazar. Badoglio, with ten combat divisions of the imperial Italian army and most of the bloody navy, has installed himself in Sicily, put Mussolini behind bars and called on the Home Army and the *Carabinieri* to throw the Germans out. Tito took Sarajevo a few hours ago. Martial law has been declared throughout the Ostmark, Albert Speer has disappeared somewhere in Sweden, and Himmler flew off at midnight, threatening to execute every slacker and absenteeist on the home front. As if all that weren't bad enough, I think I'm getting another attack of the piles."

"I have to see Donati, urgently."

"*You* have to! So does most of our top brass. No one can get to the Fuehrer—beg your pardon, His Holiness—except through that Italian Svengali. But he's locked himself up with Pope Adolf, planning his coronation, and won't have him bothered by such trifles as the botched-up offensive in Russia."

"I haven't made myself clear. It was Donati himself who sent for me. But I can't get past those Leibstandarte robots."

"Hm-m-m." Dietrich took a hand mirror from the orderly and examined his shaven jaws. "That *does* put a different complexion on it. We'd better get your message to Rattenhuber. He's at least in a position to put it on the lunch tray."

Donati greeted Kurt at the entrance to the papal apartments and led the way to a loggia overlooking the courtyard of St. Damascus. He had aged a great deal since Kurt had last seen him, five weeks back.

"We must be brief, my son. Did you see everyone on that list?"

"All of them, Father. Stuelpnagel seemed very satisfied with my report. And Admiral Canaris asked me to tell you that the asparagus is now ready for eating."

The priest's wide mouth flickered with the faintest of smiles. It opened in dismay at Kurt's next words.

"Schellenberg's men seized my sister after she'd been to the U.S. Embassy in Madrid. She died in Berlin under interrogation, Father. Canaris says she told them nothing."

Donati had lowered his head before Kurt finished. Now it drooped lower and he seemed to be praying, silently. When he looked up again, his dark-brown eyes were awash.

"I beg your forgiveness."

"She would give you hers, Father, I'm sure of it. That's what matters most to me."

"Thank you. And now *you* are in danger."

"Perhaps. It's probably why Canaris sent me here."

"There'll be no sanctuary for any of us here, my son, when the storm finally breaks." He looked away, frowning. "I don't want you to return to Germany. You must get rid of that uniform and go south."

"South?"

"To await the arrival of Badoglio's troops in Naples. See their commander. Tell him what you know. Beg him to delay his advance on Rome until the German generals have seized power. They will spare the Holy See. Hitler and his Waffen SS will bring it down in ruins about them. Go now, my son. When we meet again, the storm will have passed."

Hermann Goering's message to Hitler was an act of inspiration.

"I must return to the Reich, Your Holiness, to attend to more mundane affairs on Your behalf. But I shall be flying into danger. May I therefore crave the immense distinction of being the first person to make his Confession to Your Holiness?"

"But the Reichsmarschall is not even a Catholic, so far as I know," Donati protested after Hitler had passed him the note.

"Then we shall declare him one. The formalities can follow, elsewhere." Hitler popped a dried fig into his mouth and chewed away energetically, his eyes twinkling. "You mustn't deny Us a little harmless amusement, dear friend." He started to giggle. "Goering's confession! Be sure to interrupt us after the first two hours!"

In the event, it took only ten minutes. Kneeling on a cushion at Hitler's feet in the private papal study, the fat Deputy Fuehrer reeled off a list of minor peccadilloes, mostly to do with his looting of other people's property.

"So you've sinned against the seventh and the tenth Commandments," Hitler grunted. "Now, what about the sixth?"

"The sixth, my F—Your Holiness?"

" 'Thou shalt not commit adultery.' Make a proper confession, my son."

"But I am guiltless! I was completely faithful to my darling Karin, just as I am to Emmy!"

"May the Almighty forgive you," Hitler scowled. "Very well, then." He gave his absolution. "And for penance you will abstain from all evening meals for the next seven days." His voice rose to a shout. "And that's an order!"

Goering pushed himself, wincing, to his feet.

"Have I Your Holiness's permission to speak?"

"Two minutes."

"The Bolsheviks and the Jews are hammering at Fortress Europe. Is it Your Holiness's wish I should immediately take over the temporal leadership of the Reich?"

"I suppose so. But not the Chancellorship. I intend retaining that post." Hitler adjusted his white skull cap and slipped smoothly into the royal plural. "Did We tell you about Our plans for St. Peter's?"

"Not yet, Your Holiness."

"I sent for Speer. Isn't he here yet?"

"Speer is a traitor. He has fled the Reich."

"Then have him shot at once," Hitler snapped. "Now about St. Peter's. It's absurd that it should remain in this decadent provincial city. We're going to have it dismantled, stone by stone, and reassembled in Berlin, the capital of the New Order."

"Fantastic! Talking about Berlin, Your Holiness, the *Oberkommando* of the Wehrmacht is in complete disarray and squabbling among itself. Is it your wish I should take over from Keitel?"

"Yes, you'd better do that." Hitler stood up. "Now, if you'll excuse Us—"

"Including, naturally, the Waffen SS?" Goering, sweating freely, pressed on.

"Naturally. And don't forget to shoot Albert Speer. When I think of the honors We showered on that ingrate! . . ."

The SS orderlies attending on Pope Adolf had done a good job of wiring up the Sovereign Pontiff's study. At the monitoring desk up on the second floor of the Apostolic Palace, immediately below the study, SS Oberfuehrer Rattenhuber switched off the recording machine and put a top-priority call through to Himmler in Berlin.

There was a long silence when Rattenhuber finished his account of the Goering-Hitler dialogue. Then: "We have to be clever about this, Rattenhuber. That clown still has his public, and the way everything's breaking, back here—"

"My thoughts, exactly. I propose having my own technicians thoroughly examine the aircraft our fat friend will be taking from Ciampino. It would be such a tragedy if it blew up in mid-air."

"Unthinkable. I leave it in your hands, then. Oh, and Ratten-huber—I shan't forget this."

Feldmarschall Keitel, stunned by Goering's curt message relieving him of the OKW command and in despair of making contact with the Fuehrer, left the airport for Berlin twenty minutes after Goering took off in a converted Heinkel bomber. The news of the Heinkel's disintegration over the Austrian alps greeted him on landing at Tempelhof and, correctly identifying the cause of the tragedy, Keitel drove at once to Himmler's headquarters on the Prinz Albrecht Strasse. The Reichsfuehrer SS, whose nervous twitch had gotten worse, was hanging up the telephone as Keitel was shown in.

"That was the Doctor. We're having a meeting at his Ministry and you'd better come along."

General Halder, chief of the Army General Staff, was already at the Wilhelmplatz when they arrived, and the four men sat at a round table in the conference room adjoining Goebbels's office and began to debate what the little propaganda chief acidly referred to as "the new situation created by the untimely explosion of our Deputy Fuehrer." It was agreed that Adolf Hitler could no longer be counted upon to provide sane leadership of the Reich and that it would be disastrous if either Bormann or Ribbentrop, still hanging on in the Vatican, were to talk the Fuehrer into delegating his supreme authority to them. As to Donati, opinion was divided. Himmler and Keitel branded him as an agent of Roosevelt. Goebbels, with his Catholic upbringing, found it inconceivable that a dignitary of the Church would engineer Pope Pius's dethronement, out of whatever ulterior motive. Halder advanced no views, remaining silent until the discussion moved on to the military situation. At this point, he produced from his briefcase the latest figures of casualties on the eastern front and the shortfall of tanks, aircraft and ammunitions from the factories.

"Gentlemen, gentlemen!" Doctor Goebbels expostulated. "This is not a General Staff conference! We have to settle the vital question of leadership. What am I to tell our people—that their Fuehrer has abandoned them for higher things? That there is a leadership vacuum here in Berlin?"

Keitel was the first to break the heavy silence. His faith in the Fuehrer's genius, he said, was undiminished, and he himself was confident that Hitler would lead them eventually out of the crisis. In the meantime, however, the Wehrmacht High Command should set up a military council charged with restoring order and morale in the Reich and with securing its frontiers against all external threats. "The loyal support of the Party," he concluded, looking straight at Himmler, "and the Waffen SS, will guarantee the council's effectiveness."

"Out of the question!" Himmler snapped. "The Party is the supreme power in Germany and must remain so. Our morale and organization—unlike the Wehrmacht's—remain unshaken. The Fuehrer will decide—perhaps he already has—on a new deputy, and the Party and the SS will loyally serve that person. Even—" he favored Goebbels with a thin smile—"if it should turn out to be you, Herr Doktor."

The meeting ended as Himmler and Goebbels had planned it should end. Pending new and intelligible instructions from the Fuehrer himself, the Party Chancellery, which in effect meant the political direction of the Reich, would be in the caretaker hands of Doctor Goebbels, thus filling the vacuum created by Bormann's immobilization in the Vatican City. For his own good reasons, Hitler had already removed Keitel from the Supreme Command of the Armed Forces, and there could be no question of reinstating him except on explicit orders from the Fuehrer himself. Franz Halder must, therefore, assume immediate command of the OKW, but his authority would not extend over the Waffen SS, whose disposition would be a matter for consultation between Halder and Himmler, with the Reichsfuehrer SS making the ultimate decisions. Alfred Jodl would continue as commander in chief of Wehrmacht Operations and Friedrich Fromm as commander in chief of home forces. Halder would call a meeting of all senior Wehrmacht generals as soon as this could be arranged, and there he would explain how the leadership crisis had been solved and secure the generals' approval and loyalty.

Wilhelm Keitel, who had been sinking into a deeper and deeper depression as the decisions were reeled off, at last found his voice. "And what, gentlemen, is to be *my* role from now on?"

Halder remained silent. Himmler and Goebbels exchanged quizzical glances.

"Why not take a little time off to think things over?" the Propaganda Minister purred. "I'm sure you'll come up with something."

III

THE "ELECTION" of Pope Adolf had taken place on a Saturday, making it impractical to stage his coronation on the first Sunday following, in accordance with Vatican convention. The event was scheduled, therefore, for the second Sunday, namely October 15.

On the night of Thursday, October 12, the Military Governors of France and Belgium, Generals von Stuelpnagel and von Falkenhausen, ordered the arrest of all SS and SD personnel in the territories under their command and, in a communiqué endorsed by every corps commander of the reserve army in the West, called upon General Halder to form a Supreme Military Council for the Defense of the Reich and to take "appropriate measures against any opposition, from whatever quarter, to this unavoidable solution to the leadership crisis in the Greater Reich."

That same night, in Berlin, General Paul von Hase, commander of the capital's garrison, moved the main body of his troops into the Tiergarten and cordoned off the Deutschlandsender and Reichssender radio stations, the Ministry of Propaganda, the R.S.H.A. headquarters in Prinz Albrecht Strasse and the Berlin SS Security main office in the Anhalt Station quarter. Not a drop of blood had yet been shed when at 8:03 A.M. the following day, General Halder—preceded by the playing of "Deutschland über Alles"—addressed the nation over the radio. He called for calm and discipline in "these difficult days" and, without once mentioning the name Adolf Hitler, invited the German people, in or out of uniform, member or nonmember of the Party, Catholic or Protestant, to unite behind the new Supreme Military Council, in whose *sane*—and he stressed the word—hands Germany's honor would be upheld, her *lawful* achievements secured and her peaceful future assured.

In his private residence on the Hermann Goering Strasse, Joseph Goebbels listened to Halder's broadcast in silence while his aide Rudolf Stimmer took the speech down in shorthand. When it was over, Goebbels switched off and limped over to the window. He turned suddenly around to face Stimmer, his dark-brown eyes blazing with emotion.

"I would have followed the Fuehrer into the jaws of hell itself! He lost me when he walked into the Vatican."

"And now, Herr Doktor?" Stimmer ventured.

"Let the dice fall! In twenty-four hours' time, either you and I will be under lock and key or Halder and his generals hanging from meat hooks. There's not a thing we can do about it."

Heinrich Himmler had taken another view. Alerted by a Paris call from SS Standartenfuehrer Knochen minutes before Stuelpnagel's troops stormed his hotel on the Rue Castiglione, Himmler had ordered Rudolf Brandt to assemble a strong bodyguard and had then driven at break-neck speed to Potsdam, a hundred and fifty miles east of the capital, where the crack Viking Division of his Waffen SS was encamped. From Potsdam he had made contact with the commanders of every SS division in Germany and on the eastern front. The orders were explicit. In the event that the Wehrmacht insurrection in France and Belgium should spread, the Waffen SS would engage all rebel elements of the regular army, disarm them and execute every officer from the rank of lieutenant upward.

While Himmler was barking out his orders over one telephone, Brandt was talking over another one to General Fromm, commander in chief of the Home Forces, who currently had a whole army corps within striking distance of Berlin. Fromm, the last of the Wehrmacht generals to be sounded out by Halder and Canaris, had taken a wait-and-see attitude toward the army plot. Now he declared himself and his troops "for Himmler and the Reich." He was told to put a ring of steel around the capital and await the arrival of the Viking Division, at that moment heading in motorized columns for Berlin.

A call to Feldmarschall Kesselring, who was "mopping up" in northern Italy after his Operation Clamp-Down, confirmed his loyalty to the Party, and it was decided that he should move part of his forces into southern France to discipline and replace the Wehrmacht coastal garrisons that were now declaring for Stuelpnagel. The remainder of his forces in Italy would establish a defense system south of the river Arno and would be stiffened by the Leibstandarte division of the Waffen SS, now ordered northward from its barracks near Rome.

"Is that wise?" Obergruppenfuehrer Brandt frowned. "It leaves the Fuehrer isolated in a hostile city, with only one regiment of the Leibstandarte to protect him."

"Aren't you forgetting something?" Himmler snapped. "The Fuehrer has God on his side. He doesn't need *us* any more."

At noon the next day, October 13, Jodl sent an ultimatum to Halder to surrender himself and his staff to General Fromm and to order the troops of the Berlin garrison back to their barracks. If he failed to comply, the Viking Division, backed by Fromm's army corps, would move in, and the resulting bloodshed and destruction of civilian property would be on Halder's head.

Halder replied as Chief of the OKW and head of the provisional Council for the Defense of the Reich. General Jodl was dismissed, with immediate effect, from the post of Chief of Wehrmacht Operations and General Fromm was ordered to withdraw his troops from the periphery of Berlin.

The battle for Berlin was over by nightfall and cost the lives of the entire garrison—either before or after surrender. General Halder and his staff were strung from lampposts in the Bendler- strasse. At 11 P.M. Doctor Goebbels announced over the Deutschlandsender network that Heinrich Himmler had as- sumed all the Fuehrer's responsibilities, including supreme com- mand of the armed forces. The rebel Wehrmacht generals were invited to hand over their commands to the nearest Waffen SS generals in their regions.

The battle for Germany had begun.

CHAPTER FOURTEEN

THE CORONATION of Pope Adolf lacked much of the splendor of such occasions, notably through a shortage of ecclesiastical bit players and the conspicuous absence of a general public. A handful of terrified Roman priests, known for their Fascist sympathies, had been rounded up by Rattenhuber, whisked to the Vatican Palace and promptly ordained cardinals by Pope Adolf; but the papal knights, so colorful a feature of the procession down the aisle of St. Peter's, had disappeared into thin air, and the Swiss Guard remained confined to their barracks. However, a visible impact was made on the press by the black-and-silver-uniformed SS officers detailed to support the throne and the papal canopy, and to bear those symbols of royalty from the time of the Pharaohs, the great ostrich-feather fans. And Hitler had taken considerable pains over his costume. The new white silk slippers and the miter of golden wool had been made especially for him by Roman craftsmen under the cold eyes of Leibstandarte troopers. The papal *falda* and mantle draped him magnificently, and the pectoral cross, fashioned from his own design combining the swastika and the symbol of Christianity, had been declared by the new Pope to be "a masterpiece of the goldsmith's art."

He was not as complimentary about the new papal seals. These had been another rush job, done by a different Roman jeweler, to replace the seals taken from Pius XII and broken up. In his nervousness, the craftsman had cast the swastika the wrong way around. The unfortunate man was summarily executed in his workshop on the new pope's orders; the Leibstandarte officer whose duty it had been to supervise the work was demoted to the ranks and given a penance of five decades of the rosary.

Pope Adolf had grudgingly accepted Donati's advice to dispense with the full Coronation Mass in which he had been tutored. There was the fact that the superbly trained Vatican choir, like the papal knights and noblemen, had taken indefinite leave of absence before it had occurred to anyone in the entourage to round them up. And there was the even more inconvenient circumstance of the new Pope's total inability—rare in an Austrian—to chant his part of the service in tune. But Adolf was not to be cheated of the other theatrical embellishments proper to a full coronation ceremony. Wearing the papal alb and stole, the mantle and the miter, he had mounted the canopied *sedia* in the Royal Hall from whence he was borne by his SS elite to the entrance of the Basilica and thence, with slow and solemn dignity and preceded by his newly appointed cardinals, down the wide central aisle of St. Peter's, to the foot of the steps before the high altar. Here he was draped in the sixty pounds of gilded vestments reserved for a High Coronation Mass, and after making his bow toward the pews set up for the press and the hundred or so Leibstandarte troops assigned to "congregational duties" Adolf slowly mounted the altar steps and started to celebrate Mass.

Himmler had at least had the foresight to secure, in advance of the coronation, the services of one body of laymen indispensable to the full aural splendor of the occasion. The Vatican trumpeters, held under close SS surveillance since the "election," were in their place high under the dome of St. Peter's when Adolf raised the Host above his head for the Consecration, and the long fanfare that now resounded throughout the vast Basilica paid melodious tribute to the trumpeters' instinct for self-survival.

The mass over, Hitler was reverently assisted by his acolyte cardinals back down the altar steps and up into the *sedia* for the act of coronation.

To the hollow-eyed Bormann and Ribbentrop, from their privileged places close to the Papal Altar, it appeared that Hitler winced with discomfort when Giovanni Donati, resplendent in his cardinal's *cappa magna,* placed the weighty triple tiara on the Fuehrer's head. If so, it hardly supported his earlier reassurance to Donati: "I've had to wear a steel-lined military cap for the past four years, remember. The triple tiara will give me no trouble."

When the first distant crackle of gunfire interrupted the solemn ceremony, Ribbentrop and Bormann exchanged nervous glances and peered back over the empty reaches of the vast nave to where the armed Leibstandarte bodyguard had been posted at the five entrances to the Basilica. At the same moment, Oberfuehrer Rattenhuber left his place between Gestapo chief Herbert Kappler and Werner Voegler and strode swiftly down the central aisle, toward the nearest entrance. A few minutes later he was back and leaning over Ribbentrop to address Bormann.

"An advance column of Badoglio's troops is engaging my men at the Victor Emmanuel Bridge. I don't think they can hold out till the end of the ceremony."

"Get word to Donati," Bormann said, moistening his lips. And to Ribbentrop, whose face had turned ashen, he said, "Perhaps you and I should try to find out what the transport situation is at Ciampino."

Hitler took the whispered news from Donati without a blink of the eye. "The Leibstandarte will take care of things," he said, smiling. "They won't permit those comic-opera soldiers to upset our ceremony."

"Your men are outnumbered, Your Holiness. Rattenhuber advises postponing the rest of the ceremony."

Hitler's forefinger came up to flick gently at his clean-shaven upper lip. "They are Italian troops," he murmured. "Good Catholics, all of them. They would never invade St. Peter's at a time like this." He rose slowly from the throne, carefully balancing the triple tiara on his head. "We shall walk out there, with Our troops behind Us, and accept the Italians' surrender. They will never fire on their Pope. Afterward, we shall start the ceremony all over again for their benefit." Halfway down the altar steps he paused and called back to Donati. "But with you, as always, at Our side, Your Eminence."

The battle for the Via della Conciliazione was over by the time Hitler had completed his slow progress, shepherd's staff in hand, from the Papal Altar to the Portico of St. Peter's. Italian troops, infiltrating through the gardens of the palaces on both sides of the broad thoroughfare, had cut off the German line of retreat from the bridge and caught the remnants of the first-line Vatican defenders in a lethal crossfire. Those who had escaped encirclement were scurrying to new positions behind the colonnades of the *piazza,* which was now being swept by a hail of carbine and automatic fire from the Via della Conciliazione. Beneath the Portico, Hitler gave his instructions to Rattenhuber.

"We have changed Our mind about these desecrators of the Holy See. They shall not be invited to the ceremony, but shall be outmaneuvered as We have always outmaneuvered our enemies. Signal your men to cease firing and to spread out behind Us as We walk toward the Italians. They will lower their arms, you may count on it. When We are within close enough range of them, We shall raise this staff as a signal for Our troops to put them to rout."

"But out there in the *piazza,* with no cover! We'll all be slaughtered!"

"We are your cover, Rattenhuber. Did I tell you, by the way, I'm seriously thinking of promoting you to *Brigadefuehrer?"*

Kurt had been four days in the company of Colonel Ricardo Orlando, and if he had to listen to one more account of the dapper little commander's amorous triumphs in Cairo, he was going to have to yawn right in his face.

It hadn't been quite so bad back in Naples, where the colonel and his staff had installed themselves in a comfortable farm-house north of the city while they awaited orders to move up to Rome; between mealtimes, at least, there had been a reprieve. But they had been on the road for more than three hours now, with Kurt a captive audience in the commander's jeep, and apart from a break at Cassino for an intelligence briefing from divisional headquarters in Naples the saga of Orlando's erotic exploits had been unremitting.

Kurt made one last effort to turn the conversation to the relatively trivial matter of what lay ahead of Orlando in the Italian capital.

"This report that there are only two companies of the Leibstandarte left in the Vatican City, Colonel—I find it almost unbelievable."

Orlando gave a shrug. "Is all he needs, Hitler," he said in his halting German, "to escort him to the airport and—pouff!—off to Berlin. Why the whole Leibstandarte regiment have to fight its way out of Rome? In Germany—ha!—is where he needs them right now!"

"I think you're in for a bit of a surprise, Colonel. Hitler's completely lost touch with reality. He'll probably still be there, playing at Pope, when we arrive."

"Then I accept his surrender." Orlando's chest swelled visibly beneath his custom-tailored combat jacket. "What an honor for my regiment! Maybe the *real* Pope gives me a title—no?"

You're more likely to get a Leibstandarte bullet up your ass. Then, aloud: "Any change in the orders, I mean about Hitler and company?"

"No change. We find them in the Vatican—we take them prisoner. They fight—we fight back. We find them gone—so they are gone. The Maresciallo wants peace for Italy, not war over that madman, like you have in your country."

Kurt was standing close to the colonel when one of his adjutants drove back across the Victor Emmanuel Bridge to report that the Via della Conciliazione was now cleared of SS troops but that a force of about a hundred Leibstandarte men had taken cover among the colonnades of the *piazza* and were apparently preparing a fanatical last-ditch defense of their Fuehrer. Grenades and mortars would have to be used to dislodge them.

"Out of the question!" Orlando snapped. "Bernini's masterpiece must be preserved from damage at all costs." He raised his binoculars and trained them on the distant façade of St. Peter's. "We had better infiltrate the Second Battalion from the west, bringing them up behind the Basilica. When they are in position, I shall—" He broke off, his mouth falling open. "They're not answering our fire any more!" He lowered the glasses and motioned to Kurt. "Let's get over there, Major. They'll be sending someone to talk terms and I shall want you with me." In his excitement the little colonel was still using his native tongue, but Kurt caught the gist of what he was saying and sprang quickly after him into the rear of the command jeep.

By the time the driver had braked to a halt before the troop-carriers drawn up across the end of the Via della Conciliazione, the Italian troops had also ceased firing and were emerging from cover to gape across the vast square. The First battalion's major had been killed directing the assault on the bridge, and the captain who leaped down from the nearest truck had a field dressing bound to his head.

"What's going on, Captain?"

"I'm not sure, sir." The officer pointed across the *piazza*. "Look over there!"

From where Kurt stood, the two figures walking side by side down the broad slope leading from the Portico were far too small for identification by the naked eye. But there was no mistaking, even at this distance, the papal triple crown and shepherd's staff, or the cardinal's *cappa magna*. Orlando was hastily refocusing his field glasses. *"Dio mio,"* he breathed, seconds later. Then, thrusting the binoculars at Kurt, "Take a look, Major."

It wasn't easy, keeping the glasses steady with his one hand. But he got a fix and managed to hold it.

"Well?" Orlando yelped impatiently. "Have you identified them?"

"I have, Colonel. Adolf Hitler and Monsignor Donati."

They were making very slow progress, with Hitler's left hand occasionally reaching up to steady the huge bulbous crown. As they reached the bottom of the slope and started to move over level ground toward the central obelisk, groups of Leibstandarte troopers came streaming out from the colonnades to form a thickening spreading line behind the two magnificently robed figures. The SS men held their carbines slack and pointed to the ground. Kurt panned the binoculars swiftly over their ranks. There was no sign of Werner Voegler.

"Would you believe it?" Orlando exulted, still speaking Italian. "The great Hitler in person, surrendering himself to me, Ricardo Orlando!" He leaped from the jeep and elbowed his way through the dense mass of his troops packing the eastern entrance to the *piazza*. "Hold your fire, men!" he shouted. "This is the greatest moment in the long and glorious history of our country!"

The order was unnecessary. His troops were as men transfixed, gazing in solemn silence at the advancing figures.

Kurt had shouldered through the troops to reach Orlando's side. He was still holding the field glasses and he raised them again now and trained them on Giovanni Donati. The priest's face seemed close enough to touch; Kurt could see the moving lips, the cast-down eyes, the broad peasant's hand clasping the filigree cross tightly against the breast. He moved the glasses a fraction to the right and Hitler's face leaped into close vision. It was a face he had studied in all its changing moods for so long now that, like Bormann, he believed he could read the workings of the mind behind it. The Fuehrer's mouth was set hard, the chin tilted upward, the eyes blazing with— Quickly, Kurt swung the glasses back to Donati, to the priest's ceaselessly moving lips, and then away to pan across the shoulder-to-shoulder line of SS troopers.

"Colonel Orlando," he said quietly, in German, "Hitler is not coming to surrender."

"What's that? Why you say that?"

"It's a trick. Soon as they're close enough, they're going to open fire."

"They would not dare," Orlando muttered. "It would be suicide for them." But he had backed a pace or two and was chewing his lower lip vigorously. "Weapons at the ready, men!" he shouted suddenly. "All eyes on those Germans!" He might have been speaking Mandarin Chinese. The Italian soldiers' eyes remained riveted on the man, now a bare two hundred and fifty paces away, wearing the triple tiara and grasping the tall shepherd's staff.

Hitler had come to a halt and was transferring the staff to his left hand. His voice rang out over the square. *"Pax Vobiscum!"*

His right hand rose slowly, fingers shaped for the pontifical blessing. There was a stirring of bodies, a scraping of boots behind Kurt and, glancing quickly around, he saw individual soldiers, here and there, pushing forward and sinking to their knees. The eyes of the majority, still on their feet, were fixed unwaveringly on Hitler. Kurt looked back into the square, first toward Donati, who seemed to be gazing straight back at him, shaking his head slowly, and then at the SS men spread out behind. It was possible that only he and the little colonel standing beside him noticed the stiffening of their limbs, the stillness of their down-pointed weapons.

"Benedictio dei omnipotentis—"

"Deploy!" Orlando screamed. *"Rapid fire!"* And again, as he whirled around and plunged into the midst of his bemused troops: "Fire, *buffoni!* We've been tricked!"

Still Hitler hadn't raised the staff. It was as if he were savoring to the full this moment of combined military and spiritual authority and wanted to draw it out. Before him, an awe-stricken congregation of the faithful; simple Italian peasants in army uniforms who were no more capable of firing upon the wearer of the triple tiara than they would be of treading the consecrated Host under foot. Behind him, a company of men trained as no men had ever been trained before to obey without question their infallible Fuehrer's orders and to die for him, in a mindless state of Nazi grace, any time he gave the word.

His lips were curling into a beatific smile as his right hand completed the blessing and started to come down—only to explode in splinters of bone as it met the long stream of lead directed by Kurt from the troop-carrier's machine gun.

When the battle was over, Kurt made his way through the dead and dying Italians to the place, a few yards from Caligula's obelisk, where Hitler and Donati lay. He had no eyes for the bloody corpse of the Fuehrer or for the shambles of black-clad bodies littering the *piazza,* only for the short stout figure lying on its side, one arm flung out as if reaching for the triple tiara that had rolled to within inches of the limp fingers.

Kurt knelt down and fumbled under the twisted *cappa magna* for the wrist of the priest's other hand. It was wet and sticky and he could feel no pulse. As he let the hand go, Donati's hooded eyes fluttered and then opened.

Kurt bent closer. "It's me, Father—Kurt Armbrecht."

The tired brown eyes were trying to focus. After a little while they started to droop again, but now the lips were moving.

"My son . . ."

"Stay quiet, Father. There's a doctor coming."

". . . and you must tell them how it . . ." A weak cough brought the blood bubbling from a corner of the wide mouth.

"I shall tell them, Father."

CHAPTER FIFTEEN

I

IT WAS now a race against time. The news of Hitler's death would probably have been flashed already to Himmler in Berlin by the SS operators on duty at the Vatican switchboard. It was anyone's guess how the Reichsfuehrer SS would react to the news, but if the intelligence briefing picked up at Cassino had been accurate, and the Luftwaffe was in fact giving support to the army in its operations against the Waffen SS, then Himmler and the rest of the Party *Fuehrung* must now be in a state bordering on panic. One thing was certain: Himmler had only to take his mind off other problems long enough to issue one order to the *Totenkopfverbaende* camp commanders and every political prisoner, including Walter Armbrecht, would be butchered within the hour.

Kurt had grappled with this fear all the way up from Naples, without devising a stratagem that offered even the slightest hope of success. Canaris was dead. The rebel Wehrmacht generals, totally involved in crushing the Waffen SS, would scarcely turn from that task to the freeing of concentration camp prisoners, even assuming that they favored such action. There was now only one person with any access to authority inside the Reich he could appeal to and trust, and that was Peter Waldheim; but what could Peter do for an imprisoned professor whose son was certainly by now right at the top of the Gestapo's "Wanted" list?

The first faint glimmer of hope had come when Colonel Orlando yelled to him over the throng of soldiers crowding around the corpses of Hitler and Donati, then turned to point toward the Basilica. A detachment of the Colonel's troops were emerging from the portico, prodding ahead of them the dozen or so Nazis who had been spared the blood bath in the *piazza*. Hurrying to catch up with Orlando, now striding purposefully across the corpse-littered square, Kurt's stomach contracted at the sight of Werner Voegler, limping on the fringe of the group of captives; and a moment later the glimmer of hope took on the outlines of a possible solution. He paused in his stride to stoop and snatch a Luger P.08 from the holster of a dead SS man, and thrust it into his belt. A minute later he was standing face-to-face with Werner Voegler.

"Glad to see you alive, Voegler. We still have a score to settle, you and I."

Voegler stared back at him, tight-lipped. The vein at the side of his brow was pulsing, and it might have been from hatred but it could also have been from fear. Kurt took Orlando aside and spoke urgently into his ear.

"Va bene, va bene!" the Colonel nodded. Then briskly, in Italian, to a squad of riflemen standing by: "Accompany the Major and his prisoner—that SS pig there!—to the telephone exchange, wherever it is. You are under the Major's orders."

Slowed down by Voegler, it took them ten minutes to reach the Vatican's telecommunications center. Otto Dietrich had beaten them to it, presumably through one of the side doors of the Basilica. He had elbowed one of the male SS operators off his stool at the long switchboard and was shouting hoarsely into the mouthpiece as Kurt strode across the room, snatched the earphones from the press chief's head and ripped the live line from its plug.

"Armbrecht!" A spray of spittle hit Kurt as Dietrich kicked back the stool and whirled on him, his ashen features agape. "What the bloody hell do you think—!"

"Take him!" Kurt snapped at the Italian troopers. "If he

opens his mouth again—" he backed the command with an eloquent gesture—"shoot him!"

Two minutes later, with all but one of the SS telephonists staring into the muzzles of Italian carbines, Kurt motioned Voegler forward and ordered the remaining operator to give up his stool. "Sit down there, Voegler!" Kurt took out the Luger and put the muzzle to the Obersturmfuehrer's ear. "We're through to the Berghof exchange. I want you to identify yourself and to ask for Major Waldheim to come on the line. Then I'll tell you what to say. Try anything clever, and it'll give me a great deal of pleasure to blow your brains out."

Voegler gave his calling code to the Berghof operator and asked for Waldheim. A few seconds later, he leaned back to glare coldly up at Kurt.

"He's not on the mountain."

"Then find out," Kurt grated, "where he is right now—the location and the telephone number."

Another few seconds and, "He's at his sister's home in Nuremberg. The number is 2512."

"Right!" Kurt pulled out the lead and ordered Voegler back across the room. "Get me that number," he told the operator.

If he could now talk personally to Peter in Nuremberg—only a hundred miles north of Dachau—it was working out even better than he had hoped. But how much time was left before the main Roman exchange came to its senses and blocked all lines to Germany? Peter's voice, loud and clear, cut into his silent prayer.

"Kurt? Is that you on the line?"

"That's right, Peter, I'm calling from the Vatican City. Now, hold it—just listen carefully to what I have to say. Hitler is dead. . . . Yes, yes, I've seen the body and it's lying right now in St. Peter's Square. . . . I can't go into all that now. Just tell me quickly: what's the situation back there?"

"Confused. Chaotic, in fact. I'm staying right out of it till the picture clears. But I gather Himmler has sent Brandt to parley with the Military Council."

"I'm worried about my father, Peter. I—I guess you know where I stand now?"

There was silence at the other end of the line.

"Peter, you still there?"

"I am with you, Kurt." The words came, each one separately stressed, quietly over the line. "What do you want me to do?"

The young Luftwaffe adjutant had been weighing the odds during his breakneck drive from Nuremberg to Dachau; by the time he presented himself at the main gates of the concentration camp he had decided there was a good fifty-fifty chance of getting away with it.

Sturmbannfuehrer Helmut Brunner was hunched at his desk, fiddling with the dials of a portable radio, when Waldheim was ushered in. He glanced sourly at his visitor's credentials before tossing them back across the desk.

"You were lucky not to be shot on sight by my guards. Your brave pilots won't do as well, once this army treachery has been taken care of."

"Don't be deceived by the uniform, Sturmbannfuehrer. I'm on the Fuehrer's personal staff, remember. My first loyalty—" Waldheim hesitated, then finished the statement in a lowered voice—"has always been to him."

"Then maybe you can throw some light on this rubbish being put out over the British radio." Brunner's shifty eyes stayed level just long enough for Waldheim to read the fear in them; and his spirits rose.

"If you mean about the Fuehrer—?"

"Precisely. This cock-and-bull story about him being killed by the Italians."

"It's true. It's why I'm here."

"My God!" Brunner sprang up from his desk, rushed to the window as if to seek confirmation in the night sky, then spun around to face his visitor. His face was the color of pale putty. "There's no hope for us then! We're finished!"

"I wouldn't say that, Sturmbannfuehrer. The word was coming in, when I left the Berghof, that Reichsfuehrer Himmler is meeting with the army and Luftwaffe generals. There's still time to restore order here in the Reich and stabilize the eastern front."

Brunner was stalking about the room, shaking his head vigorously. "Finished!" he reiterated. "Without our Fuehrer—our people divided—the SS disarmed—!" He stopped abruptly, to blink across the room at Waldheim. "You say the Fuehrer's bodyguard were all wiped out?"

"I didn't say that. For example, Obersturmbannfuehrer Voegler—" Waldheim broke off to take an anxious look at his wrist watch.

"Voegler—what about Voegler?"

"He managed to get a call through to the Berghof from somewhere in Rome. He asked for me, then put me on to Kurt Armbrecht, who said he met you here with Voegler earlier this year. Is that correct?"

"Yes, yes! Go on!"

"Armbrecht has defected to the Italians. He's going to have Voegler shot if I don't fly his father, Professor Armbrecht, to Ciampino airport by dawn tomorrow."

Brunner was gaping at him, incredulously. "Are you mad? What guarantee have you got, once you hand over this professor—"

"Armbrecht and I," Waldheim cut in, "were close friends and colleagues. I know the man, and I have his word that Voegler will board my plane and that we can take off again as soon as his father is safely delivered." He took another impatient look at his watch. "I have a plane and crew standing by, fueled up, at Munich airport. We might just make Rome by dawn."

"It's out of the question!" Brunner had slumped into his chair and was pounding his brow slowly with one clenched fist. "I'm only second in command here. My chief's touring the camps in the East. I'd need written authorization from Berlin—"

"And while we wait for that, Voegler dies. Are you ready to

309

explain to Reichsfuehrer Himmler, when all this trouble is over, how you could allow that to happen to a personal favorite of his rather than part with an insignificant old professor?"

There followed a long silence, broken at last by the scraping of chair legs as Brunner lurched to his feet. "I'll need a receipt!" he shouted. "A personal receipt from you as adjutant at the *Fuehrerhauptquartier!* Plus a signed statement, putting all this in writing!"

The rising sun was curtained by rain clouds and the wind out on the tarmac at Ciampino was cold and damp. As the converted Heinkel taxied toward them, Kurt raised the collar of his borrowed raincoat and snatched a glance at Voegler, standing between two Italian militiamen, his arms folded, his head arrogantly erect.

He thinks he has won. His god is dead, his Party a shambles, his regiment decimated, his nation torn asunder. But his demigod, Himmler, still lives, which means that the power and mystique of the Schutzstaffel *will eventually triumph over all adversaries. . . . I could kill him now, and no one would stop me or punish me. But if I did that, breaking my word to Peter, then the things that Voegler stands for would indeed have won.*

His father came off the plane first, helped down the steps by Waldheim. His uncovered hair was snow white, and the suit they had taken him away in hung in folds from his wasted body. Behind him came Margit Armbrecht, her eyes lighting up at the sight of Kurt, then streaming with tears. As the three of them stood there, united in a silent embrace, Kurt heard Voegler's voice, brittle and peremptory.

"Let's get going then, Waldheim! Or do we have to wait for the violin serenade?"

"You're not going anywhere, Voegler. Not in this plane, anyway."

Gently disengaging himself from his parents, Kurt went to join Waldheim at the foot of the steps. "You can't do this, Peter," he muttered quietly. "I gave my word."

"Sure, you gave me your word. But I didn't give *my* word, either to you or to Brunner, that I'd take that swine anywhere. If you want to fly him back yourself, the plane's all yours." He turned away to call up to the flight deck. "All right, men! Welcome to sunny Italy!"

They stood by, watching in silence, as Voegler rushed limping for the stairs, dived into the plane and floundered about inside the fuselage. He reappeared in the hatchway, waving his arms and shouting for Waldheim. They stayed there watching him as the shouted demands turned to protests, then appeals, then into a stream of broken abuse. At a signal from Kurt, the militiamen went up the steps and dragged the SS officer, sobbing, from the plane.

II

In the spring of 1945, Kurt and Walter Armbrecht made their pilgrimage to Manostrana, by rail via Innsbruck and Bolzano to Venice, thence to Pescara, where Colonel Orlando, now on the headquarters staff of Marshal Badoglio, had arranged for an army jeep to be put at their disposal.

More than five months had passed since Kurt, airlifted with Waldheim from Rome to London for prolonged interrogation at Eisenhower's SHAEF, had finally been permitted to rejoin his parents in Munich. In the meantime, in Paris and Warsaw, the representatives of Germany's Supreme Military Council had been presented with, and had accepted, the Allied Powers' terms for surrender.

Most of the weight Walter Armbrecht had lost during the months of incarceration at Dachau had now been recovered, but the snow-white hair, the lagging gait, remained as legacies of his ordeal. And the light that had gone out inside him when Waldheim told him how Sophie had died would never be rekindled.

They had not spoken about Giovanni Donati during the long and wearisome train journey to Pescara. The professor had slept, fitfully, between train changes. Over snacks from the hamper prepared for them by Margit, they had talked mostly about Germany and the prospects of redemption for its people. But now, as they motored across the coastal plain from Pescara toward the towering granite peaks of the Sasso, Walter Armbrecht spoke the priest's name softly.

"Giovanni Donati . . . how I wish I could have met that man."

Kurt remained silent. His own thoughts were on that final meeting with the priest, inside the papal apartments, and on the last words he had heard Donati utter: "Go now, my son. When we meet again the storm will have passed."

And so it had, although only he and Donati had known it as they faced each other eight days later across the great *piazza* of St. Peter's.

He was assembling other memories of the priest. Berlin . . . Obersalzburg . . . Madrid . . . And he was thinking aloud now.

"You know, Father, it might take America a year—maybe more—to bring Japan to her knees in the Pacific, but as far as I'm concerned the Pact of Steel was doomed from the moment, just about a year ago now, when I watched Donati mutter those few words in Hitler's ear at the reception in the Retiro Park. The Hitler I gunned down in St. Peter's Square was a preposterous fiction. The real Fuehrer of the Reich died that evening in Madrid, from a lethal overdose of megalomania."

"And his executioner," the professor sighed, "lies unhonored and unsung. They say that even Roosevelt, right up to his death last month, still had his doubts about Donati's real motives. He inclined to the view that the story Donati gave to dear Sophie was intended as a device for bailing himself out if anything went wrong with his real plan, which was to have himself appointed Pope under the New Order."

They had reached the foothills of the Forca di Penne and were traversing the valley, toward the town of Corfinio. With sudden bitterness, Kurt said, "Roosevelt never met him. Even if he had, what would a politician know about integrity!" A moment later, in a softer voice, "It was I who brought him the news of Sophie's death, remember? What I saw in his face—" he broke off, biting at his lip. "There was one other person," he went on, "who could have silenced the skeptics, and that was Admiral Canaris—if that swine Himmler hadn't included him in his Black Friday massacre."

"And the Vatican?" his father asked. "Surely there was wisdom enough there? Charity at least?"

Kurt shook his head. "Pope Pius will have made his own private judgment, but officially it could never favor Donati. Here was a priest—a prince of the Church—who had committed, or connived at, some of the worst heresies, blasphemies and sacrileges in the history of the Church. There can be no condoning this, however noble the motive. The Vatican's attitude has to be that the Church would have survived without Donati and without those dreadful sacrileges. And who can contradict that, now?"

He had to help his father down the steep pathway, little more than a goat track, leading from the outskirts of the village of Manostrana to the small and isolated plot of land set aside for the unconsecrated burial of those fallen from grace. Within this rubble-walled area the weeds had grown knee-deep around the few mounds of earth and weatherworn headstones marking the resting places of the village's unrepentant atheists and apostates.

One grave only, at the far end of the enclosure, wore the look of being cared for. No weeds grew from it or from the ground immediately around it. The spring rains, torrential in these mountains, had made no apparent impact on the neat hummock of yellowish-brown soil.

The village stonecutter had carried out Kurt's written instructions to the letter. The marble headstone, broad and stocky as the man it stood sentinel over, was engraved with his name, the dates bracketing his time on earth, and below this, the simple inscription: DO NOT JUDGE EVERYTHING YOU SEE.

Kurt and Walter Armbrecht knelt down at the graveside. A few minutes later, as they got to their feet, the bell of the village church started to toll the Angelus.

IT MIGHT have been of some value, in rewriting the story of Adolf Hitler's last two years, to have been either an historian or a military strategist. But perhaps not all that much. The historians have made their judgments, and the facts upon which these were based are freely available to us all. As for the military strategists—and regardless of which side they were on—their record from the outbreak of World War II up until Hitler's defeat at Stalingrad was, to put it generously, less than impressive.

Hitler Has Won is a novelist's blend of truth and fiction. It freezes the march of events inside Hitler's Reich at the date in March 1941 when the Regent of Yugoslavia was first summoned to Hitler's mountaintop retreat at Berchtesgaden. Most historians agree that it was from this date onward that the Fuehrer of Germany made the mistakes that were to shatter his dream of a Thousand-Year Reich, and that the first and perhaps the greatest of these blunders was his postponement by five fatal weeks of the Wehrmacht's invasion of Russia.

The Hitler of my novel has already smashed the Red Army west of Moscow and taken the Russian capital when the story opens. He has also persuaded his Japanese ally to strike at Vladivostok rather than at Pearl Harbor. From there on the reader is invited to join the author in an exercise of the imagination. To the historian and archivist this will have been a leap into pure fantasy. To those to whom the fascination of recorded history lies in the *two* shadows it casts— the grim reality and the dreadful ponderable—perhaps the fantasy has not seemed to be so farfetched.

FREDERIC MULLALLY

315

The capitalized names below belong to characters entirely fictitious but decidedly less strange than the real-life people who make up the bulk of the cast.

ARIAS, ALBERTO	A Spanish army veteran
ARMBRECHT, KURT	Hitler's literary assistant
ARMBRECHT, MARGIT	Kurt's mother
ARMBRECHT, SOPHIE	Kurt's sister
ARMBRECHT, WALTER	Kurt's father
Badoglio, Marshal	An Italian army commander
Bevan, Aneurin	A British Member of Parliament
Bormann, Martin	Chief of the Party Chancellery
Braun, Eva	Hitler's mistress
BRUNNER, HELMUT	Deputy commander of Dachau
Canaris, Wilhelm	Chief of the Abwehr (intelligence bureau)
Cerejeira, Cardinal	Archbishop of Lisbon
Churchill, Winston	Prime Minister of Britain
Ciano, Count	Mussolini's Foreign Minister
Dietrich, Otto	Reich Press Director
Doenitz, Karl	Grand Admiral
DONATI, GIOVANNI	A Vatican diplomat
EPPLER, FRÄULEIN	Private secretary to Hitler
Falkenhausen, Alexander von	Military Governor of Belgium
Franco, Francisco	Dictator of Spain
Goebbels, Joseph	Reich Minister of Propaganda
Goering, Hermann	*Reichsmarschall*
Greese, Irma	Wardress at Ravensbrueck
GRUYTEN, HELGA	On Hitler's secretariat staff
Halder, Franz	Chief of German General Staff
Hase, Paul von	Commander of the Berlin garrison
Himmler, Heinrich	Reichsfuehrer of the SS
Hitler, Adolf	Fuehrer of the Reich

Hoess, Rudolf	Commander of Auschwitz-Birkenau
Hoffman, Heinrich	Hitler's official photographer
Hull, Cordell	U.S. Secretary of State
Husseini, Haj Amin el	Mufti of Jerusalem
Jodl, Alfred	Chief of Wehrmacht Operations
Keitel, Wilhelm	Chief of Wehrmacht High Command
Kesselring, Albert	A German field marshal
KRENKLER	A local Nazi branch leader
Maglione, Cardinal	Secretary of State to Pius XII
MASSINGBERD, ERNLE	U.S. ambassador to Spain
Morell, Theodor	Hitler's physician
Mueller, Heinrich	Chief of the Gestapo
Mussolini, Benito	Dictator of Italy
OBEHEUSER, HELGA	SS doctor at Ravensbrueck
ORLANDO, RICARDO	An Italian army colonel
Rattenhuber, Oberfuehrer	Commander of Hitler's bodyguard
Ribbentrop, Joachim von	Reich Foreign Minister
Roosevelt, Franklin D.	President of the United States
Salazar, Antonio	Dictator of Portugal
Schaub, Julius	Hitler's chief civilian adjutant
Schirach, Baldur von	Gauleiter of Vienna
Schmidt, Paul	Hitler's interpreter
SHAW, WILLIAM	A Washington journalist
Spellman, Francis J. Cardinal	Archbishop of New York
STIMMER, RUDOLF	Aide to Goebbels
Stuelpnagel, Karl von	Military Governor of France
Tisserand, Eugene Cardinal	A cardinal of the Curia
VOEGLER, WERNER	An officer of Hitler's bodyguard
WALDHEIM, PETER	Hitler's junior Luftwaffe adjutant